Bloodlines

Stephen W. Shawcross

Printed and bound in Canada.

ISBN 978-0-9867026-2-4

Cover and interior artwork by WLDesign
wldesign@sympatico.ca

Edited by J.L. Hughes

Acknowledgements

Wikipedia for references to all manner of historical minutia: 1940s fashions, slang, train schedules, restaurant menus, and the salient characteristics of various geographies.

Antony Beevor's, "The Battle of Arnhem", which provides a blow by blow account of Operation Market Garden and is a sensational read in its own right. Apologies for any artistic license taken in veering from the actual events.

"Pogue's War", based on the diaries of World War II combat historian, Forrest Pogue who captured the quotidian aspects of the front line. It was recommended years before the current project by Robert Yakas, an architectural associate, himself a Vietnam vet whose father received a purple heart for his actions in the battle of Jebsheim in the Alsace during the Colmar Pocket operation.

Charles Messenger's "The D-Day Atlas: Anatomy of the Normandy Campaign". What can I say? I'm a geographer by education. Maps are important, as are participants and dates, in creating authentic fiction.

A big shout out to my editor on this journey, J.L. Hughes, a thriller writer herself, who undertook a line by line edit, conveying the protocols of the thriller genre, and helping to craft a much more digestible read.

To friends, family and the many book sellers and purchasers who support this sideline, and in particular my partner and love interest, the lovely Linda whose pronounced Scottishness has kept me solvent and grounded, not to mention well-cared for over the last 50 years.

Also by the Author

Runaway Summer (www.runawaysummer.com)
A Fearful Symmetry (www.afearfulsymmetry.com)
Walking on the Moon
The Paintbrush Diaries (www.paintbrushdiaries.com)

Bloodlines

Stephen W. Shawcross

Calgary, Canada
2020

The Heartland Killings

IOWA,
Fall 1941

She started working on the restraints as soon as she heard the front door slam shut. Gravel crunched underfoot, and the car sputtered to life, then stalled. Her heart stopped while the engine turned over, finally catching. She expelled a long breath, and redoubled her efforts, but froze again when the engine cut out.

'Please,' she implored, 'please let it start.'

In answer there was a thunderous report as the engine exploded into life only to die a few seconds later. She heard the car door open and then the sound of the hood being raised.

She remained motionless, save for the pounding of her heart, calling upon God and all his heavenly angels to intervene just this once. She swore she'd never ask for another thing as long as she lived.

The hood slammed down, the door shut, and after several more attempts the motor belched out a cloud of acrid exhaust into the hushed farmyard. She could smell the fumes from where she lay. Coughing and wheezing like an asthmatic, the car made its way down the long driveway and out onto the county road beyond.

She tugged harder now, grunting through the pain, until her right wrist was chaffed raw and dripping. Once slick with her blood, the twine began to loosen some and roll up onto the meat of her palm. She angled her thumb to touch her little finger and began a slow, rotating motion with her hand, like a wave from a royal carriage. Agonizingly, the ligature moved upwards until it stopped just below the thumb joint. At this point she rested for a spell, to catch a second wind. Her head throbbed from the alcohol he had forced her to drink, but was clear enough for her to realize that it was now or never.

She'd seen him do it, the only witness to cold-blooded murder, and although she swore she wouldn't sell him out, she could tell by the way he looked at her with those piercing, dark eyes, that he couldn't risk it. It was only a matter of time before he slit her throat too, and did away with the corpse, buried her in the woods, or in the walls of this ramshackle old farmhouse.

She'd read about things like this in the cheap detective pulps favored by her older brother, Eldred, sitting hunched by the woodstove, squinting at the dog-eared pages. Kin, she longed for them now like she'd never done before in her short life. She didn't think she could miss anything this much.

Gathering what strength remained, she pressed her struggle against the bonds. Sweat poured down into her eyes, stinging, blurring her vision. A rivulet of blood tattooed the inside of her forearm. With a final wrenching swing, she forced the twine to relinquish its hold, and her aching hand flopped down to her side. She wiped her bloody wrist on the mattress, and then turned and kneeled, attacking the coarse twine with tooth and nail.

He'd made a major miscalculation, not securing her legs as he had on previous occasions when he'd left the property for more alcohol and tobacco. He never brought back any food. At least she never smelled any cooking. It had been five days since she had last eaten. Hunger gnawed at her gut and a wave of dizziness accompanied her renewed exertions. She shivered despite the warmth of the night, Indian summer lingering well past the harvest.

With a final tug, her left arm was freed, and she fell back onto the mattress, panting, as good as spent.

'Come on, get up,' she urged, cloudy now, head spinning. Ungainly as a just-foaled colt, she staggered to the bedroom door, and grasping the handle, clattered hard against the splintered wood. Locked! A new wave of panic swept over her. She choked out a sob, and sank to the floor.

* * *

Dawn forged the surrounding hills in bands of hammered russet, the faint light spilling onto the rutted pathway leading to the dilapidated barn, gap-toothed with missing boards. Shadbolt paused for a moment to gaze at the momentary burst of color, illuminating the bare branches that rose like tracery against the stained-glass sky. He retained the image for future reference before turning his attention back to the barn. It was obvious from his survey of the house that the girl had been held there for some time. Ligatures of coarse twine hung like gallows noose from the iron bedstead, hovering above a urine and blood-stained mattress. Discarded butts, roll-your-owns, and several empty bottles of cheap whisky littered the floor. These clues he had studied under the flickering lamplight, shadows dancing on the faded wallpaper, a pretty pattern of pink and yellow roses, reminiscent of the girl's bedroom at the back of the sharecropper's hovel. Not much more than a lean-to really, but the tidy little room spoke volumes about the hopes and dreams of the occupant, fifteen-year-old Thelma Clayborne, missing for near a week now.

* * *

She lay there for too long, drifting in and out of consciousness, delirium clouding her thoughts, dulling her instincts. At one point she thought she heard her mother calling and sat up, cocking her head at the sound. The chorus of a song from her childhood played over and over on a scratchy Victrola. Her eyes drifted to the window and on hands and knees she willed herself to make the journey, inch by excruciating inch.

She ripped away the blanket that he had used to block out the daylight and pushed upward on the sash. It raised several inches and then stuck fast. Now squatting, she thrust all her weight against the frame. Grudgingly, it conceded another inch, before jamming tight. She forced her head through the narrow opening and peered out into the murky night. Darkness obscured the ground below, which tumbled off into a thicket-filled hollow, a good three-storey fall at least. She kicked her bare leg up onto the sill, rotated her body and, feeling with her toes, directed the other leg through the opening. She pushed against the floor and slowly angled herself upward until her bottom met the underside of the window frame. Here she remained, alternately tensing and relaxing the muscles until she had squeezed her hips all the way through. She teeter-tottered on the sill before jack-knifing from the waist to slither down the wall. Her bare feet scrabbled against the clapboard, seeking a toehold, but the planks were lapped to shed the rain, and offered no purchase. She continued lowering herself, shoulders next and finally her head. She clung to the sill, legs bicycling in the air, fingers slick with blood, quickly losing their tenuous grip. Then she was falling, down and down, into the darkness below.

* * *

"Whisky with a beer chaser," he called out when the bartender finally acknowledged his presence.

"Ya gotta clear that tab, first. Old man Robinson likes his lettuce fresh."

"Money order ain't come through yet. Could be another day or two."

"That ain't my look-out, mister."

"Come on, cut a guy a break will ya. I ain't no welcher."

"I ain't sayin' you is, but I already stuck my neck out, seein' as you was kin to ol' Mrs. Huntington an' all. I gotta cover the difference myself. What do I look like, a Rockefeller?"

He narrowed his eyes to feral slits and stared up into the rube's doughy face, gum-batting away like some one-room schoolmarm. He'd heard it all a million times before. He knew the type, a little bit of authority and they thought it gave them the right to Lord it over anybody fool enough to take their guff, which included just about every chucklehead who inhabited these backwaters. Well, they sliced open like everybody else, guts spilling in ropey coils to steam away in the fetid air.

The bartender backed up a step when he reached into his jacket pocket, fishing out a bill that he smoothed out on the bar top before pushing it toward him.

"Here, take my last fin against what I owe." The bartender snatched at the five, tucking it into his shirt pocket, and turned to retrieve the bottle of Jim Beam, pouring out a measure, which he slid toward the awaiting hand. In the dim light he caught the bartender staring at his badly-frayed cuff, and knew instinctively that his suspicions had been aroused. He'd arrived in the backwater a few days ago, claiming to be a relative of the longstanding local clan, a nephew of the old bird who was the last in a long line to occupy the two hundred or so acres of prime farmland twenty minutes north of the town limits. He had chanced upon the vacant farmstead and knew enough of the local history to spin a credible yarn. So far, his story was holding up, but that couldn't last much longer.

He downed the whisky in a single gulp, the slow burn spreading up from his gut. He left the empty glass on the bar top, taking the beer to a table away from the small knot of patrons gathered around the bartender, jawing about the war in Europe and how long they figured the limeys could hold out. He had his own troubles to worry about, starting with what to do about the girl. He should have finished her off on the spot and been done with the whole shebang in one fell swoop. Now he'd complicated the issue by kidnapping her and then mingling with these rubes while he concocted a plan to make her disappear. She'd seen him stick Jeffers from behind, a swift slicing motion across the carotid; seen him drag the still twitching body onto the siding where the shunting locomotives could destroy the evidence under a moonless night sky, mangle up the corpse so bad that no autopsy could prove the rummy hadn't passed out on the tracks and met his end under the deadly iron wheels. She had been too stunned to cry out, and for all his careful planning he'd totally missed her wandering up the tracks beside the livestock pens. Now he was doing exactly what he swore he wouldn't do, hang around while the dragnet tightened, half the county out looking for the missing girl.

'Stupid, stupid, stupid.'

With one long swallow he finished the beer. No sense trying to order another. He wasn't about to start groveling now.

He pushed back from the table and, keeping his eyes on the floor, walked out into the night. Off in the distance came the mournful wail of a freight train. He shuddered as the sound burrowed into his memory, a sourness rising in his gut. He steeled his nerves as his mind leapt to the business ahead.

* * *

The fall was over in a heartbeat, one moment clinging to the second storey windowsill, and the next laying in a crumpled heap at the side of the house. Her ankle had turned over when she touched down. She heard the snap of the breaking bone before she felt the pain rocket up her leg. She started to retch, dryheaving what little remained in her belly, a pitiful amount of bile and mucus. She couldn't bring herself to look at the mangled limb. Instead, she reached down to feel a sharp protrusion where the bone had punctured the skin. A choked cry issued from her lips, and for an instant her heart sank, but there were no tears, just a steely determination creeping into her psyche, stiffening her resolve.

She weighed the options. A cluster of out-buildings sat fifty yards to her right, and the main barn another thirty yards or so beyond. Straight ahead lay the long driveway and the way back to town, provided she could flag down a passing car before he returned. What were the chances at this time of night? From far away the lonesome moan of a Wabash freighter reverberated across the hushed fields. She pulled herself up and on hands and knees began the torturous crawl to safety.

* * *

The flap of wings high up in the rafters drew his gaze. A silhouette flashed, slicing the beams. Shadbolt canopied his eyes.

There, suspended high in the apex, a cruciform shape, arms outstretched, lashed to a long-handled shovel with heavy chain, the torso hooked through the sternum, sheathed in tattered white linen, like a Eucharist chasuble. A dark pool, glinting on the floor below indicated that the body had been impaled and bled out.

A deadly signature, a calling card most heinous, ritualistic in its execution, brutal in its intent.

He walked back outside and, leaning against the weathered wood, inclined his head to feel the sun on his face. He cupped his hands and lit a cigarette, smoked it down to the end, spitting out the loose bits of tobacco, and then fired up another, and a third, all the while ruminating on the details of the killing.

His mind tracked, like a needle in a groove, every note in the score, every nuance, every subtlety, if one could use that term to describe these violent, sadistic acts. The arrangement of the bodies, bathed in streaming sunlight for maximum effect, shafts of light as if from heaven, illuminating what? The flowing vestments of white, a reference to vestal virgins perhaps, and on the head, resting like a crown of thorns, a wreath of barbed wire.

The tableaus appeared biblical somehow, but the meaning, and he believed there was one, continued to elude him. His thoughts returned to the three other victims, their similarities. This one felt different, not only the age of the victim, but the type of female. Thelma was dark-haired, and short, not even five feet, and slight of build. The others were uniformly blonde and full-bodied. Something had escaped him in the shock of the moment.

Taking a last drag, he stubbed out the butt and re-entered the barn. He climbed up into the hayloft and unhitched the rope, slowly lowering the corpse to the floor. This girl was at least five-eight and big-boned. Her blonde tresses were matted and dark with streaks of blood from the barbed wire wrapped around her head. It was definitely not Thelma Clayborne.

* * *

He raced around the farmhouse in a panic when he found her gone, not believing she could have escaped through the narrow window opening. Shouting and cursing his stupidity along with her trickery, he searched through the rooms, running up and down the staircase several times before returning to the bedroom and spying the smears of blood on the sill. He surmised that she couldn't have gotten too far, on the other hand, there had to be a hundred different places she could be hiding.

Things were unraveling fast.

With hurricane lamp in hand, he wandered out to the barn, following what looked like a trail in the loose gravel. He unfastened the cane bolts and waved the lamp about. Anxious shadows skittered around the dark interior. Impatiently, he checked the stalls and then the hayloft. Above his head came the soft cooing of pigeons in the rafters, and the night wind whistling through the chinks in the boards.

"Stupid, stupid, stupid," he hollered, lashing out at an upturned bucket and sending it clattering across the floor.

Convinced she wasn't in the barn, he returned to the house and hurriedly gathered up his things. He couldn't waste another minute trying to find her. This bird had flown.

He started up the car and after idling for several minutes while he fiddled with the choke, fled the scene, heading south to the Missouri State line. He drove through the night, sticking to the back roads that ribboned the slumbering landscape. As dawn broke, he pulled into a roadside diner, a crimson stain spreading along the horizon. He got out and stretched, and lighting up a cigarette, gazed eastward as the sun contoured the low bluffs and turned the stubbled fields to gold. He rubbed at his jaw and brushed at his hair, which immediately flopped back over his forehead. Appraising his appearance in the side-view mirror, he spit into his hands and forcefully slicked his scalp into shape. Satisfied, he walked up to the front door and entered the establishment.

An early morning crowd of truck drivers and traveling salesmen occupied the stools along the counter, and a handful of others, farmers mostly, finished with the harvest, were scattered amongst the booths by the windows. He picked his way to a table on the far side of the room, beyond the reach of the boisterous chatter and the possibility of conversation. A sleep-deprived waitress approached with coffee pot in hand, filling a mug and setting it in front of him.

"What'll it be, Shug?"

"You got a blue plate special?"

"Not for breakfast, but the steak and eggs is as good as. Only two bits. Comes with grits, green tomaters and toast."

"Sure."

"How do you like your eggs?"

"Sunnyside up."

"And the steak?"

"Bloody, and keep the joe comin', been drivin'…" He hesitated.

"You betcha, Shug."

She returned twice more to refill the mug before delivering his breakfast. He dug in. It was the first real chow in his gut for the better part of a week. With a full belly he began to think a little clearer, pondering his current predicament. The girl had by now reached local police, who would no doubt issue an all points bulletin across Iowa, but he was deep into Missouri, out of harm's way for the time being, or so he thought. Did he travel west to Kansas or east to Kentucky? He could probably get on with the ATSF in Topeka, on the rails or in the yard. His cards were up to date and he was all square with his union dues.

Rising from the table, he fished around in his pocket for the two bits and an extra nickel for the waitress. He had just finished setting it beside his plate when in walked John Q Law, square-jawed and shouldered, campaign hats tilted forward as if against a stiff breeze. The lead trooper walked to the counter and turning around addressed the diner in a loud voice.

"Who's the owner of the Cord oucha heya?" The place quieted and the trooper repeated the question, pointing out to the parking lot, "I said, who's the owner of the Cord, looks like a '29 or '30?" There was a collective shaking of heads while all eyes scanned the room. Still no one owned up. "Well it didn't just drive heya by itself now did it?"

"Mebbe the fella dun drove it ain't heya no mo," said the owner, standing by the griddle, spatula in hand. He was attired in a stained apron and greasy toque blanche, massive biceps bulging like pythons from his tee-shirt.

"That's possible I guess, but just to be sure, I'm a gonna hafta ask you gents to show me whatcha all drivin'."

From where he sat, he could tell that the owner was about to say something else, but just ground his teeth together instead, and turning back to the griddle poked at the fat back, muttering under his breath.

They started at the far end of the diner, escorting the patrons out to their vehicles, and having them fire up the engines. As they walked out with the fifth group, he got up and sauntered over to the counter where the waitress stood, hand on hip.

"Where's the john at?" he whispered.

"Out back, Shug, but you can cut through the kitchen," she pointed to the swinging doors behind her.

"Much obliged." He strode through the kitchen and out the back door, following a worn path to a rickety outhouse nestled in a clump of trees. He looked around to make sure he was alone and then lit out across the adjoining field, aiming for a woodlot and the river valley beyond.

* * *

"Take your time and try and remember everything you can about your abductor. Nothing is too insignificant: what kind of cigarettes he smoked, gum he chewed, the smell of his hair oil, anything."

"He smoked home-made cigareets. He smoked an awful lot of 'em. His fingers was all yeller from them, and his har was dark and combed straight back."

"Side part, middle part?"

"Middle, but it kep' fallin' in his eyes like Jimmy Cagney, 'cep' his face was thinner, a lot thinner, more like Jimmy Stewart." She was about as good a witness as they could've expected under the circumstances, a real trooper, perched upright in the hospital bed, busted leg in a thick plaster cast. She'd probably be walking with a limp for the rest of her life.

Shadbolt took her through the standard battery of questions, obtaining a detailed account of the kidnapper's physical appearance and motivation for the kidnapping. The location of the murder victim was exactly as she had described, although discovered by a couple of railyard bulls the day before. They still didn't have a positive identification on the woman in the barn. The state police were checking the missing persons' reports. So far, there were no matches from the surrounding counties. It could take a while.

Later as he sat nursing an over-brewed coffee at a nearby diner, he reflected on the evidence gathered at the scenes. The overlapping elements of identical ligatures, and roll-your-own cigarettes were one hell of a coincidence, that and the fact that the farmhouses where Thelma and the other victim were held were less than ten miles apart, long-deserted, and remote from neighboring spreads.

The bartender at the Oskaloosa Hotel recounted the family connection and how the man Thelma described spoke with assurance and familiarity. He obviously knew the lay of the land. The bartender went on to reveal his suspicions about the man but figured him for a grifter at worst. The guy just didn't strike him as a kidnapper and murderer. This view was consistent with Shadbolt's own feelings. Unless Thelma's abduction was an elaborate ruse to throw them off the scent, they had simply stumbled onto a parallel series of events. Shadbolt was convinced that the acts had been carried out by two entirely different individuals: one methodical, calculating and excessively-cruel, the other sloppy, and indecisive, a murderer none-the-less, but not in the same league, hell, not even in the same universe.

The victims of his investigation weren't typical runaways, abused or disgruntled adolescents; they were young but mature women, independent and unattached, a teacher, nurse and waitress from Webster City, Boone, Grinnell and now Oskaloosa. All within striking distance of Des Moines. The Bureau had been called in after the second murder given the similarities and unusual nature of the crimes along with the crossing of county lines. Chief Sloski of the Iowa State Police knew this wasn't your common or garden criminal. He was savvy enough to know when to call in the heavy hitters with their advances in police work. He told Shadbolt how impressed he had been with the Bureau's handling of the Kelly debacle back in '39.

Shortly after the interview with Thelma Clayborne, an APB was issued, and posters distributed to every post office in every backwater throughout the depression-ravaged state. The artist's sketch of the perpetrator garnered an avalanche of tips that had the state police running ragged. Shadbolt remained resolute, telegramming the section head in Kansas City for more time and resources to sift through the detritus of the crime scenes, to follow the disparate threads. Instead he received a call to report to Washington post haste.

"Local chief figures they've identified their man, just a matter of time now."

"Local chief couldn't tell shit from Shinola," Shadbolt replied. "It's about looking like you're doing your job."

"Well the Governor is thrilled that it's being dealt with so quickly. Anyway, this has got to be wrapped up tout suite. We got bigger fish to fry."

"The M.O.'s are as different as night and day. Unless the guy's a Jekyll and Hyde, we're looking at two individuals, and right now they're chasing the wrong hombre. I'm convinced there's a connection to these other homicides. The real killer is still out there, no doubt sizing up his next victim."

"Look, one more week, two at most is all we can afford. We've been seconded to Internal Affairs for another assignment. I can't say more right now: it's all hush, hush. You'll get a full briefing when you get to Washington."

"What about resources? I sure could use a couple more hands."

"I can send Perkins and Will. They're due some time off, but hell, a change is as good as a rest."

"No one else besides Mutt and Jeff?"

"Beggars can't be choosers, Jack."

"Don't I know it? Okay, Mutt and Jeff it is. Better'n nothin' I guess."

* * *

The duo arrived on the 6:35 from Kansas City the following evening. Shadbolt met them at the station, briefing them in a nearby diner over steak and eggs. Perkins was the older of the two, a real hard ass, ex-beat cop originally from Hoboken. He provided the muscle during prohibition when skull-cracking and the manhandling of bootleggers was a prerequisite for the force. Felix Will was younger than Perkins by a good ten years, a college graduate, one of the new-breed of forensic specialists applying a raft of advanced methods to evidence-gathering and interpretation. They were an unlikely pair, in Shadbolt's estimation each overly suspicious of the other, and consequently taking one step forward and two steps back with the cases they collaborated on.

"Captain says the locals have a bead on the perp," said Perkins, belching to emphasize his displeasure at being dragged out to Des Moines to do ordinary police work.

"They've got a good description of a murderer, just not the same one we're looking for."

"You mean there's two of these maniacs on the loose around here?"

"Two very similar sets of circumstances; one fits the pattern, the other is a coincidence."

"I had a chance to review the case files on the way over," said Will.

"Don't you ever take a day off, College-boy?" Perkins spat.

Ignoring the jibe, Will continued, "It has all the earmarks of a repeat murderer, someone killing for sport or to satiate some perverse fixation."

"What'er you gettin' at, we got another Whitehall ripper?" said Perkins, a look of skepticism etching his coarse features.

"Possibly, though he didn't kidnap and torture his victims as far as we know."

"He butchered 'em just the same."

"Yes, that's true, but the devil is in the details. This is more like Peter Kurten, the vampire of Dusseldorf, a textbook sadist who committed ritualistic slayings of eight people before being guillotined in Cologne in '31. Fritz Haarman was another. He'd keep his victims locked up, sometimes for weeks, engaging in brutal games of cat and mouse before finally dispatching them. He went on a killing spree in Hanover from just after the great war till 1924."

"So, we should be lookin' for a Kraut then?" said Perkins.

"Not necessarily," Shadbolt interjected, "John and Sarah Makin were home grown, and Martin O'Leary was born and bred in the Bronx. He preyed on immigrant women in the slums at the turn of the century. They have no idea how many he murdered, but several were discovered buried in the basement of the tenement he rented."

"Yes of course, O'Leary," Will continued, "and don't forget Beauchamp."

"Down in Orleans, right? Back in the 20's if memory serves."

"Correct. His victims were all single women. Kidnapped and very sadistically killed. Tortured in fact, branded, some partially skinned and hung."

"Hung?"

"Not hung by the neck, suspended, posed if you like."

"What kind of poses?"

"They're only described. The victims were taken down before being photographed, but the accounts match these recent cases very closely: arms extended, cruciform shapes."

"Hell, that's our guy to a tee. I reckoned it was something biblical. I'm just not that well-acquainted with the scriptures to identify a theme. Not that that's going to lead us to the killer."

"Not directly. However, it might help in constructing a picture, determining influences, motivations, and once we learn what makes him tick, we can anticipate what he might do next and that's how we'll nail him."

"In theory. We just don't have a whole lot of time to make this bastard."

"So, what happened to this Beauchamp fella?" said Perkins. "Did he swing?"

"No, the case never came to trial. He was identified as the primary suspect. There was corroborating testimony from witnesses and lots of hard evidence, personal effects of the victims and such, at his compound, an old plantation outside Baton Rouge. Agents tracked him as far as Lafayette and then he disappeared into the bayou."

"Disappeared?"

"They found his pirogue capsized. It was speculated that the gators got him."

"You don't suppose it could be him do you, back after a long break?"

"Not altogether impossible, but unlikely; once these types get a taste for it, there's no turning back. The thrill of the act is like heroin to a junkie. The monkey has got to be fed."

"Some monkey," Perkins scoffed.

"I'd like to start interviewing friends and workmates of the other three victims, and anybody else they had regular contact with, storekeepers, bank tellers, customers, etc., see if we can identify any changes in behavior, or routine, any new acquaintances, strangers in town asking questions. They were all held in abandoned farmhouses, big spreads, isolated from neighbors. How's he finding these places? Driving the back roads, checking the obits, foreclosures? Any one of these activities requires visits to gas stations, county offices, grocery stores and newspaper stands. We just have to find someone, anyone who might remember anything that can put us on his trail."

"That's a pretty tall order, Jack. What have the State badges turned up? Shouldn't we be talking to them first?"

"All you gotta do is look at their files. They can hardly spell the names of the victims correctly. That's why we got called in the first place. They're way out of their depth. Handing out speeding tickets, chasing stray cattle, and breaking up drunken brawls is as complicated as it gets in these parts."

* * *

Perkins entered the musty county offices through a battered screen door that moaned its displeasure, echoing his own distaste for the long, tedious hours that lay ahead. A wild goose chase if you asked him. It was his fourth stop in the last two days of combing these backwaters for information he very much doubted would lead anywhere fast, but Shadbolt was insistent, and the sooner he proved that 'Abercrombie' was barkin' up the wrong tree, the better. He sidled up to the front counter and slapped at the bell. Footsteps sounded from deep within and a disheveled-looking clerk appeared from behind the high, stacked shelves. He squinted at Perkins through a pair of coke bottle glasses that gave him the appearance of a bedraggled barn owl.

"Afternoon, what can I do fer ya?"

"FBI," Perkins growled and flashed his badge.

"Oh." The clerk flustered, fidgeting with his tie. Large, yellowy patches stained the underarms of his shirt.

"We're collecting information on recent foreclosures, farm foreclosures."

"That would be the lis pendens documents. I'll just …"

"I don't need to see the records. I just need to find out if you keep a list of people who ask to see them, or get copies, and what about the sale of the properties; do you keep records of the transactions?"

"Of course. How far would you like to go back?"

"Well, not too far, last six months probably."

"They're organized by year. I can get you this year's. It's right up to date. Miss Hutchison is very efficient."

He disappeared into the stacks and came back with several hard-backed ledgers, placing them on the counter.

"These are the lis pendens in case you need to verify anything. This is the sign-out book and the last one is the patent deeds, which show the change of ownership. The foreclosure sales are marked." He opened the ledger and pointed to a red stamp in the upper right-hand corner. "You're welcome to use the table over there," he motioned to a dilapidated relic positioned against the far wall.

Perkins lugged the tomes over to the table and, taking out his pad, checked the names of the individuals or agencies who had signed out the foreclosure registry. It didn't take long to record a hit against the previous ledger, and then he drew a sharp breath. One name appeared on the registers from all four counties where the murders had taken place.

"Bingo," he called out loud, causing the clerk to peer over in his direction. He tapped a cigarette from a soft pack of Lucky Strike and leaned back to enjoy a smoke before carrying the ledgers back and depositing them in a heap. The clerk frowned as the books slammed onto the counter. Perkins flipped open his pad. "Wilson and Partners Real Estate Agents, they've been in here a whole mess of times in the last six months. What's the lowdown on these hombres?" The clerk opened up the sign-out book and ran his finger up and down the columns.

"Yes, Ed Wilson from Des Moines, he's been in on a number of occasions this year."

"You know him?"

"Not personally, but he's done business in the county before."

"So, what's his angle?"

"What do you mean?"

"What's he lookin' for?"

"Well, foreclosures, specifically farmsteads; bank foreclosures, or court-ordered sales when the owner dies intestate. He, ah, requested that we notify him of any suitable properties. He's considered a few, but I don't believe he's closed on any yet."

"Any idea why?"

"I couldn't say for sure. Price I would guess. Until the corn market picks up it's a hard way to make a living."

"Can you confirm his address and telephone number?"

"Yes, that's it unless he's moved in the last couple of weeks." Perkins turned on his heel and strode out of the building, letting the screen door bang his goodbyes.

* * *

The clerk waited until the FBI agent had vacated the parking lot. He glanced about furtively before retreating to an interior office to make a phone call. He didn't like this one little bit, 'no sir-ee', not one little bit. What the hell had he gotten himself into? At the other end of the line, the phone continued to ring. He hung up and dialed again. Still nothing. He could feel a headache coming on, a dull throbbing right behind his eyes. If he couldn't get through, he was going to have to make a personal visit. It was against his better judgment, but this was serious.

* * *

"Mitt me, kid!" Perkins was beaming as he bounced into the diner banquette.

"What are the congratulations for? You look like the cat that ate the canary."

"I've got a bead on our bad egg."

"So fire away."

"Ed Wilson, real estate agent right here in Des Moines. He's shown up in all four counties looking for foreclosed farms. Shadbolt was right on the money."

"He played a good hunch."

"Dumb luck if you ask me."

"Dumb like a fox."

"So how did you make out?"

"Not as well as you apparently. Maybe one lead. Not sure how solid it is though. Sister of the dead waitress in Grinnell. Says she talked to the victim about two days before she went missing. The gist of the conversation was that her sister was spooked by the same vehicle being parked outside her place three nights running."

"Did she make the plate?"

"No, but she described it as a dark-colored coupe with a prominent, winged hood ornament."

"Coupe, huh? That bowsprit makes it a Chevy or Cadillac probably. Not much to go on."

"It's a start. All we gotta do now is see what model car your real estate mogul drives. Let's see what Shadbolt has to say."

"Why wait for him to take all the credit? He'll be forever interviewing the cinder dicks about that other murder in the Wabash yards. I say we pay Mr. Foreclosure a visit right now. No sense dilly-dallyin' when I've got a sweet patootie, cute as a bug's ear, gettin' restless back in Topeka."

"Alright, but let's leave him a note. Let him know what we're up to."

* * *

Shadbolt spent the afternoon scrambling around the cattle pens with the yard bulls and afterward interviewing the dead man's work mates in a drafty, makeshift office, gritty with coal dust. Jeffers, the murder victim, elicited little in the way of sympathy. He came off as a malingerer and con artist, who also had a string of charges for petty thievery and cashing bum checks. With what they told him he could've had any number of enemies from any number of past scams he was involved in, but it was the last interview that provided most of the answers Shadbolt needed.

"Yeah, he coulda had lots of fellas sore at 'im for chiselin', you know what I mean."

"Do you remember any in particular?"

"Fer sure, he told us about a clip joint he was workin' at in Las Cruces, and this one time see, he took some rube for every last dime of his weddin' money. The guy was supposed to be gettin' married the very next day. Jeffers was swappin' the dice with a loaded pair, the ol' snake eyes switcheroo, but the guy was too drunk to notice. Jeffers said he bilked him outta two hundred and fifty simoleons. Heard the guy lost his fiancé and did twelve months in stir for assaulting the doorman and manager with an axe handle the very next night. Anyway, coupla years later Jeffers spots the guy at a union meeting at the ATSF hall in Albuquerque. He found out the guy was a brakeman workin' the Albuquerque to Barstow freighters, and he figured the guy was gonna recognize him sooner or later, so he hightailed it up here to the Wabash to work the marshalling yard. Anyway, to make a long story short, a coupla weeks ago he says he sees this same fella talkin' to one of the cinder dicks in the yard."

"He was sure it was the same guy?"

"Swore it on a stack of bibles."

"Did he mention a name?"

"Nope."

"What about a description?"

"Other than he looked madder 'an hell, nope."

"So, this fella was a brakeman?"

"Yep."

"On the Atchison, Topeka and Santa Fe, out of Albuquerque?"

"That's what he said. He was pretty shook up about it too, and the next thing ya know he's pushin' up daisies."

"Sounds like our man. We've got a good description from the kidnapped girl and the motive is becoming clearer. The ATSF offices in Albuquerque should be able to provide a name thanks to you."

"Say there ain't no reward money is there?"

"Consider it a public service. One less murderer on the streets."

"So, you ain't the butter and egg man?"

"Not this time 'round, sorry."

"Just my luck."

Although Shadbolt's gut told him from the beginning that there were in fact two killers out there, past experience had taught him to check and double check all the facts before pursuing a course of action. If nothing else, this revelation in the rail yard confirmed his suspicions that the kidnapping of Thelma Clayborne was an act of desperation, had occurred purely by chance, and was unrelated to the recent string of brutal slayings. He would convey this new information to the State Police in the morning, so that he, Perkins and Will could devote full attention to the real target of their investigations.

As he entered the hotel room, he caught sight of agent Will's note on the floor. He stooped to retrieve it and took it to the desk to read. The note described a break in the case, with an address in one of the better neighborhoods of Des Moines, about a fifteen-minute drive from the hotel. At this point too bushed and grimy to venture out again, he decided to await their return.

Stripping down to his underwear, he carefully hung his suit in the closet then placed his shoes outside the door to be shined. He walked into the bathroom, dialing the shower to the hottest setting. As the wall mirror started to fog, he spied his refection staring back, eyes sunken and rimmed red as the cuts scoring the flesh of the latest victim.

* * *

He'd been on the lam for three nights since slipping out of the back of the diner, hiding during the day and travelling with the moon, mostly back roads until the sky lightened again, and then he'd find an empty barn or a copse of trees and hunker down. He'd been moving ever westward, aiming for Kansas City and eventually Topeka where he hoped to sign back on with the Atchison, Topeka and Santa Fe, if not on the engines then in the main shop, or even the yard. There were always boxcars to load after the harvest.

The temperature dipped as the sun fell, and he felt the chill in his bones as he scuffed along the dirt road, kicking out at errant rocks, trying to keep his mind off the numbing cold and hunger that gnawed at his guts. He'd finished his last cigarette yesterday and was craving nicotine like a rummy craves the hard stuff. From the verges came the lonesome call of the nightjars, and from far off, the soft hoot of an owl.

He crossed the black waters of the broad Missouri River at Waverly, skirting around the town through fields of bluestem and switch grass grown brittle with frost, milkweed pods encased in glass and ragweed furred with rime. When he reached the highway again, he walked the ditches and shoulders brushing aside the crackling stalks when they threatened to check his stride.

In the heart of the night with his hands numb and his ears stinging from the cold, he heard the rumble of a truck coming up behind him. He considered scarpering into the fields beyond, but he was dog tired and sapped of the urgency to hide. Lights washed over him, sending a ragged silhouette racing ahead in the dark. The truck rattled past and then he heard the driver downshift, and the brake lights brighten as it came to a stop up ahead. It was a flatbed covered with a flapping tarp emblazoned with old English lettering and a large golden cross. As he approached the back of the truck the passenger door opened, and an arm waved him over.

"Hell of a night to be out takin' the air," said a voice at the end of the arm.

"Yeah, my car, see, it's ah …"

"So, can we get you to where you're goin'?"

"Sure, where are you headed?"

"Kansas City."

"Me too, well Topeka actually, but K.C. will do in a pinch."

"Consider yourself pinched," the passenger said and scootched over to let him in. The cab enveloped him like a warm blanket, and his extremities began to tingle and burn almost immediately. "I'm Mick McCarthy and this here wet smack is Carter Delamare." The driver, a hulk of a man, sat hunched over the wheel, and without turning his head, grunted a hello. He hesitated for a moment, and like a trumpet player finding high C, blew into his fists, while he considered a suitable alias.

"Casper Littlejohn, Cass for short."

"Pleased to make your acquaintance, Casper Littlejohn" said McCarthy, and he stuck out his hand, commenting as soon as the gesture was accepted, "Lord almighty, those are some cold meat hooks. You don't wanna be coppin' a feel with those."

"Good advice," he said, continuing to blow into his hands. "So, what brings you out in the middle of the night?"

"The crusade is movin' on."

"Crusade?"

"The International Church of the Foursquare Gospel."

"Ah, Sister Aimee's bunch."

"In the flesh."

"I thought she didn't travel around anymore."

"She doesn't, but her number one disciple, Mother Mary Margaret McCarthy, has taken up the cause."

"A relative?"

"Just a happy coincidence. We're a big clan, the McCarthy's; no special favors, I'm sorry to say, not that I haven't been angling for special treatment mind you." He spoke with a lilting brogue that was easy on the ears and infused with equal amounts of bonhomie and bullshit. Over the next twenty minutes McCarthy practically recounted his entire life story.

"So how long you been on the sawdust trail?" said Littlejohn.

"Since the summer, all over the great plains, as far north as Saskatchewan, and all points in between. We've been travelin' through Iowa this past little while. Cedar Rapids was our last port of call. Now we're headed back to California with a few whistlestops along the way: Kansas City, Amarillo, Phoenix, San Bernardino and finally home to Angelus Temple. Say, you're welcome to join our merry band of faith healers and tongue speakers, eh Carter. We could always use an extra set of hands settin' up the show."

"No thanks, like I said, I got a job waitin'."

"Suit yourself, Casper Littlejohn, but this is your chance to be saved. Jesus is coming, are you ready?" He looked directly at Cass as he said this, and then broke into a fit of laughter, slapping at his knees for emphasis.

"Don't pay any attention to him," said the hulk at the wheel, "He's been into the sauce." Littlejohn noticed a meaty paw clamp hard onto McCarthy's thigh.

"Just a nip, so it was, hardly enough to give a schoolgirl the giggles."

"Knock it off I said. Now try and get some shut eye or you'll be good for nothing come sun-up."

"Aye, aye captain. Better do as he says, Cass. The last guy caught disobeyin' is buried back in Iowa." The remark, though tossed off in jest, hit a little too close to home, and an awkward silence followed, so he started asking questions about the work on offer just to fill the dead air and calm his jitters. The driver answered each in turn, explaining that while they typically hired locals, a permanent crew was needed and they'd been shedding bodies like falling leaves through the fall, and were now short-handed. The pay was four dollars a day and they tossed room and board into the bargain.

"You make it sound pretty tempting. How long before you get back to Los Angeles?"

"Three weeks at the outside."

"See the thing of it is, this job don't start for a while. Gotta get my union dues up to date an' all, could take me a few weeks to get sorted out. This could be a good stop-gap in the meantime."

"Why don't you sleep on it for a while? Let me know your answer when we get to Kansas City. Hopefully, I'll have found another driver by then. Can you handle this kind of rig?"

"Sure thing."

"Good. Then if you agree to sign on, you can drive us all the way back to Angelus Temple."

"Sounds promising, and thanks again. Let me dream on it a while." He had misjudged the driver as some mindless Okie, but now it was obvious who the bull goose of the outfit was. Maybe, just maybe he had stumbled into a situation that could work to his advantage. The travelling gospel show could provide him with much needed cover while the kidnapping and Jeffers business blew over. The job in Topeka wasn't a sure bet, and perhaps not far enough away from the scene of the crime. His streak of bad luck was about to turn. Lulled by the steady hum of the tires, he drifted off into a fitful sleep.

* * *

Perkins drove past the house a second time just to make sure they had the right address.

"245 Oak Street, this is the place," said Will. "Real estate business must be doing alright in these parts."

"Quite the palace." Perkins mouthed a slow whistle as he surveyed the sprawling ranch house.

"I wonder if we should have waited for Shadbolt."

"What for, we're just gonna ask a few questions."

"Looks like he might be the type to decline until his lawyer is present."

"All the more reason to put the squeeze on him now before he has a chance to call in the ambulance chasers."

"Okay, but let's tread carefully. We don't want to be steppin' on any sensitive toes." Just then the front door opened, and a man and woman came down the porch steps and got into a car parked in the driveway.

"You figure that's our guy? That dame looks young enough to be his daughter."

"Or next victim."

"Shit! Flag 'em down quick." But before Will could clamber out the passenger side, the car exited the driveway and sped past. In the glow of the streetlight they caught sight of the man, pencil moustache and snap-brimmed fedora, late middle-aged, and sitting beside him, a young woman, tall and blonde. Perkins started the engine and hastily turned the car around, giving chase.

"Slow down and tail 'em. Let's see where he's taking her. No sense tipping our hand too quickly."

"Good thinking, Abercrombie. Easy does it." Perkins proceeded to follow at a distance as they wove through the quiet, tree-lined streets. Traffic picked up as they traversed the downtown, gaudy in flashing neon. They pulled up alongside at a stoplight, viewing the girl in profile. Cigarette in hand, she was laughing, head tipped back to vent a burst of laughter. "Well, if he's kidnapping her, she seems to be enjoying it." At that moment she glanced over at Perkins, catching his baleful stare. He nodded politely and turned to face straight ahead. "Shit, busted!" Perkins hissed, sotto voce.

"Don't flip your lid; she's probably used to mashers like you ogling her."

Perkins grunted and eased away from the stoplight, allowing several cars to come between the two vehicles. It stayed this way for another two traffic lights and then the car crossed the Des Moines River and headed west and then north onto the interstate. They drove through the dark countryside, past towns and hamlets necklaced like tiny baubles along the macadam. Soon they were the only two cars on the road.

"Where the hell could he be taking her?" said Perkins after thirty long miles. "There's gotta be plenty of deserted farms around here. He's got the pick of the litter."

"Could be operating on the premise of a minimum distance from home."

"Well, let's hope it doesn't have a hundred in it."

"Look, he's slowing down and turning." Up ahead the vehicle signaled and turned west toward Ames. Perkins followed, slowing further to avoid detection. They traversed the sleepy burg, crossing a lighted bridge that led into the Iowa State University campus. The Campanile tower soared above the trees. The clock face read 7:45 and the carillon bells were peeling. Clutches of students strolled about the lawns or gathered in boisterous groups. The idyllic setting was at odds with the sinister intent they had originally imagined.

"I'm beginning to think we're on a wild goose chase. We shoulda stopped him back in Des Moines."

"Well we're here now and the night is still young."

"So, what are you sayin'; we should keep tailin' 'im?"

"For now, I got a hunch this rabbit hole might actually go somewhere."

"I thought you college boys didn't play hunches."

"It's Gestalt."

"Ge-what?"

"German for hunch. It sounds more scientific."

"Sure Abercrombie, pull the other one."

Up ahead the car slowed to a crawl as it negotiated a narrow laneway. They continued following at a distance and then pulled over when the car came to a stop behind a featureless brick storage shed. Perkins killed the lights and waited.

Before long a door opened, revealing a duster-clad figure clutching a large box to his chest. The light above the door spilled over the container, illuminating a mangle of copper piping. The car door opened, and the driver walked around to the back and unlatched the trunk, standing aside while the figure deposited the box and then retreated back inside. This routine was repeated several more times until the trunk was filled. After the final trip the two shook hands, and surreptitiously an envelope was exchanged. The driver hesitated before climbing back into the vehicle and cast a glance in the direction of Perkins and Will sitting stock-still in the gloom of the darkened interior.

"We've been thinking all along that this could be our perp, but maybe he's been scoping out these deserted farms for an entirely different reason."

"I don't follow."

"Think about it, all that copper piping, fields and fields of corn, and derelict spreads with no nosy neighbors about."

"Well I'll be a monkey's uncle; illegal corn liquor."

"Bingo. Over half the counties around here are still dry. No wonder this hombre is livin' so high on the hog."

"Probably cornered the market after the eighteenth amendment was repealed and the booze bosses had been iced or sent to the big house."

"Only one way to find out; lead on McDuff."

They waited until the other vehicle exited the campus before firing up the motor again, and then without turning on the lights followed the receding red glow back out into the night.

* * *

When Perkins and Will still hadn't returned by nine o'clock, Shadbolt began to grow concerned. Routine questioning shouldn't have taken this long unless they made an arrest on the spot. He placed a call to the downtown precinct and checked on the evening's bookings. There was nothing to report on that front, in fact, it had been an unusually quiet night according to the desk sergeant who promised to call Shadbolt back if the situation changed. The trio had established a set routine, which included a briefing of the day's findings, normally over dinner, followed by a summation of the relevant facts and an action plan for the next day. It was an important part of the process, sifting through the disparate bits of information, testing different theories and angles, Perkins typically shooting from the hip, Will applying an academic rigor, and he, negotiating the spaces in between, methodically constructing the case.

Growing more restless with each passing minute, Shadbolt threw on a shirt, and slacks and ventured down the hall to Perkins and Will's suite, using the spare pass key to enter the room. He depressed the light switch and walked over to the bureau, serving as a makeshift desk. It was obvious which side of the room each of them occupied, one as neat as a military barracks and the other like it had been hit with a barrage of shell fire.

He picked up Will's journal and started to flip through the meticulously inscribed pages, detailing the interview of the sister of the dead waitress from Grinnell. He took particular interest in the dark-colored coupe that had been seen outside the murder victim's residence. He guessed Cadillac, a '39 by the description of the hood ornament. Recognizing that this was not the lead Will was referring to in his note, he returned to the bureau top and shuffled through the mess of paper closest to Perkins unmade bed.

He recovered Perkin's logbook from the pile and extracted a sheaf of paper inserted between the pages. He took them over to Will's bed and laid out the individual sheets, each corresponding to the county where the murders had been committed. Perkins had listed all the recent foreclosures, estate and bank sales of farm properties along with the individuals or entities who had made inquiries, offers or purchases within the last six months. He had then cross-referenced the names with the same name appearing in the registers of the four counties of interest, Wilson and Partners Real Estate Agents. Perkins had circled the entries in red ink, underlining the name for emphasis.

So, this was the lead Will was referring to.

He sat back and ruminated on the information. As it turned out none of the abandoned farms had been recently purchased. All were still bank-owned and by different banks at that, more or less ruling out bank employees as potential perpetrators or sources of information. The next step would be to determine what role this Wilson and Partners outfit were playing.

Was the culprit to be found there, or were they unwittingly acting for a third party? Presumably, this is what Perkins and Will were engaged in determining right now.

He went back to Perkins list and continued to scan the entries. On his third pass something caught his eye. He dialed the operator and obtained an address on the outskirts of the City, the warehouse district if recollection served.

He gathered up the pages from the bed and set them back on the bureau, returning to his room where he donned his jacket and overcoat, and then retrieving his car keys from the desk, made his way to the lobby and back out into the night.

* * *

"He must've pulled in at that last driveway," said Will, turning in his seat to scan for the taillights they had been following for the last dozen miles.

"Not unless he's killed his lights too."

"Do you think he made us?"

"He took a long gander back there at the university."

"Must have finally dawned on him."

"Maybe, maybe not."

"Well let's go back and find out." The car slalomed to a stop and spun around, heading in the opposite direction until the driveway loomed into view. Perkins pulled over onto the narrow shoulder a few hundred feet from the opening, which was bordered by a hedgerow of stately elm trees.

"We can leg it from here, through the fields, come on to them from the rear where they least expect it," said Perkins

"What about artillery?"

"They didn't strike me as the hunting types. Our badges should be enough to put the fear of God into 'em."

"But we don't know who they might be meeting up with."

"Who are you expectin', Machine Gun Kelly?"

"No, but let's not be naïve about it. These farmers come with their own arsenals of squirrel guns. They've got a good thing going and I don't expect them to go quietly into the night."

"Alright already, bust out the twelve gauge. 'Old Betsy' is in the trunk. Just don't go blowin' your own foot off, Davey Crockett."

Will retrieved the shotgun from the trunk and together they crossed the road, clambered over the rail fence and started up a row of ragged corn stubble, brown and brittle and bearded with frost. They continued to skirt the main dwelling, sitting dark and lifeless behind the windbreak. Between the low, scudding clouds a fingernail of moon cast a wan light upon a pond grown glassy in the chill. A car door slammed, and a drift of voices sounded from somewhere within a small colony of barns, sheds and silos, embossing the night sky.

Will pulled up the collar of his overcoat, and resting Old Betsy across his thighs, blew hard into his stiffening hands. Perkins strode on ahead, motioning to a rank of storage bins on the near side of the main barn. Approaching the structures, they looked for a way into the barn. Midway along the stone foundation, the outline of a door emerged from the shadows. It led to the lower level. Perkins bent down and unlatched the cane bolt and slowly pulled the door towards him. The weather-buckled wood groaned in protest, emitting a long, discordant creaking sound like a coffin lid being lifted. He grimaced and putting a finger to his lips nodded to Will to follow.

He pulled out his Smith and Wesson .38 Special from his shoulder holster and chimneyed the barrel. They waited for their eyes to adjust before negotiating row upon row of stacked barrels, presumably containing the illegal liquor. Muffled footfalls sounded on the floorboards above their heads, and the sound of something heavy dragged awkwardly. The basso rumble of male voices drifted downward, low at first, but now escalating in pitch and volume.

An argument?

This was their opportunity.

Perkins motioned them toward an open staircase at the far end of the storage room. They ascended into the high, raftered space where under a pale-yellow cone of light a handful of figures gathered, two practically toe to toe, jawing loudly.

"FBI!" Perkins barked. "Get those maulers up where we can see 'em." The words had barely left his lips when a shot rang out from somewhere up in the loft, grazing his shoulder and causing him to pitch forward

"Perkins," cried Will

"I'm okay, I'm okay, give 'em both barrels, hurry."

* * *

Will raised Old Betsy and fired into the gloom. The volley peeled like summer thunder and was followed by a woman's scream as the gathering scattered into the darkened interior. Perkins scrambled for cover behind a nearby corn crib and returned fire, aiming for the muzzle flash. The cylindrical cribs measured six feet wide and six feet high. Fashioned from thick gauge metal wire, they were filled with drying ears, yet to be shucked and shelled. They were aligned in rows, providing Perkins with cover and a pathway to get within striking distance of the bootleggers.

Another shot rang out from above causing Will to duck back down the stairs to reload. He peeked out from the stairwell, noting the location of the muzzle flash when the shooter exchanged fire with Perkins. Resting the barrel in the crook of his arm, he took aim and let loose with another deafening blast.

From the loft there came a strangled cry and a dark form fell from the shadows and onto the floor with a dull thud, his rifle clattering down beside him. In that instant the light was shot out, pitching the cavernous space into total darkness. Shots rang out from below the loft, handguns from the sound of the reports. Will was chased back down the stairs, showered with splinters of wood. He raised his head to witness Perkins returning fire and then watched him bolt behind the next crib in the row. He could tell Perkins was aiming to get to a spot behind the shooters and catch them in a crossfire. The main barn doors, their only means of escape, were located directly behind Will, perpendicular to the stairwell. They'd have to take him out to get by.

* * *

Wilson and his moll eased their way along the opposite wall beneath the loft, heading for the barn door and freedom. So long as his partners didn't rat him out, he'd put enough of a paperwork buffer between himself and the illegal operations to avoid prosecution. He figured they could ditch the auto back in Des Moines and claim it had been stolen. Of course, getting caught red-handed would scuttle that little contingency. Once he figured they were being tailed he should never have risked the delivery tonight, but the Kelham boys were insistent, and there was some unfinished business to attend to. They were old school and used to handling this kind of predicament, but in his wildest dreams he'd never have guessed the FBI would turn up in this backwater. Surely, they had bigger fish to fry. He grabbed Delores by the hand and continued to inch along the sheltered wall. The barn door was within sight. They were almost home.

* * *

Perkins heard Will fire off another blast across the barn. He made that eight shells. He'd be down to his last two. As the culprits returned fire, Perkins made a dash down the aisle between the cribs to get within spitting distance of the shooters who were concentrating their efforts on the G-man in the stairwell. Perkins was close enough to see their outlines within the penumbra of the muzzle flash and fired into the haloed mass. The first gunman dropped to his knees, pawing at the gaping hole in his chest, and just as the second turned to fire at Perkins, Will let loose with his last salvo, catching the man with a spread of buckshot that sent him hurtling backward. A third culprit attempted to clamber up into the loft as Perkins closed in.

"Drop your weapon and come on down," commanded Perkins, drawing a bead on the hayseed who stood atop the final rung, clutching a pitchfork. It landed below with a clang, and he slowly descended back down the loft ladder.

* * *

Will advanced to where Perkins stood, shotgun raised but now empty. Behind him he heard an engine roar to life, and then he was running back toward the door, reaching for his sidearm. He took a knee, extended both arms to hold the gun steady and aimed for the rear tire. He recalled every lesson from the endless hours of target practice and squeezed the trigger. The tire shredded in a jumble of flapping rubber, sending the car careening into the hedgerow at full speed. There was a vicious sound of crunching metal, followed by a deadly fireball as the gas tank exploded. He raced across the yard and down the driveway. Tearing off his coat, he beat at the flames spewing from the shattered windshield. Then he scuttled around to the passenger side, yanking at the handle, red-hot to the touch. The automobile was a mangled heap, the concertinaed door wedged shut. Wrapping the coat around his hand, he tried the handle again. The side window disintegrated, fire belching from the opening, driving him back. He put up a hand to his face and made a last-ditch attempt to breach the blaze. The intensity of the heat was staggering. He fell to his knees, looking on helplessly as the occupants were consumed in the inferno.

They had probably died on impact. He hoped so.

His mind went to the pretty blonde, laughing only scant hours ago.

He rose to his feet and dragged himself back to the barn, finding Perkins with his boot on the yokel's throat, forcing a confession, although one was hardly necessary with the evidence at hand and the scattering of dead bodies for good measure. He wondered how Shadbolt was going to react. Sure, they had busted an illegal liquor operation, but in the process abandoned their primary mission. There would be time-consuming paperwork and a full investigation into the deaths, some of whom no doubt had friends and associates in high places.

* * *

Shadbolt drove eastward, out beyond the grid of orderly City streets with their matchbox houses of clapboard and brick and into the industrial flats between the rail line and the river, past cider block warehouses and corrugated sheds where nightshifts practiced the hard graft that was the lot of the working stiff. He'd been there at one time himself, all the way through high school and college, humping bags of seed, fertilizer and herbicide, loading boxcars and freighters, hodding bricks on construction sites and hand-mixing concrete. He knew the rhythms of the workday intimately, and the relief that a nicotine break could bring. That early experience had been all the incentive he needed to knuckle down to his studies. Although, if truth be told, he had a proclivity for research and complex analysis, which naturally led him to the Bureau right after he graduated with first class honors. All in the dim and distant past now, but he still had a large measure of empathy for the average Joe, and never forgot his humble roots.

There was another very compelling reason for his career choice, involving the untimely death of someone close to him, as close as anyone would ever get. He never spoke of it and had buried it long ago, or so he thought. But this recent spate of murders had exhumed the memory, still festering after all these years.

Just past a big tank farm he slowed to check the street sign and then turned onto a gravel roadway that wound through a series of tired-looking factories and desolate storage yards. The headlights picked out a sign at the end of the road: C and K. Salvage, and he drove through the open gates and into the yard. It was a sizeable operation, several acres strewn with piles of scrap metal, lumber, building materials and miscellaneous junk, rusted out water tanks, battered household appliances, odd pieces of farm machinery and automobile parts, all enclosed by a high chain link fence topped with razor wire. He parked in front of a dilapidated two storey structure, a workshop-garage cum office.

The garage doors were closed, but a light burned in the front windows of the upstairs, reached by a wooden stairway attached to the side of the building. He climbed to the top and knocked on the door marked office. A minute passed and he rapped again, this time more forcefully. When there still no answer, he called out and rattled the doorknob. The door swung inward. From somewhere inside he heard the muted strains of a radio; a Latin melody was softly playing. He recognized the tune, Perfidia.

"Hello," he called out, "anybody home?"

A makeshift task lamp threw harsh shadows about the dingy room. It rested on a ramshackle desk piled high with stacks of paper. He walked over and studied the piles, invoices by the looks of them. An adding machine rested in the middle of the mess, the paper roll of figures spilling over the desk and all the way to the floor like Rapunzel's hair. He bent down and retrieved a page from the closest pile. The C and K Salvage logo displayed across the top bore today's date. He carefully replaced it and called out a final time before crossing the scarred linoleum and entering the adjoining room.

He flipped on the light switch and surveyed the cramped living quarters: a quilt-covered couch, kitchen table and mismatched chairs, hot plate and icebox, unkempt Murphy bed dressed in grimy sheets, and against the opposite wall, a coal-oil furnace emitting a strong kerosene-like odor, which permeated the entire premises. There was no water closet. He surmised a bucket by the side of the bed served as a chamber pot. A door along the back wall led to an interior staircase opening onto the garage below. He tried the wall switch to no avail and so struck a match to light the way as he descended. He was in half a mind to go back up and look for a lamp or a candle when the flame guttered out, but continued down into the gloom, striking a second and then a third match. On the bottom rung, he took out the piece of paper on which he'd taken down the address and fashioned a tightly-rolled taper. As he held it above his head two automobiles emerged from the blackness, a pick-up truck facing outward, the box filled with the salvager's tools of the trade, and parked beside it, a coupe, deep-burgundy in color, the winged hood ornament identifying it as a '39 Cadillac. A wild-eyed man stared out from the driver's seat, causing Shadbolt to jump back, dropping the taper, and reaching for his gun. He barrel-rolled to the side and pointed the weapon at the windshield, now in deep shadow.

"Come out with your hands up," he barked. His heart raced as he waited for the car door to open. Then the taper blinked out throwing the garage into total darkness.

* * *

The tightly-clutched ticket, dwarfed in his meaty paws, read Des Moines to Kansas City, Union Station. He managed to secure the last private cabin on the Wabash sleeper which would deliver him to his intended destination by 6:30 a.m. He stowed the ticket in his inside pocket, and gazing into the men's room mirror, patted at his Brillianteened hair, slicked close to his skull, and giving the appearance of a too-small bathing cap struggling to contain his massive jowls. He was a man of prodigious girth and appetites which ran from the extraordinary to the excessive. Tiny, watery-blue pig eyes lay shielded beneath a massive, protruding brow, an avalanche of flesh that appeared to have slipped to the bottom of his steeply sloping forehead. Although effete and fastidious about his general appearance to the point of obsession, he could snap a neck with the merest twist of his wrist and crush a windpipe with one hand.

He glanced at his nails, freshly manicured and buffed, then carefully placing his hat so as not to mess his hair, he adjusted the brim and tossed a silver dollar to the attendant. Striding along the platform, his mind raced ahead to the sumptuous offerings of the Westport Room situated next to the great hall in the Kansas City terminal, and resplendent in its newly acquired riverboat theme of brass pillars, heavy brocade, and richly patterned carpets. He knew Chef Frederick personally, conjuring visions of his signature dishes: stuffed green peppers with Creole sauce, buttered yellow rice, grilled, chopped beef with Bordelaise sauce, and the piece de resistance, a baked gondola of lobster Newburg. The porter took him to his compartment.

"You be needin' a wake-up call, suh, or mebbe some breakfast? Ham an'eggs is mighty good on da Sleepa, suh."

In response, he gave a casual wave of the hand and tossed another silver dollar, which the porter palmed.

"Sorry 'bout that bitty bed. Married folk dun took up all dem doubles what we got." The Porter gave a deep bow and exited the cabin.

The phone call from the Mahaska County clerk in Oskaloosa to Custer had alerted him to the arrival of the FBI agent and his interest in the foreclosure files. It signaled an end to the modus operandi that had thus far served him so well. In the meantime, he had taken pains to cover his tracks and sever all connections to the business of the past few weeks. Greener pastures were calling, and he was hoping that this last campaign had satiated the visceral cravings for the time being. The period between "harvestings" seemed to be growing shorter and shorter, and the newspaper accounts ever more gruesome. He felt a familiar stirring as he remembered the latest descriptions, the haughty waitress from Grinnell in particular. She had been so reluctant, and her revulsion of him so evident. The look in her eyes when she awoke, bound and gagged, had been beyond delicious and would sustain his basest fantasies for months to come.

He had never equated the FBI with this sort of crime before, believing they were primarily concerned with organized gangs engaged in bootlegging, bookmaking, protection rackets and prostitution. Up to now he had enjoyed a clear run with nothing but the local constabulary, and sometimes the distracted State police to contend with.

That was about to change. His mind drifted back to his last brush with the notorious G-men. It had happened on June 17th, 1933, the infamous Kansas City massacre in the parking lot of Union Station, and involved the botched rescue attempt of Frank Nash who was being returned by several FBI agents to the Leavenworth penitentiary, from which he had escaped three years earlier.

He was a member of Vernon Miller's crew entrusted with the task of rescuing Nash and helping spirit him away in the awaiting vehicles after dispensing with the agents. As fate would have it, he had contracted food poisoning the night before, most likely from an over-indulgence of Quahog mussels, and so was absent when the fireworks erupted and managed to elude the subsequent dragnet, fleeing south to Baton Rouge where he became reacquainted with his current associates.

He had been lucky; he had always been lucky, and God willing, his luck would continue to hold.

He reached over and slid the window down, feeling the cold air fill the cabin. He took a set of car keys from his pocket and bending them back and forth, broke each of them in two and then flung the pieces out into the night. Octavius Cadogan, was known as "Caddy" to his associates, not so much a play on his name, but on his predilection for Cadillac automobiles, which he acquired and abandoned with regularity. He was partial to this last one, had even given it a name, Elsinore. A shame really, such a waste, but needs must. He had been in the game long enough to know that sentimentality about anything was nothing but a one way ticket to Palookaville.

* * *

Shadbolt held his position, repeating the command to exit the automobile. He shifted uneasily, keeping the pistol trained on where he imagined the occupant to be. In the darkness he cursed himself for not searching the premises for a lamp before venturing down the staircase. With his left hand he brushed at the floor in front of him, feeling for the remnant taper. On the third pass his fingers traced the outline, measuring at least two inches of the crumpled paper tube remaining. He lit the remaining stub, holding it aloft.

Wild eyes flashed from within a death mask staring straight back at him. As he edged closer, he could see blood stains on the man's shirt. Closer still, the guts coiling into the victim's lap.

He let the taper fall and lighting the rest of the matches made his way back up the stairs. After placing a call to the State police, he returned with a hurricane lamp and set about examining the crime scene.

He deduced that the murder had occurred in the last few hours. The corpse was not yet cold. There was a ligature around the neck, holding the head in place and the hands were bound behind the back. The ankles were also bound, and the feet had been nailed to a block of wood with roofing spikes.

The knots were recognizable from the other murders, handcuff knots locked with half hitches. Somebody had put the man, still alive, into the vehicle, fixed him in place and then sliced him from pelvis to sternum. The incision was surgically precise, like the markings on the other victims. It appeared to have been made with a scalpel.

When he had completed his examination of the corpse, he checked the glove compartment for any papers. As expected, there was nothing of consequence and the rest of the vehicle was devoid of any useful evidence, or so he initially thought, but mingling with the smell of leather and the rank odor of spilled intestines was the faintest whiff of floral and spice. A scent he had smelled before. More recently in the derelict room, where the school teacher had been held, cutting through the acrid tobacco residue, and once before that, years ago now, in a boarding house where one of the accomplices of Vernon Miller had been staying. Fougere Royale, an expensive French cologne, not your ordinary eau de toilette, sold in bulk at Woolworth's. It suggested an individual of breeding and money, sophisticated, intelligent, yet brutally strong and cruel beyond belief. An image was forming in his mind, a compilation of traits that served to define the killer. Identifying him was one thing, catching him had thus far proved an entirely different matter.

He shut the car door and went around to the trunk. It was locked, and with no keys in sight within the vehicle, he walked over to the work bench, selecting a heavy, ball-peen hammer. After several strikes, he removed the trunk handle and released the lid. Inside was another body doubled up on its side, a male with thinning red hair and a pale complexion. There were no ligatures or rope marks, no ritualistic cuts, but ugly purple bruising about the throat suggested that he had been choked to death, his windpipe crushed. Folding back the man's overcoat, Shadbolt reached in and extracted a hand-stitched wallet from his inside jacket pocket. It contained a few crumpled bills, a laundry ticket, and a battered business card reading Milord V. Kirkland, Head Clerk, Mahaska County.

* * *

"So, he was your guy?" Shadbolt asked Perkins when he returned from the morgue.

"Same guy, just a little less active than the last time I saw him." Perkins eased himself into the chair next to Shadbolt's desk. Shadbolt noticed that he was still feeling the effects of the bullet that had grazed his left shoulder. They'd patched up the wound and would have put his arm in a sling, which, knowing Perkins, he'd removed the moment he left the hospital emergency ward.

"How's the shoulder?"

"I'll live. I've had a lot worse."

"Make sure you change the dressing regularly. I can't afford to have you down for the count."

"Don't sweat it, Jack. I'm a fast healer."

"You're a lucky son of a bitch is what you are. A few more inches to the right and we'd be penning an epitaph for your headstone."

"It was too late to call for back up, and in case you hadn't noticed, there ain't that many phone booths out there in corn country."

"Well, as it turns out you and Will are heroes to the local law enforcement, and no doubt citations are in order, and well-deserved I might add. It's too bad Ed Wilson was such a big supporter of the mayor, along with every major charity in the county. The City folk are having a hard time accepting their knight in shining armor as the king of corn liquor in these parts. That and the fact that moonshining doesn't usually carry a death sentence."

"They fired first, and Will followed standard protocol when he blew out the tire. It was a freak accident, coulda happened to anyone, and he's been beatin' himself up about it since it happened. I've tried telling him otherwise, but you know these college boys, tend to over-think everything. A word from you would go a long way to settin' him straight and the sooner the better."

"Alright, I hear you. I'll sit him down over a beer and try to ease his conscience."

This was a side of Perkins Shadbolt hadn't witnessed before. Genuine concern and empathy for his partner. It was apparent that a bond was starting to form between them. As well, Perkins had sweated the details, had done the necessary dog work, although begrudgingly, that identified Ed Wilson as the possible suspect, one who appeared to be using the same M.O. as the killer. Solid investigative police work. And, as Perkins explained, he hadn't actually overlooked C and K Salvage in the entries; he just reckoned that they were carrying out legitimate business. He claimed he would've gotten around to them eventually.

At this juncture it was clear that the Custer in Custer and Knudson Salvage, the dead man in the Cadillac, was intimately connected to the murders, as was the Mahaska County clerk. The fact that they had been disposed of suggested an ability to identify the killer. Shadbolt had scoured the premises earlier in the day and planned to return tomorrow morning to re-examine the paperwork scattered about the office, along with a stack of ledgers extracted from a wall safe. In the meantime, Will had been dispatched to car dealerships throughout the area to see if he could match the abandoned Cadillac to a sale or a previous owner.

"I'm not sure what we might find at the clerk's place. Seems to have been pretty fastidious about record keeping, according to his boss. Chances are he might have kept something of interest about the premises. He's got the upstairs of an old house in Oskaloosa. Apparently, he shares the house with the records secretary, a Miss," Shadbolt flipped through his notebook to retrieve the name, "Hutchison, Miss Hutchison, she lives downstairs."

"Sounds like a cozy arrangement."

"Doesn't it just. You may want to speak to her as well. They might have shared more than living accommodations."

"Consider it done. I'll have that canary singing a sweet tune by the end of the night."

"Don't flatter yourself, Casanova. She's probably not your type anyway."

"Hey, they're all my type when you turn 'em up-side-down."

"Well just remember what I said about taking care of that shoulder while you're turning her up-side-down, okay."

* * *

Perkins ascended the porch steps and rang the bell. The yellowed lace curtains covering the door light were drawn back to reveal a face waging a losing battle against the ravages of time. No amount of rouge and lipstick could hope to arrest the erosion of what was once considered beautiful, a transitory state, as fleeting as the darling buds of May. Her countenance brightened at the sight of the burly G-man, and she opened the door with a flourish, standing before him in a silk kimono and a turban of a type that was popular in the '20s. A long, ivory cigarette holder dangled between her freshly manicured fingers, the nail polish a garish shade of green. Perkins entered into a cloud of cloying perfume.

"Agent Perkins, ma'am." He extended his hand, which she seized and clasped to her bosom.

"I'm so glad you're here. I've been worried to death since I heard what happened to Milord. You just can't imagine." He towered above her, nodding his concern while she continued clutching his hand, staring up into his craggy features.

"Well just to put your mind at ease, we think whoever was responsible for this is long gone."

"I hope so. I haven't been able to sleep a wink in the last two days." Reluctantly, she released her grip and ushered Perkins into the parlor. "Won't you have a seat, ah, Agent Perkins."

"Thanks, ma'am." He sank down into a low-slung divan, placing his fedora on the arm.

"Please call me Clara. We don't need to be so formal after hours." She fluttered her heavily-mascared eyes and blew a perfect smoke ring towards the ceiling. "Can I offer you a drink, coffee, or if you'd like something stronger, I've got a bottle of gin that is just crying out to be poured over chipped ice with a sprig of mint?" She gave a schoolgirl laugh and sat down next to Perkins, crossing her legs to reveal the fact that she had very little on underneath the Kimono. Her demeanor was at total odds with the image Perkins had constructed in his mind, like a cast breaching its covenant with the sculptor's mould.

"Ah thanks, that would be swell, but maybe later. Right now, I've got to take a gander around Milord's place. We think he might have got himself mixed up with the wrong types, so I'm going to nosey around a bit and see if there's anything that might help in our investigation, and afterwards, if you don't mind, I'll come back down and ask you a few questions."

"Why surely, although I can't imagine how I can be of help. I mean we worked together all these years, but Milord was a very private person. He kept mostly to himself."

"Even so, anything you can add will be a big help. Sometimes it's the smallest bit of information that breaks a case wide open."

"Alright, I'll give it my best shot."

"That's the spirit, Clara. We'll get these hombres. We always do."

* * *

She escorted him to the foot of the stairs and then watched him ascend as if he were a doughboy leaving for some distant confrontation, his life in the balance. In her blurred reality the clerk's demise, and subsequent appearance of the G-man, had opened a vent into the roiling interior of her desires, entombed for so long under the cap rock of the stultifying daily routines of the dusty county offices. She was primed for one last eruption, one last bout of searing, hot passion before all that remained of her existence were paper-thin memories worn to translucency and indistinguishable from the waking dreams that offered little in the way of succor.

* * *

The stairway ended at a broad landing, which ran back along both sides, providing access to a series of rooms. There was another steeper stairway at the opposite end, leading to the attic. Perkins moved counterclockwise through the rooms starting with a small scullery. A coffee pot sat atop the gas range and a mug and plate were stacked on the draining board. The next room was the clerk's sleeping quarters, dominated by an ornately carved, four-poster bed and several dark wood dressers, most likely family heirlooms. He checked the drawers, overstuffed with argyle socks, colorful boxer shorts and white tee shirts. The room was without a closet, but a burled walnut tallboy with maple insets held his suits, dress shirts and shoes, each one impregnated with a cedar shoetree.

Bypassing the attic, he entered a compact living room housing an overstuffed chesterfield, matching needlepoint chairs, a worn oriental rug and against the far wall, an old-style Victrola, the acoustic horn resembling a flowering lily from Brobdingnag, Gulliver's land of the giants. He walked over to view the disk on the turntable, a classical piece, Chopin's Piano Concerto Number 2 in F Minor. No hip-swinging jazz for this Abercrombie.

The final room was the clerk's office, holding a large roll top desk, filing cabinet and floor to ceiling shelving crammed with hardcover books and periodicals: encyclopedias, almanacs, atlases, textbooks on a variety of subjects and leather bound collections of the classics, Aristotle, Plato, Shakespeare, Dickens, Austen, Hardy, Proust, Hugo and the like, pristine spines lettered in gold leaf.

The roll top was opened, and Perkins started to sift through the loose papers and envelopes stacked in a separate pile. Bills for the most part, notifications from various associations of which he was a charter member, and a partially penned letter to a cousin in San Bernardino he was planning on visiting over Christmas. Perkins checked the pigeonholes and then the drawers, coming across the clerk's bank statements and pass book. There were regular monthly accounts of consistent deposits and withdrawals, but in the last six weeks, two larger deposits via check from C and K Salvage of five hundred dollars each. Not an insubstantial amount. He made note of the dates. So Shadbolt was right on the money in terms of the arrangement. Custer was the contact man, and he had retained Milord to identify and scope out the joints. But why kill him, unless he had stumbled onto something, or knew more than he was supposed to know? He continued rifling through the desk, not exactly sure what he was looking for. The bottom left hand drawer was locked, and he searched in vain for several minutes for a key, eventually prizing the lock with a letter opener.

Sitting on top of a stack of manila envelopes was a pamphlet advertising the upcoming engagement of The International Church of the Foursquare Gospel, Sister Aimee Semple McPherson's travelling road show. It was dated November 1st, one week prior to the discovery of the last murder victim.

"So, Milord was a God damned holy roller, seeking forgiveness for being on the take. Nothing but a bible-thumping accessory to murder."

He flipped through the pages. A newspaper clipping slipped out. MISSING SCHOOL TEACHER FOUND MURDERED, screamed the headline. He put it to one side, and reached for the uppermost manila envelope, unwinding the thin red string tie. It contained photographs, premium cheesecake by the looks of the first few, and then out and out pornography.

"Jesus H Christ!" This was some collection, real hardcore stuff. He hadn't come across anything like this since his days in vice back in Hoboken, before he was recruited by the agency. He wondered if this was the connection to the murder victims, a pornographic photo session gone horribly awry, or maybe the torture and blooding was the payoff for the sick bastards who collected this kind of stuff. He rewound the tie and picked up the next envelope. It was much the same as the first, variations on a few themes: fellatio, anal intercourse, multiple partners, but mostly lots of hard dicks entering willing pussies. There was no real torture or brutalization and no dates or notations on the envelopes or the photographs.

He picked up the last envelope. There in the corner was a name. He read it twice just to make sure and then opened the package. It looked like they'd been taken some time ago, maybe ten, twelve years. She was well past her prime, but nicely put together: great gams, a perfectly round ass, and a great set of knockers tipped with nipples the size of Bing cherries. He went through the photographs a third time and then extracted his preferred pose, creasing it down the middle before slipping it into his pocket. He put the envelopes and pamphlet back in the drawer and held on to the clipping, surmising that Milord must have cottoned on to the caper after the murder of the schoolteacher. Maybe he'd tried to blackmail

Custer, or whoever was behind the scheme. He'd let Shadbolt know his thoughts so he could search for a demand note at the salvage yard.

After visiting the attic, a dusty repository of discarded furniture and bric a brac, he descended to the lower level and called out for Clara. She emerged from the parlor with drink in hand and beckoned him into the dimly-lit room. His gaze followed the slow sway of her hips and he wondered how those Bing cherries might feel between his teeth.

* * *

After deciding on the smaller of the two cases, Vivian fretted all the way to Kansas City that she hadn't brought enough clothing to see her through the weekend with her sister Helen, who insisted on a new outfit every time she set foot outside her apartment. Helen was the statuesque blonde to her more diminutive and much less curvaceous frame, topped with a tangle of copper-colored curls. Helen's roommate, Sally was away visiting a sick relative up State, and as Gene, her current steady was off on a case in Iowa, she'd accepted the invitation, not wanting to spend another weekend at home alone.

Topeka, although the state capital, was a quiet backwater populated by clumsy hayseeds and raucous railway workers whose idea of excitement was getting plastered at some smoke-filled juke joint on a Saturday night. Vivian was familiar with the type, having married young to a brash Midwest farm boy who had lost everything during the great crash of '29, and instead of jumping with the rest of the bankrupt stockholders, had caressed the barrels of a loaded shotgun and left her a penniless widow. She'd gone back home at that point, mucked in with her parents and siblings and helped save the family's modest homestead from the debt collectors. She'd gathered eggs at daybreak, worked the fields till late afternoon, and spent her evenings at night classes for typing and shorthand, eventually securing a good paying job at the county courthouse. With the worst of the family's financial troubles behind her, she'd taken a nice little apartment above Lockerman's Hardware, a short walk from her office near the downtown.

Since then she'd fended off a number of suitors until he came along, a burly, ruggedly handsome, wise-cracking G-man with a fondness for the ribald and an apparently insatiable appetite for her womanly charms. The first time they had made love, he stood her up against a closed bedroom door, and with party-goers knocking to retrieve coats piled in a heap on the bed, brought her to orgasm in a torrent the likes of which she hadn't experienced up till then, and in the morning, cocooned inside his sleep-warmed bed, he took her slow and easy to states as pleasurable as could be attained, soaring breathless and euphoric, the next moment plummeting, giddy and tingling, every sense enlivened. It was a relationship cemented by pure lust that remained unquenchable and immune to the constraints of social convention. The whisperings and withering looks of the neighbors were a small price to pay for the exhilaration his monthly visits brought. He was stationed in Kansas City, a two-hour train ride from Topeka, which she took on alternate weekends.

Vivian alighted at Union Station with case in hand and strode off in the direction of the Westport Room where she had arranged to meet Helen for breakfast. She spotted her immediately, striking in an emerald green suit, her freshly coiffed tresses cascading around her shoulders in waves of honey-gold. Helen was engaged in a lively conversation with two gentlemen at the next table, both competing for her attention. She immediately jumped up when she spotted Vivian.

"Over here, sis'."

"Helen, so good to see you." They embraced and then stood for a moment appraising each other. She could tell by the set of her sister's brow that she had passed muster.

"Vivian, I'd like you to meet Al and Huey, a couple of dolls in from St. Louis on business. Boy's this is my little sister, Vivian, hands off though, she's dating a G-man."

"Wow, I'd take a bullet to pitch a little woo with 'er."

"A bullet, I'd risk the hotsquat, buddy boy." He shook his limbs in imitation of someone getting the electric chair.

"Settle down now you two, before you give the gal a complex." Then she turned to Vivian, "The boys are free tonight, so I suggested that we meet up at the Beverly for drinks and then head over to the Green Lantern for a wild night of dancing. Senor Cugat and his band are there tonight. I just love 'Jealousy'".

"I thought we were going to take it easy, a little gin rummy, just you, me and the cats."

"Don't listen to her, boys. She's a born leg-puller. She knows very well it's tango time tonight, and I don't own any cats, and simply abhor cards." Helen swiped at her good-naturedly. "So, we'll see you there about 7:30?"

"With bells on." Reluctantly, they got up to leave, tossing a couple of bills on the table, and making sure the girls got a good look at the size of the bill clip. "What about a phone number?"

"That depends on how good you boys can dance."

"Well forget the business meeting then. We're going back to the hotel to brush up on our Tangos.

They waved the St. Louis duo goodbye and placed their breakfast orders.

"Another diet?" asked Vivian after Helen had asked for a fruit cup and black coffee.

"I can't seem to keep the weight off."

"But you look great."

"Are you kidding? I need a reinforced girdle to keep my ass from busting out, and my girls are screaming for the next cup size."

"You wear it well, honestly. I just wish I had a little more insulation myself."

"Don't rub it in. I'm famished half the time, and the other half I'm dreaming about food. I could kill for a cream puff."

"Those boys didn't seem to mind one bit, and speaking of boys, what happened to Donald? Is that on again, off again thing off again?"

"I was going to tell you. He's decided to stay with his wife."

"When did that happen?"

"Oh, it's been coming for a while. He finally laid his cards on the table a few weeks back. He claimed he still had strong feelings for

Miriam and couldn't bring himself to leave his kids right now. I think he was afraid of the repercussions of a divorce. Most of the money invested in the business is from her side of the family. The house, the club, the society connections, he'd lose all those things if he left her. I guess I wasn't worth the risk."

"Oh Helen." She reached over and took her hand. "After all the plans you made."

"Remind me not to get involved with a married man again will you."

"So he called it off, just like that?"

"Are you kidding? He still wants the milk; he just doesn't want to buy the cow."

"I hope you gave him his marching orders."

"And how … but."

"But what?"

"I feel … so … I don't know, used … betrayed."

"That's only natural. You staked your whole future on that bastard, waiting what two, three years?

"Three and a half in December. I met him at that Christmas party at the Paradise Ballroom, the one Bud took me to."

"Bud, I almost forgot about him. What's he doing these days?"

"Married of course, a couple of kids and a nice little house in Ingleside." She stared off into space, thinking about the life she could be leading if not for the fateful introduction. "Hey, enough of my troubles. What about you, any plans to settle down with the G-man?"

"I don't think Gene is the marrying type, but until one of us gets tired of the 'shtupping', we're stuck like glue." Vivian made like she couldn't pull her hands apart.

"Has he hinted at anything between 'shtupping' sessions?"

"He's talked about retiring one day and going back to New Jersey, running a little diner on the boardwalk in Atlantic City. I'm not sure how serious he is because he can hardly boil an egg, not that he'd be doing the actual cooking."

"That's where you come in."

"No thanks, I plan on retiring to a life of bubble baths and bon bons."

"Yeah, you and the rest of us dustbowl daisies. Too bad there aren't enough rich guys to go around."

"Whatever happened to making it on your own terms? We pitched in and kept the farm afloat didn't we? Who says we can't put the same effort into our own business, work hard and build it up into something worthwhile?" Vivian gesticulated to emphasize her point.

"What did you have in mind, dance lessons, modeling agency for overweight women?"

"I've been giving some thought to a secretarial agency, our own pool of temps. You know, when the regular girls are sick, or on maternity leave. We've gone through a dozen typists since October, almost all off having babies."

Helen started to count on her fingers. "October means February pregnancies, Valentine's Day 'shtupping'. Those flowers will do it every time."

"So, what do you think?"

"Is there enough of that work in Topeka?"

"I wasn't suggesting Topeka; I was thinking here in Kansas City."

"But you don't know anyone here."

"That's where you come in." She pointed at Helen.

"Me?"

"You'll be the face of the agency, the front of house so to speak." Vivian pretended to ogle Helen's ample bosom as she said this.

"And what will you be?"

"The brains behind the operation of course."

"Touché, Tootsie."

"So, give it some thought, okay."

"I'll put it in my pipe and smoke it. Now back to my original question about you and Gene; has he mentioned the prospect of holy matrimony yet?"

"Not in so many words, and I'm not holding my breath. I'll take my pleasure where I can find it, for as long as I can find it. Life is too short to sit around waiting for Mr. Right."

"Listen to us, we've turned into a couple of good time girls, the kind we used to talk about in school, remember?"

"Are you comparing us to Charlotte Beecham?"

"Worse."

"Mrs. Neely?"

"Good God, we can't have slipped that far. Think of someone nicer, but not too nice."

"Sister Hortense?" This drew a sharp laugh from Helen.

"Sister Hortense, the last I heard she was involved with the Four Square Gospel bunch. Sister Aimee and company from Los Angeles, which reminds me, they're right here in K.C. this weekend."

"Really. How do you go from being a Roman Catholic to a fanatical bible-thumper?" A look of genuine puzzlement etched her brow.

"Well, you could ask her directly if you want to."

"You mean go to that circus?"

"Why not? I've heard from the girls in the typing pool that it's good entertainment as long as you don't get converted in the process."

"Well, I've no fear of that, but I'm a little worried about you in your fragile state of mind."

"Hey, I've got a great idea, let's arrive in our slinkiest outfits and cause a sensation. We'll have them speaking in tongues alright."

"Okay, now you've totally flipped your lid. I'm checking you into Bellevue tout suite."

"Alright already, new plan, we'll go in our most matronly get-ups, nothing out of the ordinary for you, and observe the show."

"Thanks for the compliment, but I left my sackcloth and ashes back in Topeka."

"What are sackcloth and ashes anyway? I've heard that expression a dozen times and I still don't have a clue what it means. The sackcloth part, sort of, but ashes? How do you wear ashes?"

"On your head I think."

"What, like a hat?"

"Not really, but speaking of hats, I could use a new one, what say we go over to Macy's and try some on right after breakfast?"

"Now you're cookin' with gas."

* * *

All eyes in the room were automatically drawn to the vivacious pair as they continued drinking coffee and gabbing till well past noon. One set of pale-blue pig eyes took particular note.

In a corner banquette, within earshot of the two sisters, Octavius Cadogan consumed the last of his lobster Newburg. The Kansas City stopover was scheduled for four days, time enough to get organized if necessary. The blonde he found especially alluring, tall, attractive and bountiful. He'd have to tread carefully though, other than the railway station and a couple of safe drinking establishments, he didn't wander too widely for fear of being recognized by associates of his old employer. It was a good seven years since the Frank Nash debacle and his untimely absence. From what he gathered many had since left the scene permanently, in handcuffs, cement shoes, and hearses. None-the-less, he'd continue to exercise caution.

Right now, he needed to get an address for the buxom blonde. He had overheard a first name and knew of several sure-fire ways of securing a last name and address. Daintily, he dabbed at his lips, wondering if the perfumery at Cocteau's drugstore still carried his brand. He was running low and wouldn't be back in Baton Rouge for another month or so. He made a mental note to place a phone call later that day. Then extracting his bulk from the banquette, he rounded a potted palm and approached the maitre d's station.

* * *

Shadbolt arose early and set out for the salvage yard while dawn stitched sky and earth along a crimson plane. This was his favorite part of the day when everything was fresh and new and full of promise. There was a stillness in the air, as if the land was holding its breath in anticipation of the reveal. Dew sparkled like diamonds in the fields, and for the briefest instant elation crowded out the dark thoughts until the verdant flood plain gave way to the belching factories and soot-scarred brick so reminiscent of the Morlock's gloomy underworld. He drove into the salvage yard and resignedly made his way up the wooden staircase, casting a final, fleeting glance at the incarnadine clouds, racing ever eastward to greet the new day.

He entered the upstairs office, and, sitting at the battered metal desk, meticulously sifted through the stacks of paper and drawers of files as one might pan a cold Klondike stream, seeking the merest glint of pay dirt in a cramped margin note; a name perhaps, initials, an address, a phone number on the back of a waybill or a business card, a date scrawled in a cribbed hand, a rendezvous point, a crudely drawn map, or scribbled on the inside flap of a book of matches, sitting right next to the ashtray: OC 10pm 2Gs.

Sometimes the clues were right under your nose if you took the time to look. Pocketing the evidence, he dialed the operator and obtained the phone number and address of 'The Birdcage' in downtown Des Moines.

* * *

Shadbolt pulled up in front of the club, situated at the end of a row of flyblown storefronts in one of Des Moine's less-savory neighborhoods. The front door swung open, and he was waved in by the owner, a stick of a man still bearing the last vestiges of sleep. Shadbolt flashed his badge and followed him into the dimly-lit interior. He took a stool at the bar while the owner stood on the serving side, out of habit. The smell of spilt beer and stale cigarettes was pervasive. Once through the preliminaries, Shadbolt flipped open his notebook.

"So was Mr. Custer a regular patron of the Birdcage?"

"Yeah, he was a reg'lar, twice a week, sometimes three or four, you know reg'lar like.

"Did he usually drink alone, or with friends?"

"Oh, depended, I guess. Let's see. Well mostly alone, right here at the bar." He gazed up at the ceiling and scratched at the graying stubble on his sinewy neck.

"Thinking back, this would have been a month, maybe six weeks ago. He met someone later in the evening, ten o'clock to be exact."

"Jeez, you're testing the ol' coconut here. We get a lot of customers comin' through the joint. I have a hard-enough time rememberin' what I et for dinner." He sucked on his teeth, no doubt trying to recall what his wife had served him the night before. Shadbolt surmised it was something feral and turnip greens. Rabbit maybe?

"Take your time. Try to remember something that doesn't fit his typical pattern. Something that stood out at the time. Something you noticed and locked away. It's in there, you just have to shake it loose. Try to picture Custer at his usual spot."

He stared up at the ceiling again. "Seems like he's been a reg'lar forever, as long as I've been tending bar, anyway. Truth of it is, I don't usually give a fella a second thought once I got his drink poured. You know what I mean?"

"I hear you."

"Sorry Chief, I ain't gettin' nothin' no how."

"Not to worry, I don't usually fire on all cylinders myself until I've had a couple of pots of coffee in the morning."

"You've got that right. Say I've got some fresh-perked in the kitchen if you'd like a cup."

"Sure thing, thanks."

"How d' you take it?"

"A little cream and sugar if it's not too much trouble."

"No trouble at all." Shadbolt could see the man was jittery, and feeling pressured, which was no doubt affecting his powers of recall. He wondered if there was something else contributing to his nervousness and speculated, he may have been one of Ed Wilson's customers. It was common practice to refill the empty liquor bottles with illegal spirits.

Shadbolt decided to change tactics at this point and started talking Big 6 football, the Iowa State Cyclones and the announcement of a new head coach after a lackluster season. Basketball followed. The man was a keen sports enthusiast. They segued into local politics and on to Washington and the numerous boondoggles perpetrated by FDR's administration. The talk expanded to the war in Europe, and whether or not America would enter the fray. In the middle of the ever-widening circle of discussion, the bartender stopped in mid-sentence and exclaimed, "Wait a cotton-pickin' minute. He was a big fella, real big fella."

"Who?"

"The guy with Custer. He ast' for some booze I'd never heard of. Yeah, I remember 'cause Ginny, the waitress rolled her eyes at me when he sent the first drink back. Well-dressed, suit and tie type, but big, real big, had to be over three hundred pounds, three-forty, three-fifty maybe. I remember, 'cause they were at a table, which was different for Custer 'cause he always sat right here even if he was with somebody." He seemed to sag then, the exertion of recall sapping him like a spent miler.

"Did you ever see him again?"

"With Custer?"

"With anybody."

"No."

"You're certain."

"Pretty sure. I mean you don't forget a guy like that."

"Okay, that's good. I think you've just narrowed our search down. Could I trouble you to use your phone?"

"No problem." The bartender reached under the counter, placing the phone in front of Shadbolt before shuffling to the end of the bar where he pretended to fuss with the liquor bottles. Shadbolt placed a call to the field office in St. Louis, asking them to comb their files of known criminals, wanted and otherwise for an individual matching the description he relayed along with the initials OC. Then he handed the bartender a card, instructing him to call if the gentleman ever reappeared in his establishment.

* * *

Shadbolt's team met up again in the evening over Scotch and too many cigarettes to review what each had uncovered that day. Shadbolt had obtained a good description of the suspect along with a set of initials. Will had a lead on the purchaser of the Cadillac from a local dealer who had matched the serial number to a car he had sold not two months ago. He said the gentleman had bought it, sight unseen, and wired the money. The car had been delivered to an address in Cedar Rapids, and the ownership papers, which they'd forgotten to include with the delivery, later forwarded to an address in Louisiana. It had taken Will the better part of the day to chase down the owner of the property, a Mrs. Elsinore Cadogan, presumably the C in OC, Shadbolt speculated. Unfortunately, the St. Louis field office had nothing on file that matched the initials, but several fit the physical profile. They were dispatching a package by Western Union that would arrive the next day.

"The clipping you found at the clerk's place suggests he had put two and two together," said Shadbolt.

"Do you figure he was puttin' the squeeze on Custer, or this OC hombre?" Perkins asked.

"Well, I didn't find anything in the way of a blackmail note at Custer's, although that's hardly conclusive. He could just as easily have delivered his demand in person."

"I'm not so sure about that, Jack. He didn't strike me as the confrontational type. More the weasely, let the postman deliver it type."

"What's your take on this, Will?"

"Maybe he wanted out after he realized what was going on. Illegal corn liquor is one thing, but murder. I doubt if either one of them had the faintest idea what they were getting themselves into. My hunch is it was always going to go down this way. The clerks and the Custer's are expendable, mere pawns in the game, if you can call it that. It wouldn't surprise me if we came across a bunch more in and around the vicinity of these murders. This is one sick, psychopathic bastard. He's got to be stopped." Shadbolt nodded in agreement, and Perkins held his tongue for once. It wasn't the time for wisecracking. They could sense the frustration building in Will.

"Are you sure chasing this car lead is the right thing? It's a bit of a haul down to Baton Rouge. What do you figure, three days there and back?"

"It's eighteen hours on the KCS Southern Belle, direct to New Orleans with a stop at Baton Rouge."

"But Felix, three days?"

"Yeah, but it's a solid lead. We'll be able to learn a lot more about our man. We might even get lucky and find him at home."

"Look, we can contact the field office in New Orleans and get them to check it out a hell of a lot faster."

"I'm not sure that's going to help us in the long run."

"We don't have a long run. We're on borrowed time as it is." Shadbolt tapped his watch for emphasis.

"But they've got no background on the file, or on this type of case for that matter. In the time it takes to get them up to speed, I can be there and back."

"I'm not so sure about that."

"It's better than sitting around waiting. I've got a strong feeling about this. It's the first slip-up he's made. A visit to his home turf by the FBI is the last thing he ever expected. Who knows what we'll turn up?"

"Alright, take the sleeper to KC and hit the Southern Belle first thing, and then get back here as soon as humanly possible."

Will finished his glass of Scotch and went to his room to pack.

Shadbolt turned to Perkins. "I'm thinking of playing another hunch. It's a long shot, but my gut tells me it just might pay off at the window."

"If it involves more late nights with the lonely-hearts club count me out."

"No this is a desk job. We'll be on the blower to every drug and department store in the State."

"Maybe I spoke too soon. The lonely-hearts club is starting to look a whole lot better."

* * *

As Shadbolt laid out the approach, something gnawed at the back of Perkin's mind. He was as close to a moment of Gestalt as one can get under the influence of too much Scotch and too little sleep. It had to do with the ritualistic nature of the killings, and Shadbolt's comments about some kind of biblical theme, and while he struggled to appreciate that interpretation, he had a feeling that he had seen a connection. But what and where?

* * *

With mounting skepticism, Casper Littlejohn watched the hordes funneling into the big top he helped erect earlier in the day. It had taken twenty of them the better part of five hours, hard work, but the grub was good, and the boarding house, where he shared a room with Mick McCarthy, clean and tidy. In the end, he signed on for the three-week stint, figuring that Los Angeles was as good a destination as any, and besides the ATSF had a big yard in Commerce City, maybe even bigger than Topeka, where he could disappear indefinitely. When the last of the ticketholders had passed through the turnstiles, he was directed to one of the rear exits to discourage freeloaders. This vantage afforded an unobstructed view of the stage and dais bathed in bright white light. Every seat in the house appeared to be occupied, and a roped-off, standing room section immediately to his right was filled to capacity with rubes rubbernecking and jostling for a better view of the proceedings.

Above the din, a voice boomed out over the loudspeakers, announcing that the service would commence in two minutes and causing an immediate rise in the excited chatter. The anticipation was palpable, frisson surging through the collective conscience, linking all within to some higher power and calling. Then the house lights dimmed and the musicians in the pit struck up a rousing rendition of 'Onward Christian Soldiers', which in turn gave voice to the assembled multitude, rising from their seats and singing at the top of their lungs.

From the wings came a burgundy-robed choir, defiling to a set of risers to the left of the dais. Here they assembled in three rows, banging tambourines in a quick-time feel as the orchestra segued into "Old Time Religion". Now the crowd began to clap and whistle and stamp their feet, a few, already moved by the Holy Spirit, performing impromptu jigs in the aisles.

By the third hymn, the entire audience was in a swoon, calling out hallelujahs, and Praise the Lords, and other less intelligible epithets. As the music rose to a fever pitch it was as if the crowd was seized by some unseen force they were powerless to resist. Female members began to faint on the spot and several were carried out to revive in the chill night air.

Littlejohn watched with a detachment born of natural cynicism and his experience on the other side of the grift. He was well-acquainted with these travelling gospel shows and the snake oil salesmen who ran them, praying on the weak, the sick, the infirm, the superstitious, the desperate and the naïve amongst the great unwashed mass.

Up to the dais he strode, dressed in a seersucker suit, a shock of snow-white hair swept up in a towering pompadour accentuating his height. He smiled, horse teeth flashing in a massive jaw, dented with a dimple as round as a bullet hole in the middle of his chin. Bible Billy needed no introduction. He was a regular fixture on Sister Aimee's radio show, broadcast weekly from Angelus Temple.

"Be seated friends," he counseled. "We have good news to share with one and all this evening, very good news indeed. For this very night, many amongst you will be saved from eternal damnation, ripped from the clutches of Satan, the Prince of Darkness, ol' Beelzebub himself, and delivered unto the Lord."

This was answered by a host of 'amen's', which went on until he raised his hands for silence.

"Friends, I am honored to be here with you tonight, in this great State of Missouri, in your beautiful city, to share the word of Jesus Christ, our Lord and savior, lamb of God, the Great Redeemer, light of the world. He has called upon me to deliver his message, a powerful message of forgiveness and hope and a chance for eternal life. I stand before you filled with the Holy Spirit, and before we end our service tonight this entire congregation will be filled with the Holy Spirit, every last man, woman and child. That's a promise."

Bible Billy preached fire and brimstone for the next forty-five minutes, before giving way to a musical interlude featuring the choir, and a costume drama based on the story of Samson and Delilah. There followed a short intermission with refreshments and more hymn singing before the lights were extinguished completely and a pump organ playing a rumbling fugue announced the star attraction.

As if by magic, Mother Mary Margaret appeared on the dais, illuminated by a brilliant white spotlight that made her gold satin robe sparkle and shimmer. The voluminous gown was topped with a fur-trimmed cape and reached down to the ground, covering her bulky form. A matching garrison cap was perched precariously amongst a riot of brassy, blonde curls and gave her the bearing of a conquering military hero, come to smite the forces of evil and rescue the masses as Moses rescued the Israelites from enslavement.

A hush fell over the audience as she bid them welcome, speaking in a voice at odds with her immensity, so gentle that they were forced to lean in, straining to hear her every word. Her message was prosaically simple, her demeanor reserved to the point of modesty. She began slowly, quoting chapter and verse from Matthew and Mark, Corinthians and Thessalonians. She recited the best-loved parables, stories most knew from Sunday school, and proverbs about how to live a godly life. Just when the crowd had been lulled into a state of complacency, prideful and self-satisfied, confident in their covenant with the Lord, she turned on them, calling out each and every one for what they truly were: drunkards and brawlers, philanderers and harlots, abusers, charlatans, cheaters, backsliders and common thieves: cruel, faithless, depraved, and worse. Mercilessly, she castigated those engaged in the seven deadly sins: pride, greed, lust, envy, gluttony, wrath and sloth. She condemned them to eternal hellfire and damnation, describing with apparent relish the horrific punishment awaiting them in Satan's realm.

It was a carefully orchestrated delivery, geared to shame, and humiliate, and cause even the most virtuous to question their character and standing in the eyes of the Lord. At the nadir of the diatribe she offered them a way out, a way to be reborn, a stairway to salvation through the healing powers of faith. Like a shepherd leading her flock, she led them to the foot of the proverbial stairs. Here she raised her arms to heaven, and in a pleading voice, beseeched the Lord to wield her as a surgeon might wield a scalpel to remove a tumor. Now, two white-clad attendants stepped forward to receive those who had made their way to the front of the stage in hopes of being healed. They had travelled untold miles for this chance after their local doctors had nothing better to offer than words of sympathy.

Littlejohn observed that the attendants were selective in who they brought forward to receive the churchwoman's ministrations. They bypassed several before selecting a frail looking woman who hobbled, with the aid of a cane, into the spotlight. Mother Mary Margaret rose above her like a breaching leviathan, grasping the woman by the forehead and snatching the cane from her hand.

"By the power of Jesus Christ our Lord and Savior I compel Satan to leave this poor soul so that she may walk in his light once more." The command was repeated like a chant for several minutes with the audience joining in as the drama intensified. Still clutching the woman's forehead and waving the cane about, Mary Margaret bellowed something unintelligible. Then she pitched the woman backward into the awaiting arms of the attendants and struck the cane against the floor, snapping it in two with a crack that resounded like a rifle shot. A collective gasp issued from the audience, followed by a deafening silence. In breathless suspense, they awaited the fate of the crippled woman. Ever so slowly she was raised to her feet, and tottering on unsteady limbs, she took her first unaided steps into the embrace of Mother Mary Margaret.

The entire ensemble erupted like Krakatoa, and a sustained bout of cheering carried the miracle out beyond the grounds and into the heart of the night. The feat was repeated with the same result another half dozen times until Mary Margaret, drenched in sweat and growing visibly exhausted, fell to her knees. As the aides rushed in to assist her, she waved them off and staggered back to her feet, insistent on one final miracle.

At the edge of the stage, a young, wheelchair-bound girl waited alongside an older couple. The girl was dressed in a pretty, pink frock, which covered her shriveled limbs, the result of a deadly car crash that had killed her parents along with three older siblings and left her maimed for life. Her grandparents had trained into Kansas City all the way from Idaho. It was their third attempt to get little Audrey in front of Mary Margaret. Surely this time they wouldn't be denied. They stood hopeful and perfectly still, lips moving in whispered prayer. All eyes were riveted on the child, another helpless invalid seeking the healing touch of Mother Mary Margaret, who stood gazing down upon the cripple. She appeared to recognize the pink dress and matching hair ribbons from past crusades. Here they were again, a hopeless case. No surge of adrenaline was going to break the chair's steely grip, even temporarily. But the crowd was waiting, expectant, anticipating another miracle. The rest of the ailing souls stepped back a little to let the child go next. With no alternative, Mary Margaret beckoned the little girl to where she knelt on the stage. The attendants, hesitant at first, lifted the wheelchair up, and pushed it into the glare of the spotlight. Mary Margaret sprang up suddenly and began to pace around the wheelchair, muttering incantations, the ritual now more Voodoo than Christian. She mopped at her dripping brow with a billowing sleeve and began to recite the Lord's Prayer aloud, exhorting the entire ensemble to follow suit. At the final Amen she launched into Psalm 23.

"The Lord is my shepherd; I shall not want. He makes me to lie down in green pastures: He leads me beside the still waters." As one voice the crowd responded. "He restoreth my soul: He leadeth me in the paths of righteousness for His name's sake. Yea, though I walk through the valley of the shadow of death, I will fear no evil."

Mary Margaret continued to circle the girl, pacing faster and faster. The girl's eyes followed her as she repeated the orbit, a giant golden sun eclipsing her tiny shattered planet.

"For thou art with me; Thy rod and thy staff they comfort me. Thou prepare a table before me in the presence of mine enemies: Thou anoint my head with oil; my cup runneth over. Surely goodness and mercy shall follow me all the days of my life: and I will dwell in the house of the Lord forever."

Suddenly, Mary Margaret dropped down in front of the child, and hugging her to her breast, lifted her up out of the wheelchair, and clutching her tightly, carried her to the edge of the stage where she hung limply, like a tiny rag doll.

"Lord Jesus, let this child made in thy father's image feel the earth beneath her feet. Let her suffer no more. Take my limbs, take my strength if you must. I will sacrifice all for the sake of this innocent child."

"No, no," many in the crowd called out, caught up in the ordeal and fearful for Mary Margaret's well-being. Slowly, Mary Margaret sank to the floor, and as she did, and the child's feet touched the stage, she remained upright, teetering and unsteady, but standing. Then Mary Margaret released her grip. The child turned, and with arms outstretched staggered toward her grandparents.

A whoop went up from the multitude that shook the very ground upon which they stood and could've been heard in towns and hamlets ten miles distant from the epicenter. The ensuing hysteria rolled through the throng like a wave of thunder. Women wailed and men shouted their praises to the heavens. Children sat dumbstruck. Even the most hardened were reduced to tears.

Most in attendance believed they had witnessed an honest to goodness miracle, several if the other, less-dramatic healings were taken into account. They flocked to the front of the stage to touch the hem of Mary Margaret's robe, to swear their fealty, and to seek a higher calling, whatever that might be, for God had spoken to them directly. He could not be denied. Many would return again the next night or spread the word to friends and neighbors. The first night was always memorable, the most dramatic, perfectly staged to ensure a packed house for the full engagement.

* * *

After the last stragglers were ushered out, and the tent cleared of debris and made ready for the next evening's crusade, Mick McCarthy took Littlejohn by the arm and in a conspiratorial whisper suggested that they go and wet their whistles before the bars closed down for the night. Littlejohn wasn't particular about the blarney-spewing Irishman, but he was craving a drink.

"I'm flat broke until I get paid."

"Don't give it a second thought, I can spot you a beer or two until then. Besides, it's unhealthy to drink alone, don't you know?"

"So where to?"

"Little place around the corner from the digs. We'll catch a ride back with Carter."

They were shuttled back into the City, bouncing around in the box of a half ton with the others at the boarding house. Along the way, McCarthy arranged for one of their company to spirit them in after hours, promising a future favor in return. They made for the front door of the boarding house under the watchful eye of Carter and went straight out the back door, scuttling through several darkened alleyways to a seedy-looking juke joint, roiling with the unwashed and the downtrodden. Littlejohn parked himself along a wall while McCarthy fought his way through the tightly-packed bar, returning with four long-necked bottles of Muelebach, the local pilsner.

"Here's mud in your eye." He tipped his head back and finished the beer in one long swallow.

"Whoa there, Irish. This ain't no chugging contest."

"Just lubricating the pipes, Cass Boy. I'm drier than Death Valley in a drought."

"Now that you mention it, I'm pretty parched myself. That was thirsty work." Littlejohn closed his eyes and took a long pull, wiping his mouth with the back of his hand.

"So, what did you make of the shenanigans tonight?" said Mick.

"Truth be told, I ain't never been to anythin' like that before. The crowd sure took to it though. Real converts."

"Swallowed it hook, line and sinker, more like."

"How do you figure?"

"That's the third time I've seen the wheelchair trick."

"It looked pretty convincing. How does it work?"

"I don't know where she finds 'em. She doesn't usually do the really bad ones. The ones up at the front, maimed, crippled, lying on stretchers, the real hopeless cases. She avoids them like the plague. But every so often, a kid will show up in a wheelchair, a pretty little thing, wearing a frilly pink dress, it's always a frilly pink dress, and you can see the crowd taking to her rightaway. And she'll ignore her till the crowd is almost delirious with hope, begging Mother Mary to make her walk again. She does the big production number every time, the chanting, the pleading, all the mumbo jumbo until miracle of miracles, that little girl gets out of her wheelchair and walks again. And everyone goes home happy."

"What about the others, the woman with the cane, and that skinny guy with the goiter?"

"Plants I reckon, or they're duped into believing they've actually been healed until they get outside and realize they've been had. By then they're too embarrassed or too dumb to call it what it is, a scam, plain and simple."

"Well you know what they say about a sucker being born every minute."

"And how."

"Any other scams I should know about?"

"It's all a scam if you ask me. There's more sinning going on behind the curtain than you can shake a stick at. Bible Billy's the worst. He's bangin' the choir girls two at a time, and anything else in a skirt for that matter."

"You've seen him with your own eyes?"

"No, not personally, but others have and on more than one occasion. It's common knowledge on the circuit. But that isn't the half of it. There's been some odd goings on this past month through Iowa."

"Odder than what I saw tonight?"

"Not on stage, that doesn't really change. You can see the patterns repeating themselves. No, it's other things, little things. It's hard to explain. They don't mean much by themselves but when you put them all together, they don't add up."

"Give me an example."

"Well, twice I've seen this car, a real fancy machine, pull away from the trailers in the middle of the night, and the second time I swear I could hear a woman screaming blue murder."

"Go on."

"I didn't think about it at the time, but on both occasions all the spare rope went missing. We had to go into town, me and Carter to get enough to see us through to the next port of call, Ames if I remember correctly."

"Could've been a coincidence. Anybody could have taken the rope."

"I suppose, but it was on the very two nights that I spotted the fancy car. What the hell would someone driving a car like that want with a bunch of rigging for the big top? And then there's the hires that quit or go AWOL. More than usual lately. This one kid in particular, Jesse something or other. He said he overheard a conversation that didn't sit right with him, and he was going to report it to Mother Mary directly. He wouldn't tell me who it was, or what exactly it was about, but you could see he was pretty shook up. Anyway, the next day Carter tells me he's quit, but the thing is, he never took his bag. He told me he wanted to be a writer, another Dashiel Hammett and he had all his notes and journals in that bag."

"Did you keep it?"

"I should've now that I think about it. The kid was pretty passionate about writing, always scribbling in his notebook. It doesn't make any sense that he'd up and go without it. And he's not the only one who's come and gone in the dead of night without so much as a by your leave."

"You told me yourself, you'd been losing crew. Hell, that's why you hired me."

"Yeah, but most guys tell you when they're gonna quit, and they pick up their pay and shake your hand and say goodbye properly."

"Well that hasn't always been my experience. I'm sure there are good explanations for these odd goings on."

"Maybe so, but you haven't heard the best one."

McCarthy took a swig of his second, long neck and then leaned in so that his head was almost touching Littlejohn's. "I came across a telescope that was rigged up behind the stage and pointing out into the audience. There was no one about so I took a gander." He waited for Littlejohn to pose the obvious question.

"So what did you gander at?"

"It was trained on this blonde number, a real tomato. I figured she must have been a plant, but I never saw her called up. Anyway, I didn't think about it again until about two weeks ago when I saw her picture in the paper. She'd been murdered."

"Murdered?" Littlejohn repeated, a little too loudly.

"Not so loud." McCarthy glanced about furtively.

"And you're certain it was the same dame?"

"I'd swear it on a stack of bibles. You see she had this beauty mark here on her cheek," he said, pointing. "I remembered it because I used to go with a girl had one in the exact same spot." The conversation had taken an unexpected turn into territory Littlejohn was trying to steer clear of.

"So, what do you reckon?"

"I'm not sure exactly. It's a funny business though, a real coincidence, don't you agree."

"Could be somethin' and nothin', hard to say. You ain't plannin' on stoolin' to the cops are you?"

"Haven't really thought about it," said McCarthy. He seemed mildly irritated that Littlejohn hadn't taken his allegations more seriously. "I'd go to the cops in a heartbeat if I could prove it was Bible Billy. That self-righteous son-of-a-bitch needs to be taken down a peg or two. No, I'm gonna bide my time. Keep my eyes peeled. And when I got the goods, I'm goin' straight to Mother Mary Margaret herself, maybe collect a little reward in the process. You ready for another?"

"Sure, just one though. No sense waking up to a hangover." He watched as McCarthy elbowed his way back to the bar. He'd have to stay on his toes, keep a close eye on the Irishman. He couldn't afford to be around if the cops ever came calling.

* * *

Octavius sensed the tail like a cape buffalo senses a stalking lion. Perhaps he'd been a little too casual in his wanderings about the City; too indiscrete in whom he had conversed with. He replayed his movements over the past two days, recalling the sumptuous repast at the Westport Room, his identification of a potential candidate, and arrangement for a "showing", a fine bottle of '35 Chateau Margaux with last night's dinner, and not fifteen minutes ago he acquired ten precious ounces of his preferred fragrance, Fougere Royale.

That was his mistake, the visit to Cocteau's Drugstore. He was spotted earlier, and watchers set up at his likely destinations. The maitre d' at the Westport was the likely source. He'd paid him to approach the sisters with two tickets to the Saturday night Crusade of the International Church of the Foursquare Gospel. The sweetener was the further offer of a car to pick them up, which necessitated the furnishing of an address. They were told that the tickets had come courtesy of a secret admirer, and they gratefully accepted.

His hotel was still several blocks away. Time enough to shed the tail, or better yet, deal with him directly. He weighed the risks before ducking into the next alleyway.

* * *

Half a block behind, an up-and-comer in the Kansas City underworld observed Octavius turn abruptly into the alley. Nicky Scarpino had received the call to watch for the big man, and to phone for backup after he'd spotted him, but he'd come and gone so quickly that he'd hardly had time to put a nickel into the slot. The guy was pretty spry for a heavyweight, and for a split second he wondered if he'd been made. It was a fleeting thought, banished the instant he rounded the corner in time to see Octavius disappear down the back steps of a building. Gotcha now, he thought and reached for his switchblade.

* * *

"You just missed him, fifteen minutes at most," said the clerk at Cocteau's after Shadbolt relayed the description of O.C. furnished by the bartender.

"He didn't by chance leave an address or the name of the hotel where he was staying, did he?"

"As a matter of fact." The clerk consulted his ledger. "He gave me a number to call after I confirmed the order. It's the Orpheus Hotel, room 306. Do you want the number?"

"Please."

"Glendale one, three, two, two, zero."

"What name did he give you?"

"Just said to make the order out for Caddy."

"As in the automobile?"

"Correct. I took it for a nickname." Caddy, Cadogan, it seemed to fit, thought Shadbolt. "Say, what's this all about?"

"Police business, FBI to be specific. I'm agent Jack Shadbolt out of the Kansas City field office. Right now, I'm in Des Moines.

This inquiry is in connection with a case up here. I'd appreciate it if you keep this to yourself for now, and if this gentleman, Caddy, should ever contact you again, I'd like you to call the Kansas City office and ask for me directly." Shadbolt passed on the phone number, thanked the clerk for his help, and pondered his next move.

The suspect, OC, Mr. Cadogan, or Caddy was in Kansas City staying at a known address. He and Perkins could take a late afternoon train and handle this themselves or have the Kansas City detachment make the arrest. On what charge though? Right now it was all circumstantial, a possible connection to an abandoned vehicle, and an affiliation with a murdered man, who was loosely associated with several foreclosed properties where a series of brutal killings had taken place. The link was clear in his mind, but would a judge see it that way? And if the Kansas City office moved in on him now, how long could they hold him for? This OC character, whoever he was, was one step ahead of them, and time was of the essence. He asked the long-distance operator to put him through to the Kansas City office and, after relaying the instructions, he made his way to Perkin's room.

"Gene, we're heading back to Kansas City, be ready in ten minutes, okay."

"What gives?"

"I'll tell you on the way. We may have the culprit in our sights."

* * *

Nicky Scarpino edged his way down the metal staircase, entering the door Octavius had gone through only moments before. His mind was already racing ahead to how the death of this 'Cornuto' would be received by Joey and the rest of the crew, and how fast he might move up the ladder past all the other 'Cornutos' standing in his way.

It was dark inside and the strong smell of beer told him he was in the cellar of a bar. He reached into his pocket, and extracting a lighter, shed a quavering light over his surroundings. Crates of beer and barrels of cheap rum were stacked to the high ceiling, latticed with pipes and wires. He looked around for a way out, and as he made to exit the cavernous space, a heavy cask came crashing down upon his head.

He fell hard onto the concrete, the lighter and switchblade skittering away from him. He lay face down for a while, and then shaking off the cobwebs, he rose to his knees and began sweeping the floor in front of him with his hands. He found the lighter first and held it aloft. In his confused state of mind, it began to dawn on him that the fat prick who had laid him low might still be in the room, waiting to finish him off. As the reality of his predicament began to register, he heard the snap of the switchblade and an arm snaked out of the darkness, and plunged it low into his abdomen, drawing a straight line up to his sternum. He dropped the lighter and clutched his gut tightly, willing the wound to close up so he could run and find a sawbones to sew him back together good as new. He staggered to his feet just as the cask crashed down on his skull again.

* * *

The tail's neck snapped under the weight of the blow as Octavius caved in the top of his head with the heavy cask. Then he reached down for the switchblade intent on sending a delicately carved message to those who might consider following in the tail's all too obvious footsteps.

Cautiously, Octavius left the cellar and made his way out into the alley, checking first to see if there was anyone about. He made a decision to avoid going back to the hotel for the moment in case other watchers were in place. He'd return under cover of darkness after completing this evening's business to the extent that the viewing was met with approval. In a million years he never expected this kind of welcome back into his old stomping grounds. It was obvious a changing of the guard had taken place, and he had a sneaking suspicion of who still might be holding a grudge after all this time.

He needed to make sure the vendetta didn't extend beyond Kansas City. Nobody was going to cramp his style and certainly no little pissant like Joey Lasorda.

* * *

The house sat well-back from the road, the once stately façade fading now like an aging Southern belle. Agent Will eased the vehicle up the driveway, parking next to a vintage Daimler, a thick coat of dust indicative of the lack of use. He ascended the stairs framed by soaring Doric columns, and raising the worn brass knocker, rapped three times. From this vantage the overall state of disrepair became more evident: paint was peeling from the soffits, the glass in the arched fanlight was cracked in several places and everywhere shutters sagged on their hinges. The air of decay was pervasive and palpable. He knocked a second time, the sound swallowed up in the cavernous interior. He waited, loosening his collar in the afternoon heat. From within he heard the whisper of shuffling feet, and the door groaned open to reveal a stooped black woman in a washed-out maid's uniform. She looked up at him like some whipped dog, her eyelids fluttering in a nervous tick. She possessed the demeanor of someone subjected to a lifetime of abuse.

"Yassuh?"

"Good morning, ma'am. My name is Felix Will. I'm here to speak with Mr. Cadogan. Is he at home?"

"Nosuh, Mistuh Cadogan ain't ta home." She began to close the door.

"Excuse me, ma'am, do you know when he might be returning?"

"Well, I don't rightly know. Mistuh Cadogan bin away fo awhile now."

"Did he leave a forwarding address?"

"Nosuh, he jus be gone like he al'ays be. One minit he be heya, and da nex'he gone, and den he be back and gone 'gen." From down the hall he heard a woman's voice call.

"Who is it Violet?" The maid turned and was about to reply, but instead let out a sigh and shuffled back down the hall.

"I's comin', Miz Cadogan." She disappeared behind a grand staircase which led to a second-floor landing. He heard muffled voices and then the sound of something, or someone, being viciously struck, followed by a mewling cry.

"Is everything alright in there?" he called out. There were more muffled voices, and then a different sound he couldn't quite put his finger on until the wheelchair rolled into view. Against the backrest a very large woman was propped. Tendrils of gray hair cascaded down her shoulders, washing over her considerable bulk. She pumped the wheels with arms the size of hams, dragging the maid along in her wake. She came to an abrupt stop in front of Agent Will, looking him up and down before introducing herself.

"Elsinore Cadogan, the lady of the house and whom do I have the pleasure of meeting?"

"Agent Will ma'am, Felix Will, pleased to make your acquaintance." He held out his hand.

"An agent provocateur I hope," she said, clasping his hand. She gave a girlish laugh and touched at her hair.

"I'm with the FBI, working a case in Iowa. I believe Mr. Cadogan may be able to assist us."

"My son, Octavius?"

"Why yes. I was hoping to catch him here."

"Violet, get our guest some iced tea. You do take iced tea, Felix? You don't mind if I call you Felix, do you? Please call me Elsie." She quickly spun the wheelchair around, and before he could respond, commanded him to wheel her into the conservatory while Violet prepared the tea. The maid turned and shuffled off down the hall. Will noticed angry, dark welts on her arms and a vicious abrasion across her calf. He stepped behind the wheelchair and pushed the dowager around the stairs and down a long hallway past several closed doors. The walls were adorned with portraits of Southern gentlemen astride impressive stallions and southern belles in antebellum hoop skirts surrounded by cherub-faced children. She commented on the provenance of one and all, reciting the family history as they made their way along the corridor. The line had been thinned considerably during the Civil War when several of the prominent male members had been dispatched at Antietam, Chickamauga, and finally Gettysburg.

"I blame Pickett," she hissed, deriding the ill-fated charge across the open fields amidst a hail of musket balls and cannon fire. "Like lambs to the slaughter." She motioned to a door on her right, which led to a conservatory flooded with late-afternoon sun. Potted orchids crowded every available surface and perfumed the air with a cloying, sickly-sweet scent.

"Please take a seat." She pointed to a threadbare divan. Will obeyed, his eyes taking in the light-filled space. Columns of dust motes rose to the ceiling, barely disturbed by the fans, moving languorously through the torpid air. Several of the panes were cracked and the mullions water-stained, adding to the general atmosphere of decay. The old South, he mused, on an inexorable decline into decrepitude and eventual oblivion.

They made polite conversation until the iced tea arrived, and after dismissing Violet with a magisterial wave of her hand, she leaned forward, and in a hushed voice, inquired what the FBI could possibly want with Octavius.

"Actually, I was hoping to catch Mr. Cadogan here. This address was provided when he purchased an automobile, which is of interest to the Bureau."

"And what interest does the Bureau have in the automobile?"

"Well, I'm not at liberty to discuss the details of the investigation, other than to tell you that the automobile in question has been associated with a number of crimes."

"You don't think Octavius had anything to do with these crimes, do you?"

"No, no. The car may well have been stolen from Mr. Cadogan, or an acquaintance may have used it. We'd like to find out when and where this might have occurred. He hasn't talked to you about it has he?"

"About what exactly?"

"The theft of the vehicle."

"No, we haven't spoken for a while now. His business takes him away for months at a time."

"If you don't mind me asking, what business is he involved in?"

"Real estate. He purchases properties for a large organization."

"Oh, and which organization is that?"

"I'm afraid I can't recall, although I'm sure he's told me."

"Do you recall what type of properties he purchases?"

"Felix, you will think me just a forgetful old woman, but we rarely talk about his business ventures when there are so many far more interesting topics to discuss: poetry, art, and history, the classics, travel. He was studying to become a doctor, you know, a surgeon, at the Sorbonne in Paris, France. He speaks impeccable French, not like this pidgin Creole they speak in these parts."

"And what happened that he didn't become a surgeon?"

"Something to do with his papers apparently, some mix up with the French bureaucracy."

"So, he didn't graduate?"

"No, it was a great disappointment to him."

"I can only imagine, but what about when he returned to the States. Did he consider finishing his studies here?"

She pondered the question for awhile. "If memory serves, it was right after his return that he moved to Kansas City."

"To study?"

"No, unfortunately, the incident had soured him for good, although I counseled him to persevere. I believe something went out of him. Some spark was extinguished. I blame the French."

"And when did he finally relocate back to the family home?"

"Let me see. He was in Kansas City for several years. It would have been 1933. Yes, the summer of 1933. I remember because we had a homecoming, a reunion of sorts with the last remnants of the family, mine and my deceased husbands. We're a dying breed, you know, the last of the old stock, the old South, gone but not forgotten."

She stared off into the distance, lost in a reverie of cotillion balls, dashing beaus, and the quotidian pleasures of the idle rich.

"Returning to the present for a moment, I take it you don't have a firm date for Mr. Cadogan's return to the estate?"

"No, I'm sorry, I don't."

"And is there no way you can contact him?"

"He doesn't give me a forwarding address and rarely, if ever, calls to let me know his whereabouts or when he will be coming home. It's the nature of the business I suppose, but it's an arrangement that suits our respective needs, and one I have never questioned."

"Fair enough, but if there was an emergency; say you were ill, heaven forbid, or there was some other pressing family matter, how would you let him know? I mean, does he have friends or relatives that he keeps in touch with on a more regular basis?"

"Well I know he's in contact with his cousins, Carter and Morgan Beauchamp, my late brother's twin boys." Will's pulse quickened at the mention of the infamous murderer's name. Could they be related?

"Do they live close by?" he continued, his mind scheming ahead on how to direct the conversation back to the identity of her late brother.

"No, in Los Angeles I believe. I have their address somewhere if you'd like it"

"Yes, certainly, that would be most helpful." She wheeled herself over to a desk that looked out onto the grounds and began rooting around in the drawers.

"Ah!" she exclaimed, "What luck. It's an old photograph album I've been searching for. Come, you can see them in the flesh." She motioned Will over to the desk. "I must have left it in here when I entered their addresses in my book. I do all my writing in the conservatory."

She laid the leather-bound volume on the desk, and opening the cover, carefully drew aside the tissue, revealing the first photograph. Will's heart thumped audibly in his chest. Staring out from the page was Julius Peregrine Beauchamp, the infamous 'Butcher of the Bayou', to the FBI at least.

"It starts in 1919, my brother had just returned from the great war in Europe. His wife, Loretta-May, had been taken up in the influenza epidemic. He was worried about the twins, so that summer he took them and Octavius to his fishing camp near Lafayette." She flipped the pages as she talked, the black and white images providing both a history and a possible series of signposts to solving the current rash of killings: Beauchamp in full military dress, an impressive collection of medals hanging from his barrel chest; Octavius, a flabby boy of ten, no doubt the butt of schoolboy pranks, looking to please his uncle and cousins; the twins, Carter and Morgan, big, strapping lads of thirteen, although there was something vaguely effeminate about Morgan, his hair was unfashionably long, and his expressive eyes were at odds with his hardening physique. The fishing camp, set on the edge of the bayou outside Lafayette, was strewn with lines of gutted fish, turtles, and 'gators. Several pages in, one photograph struck him immediately, a woman, blonde and shapely, staring out from the doorway of the cook house at Octavius and the cousins posing atop the carcass of a freshly-killed alligator. He noted the physical resemblance of the woman to the recent Iowa victims, and the equivocal expression on her face as she observed the trio, arm in arm, smeared with the blood and guts of the slain reptile. He was fast coming to the realization that he had stumbled upon a nest of vipers, the poison running deep, bred in the bone.

"Such a long time ago now," she waxed, closing the album. "Life seemed so much simpler then, don't you agree?"

Will shrugged, answering, "I suppose so, if you were lucky enough to spend your summers fishing in the bayou."

She took out an address book, and finding the twins information, slid it over to Will to copy. When he was finished, he handed the book back to her and said, "It's been most pleasant chatting with you, and thank you for the iced tea. I'll leave my card.

If Mr. Cadogan should call, please convey my details, and let him know it's an urgent matter."

"If you don't mind, Violet will show you out. I think I'll stay here and reminisce now that I've found this old album again. It brings back such fond memories."

As he drove back to the train station his mind was awhirl with what he had uncovered. The long ride back to Kansas City would give him time to sort through the details and see how the pieces fit together. Octavius' involvement in the murders was obvious, and the modus operandi becoming clearer. He wondered what role, if any, the twins might've played. The fact that Octavius was in touch with them suggested more than a supporting role, but a trio of killers didn't conform to the usual paradigm. What had they seen that summer that had put them on this heinous path?

* * *

Back in the conservatory, she picked up the album and flipped to the photograph of her long dead brother. Along with the physical resemblance, they shared certain proclivities, some best left unspoken. She turned to the photograph of the blood-smeared boys atop the gutted gator. She hadn't thought about it in a long while, but that was the summer Nell Madisson, the camp cook, disappeared.

* * *

Midway through Saturday evening's crusade, one of the set-up crew asked for Littlejohn's help to bring additional seating from the backstage storage area. As he made his way through the cluttered space, he spied the telescope McCarthy had referred to last night in the bar. Though covered with a piece of heavy felt, the tripod legs and general shape were a dead giveaway. He waved the other crew member on, and setting the chairs down, walked over to have a look. Glancing around to make sure he was alone, he lifted the material and bent down to stare through the eyepiece, but before the image could fully register, he felt a heavy hand on his shoulder, causing him to stumble and bang his forehead against the telescope. Angrily, he spun around, about to lash out at whoever had crept up on him. The heavy hand grabbed him by the wrist. It was Carter, the crew boss, and right behind him, Mother Mary Margaret herself.

"What're doin' back here?"

"I was getting some extra seats with Jones."

"It sure didn't look like you were getting any extra seats." Littlejohn shook Carter's hand away and took a step back.

"I, I used to have one of these," he lied, "just wanted to have a look."

"It's there so we can keep an eye on the crowd, troublemakers and such. It's not to be tampered with."

"Sorry, I didn't mean any harm. I was just curious."

"Well curiosity killed the cat. Now why don't you get those seats and try to stay out of trouble, okay."

"Sure, boss. Whatever you say," Littlejohn went over and picked up the folding chairs from where he had left them, deferentially nodding his goodbyes to Carter and Mary Margaret. It struck him then as they stood together, the likeness of the pair, siblings, twins even. Physically and facially they were practically identical in appearance. He took note of another idiosyncrasy as he slunk out, between Mary Margaret's sausage-like fingers dangled a roll-your-own.

Later that night, standing with Mick McCarthy in the watering hole by the boarding house, Littlejohn recounted the run in over the telescope.

"See, I told you there was something going on. Bible Billy wasn't around, was he?"

"Not that I could see."

"They were probably coverin' for him."

"Ya think?"

"That's gotta be it. He's gotta be in on the game and this is his payback, scanning the audience for conquests, and they turn a blind eye. One hand washes the other."

"So what now?"

"I don't know. But I'll figure something out."

"No cops though, right?"

"No chance of that."

"Because that could kill the golden goose and right now, I need the scratch."

"Don't worry, Bucko. I'll come up with something that won't affect your swelling bank account. Another one?"

"Sure, just put it on my tab."

What Littlejohn didn't reveal was the fact that the scope was trained on a particular spot, an exact seat to be precise, the angle fixed firmly in place, and although he didn't get a good look at the occupant, she was definitely female and blonde. There was something going on alright. He could smell a caper as surely as a bloodhound could smell a con on the run. He wasn't sure what the angle was, but he was beginning to get an uneasy feeling in his gut, and with a loose cannon like McCarthy on deck, this ship had disaster written all over it. He'd talk to Carter about an advance on his pay and reconsider the Topeka option when the troupe moved on Monday morning.

* * *

The Kansas City contingent was waiting on the platform when Shadbolt and Perkins arrived at 11:00 pm, five agents and Section Head Musgrave, conspicuous in his favored Panama hat and garish tie, this one adorned with mermaids and sea horses.

"Jack, Gene, good journey?" Musgrave inquired.

"Sure, under the circumstances."

"What's your plan, do we take him down tonight or wait till morning?"

"No time like the present. He's been a step ahead of us till now. What's the word from your man at the hotel?"

"Nothing yet. We've booked rooms at the Orpheus, and across the street at The Charles. Smith and Upshaw are there now."

"Looks like we're all set then. Let's hope he doesn't spot anything out of the ordinary and get spooked." Shadbolt purposely eyed Musgrave's Panama and cocked an eyebrow.

"Don't flip your lid, Jack. I'm going to be home in bed when this goes down. It's your show; just make sure you and Tom Mix here don't shoot the place up too bad. We haven't heard the last of the shootout at the Des Moines corral yet."

Shadbolt and Perkins made their way to The Charles on foot while the others arrived by cab and separate automobile. As promised, Musgrave headed home with instructions to phone once the arrest went down. The night air was bracing after the long train ride from Des Moines.

Perkins pulled up his collar and blew into his hands. "I think old man winter has finally arrived. It's cold enough to freeze the balls off a brass monkey."

"Haven't heard that one in a while. Do you know what a brass monkey is?"

"It's not a monkey made out of brass?"

"No, the brass holder for cannonballs on British warships. In the cold weather the metal would contract, and the balls would fall off the holder, hence the term."

"Sure, pull the other one."

"Seriously."

"Well, you've ruined a perfectly good image."

"Historical accuracy must be maintained. Otherwise we'd descend into chaos."

"Never let the truth get in the way of a good story is my motto. So, I'm stickin' with the monkey as in Tarzan's Cheetah."

They walked into the lobby of The Charles and were directed to a fourth-floor room where Smith and Upshaw were chowing down on coffee and doughnuts.

"Pull up a pew. We could be in for a long night," commented Upshaw between slurps. Shadbolt went over to the window.

"Which room?"

"Third floor, two from the top and the fourth window on your right, 306."

"Any action?"

"Nothin' yet. Desk clerk swears he's been out all day. Right now, it's a waiting game."

"Couldn't we just take him in the lobby?" said Smith.

"Too obvious and too easy for someone to tip him off. He's no doubt got a connection on the inside. Let's hope it isn't the night porter. I'm sure I've run into this guy before. Long time ago now, one of Vern Miller's gang."

Perkins turned and addressed the other two, thumbing at Shadbolt. "Can you believe this Abercrombie? He remembered the guy's brand of cologne. That's some shnozzola you got there, Jack."

"All part of constructing a profile, fellas. It's the small details, the day to day minutia that catches 'em up in the end. Unfortunately, this guy is no slouch. He managed to avoid the dragnet after the Kansas City massacre, and he doesn't show up in any of the St. Louis files. Now we've got him linked to at least four brutal murders, but only circumstantially. We've got no hard evidence yet, unless we can grill it out of him."

"Or Felix finds something down south," said Perkins

"We live in hope, Gene. We live in hope."

They took turns at the window, and later on Perkins went down to the lobby to rustle up more coffee. Smith and Upshaw dozed intermittently, drifting off in the darkened room. At 3:20 a call came in from one of the agents at the Orpheus. Shadbolt picked up the phone.

"Jack, somebody just went into the suspect's room."

"Not him?"

"We're not sure. He must have come up the back way. The guys upstairs heard him go in." Shadbolt called over to Perkins.

"Gene, did you see any lights?"

"Nothing from where I'm sitting."

"Shit, he must have killed the hall lights. We can't afford to wait around. Okay, cover the back stairs and get somebody up on the roof. We'll come in from the front in exactly two minutes."

He roused Smith and Upshaw and together they pounded down the stairs, across the road and through the lobby of the Orpheus, splitting up to take the stairs and the elevator. They converged on room 306, and throwing caution to the wind, burst through the door, sidearms drawn. It was a reckless maneuver goaded by panic at the prospect of losing the chance to collar the monster responsible for the string of brutal slayings, and there he was, sitting as calm as you please on a chair facing the doorway.

Perkins snapped on the light. He wasn't half as big as he'd been depicted, in fact he didn't come close to matching the description provided by the bartender back in Des Moines.

"Joey Lasorda," barked Perkins, gun pointed squarely at the reclining man's chest. "What the Sam Hell are you doing here?"

"Same as you by the looks of it; waiting for the fat man to show up."

"Well from here on in you'll be doing your waiting down at the station."

"Spare me the call to my lawyer will ya and pretend like I was never here."

"Sorry, but we can't afford any more screw-ups tonight. You may have already blown our cover."

"Hey, next time, keep me posted and I'll make sure to call at regular visiting hours."

"Very funny. Upshaw can you escort Mr. Lasorda back to the station," said Perkins

"Not just yet," Shadbolt interjected, "I'd like to talk to Joey one on one. Let's get back to our positions and try this one more time. How's the door looking?"

"I'll fix it good as new." Perkins fingered the bent hinges

"Okay, then hurry right back and use the alley."

"Roger that."

The hotel plants returned to their respective rooms while Shadbolt, Smith, Upshaw and Lasorda took the back alley and crossed over the road a block down. If OC had posted a watch then the stakeout was as good as scotched, but the appearance of Lasorda offered some consolation in that he might be able to shed a little more light on the elusive killer.

Shadbolt instructed the two agents to resume their positions by the window and he motioned Lasorda to one of the twin beds so they could sit facing each other in the gloom. Shadbolt lit up a cigarette and offered the pack to Lasorda. He tapped out a Lucky Strike and handed the pack back to Shadbolt. They sat smoking for a while, neither one speaking. Lasorda cut a striking figure in his navy pinstripe and highly polished shoes. His heavily oiled hair was well-barbered, and he'd be considered handsome if not for the smallpox scars that marked his ruddy complexion. They hadn't bothered to relieve him of his weapon, knowing it would be registered. Besides, he wasn't the type to risk a direct confrontation with the law of any stripe. He walked a very fine line, and over the years had ingratiated himself to the City fathers with sizeable donations to favored charities and envelopes stuffed with cash come election time.

Shadbolt leaned forward. "The faster you can tell me about our man OC here, the faster I can get you on your way home to a nice warm bed. I've got a hunch what your interest might be about, but let's start with the simple stuff first. What's OC's name?"

"Is there a prize for the right answer?"

"The prize is that we don't implicate you in the present, very nasty business our man is suspected of."

"Which is?"

"Well I can tell you it's not your penny ante, run of the mill stuff."

"Sounds serious."

"About as serious as it gets. Now, are we taking you home or down to the station?"

"Octavius Cadogan is the answer you're looking for."

"That's quite the moniker."

"Isn't it just?"

"Does he typically go by a nickname?"

"Yeah, Caddy, on account of a fondness for Cadillac's back in the day."

"Any specialties?"

"Knives, rumor has it he was studying to be a surgeon, and he could dress a side of beef better'n your neighborhood butcher."

"What else?"

"He was about the cruelest son-of-a-bitch you'd never want to meet, which made him a first-class collector."

"So, what happened?"

"That's personal, strictly between him and me."

Shadbolt's thoughts returned to the Kansas City massacre. If memory served, Lasorda had lost an older brother in the debacle.

"And when exactly did you part ways?"

"Many moons ago as my redskin friends say."

"Any idea what he's been up to in the meantime?"

"Can't say for certain. Nothing in these parts as far as I know."

"So, what's his background? Where did he come from?"

"Down south, Baton Rouge way. He's old plantation stock without the southern drawl. Claims he went to school in Paris."

Might explain his fondness for Fougere Royale thought Shadbolt.

"So how did he get mixed up with the Kansas City mob?"

"If you're referring to my business associates, we prefer entrepreneurs." Lasorda motioned Shadbolt closer, and lowering his voice said, "Why don't you let me take care of this. It would save us both a lot of time and trouble."

"No can do, Joey. Can't even think it for a minute. And besides, there are too many loose ends we need to tie up. Now what else can you tell me about him? Has he always been as big as reported?"

"He was born big with a big appetite to match. Every restaurant in KC was after his trade."

"What about women? Did his appetites extend to the opposite sex?"

"I don't remember him with any women, not that he was a fruit or anything, just too busy stuffing his pie hole."

"You're sure about that?"

"Unless he got struck by Cupid's arrow in the meantime, all I can tell you is that he had absolutely no interest in dames when he was on the payroll, and believe me, there were plenty hangin' around."

Shadbolt's mind returned to the crime scenes and the scatterings of roll-your-own cigarette butts.

"He didn't by any chance smoke rollies, did he?"

"Are you kidding me? Nothing but fancy, imported French ciggies for our boy. Used to stink the place out with those things. Git something or other."

Shadbolt mulled over this new piece of information. Something wasn't adding up, or the case was a lot more complicated than he had reckoned. The trail of evidence leading to Octavius Cadogan was starting to diverge, or he was purposely trying to throw them off the scent. He needed Will's analytical skills more than ever right now to make some sense of these contradictory facts.

"Alright, sit tight for a while. As soon as Perkins gets back, I'll have Upshaw escort you straight back home, and I want you to give me your word that you won't do anything that compromises our investigation. We need this guy more than you. Innocent lives may be at stake. This is a lot bigger than any grudge you might hold."

"That's a tall order, Jack. What do I get out of it?"

"Let's just say I owe you one. Cash it next time you're in a jam."

"You can count on it."

Shadbolt checked his watch. Perkins should've been back by now. What the hell could be keeping him? He picked up the phone and asked the operator to connect him to the Orpheus Hotel

* * *

Octavius was waiting on the porch as the taxi drove by without stopping. His contacts had identified the homes of people away in Phoenix, or California, or points further south for the winter. He had selected the most secluded of the lot, sitting on two acres of wooded slopes, the perfect spot for the planned abduction. The address on the stone entry pillar was clearly visible. How had the dunderhead missed it? He waited another ten agonizing minutes, assuming that the driver would return upon discovering his error. When the cab failed to materialize, he retrieved the stolen automobile from the side of the house and eased down the street, casting his gaze left and right. The street eventually terminated at a T-junction. Which way now? He banked right and continued the search. After driving several hundred yards, he was just about to turn around and try the other way when he spotted the blonde heading for an underpass that led to a stretch of parkland. He stopped the car, turned off the engine and securing a handkerchief and bottle of chloroform from a brown leather valise on the front seat, hurried down the pathway behind her.

* * *

The footfalls sounded again, causing her to stop dead in her tracks. At first, she thought it was just the echo of her heels rebounding off the brick walls of the underpass, but these were different somehow, like the heavy clop of horses' hooves. She didn't dare look behind her, instead hurrying on to the end of the tunnel, where she emerged in a wooded ravine. A patchy fog crept upwards from a small, gurgling creek, settling along the avenues and shrouding the oak trees whose bare branches poked through the murk, like gnarled limbs reaching out from the grave. How had she gotten herself into this mess? She'd gone to the restaurant as instructed only to be handed another note by the maitre d' along with cab fare to an address in Roanoak, one of Kansas City's swankier neighborhoods. The taxi driver had dropped her off at the dimly lit entry of a palatial residence where she stood waiting for several minutes before coming to the realization that the place was unoccupied. By then the cab was long gone and she had wandered the surrounding streets in search of a phone booth. The houses were spaced far apart and looked to be locked up tighter than Fort Knox. Now she swore someone was following her. She crossed to the other side of the park where she fancied the homes were closer, the streets friendlier. Maybe here she would find a phone booth or an errant cab.

Up ahead she saw a figure disappear into the mist. Friend or foe? Her heart hammered out a quickstep rhythm in her chest. She sought to arm herself but could see nothing about that might suit the purpose. The best she could do was the pointed end of a metal nail file in her purse. She quickly slipped off her heels. Better to catch a cold from damp feet than to attempt an escape in stilettos. She readied herself, wondering if she could outrun whoever was following, or lurked up ahead.

* * *

The click of her heels, like an auditory beacon, stopped suddenly. He couldn't track her visually, slipping in and out of the thickening fog, and now he couldn't hear her. He stepped onto the grass and waited. Still no beckoning sound could be heard. He broke into a trot, moving between the grass verges and the pavement as he attempted to close the distance between them.

* * *

In response to the approaching footsteps, she lengthened her stride, oblivious to the damage she was inflicting on her stockings, a new pair only last week, now laddered beyond repair. The figure up ahead materialized again, and she was about to draw back when she realized it was someone walking their dog. She called out.

"Hey mister!" The figure halted, and the dog, an old bloodhound, barked as she appeared out of the gloom.

"Quiet Duke," commanded the gray-haired gent holding the leash. He stood waiting as she approached.

"Sorry to be a bother. I've got myself into a bit of a pickle here. I need a cab to take me back downtown, and I can't seem to find a phone booth anywhere."

He eyed her suspiciously, like she was a working girl far from her usual prowl.

"You won't find one in these parts, missy. I take it you're not from around here."

"No, I was supposed to be meeting someone, but they didn't turn up, and my cab left. I'm kind of stuck. If I could use your telephone, or if you could call one for me, I'd be ever so … so grateful."

"Oh." He hesitated, clearly unsure whether to believe her or not. She sensed his reluctance and attempted to reassure him.

"Let me introduce myself properly, I know this must look very odd. I'm Helen Bennet. I work at Grundy and McWorters. I'm Mr. McWorters secretary, and I really was supposed to be meeting a gentleman this evening, but we must have got our wires crossed. If you could call me a cab, I swear I'd be eternally grateful."

"Grundy and McWorters you say?"

"For almost three years now."

"Well, you're in luck, little lady. I happen to know Jack McWorters. He runs a first-rate operation. Why don't you accompany Duke and I back home, and I'll drive you downtown myself."

"Oh, that won't be necessary, really. I don't want to put you out, a cab is just fine."

"The offer is non-negotiable, Ms. Bennet. Besides, I can't sleep anyway."

With the billowing fog closing in around them, Duke let out a mournful howl, the hairs on his back bristling.

"What is it Duke; you smell a squirrel?" The dog remained vigilant, scenting the damp air. The old gent tugged at the leash. "Come on boy, this is no time to be gallivanting about." Reluctantly, Duke gave up the quarry and followed at the heel as the pair sauntered along. “I’m Albert Dunvegan, Miss Bennet,” he said, offering his hand, “but you can call me Bert.”

“You’re a lifesaver, Bert. If you hadn’t a happened along, I’d a been walking in circles till the sun came up.”

“Well you were aiming in the right direction for downtown, but it’s a fair old hike, especially in stocking-feet.” She was too embarrassed to tell him the real reason she had removed her high heels, thinking that it sounded silly now. There was nobody following her, just an overactive imagination playing its usual tricks.

“So how do you know Mr. McWorters?” she asked, changing the subject rather than stumbling through an explanation of her unshod feet.

“Jack and I go way back. We grew up on the same street, just a few doors apart, on the wrong side of the tracks, if you can believe it, next to the Burn’s stockyard.”

“Really, Mr. McWorters lived in Cabbagetown?”

“Don’t let those expensive suits of his fool ya. Underneath, he’s as common as dirt.” As they walked on, he regaled her with the exploits of the boys from Cabbagetown, and how they had fought their way to the top of the heap where they resided today, a testament to their grit and determination.

* * *

After crossing several more streets, they made a turn up a long driveway, bordered by a tall boxwood hedge, arriving at a spindled porch wrapping around the sprawling Victorian mansion. Although invited to wait in the foyer, Helen insisted on remaining on the porch while Bert went inside to deposit Duke and retrieve his car keys. When he returned five minutes later, she wasn’t there, so he walked around to the side of the house, thinking she may have gone to wait for him by the garage. When there was no sign of her there either, he made his way to the other side of the house and called out. Surely, she hadn’t set out on foot again. Was it something he said, the tales too ribald? She didn't seem the type to be easily offended. Very strange, he mused, very strange indeed. He'd certainly have a good yarn for Jack McWorters the next time they dined together at the club. He climbed back up the porch steps, and that's when he noticed a strong medicinal odor. If he wasn't mistaken, it smelled like chloroform.

"Very strange", he said and went inside to bed.

The next morning when he took Duke out for his constitutional, he spotted her shoes and purse on the porch, and the trampled flowerbeds below. He went back inside and called his lawyer who arrived just before the police car pulled up.

* * *

At first Vivian didn't give it much thought. Helen was her own person, independent, headstrong. The fact that she was overly-long in returning to the apartment didn't immediately cause her concern. Helen had received a note partway through tonight's Crusade from the secret admirer who had furnished the tickets and chauffeured car to and from the event. It was a further invitation for her to meet the gentleman for a night cap at the swankiest hotel in Kansas City. She had dropped Vivian back at the apartment after Vivian insisted that Helen go on her own. It was now 1:30 and still no word from Helen. She would surely have called if she had decided to spend the evening, although that would've been a bit impetuous even for Helen. She wondered if it was all an elaborate ploy by Donald to win her back. Maybe he'd had a change of heart. That had to be it. She'd give her another half an hour before she started pacing the floor. And then what?

* * *

Helen awoke in a fog, her head pounding and the taste of vomit on her tongue. The smell of chloroform lingered in her nostrils, and she started to wretch. The ligatures binding her hands and ankles bit into her flesh. Where was she, and who had done this? Her last memories replayed, flickering across the retina like some jerky silent reel: the taxi ride through the dark streets, the shuttered house, the sensation of being followed and finally the old gent and his dog. Was he responsible? She struggled to draw herself up, pulling down on the restraints, but there was little play in the bindings. The effort caused her to wretch again, a small amount of bile pooling on the front of her dress, picked out specially to make an impression should the secret admirer reveal himself during the evening. She thought about calling out for help, suppressing the urge for fear of alerting her captor.

Ever so slowly her eyes adjusted to the darkness. She noted the vastness of the space, the ceiling soaring above her head, crisscrossed with pipes and wires. The chain that held her legs was attached to a large metal stanchion, the bulbous head covered with teeth and gears. She couldn't be in a house, an abandoned factory maybe? On the far side of the room several large, cylindrical objects lay lengthwise. Boilers she guessed, now derelict and obviously disused.

She concentrated on any sounds that might help identify her location. To what end was not immediately clear given her current predicament, but she felt the more she knew about her surroundings, the better off she would be. From far away she heard the faint rumbling of shunting trains and the distant warning bells of a railway crossing. If she tipped her head back, she could see the rope around her wrists was attached to a small metal wheel, which in turn controlled an insulated steam pipe, rising above her head to join with the tangle of pipes in the ceiling. There was a warning posted next to the wheel. In blood red letters it read "Do Not Exceed 5000 PSI". Just below was the immediately recognizable insignia of the old Kansas City Electric Light Company.

Now she knew where she was, east of the river in the dilapidated industrial compound of the long-bankrupted company.

The muscles in her outstretched arms began to ache, and the rough wooden pallet she was lying on chaffed at her bare legs. Someone had taken off her stockings and garter belt, and her underwear. She felt dampness between her legs and a mild irritation that had somehow escaped her earlier attention. Then it struck her, whoever had brought her to this desolate place had obviously raped her, and would no doubt be back for more. Her whole body shuddered at the thought. She choked down her revulsion, and with renewed urgency tugged at the restraints, cursing her assailant along with her own gullibility.

* * *

Mother Mary Margaret picked up the phone on the third ring after taking a long drag on her rollie. She was attired in a quilted silk dressing gown of shocking pink that accentuated her girth. Her hair was pulled back tightly from her face and fashioned into a long braid which hung all the way down her back. Beside her on the dresser, her public coif of brassy, blonde curls lay discarded, along with the rest of the trappings so painstakingly crafted to convey an image of piety and saintliness. In the confines of her private quarters the true nature of the beast was given license to roam.

"Uh huh."

"The lamb awaits your ministrations," said Octavius.

"And has the lamb proved a worthy convert?"

"The lamb is ready to enter the kingdom of heaven."

"The congregation will be most pleased."

"And may I be so bold as to suggest a series of verses to recite at the conversion?"

"By all means."

"Leviticus 2: verse 4; Proverbs 5: verses 3, 6, 7 and 10: Deuteronomy 7: verses 1, 2 and 5; and of course, Matthew 7: verses 5 through 9. Would you like me to repeat that?"

"No, I believe I have it as dictated, and a very fine selection I might add."

"You are too kind. Bon appétit."

She hung up the phone and felt a shiver of delight course through her being. Her heart raced and she flushed at the prospect of what awaited. It had been a rich harvest and the last of the sheaves was about to be brought in before she retired to Angelus Temple for the winter. She made a note of the time and then translated the biblical verses into the geographic coordinates of the sacrificial lamb's whereabouts. A short while later a heavy-set gentleman in trench coat and snap brim fedora made his way down the fire escape to a small, black van, idling in the back alley.

* * *

She was alerted to the sound of approaching footsteps and then the scrape of metal on concrete. A dark silhouette filled the doorway, consuming what little light penetrated the gloom. With quickening pulse, she watched as the figure picked its way across the room, skirting several objects strewn about the floor, in a meandering journey to the stanchion. He stood before her, a large man in trench coat and fedora, trim moustache affixed to an unsmiling, jowly face. Malevolent, deep-welled eyes drank her in. He was carrying a small, square medical bag, like a doctor making a house call. He stepped to one side and placed it on the floor.

"What do you want?" she said.

The man didn't answer. He opened the bag, and extracting a roundish article, noisily pulled off a length of tape, placing it over her mouth and roughly pressing it into place. Something kindled in the pit of her stomach as she gazed up into his dead eyes and knew in that instant that these next few minutes would be her last. He took several more objects from the bag and placed them on the floor beside the pallet. They rang a metallic note. She guessed they were knives. The next sound she heard was her dress being shorn off, the fabric lacerated in great strips that seemed to float, petal-like to the ground. A hand reached down and sliced off her brassiere, then gently cupped each breast, fingering the nipples. She fancied she heard a grunt of pleasure issuing from her assailant, and as she opened her eyes again, she saw that there were two of them, towering above her.

A doppelganger had entered, soundlessly. He straddled her, lowering himself to his knees until he came to rest on her thighs.

With the added weight, the chain bit deeper into her ankles, and she cried out, the scream reduced to a pitiful moan by the tape. Now the first man took hold of a crucifix and started to chant, swaying from side to side. The doppelganger took up the incantation all the while staring at her nakedness as if entranced. She forced herself to look at them both, to remain as defiant as possible. In her heart she knew it was hopeless, yet she refused to go quietly into the night. She began to buck and twist, fighting against the restraints. The doppelganger pressed down harder and struck her a blow to the head. This brought on a final desperate surge of energy to unseat him until the next blow rendered her unconscious.

When she came to, the smell of incense assaulted her nostrils, and the chanting had given way to what sounded like a sermon on the sins of the flesh. It was at this point that she realized the identity of the man delivering the admonishment. To her horror, the events of the last twenty-four hours suddenly came into alignment. A cry of anguish escaped the gag, and she saw the ease with which she had been seduced. Pityingly, the man looked down, not at her, but at the doppelganger, and in a loud voice proclaimed,

"The works of the flesh are evident: sexual immorality, impurity, sensuality, lust, drunkenness, orgies and the like. I warn you as I have warned you before, that those who do such things will not inherit the kingdom of heaven. For this is the will of God, your sanctification: that you abstain from sexual immorality; that you know how to control your own body in holiness and honor, not in the passion of lust like the sinners who do not know God. For if you live according to the flesh, you will die a thousand painful deaths."

As he uttered these final words, the doppelganger fumbled with his fly, extracting his swollen member, like an incubus at the bedside.

She closed her eyes again, awaiting the brutal thrust, the physical invasion of her person, when another sound caused them both to stop suddenly and cast their gaze to the doorway.

From outside, the footfalls of several individuals echoed in the cavernous space, drawing closer with each step. The doppelganger reached for one of the knives on the floor, and raised it, intent on delivering a mortal incision to the carotid, but her trussed arms shielded the vulnerable spot. Before he could select another target, his arm was grasped by the man. With a finger to his lips the man motioned toward the boilers, and quickly gathered up the instruments. Together they melted into the darkness just in advance of a supernova of torch beams slicing through the gloom as a cadre of gun-toting men swarmed into the room. Torchlight danced across the dark interior, eventually illuminating her naked torso until every beam was trained on the writhing form.

"What the hell have we got here?" They approached and stood there, ogling her. Someone gave a low whistle. "Not exactly what we were expecting, eh boys."

"Yeah, Joey didn't say nothin' about no dames." With widening eyes she tried to signal to the silhouetted forms, shaking her head in the direction of the boilers.

"Looks like she's tryin' to tell us somethin'." A hand reached over and roughly pulled off the tape.

"Over by the boilers!" she blurted out, "two of them."

They turned as one, aiming flashlights and drawn weapons at the rusted metal hulks across the room. Shots rang out from the darkness, and one of the figures in front of Helen slumped to the floor. The gunfire was answered by a hail of bullets from several side arms and a shotgun, lead ricocheting off metal in a staccato burst. Another of the men fell to the ground before the order came to "take cover", leaving Helen alone and exposed in the dark.

* * *

The man and his doppelganger had not banked on the tenacity or sheer firepower of the intruders, expecting to drive them off with the initial fusillade. Now they were trapped with escape by attrition unlikely given the odds. Whispering a hastily concocted plan to the man, the doppelganger crept to the derelict boiler farthest from the doorway and sent a spray of bullets towards where he imagined the girl to be. She alone could perhaps identify them. There was something in her eyes just before the intrusion that conveyed recognition of one of her assailants despite the disguise. As Lasorda's men concentrated their fire on where they had seen the muzzle flashes, he slithered back to his original position. From here the pair worked themselves towards the exit and then beat a hasty retreat, the darkness cloaking their escape into the maw of the plant and then downriver through the thick foliage.

* * *

Cautiously, Lasorda's men left their hiding places and gave chase. Sporadic shooting could be heard outside, every moving shadow a target. Eventually, two figures returned to the room to attend to their fallen comrades.

"Ah shit, Bruno is a goner. They took off half his head. Joey is gonna be none too pleased about this."

"What about Gedlaman?" They knelt to examine the prostrate form, turning him over to reveal a mortal chest wound.

"Doesn't look too good."

"Is he still breathing?"

"He ain't got no pulse." They stood, crossed themselves and almost as an afterthought, directed the flashlights back to where Helen lay, splattered with blood and brain matter. "She don't look so good either."

"Maybe not, but she's still breathing, see."

"Yeah, I see, but she ain't our problem."

"Hey, she could be somebody's dame, what Joey didn't know about. One of our guys, capiche?"

"I already told ya, he didn't say nothin' about no dame."

"Cos he didn't know, ya mug."

"So, don't snap your cap. We can't be takin' 'er to the Doc now."

"I got a better idea. Help me get her untied." They cut the ligatures with a switchblade and blasted the chain from the stanchion. Then the bigger of the two heaved her over his shoulder in a fireman's carry and took her outside, laying her down in a patch of weeds. He covered her with his expensive topcoat, after removing the inside labels.

"Joey better be good for the togs. That wrap cost me plenty."

"I still don't know why yer botherin' so much."

"Ain't you heard of the good Samaritan?"

"No, and I don't wanna hear. Now let's vamoose."

"We got one more stop to make. That gas station on the way in. There was a phone booth on the corner."

A short while later, they heard the wail of an ambulance cut through the quiet of the early morning,

* * *

Having lost Lasorda's men in the chase downriver, the man and his doppelganger doubled-back to where the van had been hidden, just outside the compound fence, screened by a section of corrugated iron.

"You're bleeding like a stuck pig. Lemme have a look." The man turned and raised his arm, cocked at the elbow, exposing the tear where the bullet had passed through the fabric. Blood was flowing freely from the wound, seeping through the material and dripping from the crimson-stained cuff.

"Who the fuck were those pissants? And how the fuck did they know we were there?"

"Octavius?"

"Obviously. He swore the place was as safe as houses. It wasn't the law, that's for certain. It had to be the Kansas City mob."

"You're right on that count. Someone must have recognized him and come to settle an old score."

"Some score. He should've realized the danger and called it off."

"That's not the worst of it either."

"What do you mean?"

"The girl. I think she made you. She had that look in her eyes just before they burst in. You should've let me cut her then and there."

"There wasn't enough time for a quick kill. We wouldn't have been able to make it to cover. Besides, you shot her, didn't you?"

"I couldn't tell if I hit her or not."

"You must have."

"Is it too late to go back in?"

"Too risky. How long before they figure out we gave them the slip and come back, guns ablazing?"

"They'll be halfway to St. Louis by then."

"I'm not so sure. Let's take a chance on your marksmanship, and the fact that she'll be describing a man who doesn't really exist." They were silent while the doppelganger helped the man remove his coat. He extracted a vestment of white muslin from the bag and applied it to the wound.

"I thought you said Oskaloosa was the last kill for the year?"

"What can I say? We got greedy, and as I recall it was you who insisted after you saw her."

"True enough. She was near perfect, a dead ringer for Nell."

"Your first sacrificial lamb."

"Our first, dear brother. Yours and mine."

"Well, yours in another, very special way I suppose." Removing his hat, the man mopped his brow with the undamaged sleeve. A sinuous, dark braid slithered, viper-like down his back.

"Looks like you could use a stitch or two. Are you going to be alright for tonight?"

"I'll survive. Besides, it's a well-known fact that I possess the God-given power to heal."

"So I've heard."

"We should leave now before the gunslingers return."

"Let's get the bleeding stopped before we get back into the van. We don't need the crew getting any more suspicious than they already are. At least that nosy Irishman won't be telling any more tales out of school."

"Thankfully. You told Octavius where to plant the evidence?"

"Even the most short-sighted flatfoot would have a hard time missing it."

"Good, good." The man stared off into space, his mind on a hundred details that needed attending to.

"You do realize he's starting to get sloppy. I keep wondering what else he's been missing. The clerk in Mahaska County could've been a serious problem."

"True, but for Octavius, not for us."

"I'm not so sure. There are too many links to the church: the tickets, the attendance at the crusades. Someone will catch on eventually. We'll have to change the way we harvest the sheaves."

"You'll come up with something. You always do."

"It might be time for another change of identity, a completely different system."

"Along with Octavius outliving his usefulness, you're becoming overly cautious. I say we stick to our trusted routines. We just need to take a break for awhile. That's if you can curb your prodigious appetites."

The doppelganger ignored the last remark. "The sun's coming up. Better lose the moustache and fedora. I'll help you with your surplice."

Off to the east dawn peered over the low hills, a finger of tangerine lifting the shuttering sky. Thirty minutes later, Carter wheeled the vehicle into the compound of trailers, where Mother Mary-Margaret disembarked, golden curls shimmering in the early morning sunshine.

* * *

Octavius ditched the stolen automobile on a secluded residential street, and made for one of the safe houses, rather than risking a return to his hotel. He contemplated an unannounced visit to the Lasorda residence for the sole purpose of extracting a measure of revenge for the trouble they had caused him, and the loss of certain personal effects, but after considering the odds of an unimpeded assault, decided to bide his time until a subsequent visit.

Fortunately, he had retained the Fougere Royal along with the tools of his trade, always kept close at hand. He negotiated a series of back alleys to a run-down apartment block, sitting forlornly at the end of a long line of ramshackle dwellings. Checking to see that the coast was clear, he mounted the front stoop and entered the foyer. The smell of boiled cabbage and rancid meat assaulted his nostrils. A far cry from his flower-filled suite at the Orpheus. By his reckoning it was time he was back in Baton Rouge for the winter, to rest and recharge and ready himself for the next killing season. It had been a long and fruitful run, and until this last stop, almost effortless; perhaps a little too easy when all was said and done. They had gotten careless, his cousins, and greedy as well.

He walked to the end of the hall and stood in front of apartment number six for several minutes before lifting his massive fist to the scarred wood. He rapped three times. There was a shuffling sound beyond, and the door creaked open as far as the chain lock would allow. Deeply-set eyes stared out from a face worn by time and tribulation to a ghoulish mask incapable of emotion, and barely able to register recognition. An arthritic claw fumbled with the chain, and Octavius entered the dank apartment.

"I need to rest up for a couple of hours before I catch the Southern Belle to New Orleans. Here, this should settle the account nicely." He handed the occupant a small stack of bills and was led to a cramped bedroom tucked away behind the kitchen. "If I'm not up by eight-thirty, come and wake me." He removed his topcoat and jacket, loosened his tie and slipped off his wingtips. The day, overly-long and fraught with a series of near misses. He was beginning to realize how fortunate he had been. Lady Luck had smiled down on him today. How long before his good fortune came to an end, and she lavished another with her favors?

The bed creaked and moaned under his weight as he lay back on the coverlet. At least the pillow slip was clean, freshly laundered by the smell. He breathed in the scent of lavender, and clutching the pillow to his face, inhaled deeply. It reminded him of his time in France, weekends outside Fontainebleu after the harvest, the wine and cheese and succulent pates. He was partial to the finest foie gras, flambéed and served with a delicate brioche, hot from the oven. He might still be on the continent, a respected surgeon, if not for his other appetites, equally as sensuous, perverse pleasures of the flesh, encouraged by his uncle and cultivated in the company of his cousins. Delicious flights of cruelty that summoned such an intoxicating rush of pleasure both in the moment and later in some private sanctum after he satiated himself with food and drink. His storehouse of disquieting images from these latest endeavors would keep him pleasured long into the winter months, and the trophies, tactile reminders of the groveling conquests, a finger, a baby toe, and an earlobe. Unfortunately, the constraints of time had prevented him from acquiring a very special souvenir from his latest quarry.

* * *

On the other side of the door the occupant waited until the creaking had subsided and a soft snoring could be heard through the keyhole. Then he tip-toed to the living room and picked up the receiver. Lasorda and his crew had been waiting for this call for the last three days, ever since the maitre d' at the Westport Room had tipped them off. There'd be a welcoming committee waiting at the station when Octavius showed up for the long train ride to New Orleans.

* * *

After Perkins returned to the lookout at the Charles Hotel, explaining that his delay was due to a problem re-locking Cadogan's door, Upshaw escorted Lasorda back to his mother's house where he resided with a large extended family that included several siblings, along with their wives and children. The rest of the night passed without incident.

At 7:00 am Shadbolt placed a call to the agents at the Orpheus who confirmed that the suspect had still not returned. Ten minutes later Section Head Musgrave called, "Jack, looks like we got another kidnapping on our hands. City Chief says it happened early this morning over in Roanoak. Albert Dunvegan's lawyer put in the call. Tread carefully, we don't want a repeat of the Des Moine situation. This guy is KC high society, Board of Governors at State University, Board of Trade, Freemason's Lodge, the whole shebang."

"I'm well-acquainted with the gentleman, but how does he fit in?"

"That wasn't entirely clear. Claims he was helping-out a damsel in distress, some girl wandering around in her stockings in the middle of the night. He was planning on giving her a ride downtown when she was abducted from his porch."

"By whom?"

"Not sure."

"Did he get the name of the damsel?"

"As a matter of fact, he did. Apparently, she works for a friend of his who confirmed her details. Her name is Helen Bennet, lives over on Grand Avenue, 1220, apartment 207."

"Bennet, that name rings a bell. Gene," he called over to Perkins, "Your girl in Topeka, Vivian, right?"

"Right, what about 'er?"

"Hasn't she got a sister here in KC?"

"Yeah, older sister. Why?"

"What's her name?"

"Helen."

"Helen Bennet?"

"Yeah, what's this about?"

Shadbolt's gut plummeted. He quickly finished up with Musgrave and then broke the news to Perkins.

* * *

Littlejohn awoke from a disquieting dream, entangled in his sweat-drenched covers. He fancied he had heard a low moan before he emerged from the depths of sleep, like a diver breaking the surface after a lung-bursting plunge. His tongue had grown a layer of fuzz overnight and he was as parched as an Arab in a sandstorm. He smacked his lips a few times and very slowly extricated himself from the tangle only to tumble back onto the mattress when his limbs failed to respond.

"Jesus, we must have tied one on last night," he said, directing his comment to Mick McCarthy, lying cocooned in the bed next to his. There was no answer and it was obvious that he was still dead to the world after last night's impressive intake of ale and spirits. He owed McCarthy a pile of dough. Not that he had any intention of paying it back before he scarpered tomorrow. When he returned from the bathroom several minutes later, he discovered the reason for McCarthy's unresponsiveness. He wasn't in the bed. Instead, the covers were wrapped around a couple of pillows, giving an appearance of the slumbering Irishman.

"What's that crazy bastard up to now?" He pulled on his trousers and headed downstairs for breakfast.

* * *

Perkins had the operator put him through to Helen's apartment. Vivian answered on the first ring.

"Helen!" she shouted with relief, ready to deliver the lecture she had been preparing since the wee hours.

"No, sugar bush, it's Gene."

"Oh Gene, it's so good to hear your voice. I've been worried sick about Helen. She went out on a kind of blind date last night and she hasn't come home yet."

"That's the reason I'm calling."

"What?" Her heart was in her mouth.

"Jack and I got back from Des Moines last night and …"

"You're here in Kansas City?"

"Yeah, late last night, we were on a stakeout, and we got a call from Musgrave about a possible kidnapping."

"No, not Helen," she almost shouted.

"Easy babe, nothing is for certain yet. Me and Jack are going to interview the guy who reported it. Can you come down to the field office? You can fill in the parts he won't know."

"What if she shows up in the meantime? I mean, are you certain it's her?"

Perkins thought for a second and then answered. "Okay, stay put. We'll swing over as soon as we're finished. Keep your fingers crossed she's out having breakfast with her blind date right now."

"Oh Gene, I'm so worried. Please hurry."

"We'll be there as soon as we can. I promise." He hung up, concern etched across his face.

* * *

Shadbolt and Perkins arrived at Helen Bennet's apartment after confirming the details of the early morning encounter with Albert Dunvegan and his lawyer. They had surveyed the trampled flowerbed, noting the evidence of a scuffle and called for a plaster cast of the deeply-embedded, size fourteen shoeprint, a testament to the enormity of the assailant. Vivian greeted them at the door, throwing her arms around Gene's neck and holding him tightly. He whispered pet sobriquets in her ear, slightly embarrassed that Shadbolt was witnessing another side to the hard ass he was used to portraying. Reluctantly, she let go, and wiping the tears from her eyes, led them to the kitchen where she poured three cups of coffee from the percolator.

Shadbolt took out his notebook, and lit a cigarette, pushing the pack toward her. She declined with a brief shake of her head. Shadbolt began, "We've got her movements from just before she ran into Dunvegan. He was out walking his dog. She told him she was supposed to be meeting a gentleman at an address in Roanoak, but he never showed. Can you fill us in on her movements earlier in the evening?"

She looked from one to the other unable to start. "Take your time," Shadbolt counseled. Perkins reached over and took her hand.

"Helen met me at the station on Friday morning."

"Union?"

"Yes, sorry, Union train station. We had breakfast in the Westport Room, a long breakfast and just before we left the maitre d' came over to our table and said that an admirer had asked him to deliver an envelope. At first I thought it was from these two fellas Helen was talking to when I first got there."

"Two men, who were they?" said Shadbolt.

"Just two sales guys in from St. Louis."

"Did you get their names?"

"No, no it wasn't them that sent it."

"And how do you know that?"

"Because we asked them that night." She hesitated, glancing at Perkins, a look of regret framing her expression. Shadbolt imagined her remorse was due to the fact that indulging in a little innocent fun was going to make her and Helen sound like a couple of floozies when she recounted the episode.

"We met them for a drink and Helen invited them to go dancing. She just broke up with her long-time steady and I thought a night out on the town would cheer her up." She looked at Gene expectantly. He nodded and gave her hand a squeeze, while Shadbolt made a note to return to the two good time boys from St. Louis.

"Do you still have the envelope?"

"No Helen kept it."

"Okay, back to the admirer, what was in the envelope?"

"Two tickets to Saturday night's International Church of the Foursquare Gospel's Crusade, and a chit for a limousine to pick us up."

"Alright, so you went?"

"Yes."

"And took in the whole show?"

"Yes."

"And did this admirer make an appearance?"

"No, one of the ushers brought another note inviting Helen to meet him for a nightcap at Delmonico's."

"And I take it she kept that note as well."

"Yes. She wanted me to come along, but I thought this was her chance to get over Donald. It seemed so romantic. Oh God, why didn't I just go with her?" She trailed off, eyes glistening with fresh tears.

"Don't beat yourself up, doll. Your intentions were good."

"Okay, let's get back to the Crusade …", but before Shadbolt could finish the thought Perkins almost came out of his seat.

"Wait a minute, Jack, the clerk from Mahaska County, when I searched his place, he had a pamphlet from the Foursquare Gospel bunch. The newspaper clipping about the dead waitress from Grinnell was tucked inside. I never made the connection. I mean it never crossed my mind, but this is too much of a coincidence."

"Only one way to find out." Shadbolt turned to Vivian, "Is the Crusade still in town?"

"As far as I know there's another show tonight. It's the last one before they move on."

"Alright, we better move fast. Gene let's get Upshaw on the maitre d' at the Westport. Vivian, do you think you'd recognize the usher who handed you the note?"

She furrowed her brow. "I think so. I remember his face was covered with freckles. Yes, I'm pretty sure I could point him out."

"The car's downstairs in the alley. Throw something on and meet us in five minutes, tops."

"I'll do it in three."

"Good girl."

* * *

Rather than risking another run in with Lasorda's men at Union Station, where he assumed they would be laying in wait for him, Octavius opted to travel by cab to Grandview, about thirty minutes south, and pick up the Southern Belle sleeper from there.

He had booked two private compartments, one under an alias, situated on opposite ends of the first-class section. In so far as he trusted the scheduled arrival of the train, he set off for Grandview, anticipating a direct boarding, unaware that the departure had been postponed, while a heart attack victim was attended to, causing a forty-five minute delay at Union Station. Once informed, he made for a crowded corner of the waiting room and tried his best to get lost in the mass of milling ticket holders, all the while keeping an eye out for any suspicious characters who looked like they might be part of Lasorda's outfit.

* * *

"He ain't here, boss. We checked everyone gettin' on the Belle. Tommy's snitch says he's got a compartment reserved, but he ain't in it, and the train's due to leave in five minutes."

"We shoulda pinched 'im when we had a chance at Grossinger's digs. What was Vinny thinkin' when he got the call?"

"He was thinkin' with his prick as usual. He had some broad he had to take care of first."

"We're gonna have to have a serious talk with Vincent after this goes down, real serious."

"You want I should take care of him now?"

"No, one thing at a time; the fat prick now, the man that thinks with his prick later. Look, maybe Cadogan got wise to the situation and figured he'd board someplace less conspicuous than Union. What's the first stop after Union?"

"Grandview I think."

"Who we got down that way?"

"That's Cortese territory, Sal and Paulie."

"Okay, give 'em a bell and see if they can spot 'im and hold 'im. Tell 'em we'll make it worth their while."

"What do you want us to do?"

"Stay put, and keep your eyes peeled. If he don't show by the time the train leaves, hustle your keester down to Grandview. I'll take

Phil and Serafino and head down there now. I'm bettin' on the Grandview angle, but stay sharp, just in case."

"Don't worry, we'll stay sharp as knives."

* * *

As the train pulled into Grandview Station, Octavius stood, and quickly scanned the crowd. Satisfied that he wasn't being watched, he picked up his valise and attempted to insert himself into the clutch of bodies surging toward the platform. It was a short stop for boarding passengers only, so ticket holders made smartly for the carriages, aided by a legion of red caps and porters who hurried the dawdlers along. By the time Octavius reached the first-class section, the encircling crowd had dissipated to a handful of fellow travelers, leaving him momentarily exposed, a leviathan in full breach. Coming from the opposite direction, three hard boiled types in trench coats and snap brim fedoras spotted his entrance, and calmly made their way toward the coach. Once inside, Octavius quickly headed for the suite he had secured under an alias, which was situated at the opposite end of the first-class section from the suite bearing his name on the reservation docket.

* * *

Arriving moments later and oblivious to the deception, the trio bulled their way along the corridor to the compartment number provided by the snitch. They waited until the coast was clear and then knocked, calling out "porter" in hopes of gaining entry. When there was no response, one of them tried the door. It was unlocked and swung inward revealing an empty compartment.

"Maybe he went straight to the dining car. The little fella looked like he could use a meal."

"Looks like he never missed one."

"You got that right."

"So whadda we do now?"

"Okay, Lenny you stay here. Me an' Sal will go check out the dining car. If he shows, just hold 'im here 'til we get back. Sam says Lasorda wants 'im in one piece. Capiche?"

"What if he don't show before the train leaves?"

"You saw 'im get on. He's gotta be in here somewhere. The fucker's too God damn big to hide."

"Yeah, but we only got a coupla minutes."

"So, a coupla minutes is all we'll take.",

The mouthpiece and his accomplice exited the suite and hurried along to the dining car, while Lenny made himself comfortable. When they hadn't returned in the allotted time, he ventured out into the corridor, and encountering a porter, asked if the man had seen anyone matching Octavius' description.

"Sho nuff, las suite in fus class, suh."

"Thanks. Say sport, my associates should be back any minute. Can you hang here for a tick and let 'em know where I got to?" When the porter hesitated, Lenny reached into his pocket and extracted a roll of bills, peeling off a sawbuck, which he stashed in the porter's jacket pocket.

"Betta hurry now, train be leavin' showtly."

Lenny hustled off down the corridor and entered the next carriage through the gangway connection. By the time he had reached the second gangway the train had started to roll. He carried on to the third and final first-class carriage, slowing as he approached the door to the last suite. Here he stopped and waited for the other two. He was uncertain about making the collar on his own. On the other hand, he could hardly afford another screw up. He was already in deep Dutch with Sam Cortese. He stepped up to the door and in a loud voice called out, "porter". It was only after he had leaned in closer that he noticed the peephole. In that instant the door flew open and, as he was jerked clean off his feet, he felt a searing pain in his gut.

* * *

By this time the other two had made it back to the original compartment, having combed the dining car and passenger coaches to no avail. They arrived to find the porter sitting at the window-side table gazing out at the retreating station grounds.

"Fella sez, to tell y'all he dun gone to the las suite, three cars back."

"What's back there that's so important?"

"Big fella, he was lookin' foh."

"You don't say."

"Yas suh, great big fella." Off they hurried down the corridor, leaving the porter sitting there, no doubt dreaming of the day he might be able to travel in such high style, just like them and all the other rich white folks.

* * *

Octavius eased Lenny's limp body to the floor once his bicycling legs ceased to kick. He left the blade lodged deep in the sternum while he retrieved a towel from the bathroom to staunch the inevitable flow of blood. He was just about to extract the knife when the door burst open and he was set upon by Cortese's buttons.

He concentrated on Sal, who was in the process of drawing his weapon, while the mouthpiece rained down haymakers on his unprotected head. He took a good number of jarring blows before he managed to wrench the shooter from Sal's grasp. Seeing his blows bounce off the Octavius' head like raindrops off a tin roof, the mouthpiece reached inside his jacket to draw his pistol. Octavius caught him with a vicious backhanded swipe, sending him toppling over Lenny's supine corpse. With his free hand Octavius seized Sal by the throat and threw him on top of the mouthpiece just as he was lining up Octavius for a bullet to the shoulder. A shot rang out, splintering the door frame behind Octavius. He didn't have time to cock and fire Sal's piece. Instead, he ducked out the open door, took three ravenous strides and crossed the gangway connection into the observation car, the last carriage on the train. Octavius flipped the deadbolt before sprinting to the end of the compartment, empty save for an attendant, arranging refreshments behind a small bar.

"Hey, whachu doin'? We ain't opin yet."

"Don't let them in. They've got guns," barked Octavius before stepping out onto a small veranda.

He gauged the speed of the train at just under 50mph, serious leg-breaking velocity on the unforgiving clinker bed unless he could hurl himself into the grassy verges beyond. He couldn't risk it. But what if he climbed up top and made it to the engine? With Sal's gun in hand he could convince the engineer to slow down and attempt to jump clear at a less-deadly speed. He grasped the metal ladder rungs and hauled himself onto the roof of the swiftly-moving carriage.

* * *

Back inside, Cortese's buttons pounded on the locked door, finally blowing off the deadbolt when the attendant failed to heed their shouted commands. They tore to the back of the carriage.

"Shit, he musta jumped," said Sal, scanning the borders of the receding track.

"Where? I can't see 'im. We'd see 'im if he hadda jumped."

"Up top?"

"Go have a look see." Sal climbed up the ladder and peered toward the front of the train in time to see Octavius clear the second gangway opening.

"He's headin' to the front of the train."

"Can you get a clean shot, somethin' to slow 'im down?"

"Gotta get closer. This thing is movin' too much."

"Okay, here take my piece and see what you can do. I'll head up front and see if I can cut 'im off."

* * *

Up above, Octavius leaned into the vicious headwind, which tore at his clothing, and despite his bulk, threatened to lift him clear off the roof as he leapt from carriage to carriage. On his third jump he landed awkwardly on the swaying coach and pitched sideways, rolling to the edge before he managed to grab hold of a protruding vent. He crawled back to the middle and slowly raised himself up. A shot cracked from behind, the bullet passing through his pant leg. He immediately hit the deck and turned to see one of his assailants kneeling on the roof of the observation lounge, several cars back. He witnessed another muzzle flash and heard the report as the shot ricocheted off the roof inches from where he lay. He returned fire, then pushing himself to his feet, took half a dozen rapid strides and launched himself across the gangway to the next carriage. When he looked back, he saw that his assailant was walking gingerly toward the edge of the car in obvious pursuit. He took this reprieve to run the length of the carriage and leap across the gaping chasm once more. The engine was still a ways off, six more carriages to go. He quickly made it five and was a good three quarters of the way along when up ahead another figure emerged from the car immediately behind the engine and started to walk towards him. Octavius turned to see his other assailant jump to the next car. He wasn't firing anymore or even attempting to shoot. Then it dawned on Octavius that they'd been instructed not to kill him. Wound him maybe, rough him up some, but take him alive and deliver him to Lasorda for some serious retribution.

"Don't shoot," he called out to the mouthpiece. "I'll come quietly."

The mouthpiece moved to the edge of the carriage and yelled above the din of the speeding train. "Drop Sal's gun."

The train thundered around a sharp bend and started to descend into a wooded valley, the howl of the wind and the metallic thrum of the wheels, obscuring the shouted command. Octavius feigned ignorance, cupping his hand to his ear. He wanted to get the mouthpiece close enough for a clean shot.

"Drop Sal's gun, now!"

No sooner had the words left his lips than from out of the screen of trees a hump-backed bridge appeared where a stretch of road crossed the narrow valley. Behind Octavius Sal furiously waved his arms to warn the mouthpiece, facing them and totally oblivious to the onrushing danger. Too late. The carriage was swallowed up in the tunnel, which caught the mouthpiece at shoulder height, shattering his spine and sweeping him from the roof. Octavius pivoted and hit the deck, squeezing off a shot at the crouching assailant, himself in the process of flattening against the roof. Octavius pressed his jowls into the metal and willed his bulk to achieve the clearance. The shadow of the bridge passed in a heartbeat, providing Octavius with the advantage of an unobstructed shot at the prostrate gunman. The instant he emerged from the short span of tunnel, Sal raised his head. Octavius took careful aim and squeezed the trigger. Then he turned and resumed his perilous flight toward the engine. But now two more figures emerged from the first carriage; railway detectives no doubt, alerted by the gunfire. For a brief instant he considered the diminishing odds of his remaining options before hurling himself into a stretch of marshland flashing by.

* * *

It was purely by chance that Littlejohn was in the vicinity of the trailers when two cars pulled in, parking on either side of where he stood. Two big, broad-shouldered characters with a pretty dame in tow, emerged from the first vehicle. Out of the second stepped an older gentleman, sporting a broad-brimmed Panama hat, and a noticeable bulge where his sidearm tented his suit jacket. They had law enforcement written all over them.

Instinctively, he dropped to his knees and began brushing at the grass as if looking for something on the ground. He bent lower and hunched his shoulders, like a turtle retreating into its shell. He didn't need a second warning. He waited for them to disappear into the trailer that served as an office and then high-tailed it back to the main tent. After feigning illness to one of the crew, he walked out the rear exit and then through the surrounding fields to the highway, hopping the fence to face the oncoming traffic in the northbound lane. They were closing in and Topeka was just too damn close. He considered his options and stuck out his thumb. After several minutes a long-haul transport pulled onto the shoulder.

"Where you headed?" asked the trucker.

"Where you goin'?"

"Montana, Billings, why?"

"That's exactly where I'm headed."

"Well ain't this just your lucky day."

"You said it, Jackson."

"Can you drive, 'cause I'm behind the eight ball and I could use a little shut eye."

"Sure thing."

"Then hop aboard. We can switch at Omaha."

* * *

Shadbolt hesitated for an instant, something about the man combing the grass in front of him just before he had fallen to his knees. The sensation was fleeting. He climbed the steps to the trailer and held the door for Vivian and Perkins. Section Head Musgrave followed. The office was manned by a primly-dressed woman whose pursed lips suggested she had been sucking on lemons for the better part of the morning. Before Shadbolt could make an introduction, Musgrave blustered, "We're looking for whoever runs this outfit."

"Mother Mary Margaret is in charge, but Mr. Delamare handles the day to day affairs. Do you gentlemen have an appointment?" She didn't acknowledge Vivian, her dress and demeanor not reverent enough for a Sunday morning. Instead, she gave her a disapproving look and clucked her tongue.

"No, and we don't generally ask for one."

"Well, it's very unlikely that he'll see you."

Musgrave leaned forward, "Sorry to spoil his Sunday morning, but we're FBI and need to talk to whoever runs this circus right now, if not sooner. Now, if you would be so kind as to round up one or the other." She was taken aback his brusqueness.

"Well I never." She turned away and called to someone in the back room.

"Gertie, Gertie!" Out sprang a young, pig-tailed sprite, who had obviously heard the strong rebuke from Musgrave. She wore a poplin dress of yellow gingham and a smile from ear to ear.

"Go over to Mr. Delamare's trailer and tell him to come right away. It's important and wipe that stupid grin off your face before you feel the back of my hand." The child scampered down the steps unable to contain her glee. Old lady Purcell getting a telling-off didn't happen everyday. As the woman went back to her paperwork, Shadbolt stepped up to the desk.

"Excuse me ma'am, but we're also looking to speak to one of your ushers. I'm sorry that we don't have a name, but he's a young, red-headed kid with a face full of freckles."

"Sounds like Kenny Aldridge. He's boarded out with some of the others at Mrs. Kodors' place. Let me check." She consulted a ledger on the desk, running her finger down a long column of names. Regaining her composure, she nodded before proclaiming in her most authoritative tone, "Yes, he's definitely boarding at Mrs. Kodors."

"And when do you expect him?"

"Not for a while yet."

"I don't mean to badger you, but could you be a bit more specific."

Clearly annoyed at the continued imposition, the woman huffed and puffed, and with her face turning bright scarlet announced, "Sir, I am not my brother's keeper." Standing quietly behind Shadbolt, Vivian couldn't contain her annoyance any longer. Her sister's life hung in the balance.

"Oh, for Christ's sake you officious old bag, go and find out when the fucking usher will be here, or give us the address where he's staying." The woman drew back in shock and was about to respond when Perkins entered the fray.

"You heard the lady. Move your ass before I give it a swift kick." She literally flew out of the trailer, muttering to herself. Musgrave gave Shadbolt a sideways glance, eyebrows arched below the brim of his Panama. Perkins let out a long breath and laid his hand on Vivian's shoulder. "We'll find her, don't worry."

The sprite returned ahead of the sourpuss and bounced up to Musgrave. "He ain't in the trailer, mister, and I dun asted and they said he went out and he ain't come back yet. You got a candy for me? If you ain't I'll take a nickel."

"I'll just bet you will too." He fished about in his pocket and flipped the coin into the air. She snatched it in mid-toss and ran right back out again, almost bowling over the sourpuss, who stomped up the stairs with a freckle-faced youth in tow. She pushed him in front of Shadbolt.

"Here he is in the flesh, Kenny Aldridge. Now if you don't need anything else, I'll be in the back." Without waiting for a response, she hurried into the adjoining room and closed the door, sliding the deadbolt into place. Shadbolt opened his notebook and instructed the boy to sit down, but even before he had a chance to introduce himself, or pose a question, the boy began to profess his innocence.

"I never done nothin', honest injun."

"Easy there, son, we never said you did. We just want to ask you a few questions."

"But I bin on the straight and narra ever since the last time." He looked from one to the other, searching for an understanding soul and finally settling on Vivian. "Honest injun, ma'am. I swear it on a stack of bibles."

"Relax, kid, we believe you," said Musgrave. "Just answer the man's questions."

"Kenny," continued Shadbolt, "Miss Bennet here says you handed an envelope to her sister, Helen, at the crusade last night. Do you recall the incident?"

"Incident, I don't remember a incident," he replied in a quavering voice.

"Let me rephrase that. Do you remember giving an envelope to a blonde lady last night?"

"I didn't do nothin', honest injun."

"Kenny, son, you're not in any trouble. We just need to know who gave you the envelope that you took to the blonde lady."

"Sure, the blonde lady. Now I remember."

"Good boy. So, who gave you the envelope? Was it a big gentleman, a really big fellow?"

"Perhaps I could be of assistance," came a voice from the doorway. "Carter Delamare at your service." They all turned to look, and Musgrave stepped to one side as he strode into the room, jacket straining to contain his massive shoulders. "Kenny, tell these gentlemen who gave you the note that you handed to the blonde lady." Shadbolt hadn't mentioned a note. He scribbled something in his pad.

"It was the new guy, Casper Littlejohn."

"And did he say what it was about?"

"No, he just said to give it to the blonde tomato down in front."

"Now was that so hard?"

"N, n, no, Mr. Delamare, sir."

"Will that be all for Kenny, gents. He's got a lot of work to do to get us ready for tonight's crusade."

"As a matter of fact, I have a few more questions for the boy. Special Agent, Jack Shadbolt," He stood, hand extended. "This is Agent Gene Perkins, Section Head Musgrave and Miss Vivian Bennett. Miss Bennett's sister Helen has gone missing. She attended the crusade last night and received a message from someone here. We need to talk to that someone. This Casper Littlejohn the boy mentioned, is he on the premises?"

"He was setting up in the main tent last time I looked. I can take you there now if you like."

"In a moment if you don't mind." He turned back to Kenny. "Did Casper say anything else about the envelope, if it was from himself or if he was just passing it on for someone?" The boy thought for a moment before answering.

"Um, he didn't say nothin' 'cept for me to give it to the lady."

"Okay, so he just handed it to you and told you to give it to the lady without any further explanation."

"Yes sir."

"And has he or anyone else ever asked you to give an envelope to a lady in the audience?"

"No sir."

"Not even one other time before last night?"

"No sir."

"Alright, I've just got a couple more questions for you, Kenny. Is that okay?"

"Sure."

"Now did you see him with anybody else that night, not someone from the crusade, but a stranger, like the big guy I asked you about earlier?"

"Gosh, I don't rightly remember."

"Think Kenny, think. This is important. It'll really help us to find Miss Bennett's sister."

* * *

The boy scrunched up his face, concentration etched deep into the furrows of his brow. In truth, he could barely remember delivering the envelope, let alone tracking the movements of a workmate he barely knew. Most nights were pandemonium under the big top and since he had joined the tour back in Sioux Falls, in his mind it had become a seamless blur. But he didn't want to disappoint his inquisitor or the nice lady awaiting news of her missing sister, so he fashioned a response that served to deflect the investigation from the trajectory, so carefully constructed by Shadbolt and his team, by creating a fictitious link between Octavius and Casper Littlejohn .

"Yeah, now I remember. It was near the end of the night."

"Go on."

"He was talking to a big guy in a suit, togged to the bricks, real smooth." Kenny warmed to the recollection embellishing the encounter with fanciful details, some veering into the phantasmagoric. "They seemed real friendly like, you know bosom buddies. I seen the guy slip the envelope to 'im, and then he gave him a fin, least I thought it was a fin."

"And then Casper passed the envelope to you after the exchange."

"Yeah, that's right."

"And then what did they do?"

"Uh, well they was gone when I got back from givin' 'er the envelope."

"Did you see them leave together?"

"Yeah, I seen 'em leave together."

"But you just said they were gone when you returned from delivering the envelope."

"Did I? I meant they wasn't right there where I left 'em. They was walking away."

"Together?"

"Yeah together, Casper had his arm around the big guys shoulder."

* * *

From the sidelines Carter portrayed the impassionate observer, allowing the boy to prevaricate at will, slowly tightening the noose around the transient dupe and Octavius. He'd been a good and faithful servant, but it was time to sever the bonds before he led them to the real culprits, his beloved cousins.

The FBI agent closed his notebook, signaling the end of the interview. "Alright, let's go and find the gentleman who delivered the note."

They ventured outside, where he led them along a well-worn pathway through the rag tag collection of trailers and tents to the rear of the main tent where the work crews were preparing for the evening's show. He approached one of the men and enquired after Littlejohn. It was he who had asked Littlejohn to pass the envelope to the usher, and he would have to provide a plausible explanation when questioned about it later on, but, as luck would have it, events were unfolding in his favor. Littlejohn was no longer on the grounds.

"The crew boss tells me he was under the weather and has gone back to the boarding house to rest up until tonight. I take it you'll want to talk to him right away."

"That's correct. He's a key to this investigation."

"Okay, let's head back to the office, and Miss Purcell can provide you with the address."

"Yes, and we'll need to talk to you and some of your other staff when we finish up with Casper."

"Certainly, whatever you need. Like I said, I'm at your service."

* * *

Too late Shadbolt realized that he had overplayed his hand with the usher, and in so doing, planted an errant seed in the consciousness of Section Head Musgrave. The Crusade manager had been quick to offer his assistance, but Shadbolt was skeptical. There was something about the man that struck him as odd.

* * *

Having dispatched Perkins and Vivian to Del Monico's to interview the Maitre d', Shadbolt and Musgrave made their way to Mrs. Kodors' boarding house. The rambling Victorian dwelling occupied an overgrown lot in a once prosperous part of town, now the domain of blue-collar families and down and outers, renting rooms by the week or hour. Seedy taverns dotted the small community, providing a respite from the squalid conditions with cheap beer, nickel jukeboxes and backroom games of chance. Generally given a wide berth by the local law enforcement, who never ventured in alone, and only under duress.

They ascended the rickety porch stairs and rang the bell. Several minutes passed before an unkempt woman in a food-stained apron answered the door. Musgrave made the introductions and then inquired after Littlejohn.

"He left this morning with the rest of the crew, and nobody's come back since."

"Is there any way he could've re-entered the premises without you noticing?" said Shadbolt.

"I don't give out keys, and the door is locked at eight o'clock sharp."

"Do you mind if we take a look?"

She gave them a scowl. "Go right ahead, if you don't believe me."

"It's not a case of disbelieving you. We need to have a poke around even if he's not here. He's implicated in some very serious goings on, and this could be helpful to the case."

"I don't want no trouble now. I run a tight ship; you can ask anybody. I don't stand for no tomfoolery."

"We fully appreciate that ma'am, and this has no reflection on your fine establishment. It's strictly a police matter between Littlejohn and us."

"Well like I said, I don't want no trouble."

"And you shall have none; now which way to his room?" Together they climbed the steep back stairs and traipsed along the threadbare runner to a door at the far end of the landing.

"You'll have to excuse the mess. I haven't had a chance to make up the beds yet. My regular colored girl, Minnie, is away looking after her sick mother."

She knocked and then called out before inserting the key and turning the handle. The room gave off a sour, sleep-stained, odor.

"Demon drink," she cursed, going straight to the window and hefting the sash as high as it would go. The bustle of the surrounding streets and alleyways seeped into the room.

"Who does he share with?" said Shadbolt, eyeing the adjoining bed.

"A drunken Irishman. Mick McCarthy's his name. A bad lot if you ask me."

"Is there any reason the pillows are arranged to resemble a sleeping man?"

Mrs. Kodors pondered the humped form under the coverlet.

"Is that how they're usually left?"

"It's the first time I've noticed them like that."

Shadbolt walked to the other side of the bed and pulled back the covers. Mrs. Kodors brought her hand to her mouth to stifle a cry, her eyes widened in disbelief. The bottom pillow was soaked with blood.

"What the hell have we got here?" croaked Musgrave.

"Nothing good; that's for certain." Shadbolt reached down and opened the pillow cover. He took a quick look inside and closed it up again, shaking his head. He glanced over at Musgrave. "We better get some more of the team down here, forensics and the county coroner. Ma'am, we'll need to use your telephone and while we're at it, do you have a cellar?"

"Yes … why?"

"Just playing a hunch. Let's make the calls first and then we'll have you take us down there."

"I need to clean up this mess," she pleaded.

"Not just yet. This is a crime scene. We need to process it first."

"But I have a boarding house to run, and guests who have paid in advance."

"Sorry, ma'am, we may have to commandeer the premises until we sort this out."

Once they made the necessary calls, she led them down the back staircase, the means by which the hired help of former households negotiated the premises without interacting with the owners. Arriving at a padlocked door, she reached into her apron pocket and took out a ring of keys.

"No need," said Shadbolt, "the lock's been jimmied." He reached out and fingered the shackle. "Crow-barred by the looks of it."

"Oh my." Reluctantly, she removed the lock, pushed the door open, and switched on the overhead light. A dim bulb flickered in the ceiling, revealing rows of shelving lining a long corridor. She remained on the threshold, unable or unwilling to venture further into the shadowy space, afraid of what they might uncover.

Shadbolt stepped past her, advancing along the narrow passageway into the center of the cellar, where a large coal furnace sat, like some hideous deep-sea creature with outstretched tentacles probing the joists. To one side, below the coal chute, sat an open stall, containing a large mound of anthracite. He walked over and, picking up a shovel, stabbed at the pile. Satisfied that nothing lay buried beneath, he replaced the shovel and moved to a series of doors ringing the walls.

"What are in the rooms?" he called back to Mrs. Kodors, still rooted in the doorway. Musgrave wandered back and coaxed her to the end of the shelving.

"We're sorry to put you through this, ma'am, but we're going to need your assistance."

"The first two are storage for the house, extra furniture, mattresses and chairs and such like. I keep them locked."

"I can see that. Doesn't look like these have been tampered with. What about the far one?" He pointed to a door at the very end of the row.

"That's the root cellar."

Shadbolt walked over and inspected the lock. It had been forced and then bent back into shape and refastened.

"Can you unlock this one for us?"

"I'd rather not," and she held out the keys for Musgrave, who brought them over to Shadbolt. He inserted the bit and turned, but the lock failed to open. It was obvious that the locking mechanism had been broken when it was forced and jammed back together.

"Can you bring me that shovel, Clarence?"

Musgrave retrieved it from the coal pile. After two swipes, Shadbolt succeeded in removing the lock, which clattered to the floor. He opened the door and a blast a cold air hit him in the face along with the earthy smell of onions and turnips and cabbages. He brushed the inside wall, seeking the light switch. A dark silhouette entered his vision an instant before the room was filled with light, revealing Mick McCarthy's bloody corpse suspended from the rafters. Mrs. Kodors gave a sharp cry and fled back down the corridor, while Musgrave craned his neck to get a better view of the dead man. There on the floor in a smattering of congealed blood was the Irishman's tongue, along with the weapon, a short-bladed hunting knife, bearing the initials CL. McCarthy's torso was scored with dozens of punctures, and a gaping cavity yawned in the middle of his chest where a beating heart had resided. As Shadbolt paid heed to the details of the brutal execution, an ever so subtle floral note emerged above the pungency of the root vegetables, the unmistakable whiff of Fougere Royale.

It was a moment of enlightenment for Shadbolt, confirming his earlier suspicions about the murders. He had no idea what unearthly set of circumstances had caused their paths to intersect as they obviously had. In some bizarre twist of fate, Casper Littlejohn had become ensnared in the web of murders perpetrated by Octavius Cadogan and a possible accomplice. Unravelling the tangle and apprehending the true culprits was proving to be a much more difficult task than he had ever imagined, one that was testing every ounce of his experience and know how. He was becoming desperate for the return of agent Will to see what light he could shed on the growing complexities of the case.

He turned to Musgrave, "When was the last time you recall a murderer leaving his murder weapon in plain view, a murder weapon that also happens to bear his initials?"

"What are you getting' at, Jack?"

"It's too pat is what. We're bein' played."

"You heard the kid, Littlejohn handed him the note. He's been made by the Clayborne girl and now this. Maybe you're over-thinking it. Sometimes it's exactly what it looks like. It's obvious to me that these bastards are in cahoots, Casper Littlejohn and this Octavius Cadogan, and the sooner we bring 'em in the better."

"I'm with you there, if only to get to the truth of the matter."

"Let's face it, they're both gonna fry."

"Agreed, but there's more to this than meets the eye, and I've got a ten spot says they aren't connected. Cadogan is working on his own or with an accomplice. Casper Littlejohn is a handy stooge, who just happens to be in the wrong place at the wrong time. I'll grant you that he's a murderer, but not of these four women, and we're gonna prove it."

"I admire your determination, Jack, but I ain't convinced yet, and time is running out."

"Don't tell me that, Clarence, not when we're this close."

"You know if it was up to me I'd let you play it out, but ultimately it's up to Washington. My hands are tied."

Once the other agents arrived, Shadbolt went over the crime scene with a fine-tooth comb, dusting for prints, and checking for blood along with any evidence of a forced entry into the premises, which would rule out Littlejohn for obvious reasons. He found what he was looking for when examining the trap door of the coal chute. It had been prized open from the outside and the inside catch bent back into shape after entry into the cellar had been gained.

Just after 1:00 pm, Shadbolt and Musgrave returned to headquarters, receiving news that Helen Bennett had been found and taken to Kansas City General Hospital.

"This could be the break we've been looking for. I better contact Gene and her sister with the good news. They didn't say how bad she was, did they?"

"Took a bullet was all they would say. Tell him to get over there and report on the situation. See if there's anything he can get out of her now if she's able."

"We may have to give her a day or two depending on the severity of the wound. Doesn't sound like the usual M O."

"No, it doesn't. Ambulance attendants reported that it was called in."

"By whom?"

"That's for us to find out."

"The plot thickens."

"You can say that again."

"Okay, I'll make the call to Gene, and after Will gets back, we'll pay a return visit to the Foursquare Gospel bunch, Mr. Delamare in particular. Something about him struck me as off kilter, and these murders, the biblical imagery. It's starting to fit; the crusade has been traveling through Iowa. Perkins found one of their pamphlets in the murdered clerk's apartment and now Helen Bennett is kidnapped after receiving tickets to one of their shows. I suspect if we go back and check, the other victims will have attended as well."

Musgrave just grunted an acknowledgement and then called out to his secretary to bring him a coffee.

* * *

Agent Will watched from his table in the dining car as the countryside flashed by. He was on the last leg of the return journey with a clear picture in his mind as to the likely culprits, all of whom shared lineage with one of the most notorious murderers in American history. A lethal bloodline. He was convinced the cousins were perpetrating the gruesome killings with Octavius acting as procurer of both the victims and the venues. He speculated the trio was travelling through the land under some legitimate guise as salesmen, property speculators or commodities buyers, stopping long enough to establish a temporary base of operations, secure an appropriate setting, select and mutilate a victim of a very specific type, and move to the next port of call. With Octavius' medical background, a travelling medicine show was another possibility, although in retrospect, that type of exposure would probably draw too much attention.

He sketched out a work plan to revisit the towns where the victims had lived to investigate what types of transient businesses were frequenting the territory when the crimes had been committed. In addition, he enlisted the New Orleans and Los Angeles field offices to apprehend and hold Octavius and the two Beauchamp's for questioning, if and when they returned to their known addresses.

He finished reviewing his notes over coffee and then tucked them back into his leather portmanteau. It was a graduation gift from his father, who had envisioned his talented son entering the family business, and not some plebian pursuit like law enforcement. The last time he had seen him they exchanged harsh words. He was hoping that by breaking this case, that was starting to gain national exposure, he might be seen in a better light, worthy of his father's pride. He returned to his seat, his mind continuing to sift through the details of the investigation.

With the clickety-clack of the wheels sending out a hypnotic rhythm, he drifted off into a troubled sleep plagued by an ominous dreamscape, depicting scenes of savage debauchery. Horrific images flickered as if on a movie screen: Nell Madisson laying spread-eagled on a narrow iron cot, limbs held fast with ligatures of coarse rope, body slick with sweat; Beauchamp ravaging the helpless woman and then forcing the twins to take part in the degradation; berating the reluctant one when he didn't comply; and Octavius looking on, wide-eyed. The final image replicated the photograph of the boys atop the gator only this time the gutted corpse was that of Nell Madisson.

He was jolted awake, torn out of the disturbing dream by the lonesome whistle blast of the engine as the train thundered toward Joplin. Several minutes later the Southern Belle eased into the Joplin station for a seven-minute whistle stop. Shaking off the last vestiges of the disturbing visions, Will glanced out the window to see clutches of passengers and greeters milling about the platform, engaged in animated conversation. There had been rumblings of something back in Texarkana, but he hadn't paid it much mind, engrossed as he was in his report. Finally succumbing to curiosity, he enquired of one of the alighting passengers as to the source of the commotion. The ruddy-faced gent looked at him incredulously,

"Ain't you heard? Pearl Harbor got bombed this morning."

"By who?"

"Japs."

"You're kidding, where'd you hear that?"

"This ain't no joke, mister. It's all over the radio." He sat back, stunned, while the man took a seat further down the aisle, continuing the conversation with the surrounding passengers. In seconds the whole car was abuzz with the news. Like jungle telegraph it travelled through the train, from porter to ticket taker to engineer and brakeman and back again, gaining in urgency as it ricocheted between engine and caboose. For a split second he contemplated racing to the bank of telephones in the waiting hall but speculated that he might not be able to get through and then make it back onto the train it time amidst the growing pandemonium. He began to wonder how his latest revelations would be greeted in light of this earth-shattering news, and what it'd mean for the investigation. He was aware that they were overdue in Washington to take on a big, important assignment. In that instant the reason behind the call-up became abundantly clear. He desperately needed to talk to Shadbolt.

* * *

"We're getting some disturbing news on the wire, Jack, from Hawaii. An attack on Pearl Harbor." Musgrave loosened his tie.

"The Pacific Fleet?"

"Yes."

"What sabotage?"

"No, an air attack, planes, bombers."

"What does Washington say?"

"The lines have been tied up for the past hour. The wire feed is from St. Louis."

"Any other details?"

"Not more than an hour ago, the Japs, massive air attack. The whole fleet's been crippled, hundreds killed."

"Good Lord. So, it's not just speculation, we're in a shooting war."

"As good as."

"Was this the reason for the urgency to get to Washington; I know we've been keeping tabs on the Germans?"

"Something to that effect, I just wasn't expecting anything like this."

"We should have guessed after Nanking. They've had aspirations in the Pacific for a long time now."

"Sneaky cocksuckers." The door to Musgrave's office burst open and an agent pointed to his phone.

"Call coming in from Washington, Chief. They say it's urgent."

"Okay." Musgrave picked up the telephone on the first ring, a concerned look creasing his brow. After several "uh huhs" he replaced the receiver and slumped back into his chair. "It's the brass, Jack, they need you right away, and some of the others, Gene and Felix included. The old man himself has given the order. It countermands all others."

"But what about these murders; we can't just leave in the middle of the investigation?"

"Look, you and your team have done an outstanding job on this. We've got the perpetrators identified and on the run. Between myself, and the State police, we should be able to make the collar."

"Jesus, Clarence, Will is due back later today. Let us compile our findings and have a final briefing tomorrow morning. We should at least see what he's turned up. It could help us wrap this thing up in a nice, neat bow for you and the Staties."

"You're gonna cost me my badge, Jack. Swear to me that you and your musketeers are gonna be outta here by tomorrow noon at the latest."

"I swear."

* * *

Shadbolt and Perkins were waiting on the platform when the Southern Belle pulled into Union Station at 7:55PM. Special Agent Will hadn't been expecting a greeting party, but their concerned expressions told him the news wasn't going to be good. He reached for his case in the overhead rack and quickly exited the carriage.

"I heard," he said as he stepped down. "Pearl Harbor, how bad is it?"

"Real bad. President Roosevelt will be addressing the nation tomorrow. We've been ordered to Washington immediately."

"What about the investigation?"

"It's out of our hands as of noon tomorrow."

"But who'll …"

"Musgrave and the Staties. Oh, and we had another incident while you were gone, Gene's girl's sister of all people."

"Good Lord, murdered?"

"She's in hospital, but it looks like she'll pull through."

"I'm so sorry, Gene. That's getting too close to home."

"She's one tough tomato. When she's right again she should be able to help fry these bastards."

"How'd she manage to get away?"

"Someone, and we have a good hunch who, came to the rescue. We'll debrief you in the car. We've got one last port of call before we hand this over to Musgrave."

"I've got some pretty important revelations myself. You're not going to believe the connections I turned up in Baton Rouge." They piled into Shadbolt's car and headed to the Crusade site on the outskirts of the City. Along the way Shadbolt related the most recent events, with Will reciprocating in kind.

"Beauchamp!"

"Twin sons and a nephew. The apples have fallen directly beneath the tree, and they're rotten to the core."

"Son of a bitch."

"And the Foursquare Gospel cover fits perfectly with your biblical angle."

"I should've put that together a lot sooner."

"That makes two of us," said Perkins.

"Don't beat yourselves up," said Shadbolt. "Who'd suspect a bunch of travelling bible thumpers?"

"I was speculating some sort of job involving travel: insurance, door to door sales, commodities buyer, but I have to agree, no one would have given a travelling gospel show, and a well known one at that, a second look."

"It's guaranteed if we go back and check, all of the victims will have attended the Crusade in the days before their abduction."

"The pattern should've been obvious, but I don't recall any of the witness statements mentioning that fact."

"Didn't think it was relevant, or just didn't know would be my guess."

"You know the other thing that strikes me as particularly odd is the fact that the three of them are working in tandem. I haven't come across anything like this in the cases I've studied. It's usually a lone wolf, or a mentor and disciple."

"Agreed. This is a whole new ball game and we don't have a program to identify what position the players are playing. By my reckoning it looks like Cadogan is the procurer for the other two, but the knife work suggests he's playing a role in the final mutilation as well. I believe we came into contact with one of the cousins at the Crusade grounds. He runs the outfit, well manages it for Mother Mary Margaret, the faith healer. Goes by the name of Carter Delamare."

"So he kept his first name."

"Appears so. Easier I guess, less opportunity for slip-ups."

"What about the other twin, Morgan?"

"No sign of him on the last visit, but no doubt he's lurking somewhere in the background. By the way, there was one other really strange coincidence: Casper Littlejohn."

"Our parallel kidnapping murderer?"

"One and the same."

"But how?"

"He showed up on the Crusade's work roster, a general hand. Seems like they took him on right after the Oskaloosa caper. He's also implicated in another murder, either that or he's being set up, which is my theory, though not fully endorsed by Musgrave as yet."

"Who was the victim?"

"Another hand, older Irishman with a less than savory reputation. We've got an APB out on him. Hopefully, he won't slip through our fingers again. Now all we have to do is turn up something on Mr. Carter Delamare, a.k.a. Beauchamp, and his brother before the night is out."

"Do we have enough to hold 'em for the time being?"

"All circumstantial I'm afraid. It took us the best part of the afternoon to convince Judge Stoneham to issue a search warrant. Musgrave was practically down on his knees by the end. We've got to tie them to Cadogan or better yet, any of the victims, but that's going to require something concrete, and if not, Gene has a little insurance policy up his sleeve, obtained from the latest victim."

"Should I really be hearing this?"

"Desperate times call for desperate measures."

* * *

When they arrived at the field that served as a parking lot, the first thing they noticed was the lack of vehicles. The grounds were virtually empty, and the area around the big top dark. As they approached the entrance, they saw the sign, "Tonight's Crusade Cancelled Due to Illness," and underneath in hastily scrawled letters, "See office trailer for refunds." They made their way to the trailer they had visited earlier in the day and entered to find the sourpuss sitting behind her desk refunding pre-purchased tickets to a couple who claimed to have driven most of the day to attend and couldn't comprehend how a faith healer was incapable of healing herself.

"No, like I said, she got into an accident and has a deep cut on her arm."

"Well, could we jus' see her. You know, jus' pay our respec's. May-Jean has got the arthritis real bad. A short, little visit is 'bout all she needs."

"I'm sorry sir, that isn't possible. Can you imagine if we granted everyone personal visits? And besides she isn't here at the moment." The rube continued to wheedle until, at the end of her patience, she shooed them away as one would petulant children. Looking up from the cashbox she blanched when she recognized the agents from earlier that morning. She sat up ramrod straight.

"Ma'am," Shadbolt nodded, "It's Miss Purcell, right?"

"That is correct. I take it you're not here for a refund?"

"No, we've come back to speak with Mr. Delamare."

"Oh, well he's not back yet. He took Mother Mary Margaret to the hospital to get her arm seen to. He said she needed stitches."

"How did it happen?"

"I believe it was a fall. She suffered a nasty gash and wasn't up to this evening's performance. All these miracles place a great strain on her. I don't know how she keeps it up night after night."

"Do you know which hospital she was taken to?"

"I'm not sure. Somewhere in the City I suppose."

"There are at least four in the City. Do any of these ring a bell: General Hospital, St. Joseph's, Trinity Lutheran or The Christian Hospital?"

"I'm sorry, he just said hospital and that they'd be back after she got stitches. Maybe it was worse that he thought, the cut. He's been gone over three, no four hours now."

Shadbolt turned to Gene. "We better follow up on this. I have a sneaking suspicion Mr. Delamare may be avoiding the interview we promised. Ma'am do you have a telephone on the premises?"

"There's one in Mr. Delamare's trailer, but you'll have to wait for him to return."

"I'm not sure if you're aware of this, but we're investigating a kidnapping and murder of one of your employees. We'll need your full cooperation, including access to his and any other trailers of interest. I have a search warrant here that authorizes complete access to all your facilities." He took out the folded document and held it up for her to see. "We can't wait for Mr. Delamare to return, so if you would be so kind as to take us to his trailer, and if you are able, unlock the door. Once we're finished, we'll let you know what else we need to look at. I take it you'll be here for the duration?" She replied in the affirmative, reaching into her desk for a ring of keys. Then she led them down the pathway to a large, modern trailer, sausage-shaped with polished aluminum coachwork. The insignia read Air Stream Clipper. She unlocked the door and stepped aside to let them in.

"Please be careful in there. Mr. Delamare is very particular."

"He won't even know we've been here. I promise."

They entered and Shadbolt snapped on the light to reveal a well-appointed interior of solid mahogany millwork, and all the latest appliances.

"Looks like our friend has a taste for the high life."

"Pretty slick. This place is better equipped than my apartment."

"Okay Will, you take the bedroom. I'll start in here; Gene, you start calling around and see where these hombres ended up."

Shadbolt began opening doors to the built-in cabinets and meticulously sifting through the contents. He moved to the dining table cum desk and searched through the drawers built into the bench seating. In the meantime, Will scoured the bedroom, seeking anything vaguely construed as incriminating: paperwork, receipts, financial statements along with hard evidence: weapons, restraints, and articles from the deceased.

After a half hour of fruitless telephone inquiries, Perkins called over to Shadbolt, "No sign of 'em at any of the City hospitals. Do you think they may have gone to a private clinic instead?"

"That's a possibility, but you heard Miss Purcell yourself. She definitely said hospital."

"Well, they haven't showed up at any in this burg unless they built a new one while we were in Iowa."

"Jack," shouted Will from the bedroom.

"What is it?" He stopped what he was doing and moved toward the door.

"I'm not certain. Have a look at this." He handed Shadbolt a sheaf of black and white photographs, autographed publicity shots of Mother Mary Margaret and some of the other crusade performers, Bible Billy, three of the featured singers and the orchestra leader. Standing just behind the group was Carter Delamare, the crusade manager. "Does anything catch your eye?" Shadbolt stared hard for several seconds.

"Son of a bitch," he spit, "Mother Mary Margaret and Carter could be brother and sister."

"Or twins."

"What are you sayin'?" Perkins bellowed, bending lower to get a better look. "That Mother Mary is a kiki, a queen?"

"Exactly. Mother Mary fucking Margaret is Morgan Beauchamp in drag."

"A transvestite?" queried Shadbolt.

"Either that or a full sex change. There are clinics in Europe, the Hirshfield Institute, I believe, that specialize in the procedure. It involves castration and the construction of a vagina from the scrotum."

"So, the he could now be a she?" Perkins seemed horror struck.

"Not unless there's another cousin, or a sister, but I think it's pretty obvious, and I think a nosey around her trailer will seal the deal."

"And I thought I'd seen it all on my old beat in Hoboken."

"Gene, go and get Miss Purcell to open up Mother Mary Margaret's trailer," said Shadbolt.

The sourpuss was even less inclined to cooperate with the unlocking of Mother Mary Margaret's trailer, but finally relented after Perkins fetched Shadbolt, who waved the search warrant in her face. They entered the largest of the trailers and flipped on the light switch. A crystal fixture cast shards of colored light throughout the garish interior, reflecting off a hundred shiny surfaces. It was gaudy in the extreme, exuding a garish opulence at odds with the abstemious ethos of the church. An ornate make up table festooned with a platoon of mannequin heads, modeling blonde wigs occupied a long stretch of wall. Opposite sat a gold brocade divan and a liquor trolley of sterling silver.

Shadbolt started opening drawers while Perkins inspected the tall closet and Will made for the bedroom. It didn't take long. Beside the telephone something was scribbled in code on a notepad, and at the bottom, directions to the old Kansas City Electric Light Company.

"We've got it," said Shadbolt. "This is the link we need, the location where Helen Bennett was held."

"And this," said Will, emerging from the bedroom holding up a rollie. "By the looks of the mess in here, I'd say they left in one hell of a hurry."

"I had a sneaking suspicion they wouldn't be coming back after Miss Purcell told us they'd gone to the hospital. We better get an A.P.B. out on them."

"I've got the New Orleans and Los Angeles field offices conducting surveillance on Octavius' and the twins' last known addresses."

"I doubt if they'll return to any familiar domiciles, at least not in person."

"So, it's up to Musgrave and the Staties now," Will scowled.

"Afraid so."

"We were so close."

"Close only counts in horseshoes," commented Perkins

"Okay, let's get our evidence in some semblance of order. If we meet with Musgrave at 8:00 o'clock tomorrow morning, we should have enough time to get him up to speed before we leave."

"That means we'll be pulling an all-nighter," Perkins stated matter-of-factly.

"Looks like."

"Do you mind if I give Vivian a call first?"

"Sure, go ahead, and let Musgrave know the plan. We'll see you back at the car."

* * *

YESTERDAY, DECEMBER 7, 1941 A DATE WHICH WILL LIVE IN INFAMY THE UNITED STATES OF AMERICA WAS SUDDENLY AND DELIBERATELY ATTACKED BY NAVAL AND AIR FORCES OF THE EMPIRE OF JAPAN …

* * *

The trucker eased the rig into the yard and, with Littlejohn directing, backed up to the loading dock. A fresh fall of snow covered the rooftops, and along with the colored lights and conifer branches decorating the lamp posts, imbued the City with a gay, festive air.

"What say we grab us some chow at Lou's Diner. It's just down the street."

"Sure, but I'm a little light. Could you spare me two bits? I promise I'll pay you back as soon as I get me a little scratch together."

"Hey, it's on me, buddy. You saved my bacon. In fact I might even be in for a bonus on account of bein' early and all."

"Well I'm not one to look a gift horse in the mouth. Lead the way, Al." They exited the cab and trudged around to the front of the building where the trucker dropped off the bill of lading. He jawed good-naturedly with the secretary and then slapping Littlejohn on the back started to jog toward the flashing red neon. Littlejohn bent down and grabbing a handful of snow, hucked an icy projectile at the trucker, hitting him square in the back. He returned fire, laughing, caught up in the horseplay, the boisterous camaraderie of a new-found friend. They continued with the snowball fight all the way to the front door of the diner.

* * *

THE UNITED STATES WAS AT PEACE WITH THAT NATION AND, AT THE SOLICITATION OF JAPAN, WAS STILL IN CONVERSATION WITH ITS GOVERNMENT AND ITS EMPORER LOOKING TOWARD THE MAINTENANCE OF PEACE IN THE PACIFIC …

* * *

Octavius followed the creek upstream for several miles, dragging his injured leg every excruciating step of the way. He'd come down heavily and felt something in his knee give out, the cruciate ligament he surmised. He was perspiring heavily, and constantly mopped at his brow. He stopped for a while to catch his breath and rest his aching limb. The respite was cut short when he was startled by the crack of a branch, ducking down behind a copse of hornbeam in case he was being followed by one of the buttons, or the railway police. It turned out to be a doe and fawn, journeying through the woods in search of fresh browsing. He watched them disappear into the brush, and then continuing through the trees, came upon an expanse of open water, surrounded by marshes. There was a stop-log structure controlling the outlet where the stream began and a sign identifying the water body as La Cygnes Lake. Off in the distance he spied what looked like a cabin, sitting by the shoreline, a tendril of smoke curling lazily from the flue. He gauged the distance at three quarters of a mile. Then patting at Sal's gun in his belt, he began the arduous trek toward sanctuary.

* * *

AS COMMANDER IN CHIEF OF THE ARMY AND NAVY I HAVE DIRECTED THAT ALL MEASURES BE TAKEN IN OUR DEFENCE. BUT ALWAYS WILL OUR

WHOLE NATION REMEMBER THE CHARACTER OF THE ONSLAUGHT AGAINST US …

* * *

The old fishing camp outside Lafayette looked none the worse for wear despite the fact that it had sat unoccupied for several years. Rufus, the family retainer had kept it in reasonably good repair in their absence, although his and the twins' version of ramshackle occupied opposite ends of the "Good Housekeeping" spectrum. Carter parked the vehicle, stripped of its plates, behind the boathouse, and immediately covered it with a tarpaulin.

"We'll take one of the pirogues to the island. It'll be less conspicuous than the jet boat."

Morgan nodded in agreement. He wandered over to the dock, and staring into the still waters, observed his alter ego. He peeled off the moustache, removed his hat, and shook his hair free. The hunger had passed for now. It was time to hunt a different kind of prey.

* * *

NO MATTER HOW LONG IT MAY TAKE US TO OVERCOME THIS PREMEDITATED INVASION, THE AMERICAN PEOPLE IN THEIR RIGHTEOUS MIGHT WILL WIN THROUGH TO ABSOLUTE VICTORY. I BELIEVE THAT I INTERPRET THE WILL OF THE CONGRESS AND OF THE PEOPLE WHEN I ASSERT THAT WE WILL NOT ONLY DEFEND OURSELVES TO THE UTTERMOST BUT WILL MAKE IT VERY CERTAIN THAT THIS FORM OF TREACHERY SHALL NEVER AGAIN ENDANGER US …

* * *

Gene and Vivian embraced a final time and then he climbed the carriage steps to join Shadbolt and Will inside. She dabbed at her eyes and after waving him off, left the station and made straight for the hospital. Her sister wasn't out of the woods yet. Inside the private compartment, Shadbolt was apprehensive. All four suspects were on the run, and with the exception of Casper Littlejohn, extremely dangerous. He didn't trust Musgrave or the state police to bring this to a successful conclusion anytime soon, meaning more lives would be at risk. For although they had broken the case, Octavius and the Beauchamp twins were a sophisticated trio of brutal killers, capable of eluding detection through sheer guile and chameleon-like deceptions. They needed every agent in the country to be on high alert if they hoped to capture them. Unfortunately, the declaration of war with Japan had scuppered that possibility.

* * *

HOSTILITIES EXIST. THERE IS NO BLINKING AT THE FACT THAT OUR PEOPLE, OUR TERRITORY, AND OUR INTERESTS ARE IN GRAVE DANGER. WITH CONFIDENCE IN OUR ARMED FORCES AND WITH THE UNBOUNDING DETERMINATION OF OUR PEOPLE WE WILL GAIN THE INEVITABLE TRIUMPH SO HELP US GOD.

* * *

Musgrave saw the boys off at the station and returned to his office. It had been a long briefing that morning and he was dog-tired. The case files were stacked on his desk, pages and pages of hand-written notes and forensic reports, and more bizarre twists and turns than you could shake a stick at. The office was going to be on skeleton staff until he could replace the seconded agents. He wasn't sure he had the energy to give this the attention it needed. He pushed his favored Panama hat back and mopped at his brow. He was sweating like a race horse. He hoped he wasn't coming down with anything this close to Christmas. Picking up the phone, he started calling around to the other field offices. They had all bled agents to internal affairs, but the New Orleans section head said he could spare a man for a month, a long-serving agent with an eye for detail. Musgrave gladly accepted and to make things easier he promised to forward the files, which he had his secretary bundle up and ship right away. In the general disruption of the first few days of the war, the files never did arrive, and Musgrave succumbed to a massive heart attack that very evening after dinner.

* * *

The Hedgerow Mutilations

NORMANDY,
June 6, 1944, two and a half years later

The plane bucked and yawed in protest as the pilot sought to evade the heavy flak, lighting up the sky like a fourth of July celebration. Banking sharply, he dropped steeply through the worst of the tracers, finding a quiet pocket between the batteries, a momentary respite from the incendiary bursts. Inside, the C-47 was deathly still; conversation had ceased as the platoon neared the drop zone. Twenty-seven paratroopers sitting mute in the darkened interior, ribbed like the belly of a whale. The 502nd Paratroop Infantry Regiment, the five-o-deuces of the 101st Airborne, the Screaming Eagles, they were the first wave of Operation Overlord, landing behind German coastal defenses in the dead of night to secure access for the forces that would assault Utah Beach later that morning.

While tracers continued to illuminate the sky, the C-47 swung in low, through a bank of clouds, and out they dove into the dark night, floating down and down, gentle as butterflies emerging from the chrysalis, spores on the wind.

His own metamorphosis was now complete. He had shed one hundred pounds and sported a classic Mohawk, a strip of dark hair striping his shaved skull. His face was covered in war paint, bold slashes of red and black. Gone the jowly, sagging flesh, replaced with rock-hard muscle and chiseled features. A long, fallow stretch of convalescence and subsequent training. The time had come to harvest the sheaves once more.

The ground rose up to meet him, an open field of ripening hay. He hit and rolled, distributing the impact across his large frame, then he gathered up the parachute, and moved swiftly to rendezvous with a pair of dark shapes off to his left. A small group quickly assembled, and reconnoitering the immediate landscape, realized that the pilot had missed the drop zone by a good two miles. They set off heading north for the beaches and met up with several other small groups until a Lieutenant-Colonel finally took charge and directed them to their respective missions. By 3:30 am they had taken a lightly-defended village in a brief firefight, and afterwards he volunteered to join a patrol charged with seizing a nearby panzer barracks.

Under the command of a staff sergeant, they crossed a series of open fields, battling through almost impassible hedgerows to arrive at a large farmstead. The patrol split up and advanced to their intended targets, the main house, a stone barn containing the barracks, and a small shed. On hands and knees, he crawled to a lit window at the back of the house. Peering inside, he noted several panzers in various states of undress, eating around a kitchen table. He could almost smell the coffee and taste the pork and eggs frying in a large, blackened skillet.

For the briefest instant he was reminded of his gluttonous past, the sensuous pleasures derived from food and drink. That changed through the privation of the military and his own self-imposed restraint.

But certain appetites could only be stayed for so long.

He motioned to the other two paratroopers to follow him around to the back door, where unannounced, they burst into the room, serving an appetizer of hot lead to the awestruck panzers. Within seconds the kitchen was reduced to a heap of splintered furniture adorned with a scattering of bloody corpses. Total carnage, which continued virtually unopposed as they swept through the compound. No one was spared. There was no time to take prisoners.

Afterwards the patrol returned to assist the main body of paratroopers in establishing a thin line of defense between two villages providing access to Utah Beach. But his blood was up, and not content to sit and wait for further action, he moved along the line and positioned himself beside a stonewall, overlooking a field that he surmised would serve as a natural escape route for panzers fleeing from the village.

He didn't have long to wait.

Off to his right he caught movement in the hedgerow, branches parting to reveal the iconic, coal-scuttle helmet. He loaded the magazine, the rounds scored with an x to maximize the spread and hence the amount of tissue damage wrought by the shell. He drew a bead and waited, willing the slowing of his heart as he followed the panzer in his crosshairs. Midway through the open field the infantryman turned and signaled the all clear to his comrades. One by one they emerged, taking tentative steps, nervously scanning the horizon. He waited until the last of the ragged group had left the protection of the undergrowth before gently squeezing the trigger. The rear panzer's head exploded in a pink mist. The second fell clutching at his heart; the third at his spilling guts, and likewise the fourth, the dum-dum opening up a gaping crater from front to back.

Exposed and totally vulnerable in the open pasture, the lead panzer turned as if ready to sprint for the cover of the far hedgerow, but realizing the futility of this action, went down on one knee and started firing willy-nilly, quickly expending his magazine. The panzer cowered there in the grass, muttering hurried prayers as he fumbled about his belt for fresh cartridges.

In the next instant his knee was blown off and then most of his right hand.

Unsheathing his knife, the war-painted G I slipped from cover and slowly walked toward the writhing form. A wheedling plea could be heard, followed by high-pitched shrieking and then deathly quiet save for the rustling of the leaves in the treetops and the lonesome cooing of a mourning dove.

* * *

When the advance platoon of the 4th Infantry Division passed through later that day, they spied the panzer's corpse suspended from the lower limb of an ancient sycamore, arms outstretched, lashed to his carbine, and his right leg dangling by a single ligament. His chest was carved open, and in the cavity where his heart once resided, a bunch of wildflowers had been placed. The commanding officer made a mental note. This kind of behavior was not only against the military code of conduct but morally repugnant, if such a thing was possible in a theatre of war. Macabre in the extreme, as time went on, he recognized the cruciform signature, trailing in the wake of the five-o-deuces.

* * *

The Airborne pushed on to Fourcarville, flushing out the rag tag resistance in short order. They came stumbling out of doorways and scrambling up from cellars, dirty and dark-eyed, their long occupation ending in tepid submission. This time the prisoners were sent back down the line under guard while the rest of the platoon was ordered to hold their position until Captain Brubaker received further orders. Once the perimeter had been secured and lookouts posted, the Captain led a contingent of men to the dusty town square where a statue of long-dead revolutionary figures occupied a crumbling pedestal surrounded by the gaping windows of empty shops.

The village had suffered only minor damage from shell fire and still housed most of its inhabitants. Life went on much as before, the daily rituals of morning bread and evening wine largely uninterrupted. Sunbeams tripped through lines of washday linen, fluttering like tethered clouds in the warm breezes.

With white flag in hand, the mayor emerged from one of the larger stone buildings trailed by a coterie of local dignitaries, hailing the conquering heroes with shouts of “Vive Yankees”. Amongst the smiling throng she stood, statuesque in a green woolen suit, her blonde tresses shimmering like spun gold.

He drank her in, in one long swallow.

He began weighing up the risks and the heady reward, intoxicated by the prospect of her pleading cries and delicious surrender.

The platoon was escorted to the mayor’s impressive quarters and offered food and drink: cheese and sausage, and bread, and the local vintage. In turn the men responded with chocolate and cigarettes. He took this opportunity to approach the woman in green.

"Cigarette, mademoiselle?" He held a soft pack of Camels out to her.

"Merci." She flushed slightly as she retrieved the offering. He took note of her long, slender fingers and manicured nails.

"I'm Serge Tremblay. It's my pleasure to meet you."

"You speak French?"

"Un soupçon. Just enough to get me into trouble."

"You speak it very well."

"I spent some time in Montreal. It's Canadian French, probably a little harsh on your ears."

"No, no, it is like sweet music after four years of living with these Boche pigs." She reached out and touched his arm. "Words can't express how grateful we are, all of us, all of France."

"Well it's not over yet, but between Ike and Monty we're gonna kick their Kraut asses all the way back to Berlin." She gave a laugh and tossed her head back before bending close while he lit her cigarette.

"I see you have met Mademoiselle Riberry," said the mayor, placing a proprietary hand on her shoulder.

"Our friend speaks French, Jacques."

"You are French?"

"No, no, as American as apple pie."

"Sacre bleu, a hero, and speaking French too. You will capture many hearts on your way to Berlin, mon ami." Then turning to Mademoiselle Riberry, he said, "Now we must let our liberators get some rest for the battles that still lie ahead," and placing a hand on the small of her back, he gently led her away.

She gave a shrug and cast a long last look at Serge before departing the room.

* * *

"Well Frenchie, looks like you made quite an impression with the local talent," said the Captain, unable to contain the smile poking its way through several days of bristly growth. He slapped

Serge on the back as he made his way toward the fire. The platoon was being boarded in the reception room of a large house commandeered for the evening.

"It was love at first sight, Captain. I saw Cupid's arrow strike him right in the heart."

"More like right in the pecker."

"You said it, Jackson." The good-natured banter continued until the Captain signaled for quiet.

"Okay, sack out where you can; we could be on the move in a few hours."

They settled into commodious armchairs and settees, and along the floor by an ornate stone hearth. Dreaming of home, and sweethearts, their snoring soon filled the room. Serge bided his time, and then with boots in hand he tiptoed into the hallway and slipped out the front door.

He reconnoitered the narrow streets, still lifeless after the brief siege. Curtains fluttered as he passed by and now and then he fancied he heard voices, but no one appeared. He was just about to give up when he spied her through the bars of an iron gate, sitting in a grand though somewhat unkempt garden surrounded by high stone walls. She was smoking, and in her hand a long-stemmed glass of red wine. The bottle rested on the table in front of her. She had kicked off her shoes and her stockings were rolled down to her shapely ankles. He felt his pulse quicken.

There wasn't much time and there were so many things he needed to do.

* * *

Her body was discovered when the mayor paid his weekly visit three days later. An arrangement had been struck shortly after Monsieur Riberry was taken into custody and dispatched to a concentration camp for his dissenting political views. He glanced about hurriedly before letting himself in. He noticed the empty bottle of wine on the dining room table and two glasses, one with traces of lipstick on the rim. In the ashtray were the crushed remains of several American cigarettes. Could the Captain have paid a visit, or perhaps the other big fellow, the one she claimed could speak French? A seed of jealousy took root. He imagined the shared intimacies he assumed were his alone. If this was how his generosity was repaid he might have to reconsider the arrangement. Then he thought of how the sunlight played on the golden hair of her pubis, her uninhibited lovemaking and soft cries when he entered her.

No, he couldn't give that up, perhaps a scolding, just to reassert his proprietary rights.

After all he was the mayor, the most important and influential man in the village, he muttered to himself ascending the stairs. He puffed out his chest like a preening peacock and threw open the door to her bedroom. His eyes widened in disbelief at the sight before him. She was suspended, spread-eagled from the ceiling by her feet, ligatures around both ankles and wrists. Her blond tresses dangled above a dark pool of blood covering the floor. She had been sliced from ear to ear, and a deep cruciform incision scarred her abdomen. Stifling a cry, he clutched at his throat, staggered backwards and tumbled awkwardly down the stairs.

* * *

In the heat and turmoil of the campaign, especially the early going when victory hung in the balance, and atrocities on both sides of the conflict were commonplace, the spate of ritualistic killings went largely unreported, confined to random entries in journals and diaries and fleeting observations of men becoming hardened to the tribulations of warfare. It was Major Berry who made the connection purely by chance on overhearing one of the radio operators describing a civilian casualty that was being attributed to the American forces in that sector.

"Say that again, Corporal."

"Hung apparently, upside down and butchered."

"Good Lord. And they're sure it wasn't retaliation for collaboration with the enemy."

"No, the complaint was lodged by the mayor of the village, vouched for the woman himself. He reported that the murder happened right when the 101st came through."

Berry stroked at his chin. The second civilian murder under similar circumstances on top of a report by a Captain Brubaker of atrocities being committed along the front.

The modus operandi was too close to be a coincidence.

Major Berry led mop-up operations in the wake of the advance of the 4th Infantry Division. A Yale graduate and seasoned criminal lawyer, he retained his boyish good looks and college physique into his 30's. He could've taken an easy commission but opted for active combat duty. He'd lost two nephews and a brother in the Pacific theatre. By his reckoning, he owed it to them.

* * *

Sergeant Mankofsky shifted the jeep around the rickety cart piled high with furniture and squalling children. Its driver sat hunched over the reins, urging his emaciated horse forward. They were part of a ragged convoy fleeing the hostilities. Mankofsky double-clutched, jerking the jeep forward until it settled into the ruts once more. At this rate Berry figured his kidneys would give out long before a bullet found its mark. He'd been called back to H.Q. for a briefing with the top brass.

From what he gathered headway was being made in all sectors. The Contentin Peninsula was as good as secured and Cherbourg in the crosshairs. With some of the early pressure dissipating, he contemplated raising the issue of the rogue murderer. He wasn't sure what action would be warranted or even sanctioned given the larger issues at stake, and at this point he was playing what would appear to the uninitiated as a hunch. Still, something gnawed at the back of his mind, an old case he had studied while in law school, a series of murders in the south characterized by ritualistic treatment of the corpses, posing as he recalled, not unlike the scenes that were being reported here.

He spotted the H.Q. trailer and tents of the sector under a bosque of trees beside a cow pasture. The guards waived them through the mud to the front of the trailer. Berry stepped out of the jeep and glanced skyward. The rain was starting up again. He hunched his shoulders and sprinted the short distance to cover. Inside, ten men were crowded around a wooden table, studying the map spread out in front of them. The mood was somber as they discussed the latest action and the impact of a vicious Channel gale on the construction of the Mulberry harbors, critical for the continued delivery of men and materiel to Normandy.

He listened intently, kept his answers short and sweet when questioned, and early on in the proceedings, decided to withhold the report of the brutal killings for the time being. They had enough on their plates without being distracted by this sideshow, insignificant in the grand scheme of things. He'd do a little more digging, see if he could get to the root of the allegations before troubling the brass.

He found Mankofsky under the shelter of the trees, sharing K rations with another driver. They were in the process of heating water for coffee with a sterno kit. It was slow going so he lit a smoke and waited for them to finish. On the drive back he decided to contact Captain Brubaker directly. For the time being the 101st were out of the front-line action, assuming defensive positions across the peninsula. He believed Brubaker's company was holding just north of Carentan. He contemplated a visit sometime over the next few days.

* * *

"Hey Frenchie, who you tryin' to impress?" The query spit out through the blackened stumps of a mouth as foul-smelling as it was ugly.

Octavius glanced up from the shard of mirror in his hand. He was shaving for the first time in over two weeks, not only his beard, but his skull, refreshing the Mohawk that was favored by his platoon, now referred to as the "Raging Redskins" on account of the distinctive hairstyles, war paint and penchant for mayhem both on and off the battlefield. Having slept in his clothes since the hostilities began, he was stripped naked, preparing to bathe out of his helmet. He was using his sterno kit to heat the water for his ablutions, preferring a good scrub to a hot meal, if the congealed mass of chopped egg and bacon in his K rations could be considered food.

"Haven't you heard, cleanliness is next to Godliness, and you're beginning to reek like a moldering old Billy-goat."

The trooper disregarded the insult and moved off, drawn by the smell of brewing coffee further on down the line.

Although it was rumored to be the driest spring in fifty-odd years, showers occurred several times a day, soaking the men, dousing fires and turning foxholes and tent sites into mud pits. Today the sun had finally broken through, so the work on defensive emplacements was interrupted while everyone caught up with bathing and washing their clothes and bedding, laying the laundered items out on the grass to dry. The encampment was beginning to resemble a tenement wash house as opposed to an orderly military bivouac.

Fighting was proceeding on the British front towards Caen and on VII Corps front toward Cherbourg, but little was occurring in their sector other than the odd flyover by the severely depleted Luftwaffe, which had little real impact other than to rob the troops of their much-needed sleep at night.

Octavius was pulling on a clean tee shirt when he was approached by two urchins, local children who had taken to wandering about the area, scavenging for food along with chocolate and cigarettes, which they took back to the village and sold. The two of them had acquired US service caps, now decorated with all manner of regimental insignia. Underneath their filthy black smocks, they were rail thin and their unshod feet were encrusted with mud. Brothers he surmised, like two peas in a pod.

His mind shifted to another two brothers, his twin cousins, Carter and Morgan. They had remained incommunicado since Kansas City, failing to respond to messages left at various safe houses.

When he had eventually recovered enough to visit the local library in Fort Scott, the back issues of the Kansas City papers detailed the Crusade killings, attributing them to one Casper Littlejohn and an unnamed accomplice, still at large. As to Mother Mary Margaret, the story being spun by the Church of the Foursquare Gospel was that she had become unnerved by the murders and had taken herself off to a religious retreat somewhere south of the border.

Octavius had ventured as far south as the fishing camp outside Lafayette, and while it was obvious that they had spent time there, the trail had grown cold. No indications as to where they might have gone and still no response to his inquiries. He contemplated a trip to Mexico City or Buenos Aries and then circumstances intervened.

The urchins had picked up a smattering of English, enough to voice the usual requests. Effecting their most endearing expressions they asked, "Cigarettes for papa?" Octavius motioned for them to stay put while he rummaged about in his duffel bag. He extracted a soft pack of Camels and split the contents between the two of them. Their eyes lit up at the unexpected bounty and he was showered with "merci's" from the ecstatic pair. He reached down to tenderly pat their heads and called out "Bon chance" as they scurried off back to the village.

* * *

From the shelter of the bosque, Brubaker witnessed the scene, noting the incongruity of the ruthless killing machine displaying such obvious compassion. A lot of these hard-boiled types were teddy bears under the steely carapace, and by the looks of it, Tremblay was no different. Brubaker was considering him for a citation for his part in the assault on the barracks and his bravery on the Carentan causeway, where he led a successful charge against a machine gun nest.

Brubaker's ambivalence related to the fact that it was reckless in the extreme, and Tremblay had shown no mercy when it was obvious that the enemy was ready to surrender. By the time he and the second wave of attackers arrived, the panzers were all dead, one holding a conspicuous white flag.

The Raging Redskins were fast gaining a reputation for bravado and brutality in equal measure. Most, it seemed, were anxious to return to the front and openly disdained their current defensive role. Of late they had taken to amusing themselves with a particularly dangerous version of mumblety-peg, using razor-sharp bayonets as opposed to the much less deadly penknives.

More disturbing were the reported instances of mutilated corpses amongst the enemy casualties and now there were rumors of barbaric civilian deaths in their turbulent wake.

He'd already dressed down a handful of the war paint platoon, but he feared he'd have to resort to more drastic measures to re-establish order and discipline. He moved on down the line.

* * *

Octavius sensed his presence, a shadow passing through the trees. He'd need to be on his guard. He had the distinct impression that Brubaker's suspicions had been aroused as word filtered back about the civilian deaths trailing like flotsam in their slipstream.

He'd need to change his approach with the next victim.

Later that afternoon, they got the order to move on up to Cherbourg and relieve the 4th Infantry Division, who, along with the 9th and 79th, had succeeded in taking the strategic port after a two-week siege.

* * *

Octavius surveyed the bombed-out city from one of the few remaining bell towers. The last surviving pockets of resistance had been flushed out before they arrived, so this was a strictly defensive operation while the army engineers cleared the harbor of scuttled vessels. Earlier in the afternoon he slipped away from his detail to get a better idea of the layout, and the bird's eye view afforded by the church tower provided a clear picture of the labyrinthine arrangement of streets and alleys.

Everywhere he looked the streets were strewn with rubble, making travel by vehicle almost impossible. Here and there roving gangs of laborers, aided by whatever heavy equipment could be spared by the army, attacked the piles of debris. Despite these disruptions, he noted quite a bit of activity in and around the Hotel de Ville. The establishments in the general vicinity seemed almost unaffected by the siege, with clutches of patrons, both men and women, coming and going in an endless stream.

Later on, as he sought to catch up with the patrol at a pre-designated rendezvous, he passed one of the busier spots, the Brasserie de la Paix, just in time to witness a coterie of French women entering, their laughter reverberating like birdsong in the waning afternoon.

* * *

Two nights later after a hot bath in a real tub, and a change of uniform, Octavius made his way from the barracks to the Brasserie de la Paix. The joint was literally bursting at the seams with jubilant locals and allied troops, men from the 101st, 9th and 79th divisions along with the British number 30 Commando Assault Unit who had engaged the right flank of the German defenses in the battle for Cherbourg. It was one big, boisterous affair with commissioned officers mixing freely with the common soldiery.

Octavius scanned the room, his eyes eventually alighting on a group of females exchanging comments with their liberators, who flitted around the edges like moths drawn to the flame. When he saw what he was looking for, he made his way over, addressing her in French. She was dark-haired, but with generous curves and a somewhat haughty manner. He sensed that she eyed him somewhat indifferently at first. He was not conventionally handsome with his protruding brow and small, pale eyes, but his size was impressive and the "cheveaux de Mohawk" denoted him as the bravest of the brave.

He exuded an air of daring and defiance with another more subtle undertone that most had a hard time defining. Danger perhaps?

With Octavius' command of the language, they fell into an easy dialogue. Once over the preliminaries they ventured into topics of mutual interest, sharing an appreciation for impressionist art. Octavius described his previous stay in Paris, though he avoided elaborating about his time at the Sorbonne. She too had attended school in Paris, but for more modest pursuits and was now employed as a "stenographe judiciaire", a court reporter. Octavius pressed her for salacious details about some of the more risqué cases. She demurred with what he took as feigned modesty, not wanting to give him the wrong impression so early in the flirtation. At an appropriate pause, he took leave of his companion to buy another round of drinks. As Octavius placed his order at the bar, he was approached by one of the British commandos, a lone French-Canadian, who assumed he was in the company of a fellow Quebecer.

"Canadien, Monsieur?"

"Oui."

"Where from?"

"Montreal."

"La meme chose, what district?" The inquiry had Octavius momentarily stumped. He hadn't banked on running into any Canadians with the 101st, especially French-Canadians. He answered evasively, making light of his family's peripatetic existence.

"We were like gypsies always on the move."

"We lived on Atwater, just down the street from the Forum. Were you a fan?" He was referring of course to the Montreal Canadiens' hockey team, who played their home games at the Forum.

"Oui, who wasn't?"

"Did you get to many of the games?"

"Once in a while."

"What a season last year, eh?"

"Yeah, great."

"And that new kid, Richard, thirty-two goals and another twelve in the playoffs."

"Yes, he was something else alright."

"What did you think of him with Blake and Lach?" The conversation was taking a dangerous turn, venturing into an area that was totally foreign to him, ice hockey of all things. He needed to extricate himself from the situation without appearing disinterested or too abrupt.

"Incroyable, absolument!" Once again, he was purposely vague, but tried to match the commando's obvious enthusiasm. This only led to more probing about who had distinguished themselves in the playoffs, and who might be traded in the off-season. Octavius waved off the queries, and pointing to the far end of the room, apologized that he had to get back to his companion. But the commando was insistent and continued to press him, growing annoyed that a fellow Montrealer would choose a French femme over the beloved Canadiens. Finally, at wits end, Octavius made to return to his party. The commando reached out and grabbed him by the arm.

"Let me at least buy you a drink, monsieur."

"Non, no it would be my pleasure, mon ami."

"No, I insist."

"Just one then, I really must get back to my companion." Once more he gestured to the far end of the room. The commando ordered two glasses of cognac, passing one to Octavius. "What should we drink to?" Octavius asked.

"To another cup of course."

"Alright, to another cup then." Octavius raised his glass and was about to drink when the commando suddenly reached up and grabbed his wrist, causing the cognac to spill over his uniform.

"The cup has a name, monsieur." Octavius brushed the liquid from his lapel and once more raised his glass.

"To the most treasured cup in all the sporting world."

"Non, you must name the cup."

"Why don't you make the toast then. Toasts are not my strong suit"

"You don't know the name of the cup do you?" he snarled.

"It has escaped my memory for the moment."

"Are you even from Montreal?" The commando put down his glass and this time grabbed Octavius by the lapels, his eyes bulging. "You are an imposter, monsieur, a phony."

Octavius reared back and head-butted the commando, sending him sprawling into a crowd of soldiers at the bar. They picked him up and sent him back towards Octavius, but before he could reengage some of the more level-headed in the assembly intervened, ushering him back to his comrades on the other side of the room.

* * *

From his place at a nearby table, Captain Brubaker witnessed the exchange and afterwards sought out the British commando.

"I'm sorry for the trouble. You'll have to excuse these guys. They're itching for action."

"Tell dem to save it for the Jerrys."

"You seemed pretty upset. Was it something he said to you?"

"Da guy says he's from Montreal like me, but he's lying. I don't know why. I doubt if he's ever been dere, and besides he don't sound like any Quebecer I know."

"Really?"

"Yeah, sounds more like from down south, Louisiana.

"You mean Cajun?"

"Yeah, Cajun."

Tremblay claimed he was from Maine, of French-Canadian parentage, and had spent a lot of time in Montreal, an obvious lie according to the commando. Brubaker pondered the deception. Something in Tremblay's past perhaps. But what exactly?

* * *

Octavius fussed with the stain on his lapels and then with drinks in hand returned to where his companion awaited, unaware of what had transpired. At the end of the evening he offered to escort her home. She declined as politely as possible, indicating that it was too far for him to walk and besides, she whispered discreetly, it would make the others jealous. He didn't press the point, realizing that he would miss curfew if she eventually accepted. Instead, he arranged to meet her again. She was coy about the next possible rendezvous, feigning indifference, but Octavius guessed it was because she did not want to appear overly-eager. The trap was baited. It was only a matter of time and circumstance until it snapped shut.

* * *

During patrol the next day, Octavius came upon an open excavation where workmen were repairing a bomb-damaged sewer. He called down to inquire about the extent of the damage and was given a history lesson on the construction of the extensive network of tunnels which ran beneath the City, rivaling the one in Paris. He made a point to explore this situation further, and two days later, during his free time, set off exploring the subterranean world of Cherbourg, entering an outfall that discharged above the harbor. He spent several hours traversing the miles of brick-lined tunnels and cavernous vaults, many of which looked neglected, or rarely visited for repair. He eventually surfaced through a loose manhole located on a quiet street beside the Basilique de Sacre Coure, with a crudely drawn map in hand and a half-formed plan swirling in his fevered mind.

He deliberately avoided the Brasserie de la Paix for the next three nights, not wanting to appear too desperate in his pursuit of the handsome French woman. On the fourth night he took a circuitous route to her small retinue and reintroduced himself, exchanging pleasantries with every female in the gathering. When he made to walk away, she reached out and touched his arm, perhaps a little too quickly. He pointed to an empty banquette and gently steered her away from her friends for a more intimate tete-a-tete.

* * *

Feeling ever more comfortable with the big G.I., she shared feelings and desires, until now, suppressed in the stifling atmosphere of the occupation. Her animated discourse was punctuated with bouts of raucous laughter as the weight of the world was slowly lifted, Atlas-like, by the charming American.

At the end of the evening she allowed Octavius to walk her back to her apartment in the Rue Collard, several blocks away. She considered inviting him inside, but instead bestowed a chaste kiss on the cheek. After consulting her diary, she accepted an invitation for another assignation the following week. She could borrow a new skirt from her good friend Marise, and she had seen a pretty scarf in Madame Rousseau's shop window. A few days were all she needed to prepare for the consummation of the budding relationship. She smiled, as she ascended the stairs, secure in the knowledge that the snare had been set and was about to close on a most worthy quarry, someone of means and good breeding.

That night she dreamed of the columned, white mansion he had so eloquently described.

* * *

The timing of the next rendezvous with Mademoiselle Bernier would give Octavius time to prepare. He'd need to put his hands on some rope, torches and ether or chloroform. He made a note to visit the field hospital that had been set up in a primary school on the outskirts of the City where the damage from shelling was less severe. One of the Raging Redskins was convalescing there, so he had a perfectly legitimate reason for the call.

That night he dreamed of Nell Madisson, awaking in a cold sweat, his mind fevered with images of her savaged torso and pleading cries.

* * *

"You'll have to back up and try that other street," Major Berry instructed Sergeant Mankofsky, who chomping down hard on his unlit stogie, spun the jeep around. Berry hung on with both hands as the vehicle bucked through the rubble-strewn thoroughfare. Berry needed to get to the five-o-deuces before they were dispatched back to England to re-equip and rest up before their next mission. He had prepared a full report on the three civilian deaths and the atrocities reported in the field and wanted to consult with Captain Brubaker to get his insights into the events before he took it before the brass.

* * *

For his part, Brubaker continued to keep an eye on the Raging Redskins and in particular Corporal Tremblay. The comments of the British commando had further aroused his suspicions about "Frenchie" and his possible Cajun rather than French-Canadian background. The obvious deception suggested a less than savory past, something the recruiters must have missed. He was penning a request for Tremblay's full, service records when an adjutant arrived at the door.

"Sir, visitor to see you, sir."

"Does he have a name, Jennings?"

"Sir, Major Berry, sir"

"Send him up then. Oh, and have the canteen bring us some coffee, will you. Thanks."

"Yes sir."

A few minutes later a well-groomed officer filled the door frame.

"Captain Brubaker I presume?"

Brubaker rose to meet him, snapping off a smart salute before extending his hand.

"At your service, Major Berry. I've got coffee on the way, or if you'd prefer something with a little more bite, I've got some French brandy that I swear could strip old furniture."

"Why not, I was raised on bath tub gin, so anything is a step up at this point."

Brubaker reached into his desk for the potent libation and poured two stiff measures. He handed one to Berry and raising his glass said, "Here's to an early Christmas with Herr Hitler in Berlin."

"His goose is as good as cooked if we follow your example at Carentan. You boys did a hell of a job."

"And paid a high price."

"Duly noted and much appreciated I can tell you." They downed the shots in a single gulp and then Brubaker refilled the glasses. "I think I'll save my stomach and just sip this one." Berry set his glass to one side.

"A wise choice. So, what brings you to our neck of the woods?"

"A bit of unpleasantness unfortunately. The atrocities you reported in the field seem to coincide with a string of civilian deaths, both in time and technique, if I could put it that way."

Brubaker sat back and gave a low whistle. "And you're sure it has to do with the five-o-deuces?"

"Look, I'm far from convinced at this point, but the similarities are hard to ignore and if we continue to ignore them we do so at our own peril, in terms of our primary mission and our obvious moral obligations."

"Well we've got some real firebrands in our division. It pains me to think it could be some of them."

"From what I know about this sort of thing, and I'm hardly an expert, it's more than likely to be a single individual, obviously disturbed, acting alone."

"You've come across this kind of thing before?"

"Back in law school, a case study of severe psychopathic behavior. It happened in the twenties in the deep South. I took the time to look into it again. Repeat offender by the name of Beauchamp. The mutilations and hanging of the victims match these to a tee."

"Tell me about the civilian deaths."

"Three, all women. One after the other in the villages the five-o-deuces passed through. All butchered the same way just like the panzers you described in your field report."

Brubaker stroked at his chin. "The deep South you say, this repeat offender, Beauchamp."

"Yeah, Louisiana, Baton Rouge, why?"

"Just a hunch. I've got a possible suspect. Claims to be from Maine originally, of French-Canadian parentage, but according to one of the Brits, an actual French-Canadian, his patois is Cajun. You don't think it could be the same guy do you?"

"No, no Beauchamp would be in his fifties by now, and besides he perished in the bayou, or so they say."

"Of course, what am I thinking? My guy, Tremblay, is twenty-five, twenty-six at most."

"So what's the dope on your possible suspect, this Tremblay character? Being from the same neck of the woods doesn't necessarily make him a murderer."

"That's true. As to my suspicions, I can't quite put my finger on them. A bunch of stuff I guess."

"Well, start from the start and let's see what shakes out."

"He's a big brute, goes six-five, six-six of solid muscle. Sports a Mohawk and war paint when he's in action."

"War paint, not exactly government issue."

"Tell me about it. There's a bunch of them, the Raging Redskins. You'd want them on your side every time when you're in the thick of it. Tremblay is due for a citation, hell two at least for his actions under fire. He's absolutely fearless, but reckless beyond belief, and barbaric, a real killing machine. There was an incident where he took out German troops who I'm sure were surrendering. By the time I arrived on the scene with the second wave, they had more holes in them than Swiss cheese. And that wasn't the first time I'd seen him empty a magazine into a corpse after he'd made a kill shot."

"Hhmmm."

"But he's got another side. You wouldn't know it by looking at him. There's real intelligence under that brutish exterior. I've seen it when his guard is down. I've witnessed him assisting the medics, directing them actually. I could swear he's had medical training, serious training, which squares with the incisions on the corpses. They're surgical, and from what you tell me, similar to the ones on the civilians."

"That's a coincidence that's hard to ignore. Anything else not exactly as it seems?"

"The first victim, what village was that?" Berry consulted his notes

"Fourcarville, why?"

"He was talking up one of the French women, a real looker as I recall. Took quite a ribbing from the rest of the company afterwards. I didn't catch a name, but I'm sure I'd recognize her. I don't suppose you've got a photograph?"

"Just a name for now, Jeanette Riberry, but I could request one from the French authorities. It might take a while though."

"So what do we do in the meantime?"

"I'd like to interview him. Get an impression before we take any further action."

"Does anyone else know about this?"

"No, I haven't shared it with the brass yet. They've got a war to win and I want to be absolutely certain before I make a recommendation for a Court Marshall."

Brubaker sat for a while, pensively stroking at his chin, before he spoke again. "We've got to tread carefully. We don't want to arouse his suspicions. Like I said, he's not lacking in the gray matter department. Under what pretense do we interview him?"

Berry stood up and started to pace. He pivoted suddenly and sat back down, facing Brubaker, his eyes alight. "It could be related to the citations. You know, getting all the details from the selected recipients. It's not like we hand 'em out like candy. Do you have any other candidates?"

"Yeah, one or two others."

"Legitimate candidates?"

"One for sure. The other is a strong maybe."

"Alright, let's set up three interviews for tomorrow right after morning mess."

* * *

Brubaker's body language was at odds with his jovial demeanor as he kibitzed with Octavius on the way to the meeting room. He was a straight shooter by nature and the impending deception had him on edge, nervous as a kitten and barely able to disguise the quaver in his voice when he introduced Octavius to the visitor.

"Er, Corporal Tremblay, ah, I'd like you to meet Major Berry from 4th Division. He's here to talk to you about the citations ah, I mentioned. Get some more details before a final decision is made, not that there's any doubt as far as I'm concerned. He just needs some ah, further clarification on what I've already written up."

"Major Berry, sir." Octavius snapped off a crisp salute.

"At ease, Corporal. We'll try and keep this as informal as possible."

"Sir, thank you, sir."

"Take a seat. Cigarette?" Berry proffered a soft pack of Lucky Strike.

"Thanks, but I prefer the French ones when I can get them." He took out a package of Gitans and bent forward to accept a light from Berry.

"The Captain tells me you're from Maine, up around Jackman."

"Yeah, the end of the world as we know it."

"Near enough I suppose. Good timber country. So what did you do before you enlisted?"

"A little bit of everything: lumberjacking naturally, rail yards, some warehouse work."

"In Maine?"

"Sometimes, and other times in Canada, Montreal mostly."

"Any medical training?"

"Why do you ask?"

"Captain tells me you've been a big help to the company medics with the wounded men."

"Must be from all the nurses I've dated."

"So no formal training?"

"Only what the nurses passed on when we were discussing anatomy, usually theirs."

Berry let out a big belly laugh. He was trying hard to loosen Octavius up, to get him relaxed and off guard, but the big Corporal was playing it close to the vest.

"And how do you come by your French?"

"Both parents are originally from the Gaspé. It was the tongue spoken around the house."

"Must come in handy for conversing with the locals."

"When they can understand the dialect. It's a different animal to what they speak in these parts. But it gets me by."

"You're far too modest. The Captain tells me you've been invaluable in gathering critical information about enemy movements and strength."

"I do what I can. I have a vested interest in staying alive."

Berry referred to his notes once more. "Captain Brubaker has cited you twice for actions above and beyond the call of duty. First for volunteering to take out the Barracks at Mesieres and the second, your charge and single-handed destruction of the machine gun nest on the Carentan causeway. The only question I have is about the white flag one of the panzers was holding."

"I don't remember seeing a white flag."

"The rules of combat, according to the Hague Convention, Article 23c, prohibit the killing or wounding of an enemy, who, having laid down his arms, or having no longer means of defense, has surrendered at discretion."

"If I had seen it, I would have held my fire and accepted the surrender."

"I believe one of the other witnesses stated that he saw the white flag quite clearly."

"I don't want to dispute what someone else thought they saw at the time. It was 'shit-house rat' crazy out there. Things happen pretty quickly as I'm sure you'll appreciate. All I saw was a muzzle spitting hot lead at our boys."

"Fair enough. We don't always see the same things in the same timeframe. And the charge itself, it was reported that you ran straight into the line of fire and didn't stop for cover once. There's a fine line separating bravery and recklessness."

"I honestly don't remember. The objective was to disable the battery, and as a unit we accomplished the primary objective. I wasn't the only one dodging lead, and if it's all the same to you, I'd just as soon you give whatever hardware is up for grabs to the guys who paid the price, the ones who won't be going home."

"That's a very noble gesture, Corporal, but that's not up to me and it's not how we do it, although I'm going to note that sentiment in my report."

"Will that be all, sir?"

Berry hesitated and pretended to be studying his notes again. "There is one more thing. It's not related to the citations, but we're making inquiries of all the men. There have been reports of atrocities in the field, dismemberment and brutalization of corpses along with civilian deaths, three to be precise. All occurring in the path of the 101st, five-o-deuces, and all butchered in the same manner. Have you seen or heard anything in your travels?"

"Well, I saw the Panzer strung up in the tree when we marched out of Fourcarville, but it's the first I've heard of any civilian deaths."

"No loose talk around the mess hall or the latrines?"

"Like I said, this is the first I've heard of it."

At that moment Brubaker was struck by the memory of Tremblay talking to the tall, attractive blonde who was part of the mayor's welcoming committee and had, in fact, been introduced as Madame Riberry. Now he remembered, and in his mind's eye her exchange with Tremblay came into focus. They were sharing a cigarette, speaking French and joking around. He recalled her throaty laugh and how at ease she seemed in the company of the big Corporal. Berry didn't seem to be making much headway with his line of questioning, so Brubaker leapt in with both feet.

"Oddly enough Corporal Tremblay, the woman you were conversing with in Fourcarville, Madame Riberry was the first victim."

Octavius didn't flinch. "Sir?"

"Madame Riberry, the big blonde, don't you remember the ribbing you took afterwards?"

"Which woman was that, sir? I've spoken to quite a few since we landed."

"Surely you remember her. She was practically seducing you on the spot."

"I'm pretty hazy on those first few days. It's all a bit of a blur."

"You don't seem to have any trouble disputing the white flag," Berry interjected.

"That was in the heat of battle. Those images are etched in granite. The other stuff, the day to day is gone like a puff of smoke." Octavius shrugged his shoulders. "I have a very vague recollection of speaking to a woman in Fourcarville, a fleeting memory at best. I'm sorry to hear she met with an untimely end. But that's war isn't it. You don't think it was some sort of vendetta for collaborating with the enemy, do you? I've heard there's a lot of that sort of thing going on. It's entirely logical that it happened after we passed through, with the Krauts gone the locals had an opportunity to meat out some good old vigilante justice."

"That's not entirely out of the question I suppose, but we can't rule out anything just yet. That's why we're asking and why it's important to keep an ear to the ground."

"Understood, sir."

"I think I've got enough information for now. You'll be getting an official notification in a couple of weeks. These things have to get run up the flagpole you understand. On the other matter, please report anything you hear to Captain Brubaker, no matter how trivial."

"I will sir. You can count on me."

"I'm sure I can. Dismissed, Corporal."

Octavius stood to attention, saluted them both and strode out of the room.

Berry raised his eyebrows as Octavius departed. "Why didn't you elaborate on the Madame Riberry incident before now?"

"The details had slipped my mind. I suddenly put a face to the name and it came back to me. I take it she was the first victim?"

"The first that we're aware of at least."

"I hope I didn't let the cat out of the bag."

"Wouldn't have mattered. I don't think I've ever met a cooler customer, or a more skilled defendant."

"Do you think he bought it, about the citation?"

"Not a chance, and I didn't buy his back story either, the whole salt of the earth routine. This character is educated and sharp, very sharp."

"So what do we do now?"

"We keep an eye on him."

"That's not going to be easy in the field and we've got a war to fight."

"Let's see what I can pull up on him. I'll make some inquiries State side."

"Internal Affairs?"

"Not yet. I've got a good contact in the Bureau, my old college roommate actually. We played football together. He would have made one hell of a lawyer, but he chose law enforcement instead. A personal tragedy caused the switch. The death of his sister. They were very close. In fact, he practically raised her after their parents passed away. Typhoid epidemic. Last I heard he was up in Washington chasing down spies and saboteurs. I'll send him a wire."

"And in the meantime?"

"Keep the Corporal on a short leash if you can. HQ say's you'll be heading back to limey land by the middle of the month. At least he'll be on ice for a while. It'll give me time to make the necessary inquiries. I'll be in touch."

* * *

So, they were on to him. He'd been aware of Brubaker's suspicions for a while, but now more senior brass had entered the frame. Their little charade had been paper-thin. Rank amateurs. His only concern was if they started to dig a little deeper into his past, albeit an appropriated past. Stumbling upon Serge Tremblay at La Cygnes Lake had been most fortuitous at the time. The sole occupant of the remote cabin was a solitary figure, virtually unknown to his scattering of neighbors. He was glad of the company and overjoyed that he could finally converse in his native tongue. Living outside the usual strictures of society himself, he didn't question the sudden appearance of an injured man, obviously on the lam. He was a trusting soul, so naïve. He never saw it coming.

* * *

Shadbolt read the wire again. It was from his old college roommate, Ed Berry, a Major no less, in the 4th Infantry Division. The request was a strange one, a full background check on a Serge Tremblay from Jackman, Maine, born December 2nd, 1919. He was the prime suspect in three civilian deaths and several battlefield atrocities, specifically the sadistic mutilation of enemy corpses. The last line caught Shadbolt's attention. It had been two and a half years since the Iowa murders and although his team had been removed from the investigation, he'd kept an eye out for any re-occurrence employing a similar M O. He'd have to get more details from Berry along with clearance from the brass. Things had slowed down considerably in the last six months since the capture and incarceration of Hans Sahlen and his associates, a German spy ring attempting to infiltrate a top-secret project out in the New Mexico desert. Now his team was back in Washington, essentially waiting for their next assignment. He re-read the wire and then walked down the hall to speak with Perkins and Will.

* * *

He'd been on a short leash since the interview, pulling guard duty and KP with a regularity that far exceeded the normal rotation. It seemed there were more bodies about and he didn't have the freedom he'd enjoyed at the beginning of the posting. Now he'd just learned that they were scheduled to leave for England in another few days, putting a crimp in his well-laid plans. He'd had his sights set on Mademoiselle Bernier from the outset. The build-up had been carefully planned, the anticipation delicious in the extreme, his whole being primed for execution of the ritual slaughter. He considered the risks and the heady reward, deciding then and there on a course of action.

* * *

Brubaker was about to leave the Brasserie de la Paix when Tremblay entered with the French woman in tow. He'd seen the pair of them together now on two separate occasions. Tremblay seated her at a table and then sidled over to the bar to order drinks.

What surprised Brubaker was the fact that Tremblay had been assigned guard duty for the week. It was possible that he had traded shifts with someone else, strictly against regulations.

He'd have to speak to whoever had authorized the switch.

His first instinct was to confront Tremblay on the spot, but as he continued to observe the pair, he decided to bide his time and see how things played out. He didn't have long to wait, for once the initial round had been consumed, the woman collected her things and together they left the premises.

Brubaker waited a tick and then followed them outside, lingering on the pavement to light up a cigarette, while as surreptitiously as possible, he noted their direction of travel.

They were northbound, heading toward the harbor.

He set off after them, keeping a good distance back to veil his pursuit. They wound through the streets and alleys in a haphazard fashion, stopping to embrace along the way. She appeared to be leaning heavily on the big corporal, her gait growing more unsteady as the minutes passed.

At one point, Brubaker thought he had lost them when they disappeared down a particularly dark stretch of road. He was momentarily panicked and about to call out when he heard footfalls off to his right. He turned in time to see them climbing a set of stairs punctuating a long row of buildings.

Tremblay was practically carrying the woman.

As they disappeared into the shadows, a window opened above Brubaker's head and a soft voice addressed him,

"Americain, you want fuck avec moi?"

Before he could decline the salacious offer, the window of the next apartment opened, and a rotund woman in face cream and curlers started to berate him and his would-be paramour. He was about to proclaim his innocence but didn't trust his French well enough to provide a suitable explanation, so he waved his arms for silence, and then high-tailed it across the street in order to avoid further commotion. In his wake the harsh words of the feuding neighbors reverberated, causing other windows to open and other voices to join the cacophony.

He ascended the stairs two at a time, stumbling as he reached the top. The narrow passageway was hemmed by a half-height wrought iron gate.

Something hung from one of the pickets.

Brubaker reached out and took hold of a silken undergarment. It was warm to the touch. He hurried on, stuffing the article into his jacket pocket.

Now the path descended sharply as he made his way along the side of a featureless brick building which terminated at the precipice of a steep hillside. He looked out over the harbor, scanning the incline for any sign of the pair. Off to his left came the sound of tumbling water. Its source was an outfall, a massive dome-shaped tunnel conveying a steady stream of raw sewage from the very bowels of the City.

As he ventured closer, he took out his lighter and held it over his head, revealing a brick-lined channel bisecting the floor of the structure with a walkway on either side.

Had Tremblay taken her inside?

Surely not, the smell was overpowering. Unless he had knocked her unconscious and was carrying her off to have his way with her.

And afterwards?

Images of the battlefield atrocities filled his head and a shiver ran up his spine. He cupped his ear and strained to hear above the rush of the flow. Ever so faintly, footfalls echoed from deep inside. He pulled his jacket over his nose and mouth, and with lighter held aloft, entered the opening.

The floor of the tunnel was relatively dry save for the occurrence of small pools of water here and there along the walkway. He fancied he saw the occasional footprint, but there was no trace of the tread common to the standard issue boots worn by the 101st.

Could Tremblay have changed footware or sheathed his boots to disguise the prints?

The flame guttered as he stood observing the marks on the tunnel floor. He wondered how long his lighter fluid would last. If he was going to overtake his quarry, he'd have to pick up the pace.

He cupped the flickering flame and broke into a trot all the while wondering how Tremblay was managing in the dark. He'd be laboring under the same conditions but with a visibly drunken companion adding to his burdens.

How was he moving so quickly?

He stopped to examine the walkway once more. There was nothing to indicate that her feet were actually touching the ground, so Tremblay must be carrying her, he speculated.

Up ahead the main tunnel branched with the adjoining fork narrowing considerably. Brubaker pressed on, guessing the big corporal would have stuck to the larger passageway. Here the stench he had encountered at the outfall was replaced by a fusty, pungent odor and the flow, while still murky, looked to be made up mostly of rainwater rather than sewage.

Along this stretch stalactites hung from the ceiling like alabaster icicles, and he was reminded of the grade school rhyme, "when the mites go up the tights come down", as a way of differentiating stalactites from stalagmites.

As he ventured deeper into the system, he extinguished the flame for the longer stretches of straight runs in a bid to conserve his light. It was disorienting and several times he came close to tumbling into the murky flow.

At the next junction, several smaller branches entered the main tunnel, which began to curve off to the left. There was a set of steps leading to a raised platform which crossed over the channel as the walkway on the right terminated.

He followed the curving tube for some distance to a high vaulted chamber where another channel entered the first at right angles. A single bulb suspended from the central arch like a gallows' noose cast a wan yellow light over the interior.

Brubaker snapped his lighter shut and took in the surroundings.

Against one wall a set of metal stairs led upwards, he presumed to the street. He walked over to inspect the treads to see if the pair had gone that way, but could detect nothing that suggested their ascent.

Undeterred, he advanced once more into the black maw of the tunnel and was quickly swallowed by darkness, his lighter barely penetrating the gloom.

At intervals he heard the scurrying of rats, catching glimpses of matted fur and worm-like tails as they scuttled into dank crevices or plunged headlong into the effluent. Underfoot the walkway became slippery, and he slowed his pursuit, treading cautiously around shallow pools and slick mats of sludge. The footing was precarious and here and there piles of detritus carried by surging storm waters further impeded his progress.

Twenty minutes had passed since Brubaker entered the sewer and he had not seen or heard the pair again during that time. He was questioning the source of the footfalls that had led him into this labyrinthine netherworld in the first place. If he turned around now, he might have a chance of making it back to the entrance before his lighter ran out.

But what of Tremblay's victim; could he take the gamble that they had somehow eluded him?

In all good conscience he couldn't abandon her now to a fate worse than death.

"Okay, ten more minutes," he said aloud. If he didn't catch them up by then, he'd turn back and go straight to the base MPs for assistance.

From up ahead came the sound of tumbling water. As he closed in on the fountainhead his face was bathed in a mizzle of mist. He raised his arm and snapped his lighter once, twice, snick, snick. The insipid flame revealed another vault, containing a large pool where several smaller sewers emptied their loads, cascading over a steep vertical drop.

The roar of the water was deafening as it reflected off the unyielding brick surfaces, rebounding and amplifying, the din assaulting him from several directions at once. It was disorienting in the extreme, and in that instant, he felt dangerously isolated and alone.

He turned his gaze to the pool. There within the wavering rim of light something floated just beneath the surface.

The body of a woman.

He passed the lighter into his left hand and drew his service revolver, instinctively crouching in the process. From above he caught sight of a muzzle flash a split second before he was sent reeling backwards clutching his chest.

* * *

According to the locals around Chilton Foliat, that July was the hottest on record for their little corner of England, utterly stifling they complained, fanning reddening faces with anything at hand, and scurrying to the shady side of the street as they went about their daily business. Octavius barely noticed it, habituated as he was to the smoldering summers of his youth in the bayous of

Louisiana, and later on, cruising the French Quarter in the heat of the night.

He crossed over the stile and skirted the next field, following a worn pathway between villages. He had been out for the past two hours, reconnoitering the countryside, a patchwork quilt of farm fields, undulating downs and woods nestled in secluded vales. He was looking for abandoned out-buildings and little-used sheds.

The 101st had returned to England some two weeks ago to replace men and equipment, and recharge in anticipation of the next operation. But Octavius was restless. His appetites, dormant for so long, had been aroused amid the carnage of D-Day.

He checked the ordinance map and took a sip from his canteen. Overhead he witnessed a hawk circling lazily before disappearing into a stand of big belly oak. He set off in that direction, cutting across a sheep pasture and then another stile, breaching the low stone wall separating the fields. From here the land fell sharply toward the woods, where nestled in a copse of trees at the bottom of the dip, stood a derelict stone structure. The roof was swaybacked and badly weathered and there were no windows to speak of. He moved closer, steadying his breathing in an attempt to slow his racing heart.

* * *

"Cathy, can you take this over to the Vicar's when you go down to the village this morning?" Her father stood in the doorway of the greenhouse, holding out a clay pot, the white shoot of the bulb pointing like an accusatory finger.

"What are you giving him now, da?"

"It's that hybrid I've been experimenting with, Brasovia nodosa." He stared off into the distance trying to recall the common name for the orchid, "Lady-of-the-Night."

"Do you think that's appropriate for the Vicar?"

"What do you mean?"

"Lady of the night." She arched her eyebrows to emphasize the point.

"It's not that kind of lady. It's because the fragrance is released at night, you daft ha'porth. And what do you know about ladies of the night?"

"Da, I wasn't born yesterday."

"So you're fond of telling me."

"Oh alright, I suppose it'll fit in my basket."

"There's a good girl. Try not to shake it about too much."

"I'll wrap it in an old blanket then. It'll be safer than a babe in arms."

"I've got some sacking inside that should do the trick."

She followed him back into the greenhouse through the heady bouquet of his prize-winning orchids. He confessed to her that he was determined to take another prize at this year's fall fete to add to his impressive collection of silverware, along with bragging rights at the horticultural society of which he was the treasurer. It was a conceit that he readily admitted to, but what else was a retired professor of botany from Cambridge to do with his waning years?

Within seconds she was damp with perspiration. It was like the tropics inside the glass enclosure, the July heat amplified to jungle-like intensity. At this rate the Rita Hayworth wave in her golden tresses, that had taken her all morning to achieve, would be as limp as a dishrag. She had been trying to catch the eye of a certain American Lieutenant during her shift at the Blue Boar, which had become the home away from home for the commissioned officers of the 101st Airborne stationed in and around the Village of Aldbourne.

She was as determined as her father, stubborn some might say. Oh well, I'll reset it later she thought to herself, and stashing the pot in her basket, set off toward the vicarage.

* * *

He knapped at the flint, fashioning the rock so that it fit seamlessly into the final course along the west wall of the Vicar's fine home. He was a skilled stonemason, one of the finest in the county, continuing the tradition of his father and his father's father before him, all the way back to his Saxon ancestors who had fashioned the first stone churches and manors, iconic to the region. He was descending the scaffolding when Cathy rode into the yard to deliver the Vicar's orchid. In the heat of the day he had removed his shirt and stood glistening with sweat, a gritty Adonis, and somewhat embarrassed to be caught half naked by the very girl whose heart he hoped to capture.

"Look at you, standing there like a young Greek god," she teased. He reddened and crossed his arms in a show of modesty. "If muscles were money, Eddie Longstaff, you'd be the richest man in all of Wiltshire."

"Get away with you, Cathy. You'd make a sailor blush, so you would. Let me get decent." He reached for his shirt.

"Don't get dressed on my account. I could look at those muscles all day."

"'ush now, girl. You'll 'ave the 'ole village gossipin' and 'ere in the Church yard for 'eaven's sake."

"They can gossip till the cows come home. It's not going to stop me from gawking."

"So what brings you 'ere besides takin' the mickey outta me?"

"Orchid for the vicar," she replied, unraveling the pot.

He drank her in. She was radiant in her summer frock which clung like a second skin to her generous curves. She took off her kerchief and shook her thick mane of hair, waves of gold cascading to her shoulders. Dancing eyes of violet and a perfect rosebud mouth seemed to mock and beckon at the same time. She was poetry in motion, and he was well and truly smitten.

"Will you be doin' a shift at the Boar tonight?" he said, a slight quaver in his voice.

"Aye, six till closing."

"I can see you 'ome afterwards like, protect you from all them Yanks."

"Thanks all the same, but you can do another favor for me."

"Go on, I'm all ears."

"Well, we've got an American servicewoman coming to stay with us. She's in the medical unit attached to the 101st.You could play the good host and protect her from all 'them' local lads."

"I wouldn't know what to say to 'er."

"Just take off your shirt. You wouldn't have to say a thing."

"Cathy!"

"So I can count on you?"

"Oh, alright then."

"You're an angel." She stood on tiptoes and quickly kissed him on the cheek.

"Come around at half five and we'll all go to the Boar together."

He watched as she walked toward the rectory door, transfixed by the gentle sway of her hips and the lingering scent of her perfume. His mind was already racing ahead to the evening and how he might entice her to accompany him on a Sunday outing after service. He knew of a perfect spot, cool and secluded in a glade between pastures just out of the reach of prying eyes and wagging tongues.

* * *

The sun was still shining brightly, spangling off the bay windows when Eddie arrived at the front door of Braestead cottage. Overhead the mourning doves cooed and called from the massive chestnut trees lining the drive that led to the greenhouses. It was shaping up to be a warm evening and he was stifling in his jacket and tie, and already beginning to regret his acceptance of Cathy's request.

He wiped his face for the umpteenth time with his handkerchief, now ringing wet. He raised the knocker and rapped three times. Before he'd even had a chance to lower his hand, the door flew back, and Cathy reached out and unceremoniously grabbed him by the arm.

"There you are," she said, giving him a quick appraisal "all done up like a dog's dinner. We were beginning to think you'd been kidnapped by gypsies."

Before he had time to explain, she ushered him into the sitting room where the professor was subjecting an attractive female attired in military dress to a lecture on his pet subject, rare orchids.

"Alright da, we've got to get our skates on. Eddie, I'd like you to meet our American guest, Miss Vivian Bennett."

There was a look of relief on her face as she stepped toward him, offering a firm handshake before breaking into an engaging smile.

"Pleased to meet you, Miss Bennett."

"Call me Vivian." She looked him straight in the eyes as she continued pumping his hand. In that instant something passed between them, something indefinable, yet as substantial as the stones he worked with every day. Suddenly the chore he had been dreading had taken on an entirely different complexion.

Cathy hurried them out the door and then announced that she would have to bike to the Boar for fear of being late for her shift.

"I'm sorry for the rush, but old Mister Evans is a stickler for being on time and it'll be absolutely heaving tonight."

"Don't worry, Cathy. I'm sure Eddie won't get me lost, and it'll give us a chance to get past the preliminaries."

"You're a doll, Vivian Bennett. See you there." In a flash she was down the lane, pedaling like mad to the village."

"I'm the one 'ooh should be apologizin' for bein' late. If truth be told, me brotha beat me to the bath." For some reason he wasn't embarrassed about making this confession to the lovely stranger.

"Hey, welcome to the club. My sister Helen and I were at war for years over whose turn it was for the hot water on a Saturday night."

After those confessions, they fell into an easy dialogue, exchanging tales of sibling antics and rivalries as they made their way to the Blue Boar.

On this night the favored drinking establishment was packed to the low-slung rafters, commissioned officers of the 101st Airborne comingling with the natives in a high-spirited mix of bonhomie and the local ale, drunk lukewarm. After seating Vivian, Eddie sidled up to the bar, exchanging greetings with the regulars. He returned with drinks in hand, a stout for him and a lager and lime for her. She raised her glass,

"Here's to a quick end for Hitler and his henchmen."

"I'll second that." They each swallowed a long draught.

"Were you a nurse before the war?" Eddie inquired.

"Whatever gave you that idea?"

"Oh, sorry, Cathy said you were in the medical unit."

"That part's true, the 326th Airborne Medical Company of the 101st Airborne, but I don't do any nursing, or parachuting, thank God. I'm the commanding officer's secretary, strictly office work."

"Still important."

"In its own way I suppose. On the other hand, Cathy tells me you were quite the hero at Dunkirk."

"She exaggerates. I was jus' one of the lucky ones, 'ooh made it back alive."

"Don't be so modest. Not everyone gets awarded a Victoria Cross. She says you helped evacuate hundreds even though you were badly wounded."

"Yeah, they tried blowin' me 'ead off, but missed an' 'it me leg instead."

"Well I can see you're not holding a grudge."

"Not a chance, I could kiss the square 'ead for bein' such a poor shot."

"But you're okay now aren't you?"

"It's taken three years to come right. It still pains me in the damp, but I'm not complainin'. The doctor tells me I could be fit enough to re-join me old unit in another six month or so. If it lasts that long."

"You've done your part. Now it's our turn. We should've been in this dog fight from the get go."

"That's the spirit, my American cuzin. Can I get you another?"

"Hell, I'm in for the night; make it two."

"You know when Cathy asked me I didn't know what to expect, but you're alright in my books."

"Glad you think so. You're alright yourself."

* * *

He reddened at her compliment. Then he pushed back from the table and ambled toward the crowded bar once more. She watched as he made his way across the room. He was working hard to hide the slight limp. She was drawn to his rugged physicality, and self-deprecating manner. She also sensed a mutual attraction, a raw sexual energy flowing freely between the two of them. It had been months since Gene's last visit while she was still in training, and although she didn't want to give the rest of the American girls a bad reputation, she had needs of her own.

* * *

As Eddie made his way to the bar his mind was in a bit of a muddle. He hoped he hadn't spoken out of turn. He wasn't used to being quite so open and direct, but there was something about Vivian that allowed him to speak freely, encouraged him almost.

He returned to find her in animated conversation with a couple of GIs trying their best to make an impression. Cathy needn't have worried; Vivian was more than capable of looking after herself when the patrons got a little too friendly. In fact, she could be downright intimidating, possessed as she was with a razor-sharp wit and acerbic tongue. She matched the GIs quip for quip, until, deflated as punctured barrage balloons, they drifted away in search of easier conquests.

He resumed the getting to know you routine and was eventually joined by some of his mates, happy to be in the company of such an attractive female. This gave him a bit more leeway to concentrate his gaze on Cathy. She seemed to be focusing a lot of her attention on an American officer who appeared to be permanently stationed at the bar. From where he sat it was obvious she was flirting with him, encouraging his overtures. He experienced a twinge of jealousy and suddenly excusing himself from the table, strode up to the bar, interrupting the conversation between Cathy and her admirer.

"Sorry to butt in, but Vivian says she's got a day off tomorra and was wonderin' if we could take 'er out an' about for a bit."

"Weren't you supposed to be keeping an eye on her?" said Cathy, clearly annoyed.

"It'll take more than that lot to give 'er any trouble, believe me. What about Savernake Forest or Stone'enge.

"What about them?"

"I could take me 'amma an' chip 'er off a souvenir"

"What on earth are you going on about?"

"You, me and Vivian. A day out … tomorra."

"Oh … ah … well I'm not sure our petrol ration will get us as far as that."

"We could ask around, see if anyone's got any to spare."

"What about somewhere closer? We could take our bikes and have a picnic."

"I know just the spot, a nice little wood by the river, 'alfway between 'ere and Chilton Foliat."

"Are you game, Mike?" she said, turning to the lieutenant.

Eddie hadn't banked on a foursome.

"Eddie, this is Mike Kemper, he's stationed here in Aldbourne. Mike I'd like to introduce you to Eddie Longstaff. Eddie was a hero at Dunkirk."

The lieutenant extended his hand. He was the perfect image of a dashing officer attired in knife-edged khaki's, gold bars gleaming.

"My pleasure, soldier." He gave Eddie's hand a couple of hard pumps and turning back to Cathy said, "That sounds like a swell idea. What can I bring?"

"Just your appetite. Our housekeeper, old Mrs. Sharples has been baking up a storm. We'll be eating her wares for weeks if you don't give us a hand, and how's a girl supposed to keep her figure otherwise?" She placed a hand on her hip and batted her eyelashes. "Eddie can you bring some scrumpy? It's rumored Eddie's da makes the most potent in the county."

"We've got a fresh crock in the cella'. Should do us nicely."

"Alright, we're all set them. What time?"

"Right after church?

"Can you meet us there, Mike, St. Mary's, say quarter to twelve?"

"It's a date."

* * *

"Is it much further?" Eddie heard Cathy call out. He turned to see that she'd fallen behind the others. Having overloaded the basket on her bicycle, she was having trouble negotiating the tussocked pathway through the pasture.

"Here, let me take some of those things," Mike volunteered, though from Eddie's vantage, he seemed to be having troubles of his own staying upright with the knapsack holding the crock of cider swaying precariously about his back.

"We're almost there," Eddie shouted over his shoulder.

He was piloting them to a secluded spot on the banks of the River Kennet and had decided to take a shortcut across the fields. The terrain was a bit more of an ordeal than he bargained for with everything, but the kitchen sink, stashed in panniers, baskets and knapsacks. Cathy insisted on a full spread served on the very best China, whereas he was used to a simple pastie jammed into his jacket pocket along with a drink right out of the river.

They paused to lighten Cathy's load and then continued down a wooded slope to a quiet bend where dappled light sifted through the canopy of towering oak and chestnut trees. Here, the blanket was unfurled, and the vittles laid. Once settled, conversation was lively, and flowed as easily as his da's scrumpy, drunk from crystal goblets Cathy had secreted in her carrier.

"She doesn't do anythin' by 'alves, our Cathy," Eddie commented.

"This is absolutely delicious," Vivian enthused. "Do you always eat this well?"

"I second that," Mike chimed in. "How are Vivian and I gonna go back to army chow after this feast?"

"We're not rationed as badly here as in the bigger towns and cities. There are plenty of farms hereabouts, and we have the greenhouses when father isn't cramming every square inch with his orchids."

"Well, you're spoiling us to no end." Mike recharged their glasses and then propping himself up on an elbow said, "Ladies and gentlemen will you please join me in a toast to our charming hostess, and number one bootlegger and intrepid tour guide. May the road rise up to meet you. May the wind be always at your back. May the sun shine warm upon your faces, the rains fall soft upon your fields, and until we meet again, may God hold you in the palm of his hand."

"Aye to that."

"Amen," said Vivian, crossing herself with a mock gesture.

"Oh, I don't think I've heard that one, Mike. It's lovely and the perfect sentiment on this gorgeous day." Cathy was relishing the compliments, her high beams trained all the while on Mike.

"Just something my great uncle Sidney would cite on special occasions."

Into the heart of the afternoon the bonhomie ebbed and flowed. All the while Eddie was angling for a quiet walk with Cathy. His intended destination an abandoned stone hut, a former shelter for herders, that would provide the privacy he so desperately craved. When she failed to take the hint, he posed the question directly only to receive a demure refusal. In the awkward silence that followed, he came to the sudden realization that for all her playfulness, her attentions were obviously elsewhere, and his suit, though sincere and heartfelt, was foundering badly. He masked his disappointment with a drawn out 'shaggy-dog' yarn, triggering a gale of laughter at its conclusion. With spirits buoyed once more, Vivian turned to him.

"Come on then. I need to walk off some of this cake." She patted at her stomach.

"You sure?"

"Never been surer, Eddie. Lead the way."

"Alright then." He turned to Cathy, "we shouldn't be gone too long."

"Take your time, we've got all afternoon."

"Ta you two. See you in a bit."

He checked his watch and then with a wave, set off following the lazy currents downstream. He stuck close to the bank for half a mile or so, helping Vivian over rocks and sweepers. At the confluence of a small creek bed, reduced to a trickle in the heat of summer, he turned away from the river and tracked along the narrow depression until the hut came into view. As he made his way towards the structure, there was a sudden movement in the surrounding brambles. He caught a glimpse of a tall figure dressed in what appeared to be fatigues moving away from them at speed. Behind him Vivian gave a start.

"What was that?"

"Probably some ol' tramp."

"I thought it was a wild animal."

"None of those around 'ere. The worse you'll get is a mangy dog or a randy ram."

"Well that's a relief." She walked past him to the doorway of the hut. "This looks very cozy." She held out her hand. "Would you like to step into my parlor, said the spider to the fly." He let her lead him inside. It was cool and fresh straw covered the dirt floor. She turned and he was drawn into her warm embrace. He didn't resist as she eased down into the straw, parting his lips with a skillful tongue. It was obvious that she knew exactly what she wanted, and he was helpless to resist, a willing partner in the seduction, ensnared in her web of guilty pleasures.

* * *

As noiselessly as possible Octavius circled around the shelter and made his way back to the river, re-tracing the very route Eddie and Vivian had just taken. His chosen hideaway was not as secluded as he had originally thought. From here on in, he would have to exercise extreme caution in carrying out his plans, especially during daylight.

The extended absence from front line action had only served to intensify his hunger. As the hiatus dragged on, his waking hours were consumed by visions of past exploits, and his nights enflamed by dreamscapes of the most debauched fantasies. He began to wonder if the cravings could ever be sated; gluttony replaced by unquenchable desires of the flesh, and the discipline he had exhibited in curbing his excessive intake of food, failing miserably. His last days in France had done little to stem the heinous impulses. Brubaker had seen to that, foiling his intended plans for Mademoiselle Bernier before meeting his own end. He derived little pleasure from the ritualistic brutalization of her corpse, and took it out on Brubaker, still clinging to life with a bullet lodged deep in his chest. He sliced him, still conscious, from pelvis to sternum and hung him, with entrails spilling, alongside her savaged torso from the apex of the sewer vault.

* * *

Tracing a final sweeping curve in the river, he almost stumbled upon another couple entangled beneath the trees. He didn't see them until the last minute and stopped short just a few feet from where they lay. The woman sat up, startled, a long stretch of thigh showing where her summer frock had risen above her garter.

"Awfully sorry, sir, ma'am, didn't see you there."

"At ease soldier." Mike raised up on an elbow.

Octavius drank her in, every inch. He couldn't help himself; she was the spitting image of Nell Madisson, his first, his introduction into the twisted world of the Beauchamps. His mind raced as he stepped forward and held out his hand.

"Sergeant Serge Tremblay of the five-o-deuces."

"Cathy, Cathy Yates, pleased to make your acquaintance."

"Lieutenant Mike Kemper, five-o-sixes." He flashed his insignia.

"I'm sure I've seen you before," said Octavius, looking directly at Cathy.

"Probably at the Blue Boar. I'm a barmaid there, but I live in Chilton Foliat."

"So do I, I'm stationed there, at Hart House."

"You're just down the lane. I'm at Braestead Cottage."

"The place with all the greenhouses?"

"That's us. My father and I, and his prize orchids of course." She laughed.

"Maybe I'll see you around the village."

"You just might, Sergeant Tremblay."

"My apologies again, I'll try and be a little more careful next time."

"Don't think anything of it." She reached for the picnic basket. "I couldn't tempt you with a piece of cake could I? We've got more than we can eat."

"No ma'am, that's very kind of you, but thanks all the same."

"It's good cake, soldier. Better get it while you can. You'll be back on K-rations before you can say Jack Robinson."

"Do you know something I don't, Lieutenant?"

"Loose lips sink ships, so you didn't hear it from me, but you'll be getting a briefing soon. We're heading back into the action, details to follow. That's all I can say for now, so keep it under your hat."

"Will do, sir." Octavius saluted and moved off up the slope, his mind on fire. He had his next victim squarely in the crosshairs, his only concern the timing of the next campaign.

* * *

The cabin was set well back from the road and reached by a narrow dirt track with scrub closing in on both sides. It hadn't been used in a season or two by the look of the undergrowth and the low-hanging branches brushing against the windshield. Halfway in, Shadbolt's progress was halted by deadfall lying across the track.

He clambered out of the vehicle and continued on foot for the rest of the way. The verges were strewn with thistles, burrs and beggar's ticks sticking fast to his pant legs. Overhead the ragged cawing of a raven broke the stillness, its call like a warning, or an omen, before it took wing and flew off into the dark heart of the afternoon.

Shadbolt took it as an omen, although exactly what it portended remained hidden for the moment.

Rounding a final, sweeping curve, the cabin came into view, situated on a low rise overlooking the lake. The front windows of the weathered structure were shuttered, and the screen door hung limply on rusted hinges. He walked around to the lake side where several boats lay upended in the long grass. The land fell off quickly to a small jetty extending out into the water. Shadbolt walked to the end of the jetty and lit a cigarette.

Scanning the shoreline, he could view a good third of the water body, but no other cabins were visible from this vantage. He finished the smoke, flicking the butt out into the water and made his way through the tall grass to the back door.

It was padlocked.

He rattled the ancient fastener, rust flaking off into his hand, which he brushed against his thigh, leaving a russet smear, like a ferric stigmata. He looked around for something to jimmy the latch, settling on the long shaft of an oar lock from one of the upturned boats. After a few minutes the ancient padlock relinquished its hold and the door swung inward.

It was obvious from the thick layer of dust covering the floor that the cabin hadn't been occupied in a long time. The main room was sparsely furnished, a large pot-bellied stove taking pride of place between a stack of wood and another of newspaper. Shadbolt rifled through the broadsheets, checking the dates.

The latest one he found was April 15th, 1942.

Next, he opened the closet of a battered chifforobe, listing precariously to one side. In it were assorted mackinaw shirts along with two pairs of worn work trousers, and stacked in the corner, several boxes of shells for the twelve gauge and hunting rifle that hung on the opposite wall. The first three drawers of the chifforobe held tee shirts, socks, long johns, and some crudely-knitted sweaters, but the bottom drawer was empty, giving Shadbolt pause for thought.

He moved on to the only other room in the cabin reached via a short hallway at the far end of the main room. An iron bedstead stood sentinel beneath a large crucifix. It had been stripped of linen, which was piled neatly at the end of the cornshuck mattress. A washstand with bowl and jug and a chamber pot were the only other articles in the room, and apart from the chifforobe, there were no other drawers or cupboards to house the personal papers and documents one would normally expect in a typical abode, even one as basic as this.

Playing a hunch, Shadbolt walked back into the main room, and going over to the stove, unlatched the grate. There amongst the ashes were several remnant scraps of paper. He reached in to retrieve them and then his fingers brushed against a larger article, a badly charred, leather bound book. He fished it out and blew off the dust and ash.

It was a bible.

Though difficult to make out, the scorched inside cover bore an inscription written in French. Shadbolt determined it had been presented to Serge Rejean Tremblay on his, 'vingt et un', 21st birthday.

What would possess him to burn his bible along with the rest of his personal papers?

It was obvious he was a recluse, but to purposely eradicate all traces of his history, his identity, pointed to something much more sinister.

Satisfied that there was nothing else to be gained inside, Shadbolt exited the backdoor and approached a nearby shed. The outside wall was festooned with antlers, some impressive seven-pointers amongst the racks. Inside there was a large wooden table for butchering and dressing meat.

Several deer carcasses hung from the rafters along with pheasant and wild turkey, now blackened with age and severely desiccated. The air was rank with the smell of the rotting flesh, and on closer inspection he saw that the deer carcasses were riddled with maggots. He covered his nose and continued his inspection of the premises.

When he was finished, he stepped outside and fired up another cigarette, the smell of tobacco bringing welcome relief.

He widened his search of the property, looking for any signs of disturbed earth. The wooded areas around the cabin revealed nothing but dense mats of last year's leaves.

He considered another angle, posing the simple question: if one wanted to get rid of a body, where would one hide it? Where was it unlikely to be discovered? Out in the middle of the lake, in the deepest part? Or closer to the cabin where fewer fishing rods were likely to disturb it?

He noted several 'No Trespassing' signs in and around the property and so decided to explore the shoreline in the immediate vicinity. He hauled one of the small skiffs to the water's edge and pushed off. Within a hundred yards of the cabin he came upon a narrow inlet, the opening overgrown with willow and alder.

He nosed the prow through the pendulous curtain of greenery, entering a small pool of stagnant water. It was oblong in shape and measured about six hundred square feet. The surface was covered with duckweed. Shadbolt poled the oar, hitting bottom just before the shaft became fully submerged. Ever so slowly, he tacked back and forth across the pond, probing with the oar, disturbing the mud which rose to the surface in murky tendrils.

Finally, the oar contacted something solid, a rock perhaps, and then something metallic. Shadbolt guessed a chain by the way it moved under his prodding. Very carefully he tapped at the area around the obstruction.

It measured approximately six and a half feet by two to three feet, narrowing to less than a foot across at what he surmised was the head end.

He considered stripping off, but diving to the bottom would only confirm what he already knew was down there. Mentally, he marked the spot, measuring from easily recognizable benchmarks.

Then he rowed back to the dock. It would take a day or two to arrange for a diver and then there was the issue of identifying the corpse. They'd be relying on dental records or other distinguishing features, old injuries or tattoos. Shadbolt would need to travel to Maine to interview Tremblay's parents and hope they could provide the required information.

* * *

Three days later, the State police divers recovered the remains of what was once a large male from the secluded inlet. Crawfish and snapping turtles had made short work of the flesh, which had been picked clean off the bone. The coroner determined that the corpse had been in the water for at least two years. It had been weighted down with chain and cement blocks.

Scarring of the neck vertebrae suggested a deeply cut, throat wound, close to decapitation in fact.

"The good news is he's still wearing a partial dental plate, uppers, appears well-made, plus two gold fillings."

"Well that's a start at least. Any other noteworthy marks, former breaks, or new ones?"

"Afraid not."

"How long before the photographs of the jaw and teeth are ready?"

"We can have them ready for you later this afternoon."

Shadbolt pocketed the dental plate and walked out of the coroner's office. There was a diner two blocks away that claimed to serve the best chicken-fried steak in all of Kansas.

* * *

The Canadian countryside flashed by, all ablaze in the rich, red hues of Indian summer, smoldering late into the equinox. Shadbolt had spent the better part of August in the backwoods of Maine and Vermont, tracking down and interviewing Serge

Tremblay's acquaintances and aged relatives, those that were still on the green side of the grass. He had eventually gained an address in Montreal where his mother, in pidgin English, had told him he had resided before the trouble with the 'gendarmes', as she put it.

From what he could gather, Shadbolt surmised it had been an affair of the heart that had ended badly. There was a pending court case, but just before he was due to testify, Serge had fled south into the heart of the American midwest and hadn't been heard from since. As to distinguishing features or dental work, they claimed ignorance. Other than the occasional Christmas card they hadn't laid eyes on their boy since he left for Montreal in '37, and they contended his previous gap-toothed smile was the result of a hockey brawl in his youth.

A simple photograph might have helped the cause, but other than studio portraits of a babe in arms, there were no other images of the elusive absconder.

The interview became awkward and emotional. Until he was able to obtain a match with dental records, he couldn't confirm with any certainty that the recovered corpse was in fact Serge Rejean Tremblay, or whether he was currently fighting with the 101st Airborne in the European Theatre.

Now he was joined by Perkins on what he hoped would be the final leg of the overly-circuitous journey.

"Let's hope this address leads us to the tooth-yanker, and he can identify his own handiwork." Perkins slouched in the passenger seat, empty soda bottles, cigarette butts and candy bar wrappers gathered about his feet.

"Our Mountie contacts are providing a list of dentists practicing in the City. My guess is it'll be someone in the immediate vicinity, provided they're still in business."

"Any chance it was a backroom job?" said Perkins, firing up another cigarette.

"Not according to the folks I've talked to. The dental plate is first rate, a real professional piece of work."

"Well, this sure beats sittin' on our hands back in D.C."

"I'm with you there."

They travelled on in silence for a while, admiring the autumn finery on display. As they approached St. Hubert, Perkins consulted the road map.

"Turn left and follow the signs to St. Lambert. That's where we cross over the River, the St. Lawrence." He rolled his eyes for effect. "What's with these Mackerel-snappers anyhow? Everything is Saint something. I didn't know they even had this many saints."

"Easy now Gene; let's not be offending the locals before we get what we came for. Afterwards you can be your charming old self again."

Perkins grunted a response and continued eyeing the map. Then he turned to Shadbolt. "So which one of our three prime candidates do you suspect is impersonating the big frog here? Actually, you can make that two. I can't picture that blonde wig under a tin pot."

"Nothing is certain yet and I must admit, I'm playing a hunch, but it's a calculated hunch and everything is starting to line up. Major Berry's description from the interview doesn't match Octavius Cadogan unless he's been on a crash diet, but I somehow can't see the twins separated, and as far as we know they're still south of the border."

"That's what the gospel bunch would have us believe, right? Too bad we couldn't get 'em extradited after they did the midnight flit."

"Unfortunately, when the files disappeared after Musgrave bought the farm that possibility went out the proverbial window. It would've been purely circumstantial, our word against the word of God. The Church of the Foursquare Gospel is well-connected. Once they closed ranks, well Clarence Darrow himself couldn't have gotten a conviction."

"True, I suppose."

"It's a bit of a long shot, but I'm guessing Cadogan, although for the life of me I can't fathom what he's doing on the front lines with the Screaming Eagles."

"Easier pickin's? It sure can't be the K-rations."

"Felix has some theories of his own on that score."

"He's got some doozies alright. He's even got a name for these hombres, serial killers."

"Yeah, I know. He's been working with a couple of psychologists from Yale."

"Head shrinkers?"

"They're developing personality profiles to help identify these types, see what makes them tick. It's a direction the Bureau may be headed in the future."

"Way above my pay grade, besides I should be long gone by then."

"Still thinking about running that boardwalk diner in Atlantic City?"

"As soon as this dog fight is over and Vivian is back in my arms again."

"One thing at a time. Let's see if we can make some headway on this caper first."

"Speaking of headway, what's the low down on Felix's leave? Shouldn't that Abercrombie be out here beatin' the bushes with us?"

"Well I guess now's as good a time as any to let you in on our covert operation of two, strictly confidential."

"I'm all ears."

"He's headed south, down Mexico way to do a bit of sleuthing under the guise of R and R."

"Why you dirty little schemers. But what's with the secrecy?"

"Couldn't risk any slip-ups. J. Edgar would have our heads if he knew what we were up to."

"I'm hurt, Jack, that you couldn't deal me in." He feigned indignation.

"Sorry, but it was a last minute decision, and I didn't want you implicated if our caper came unstuck. Right now, we don't even know if we can find them let alone link them to anything untoward. If nothing else it might confirm my suspicions about Octavius Cadogan, and we'll have a bead on them for later when they try to re-enter our jurisdiction."

"I'd pay to be on that welcoming party. Those cocksuckers would never walk again."

"Amen to that, Gene."

They crossed the broad back of the mighty St. Lawrence along the impressive Victoria Jubilee Bridge and proceeded through the bustling port district, arriving at the Royal Canadian Mounted Police headquarters in a leafy suburb outside the downtown core. Shadbolt parked the vehicle and they entered the stately, brick building, clearing security before being directed to an office on the second floor. They were greeted at the reception desk by an officer in a brown tunic, who escorted them down the hall. Perkins turned to Shadbolt and whispered, "I thought these guys wore red uniforms like Nelson Eddy in the movies?"

"Strictly ceremonial, Gene."

"Say goodbye to another fantasy."

The officer stopped at a frosted glass door bearing the name of Inspector R.A. Turcotte. He knocked once, and then waved them into the office.

"Gentlemen."

"Inspector Turcotte, Special Agents Jack Shadbolt and Gene Perkins of the Federal Bureau of Investigation. Thanks for agreeing to help us out." They shook hands all around and Turcotte motioned for them to take a seat.

"We've prepared a list of local dentists and I've assigned one of our men to accompany you on your inquiries."

Shadbolt considered the list and gave a low whistle. "Looks pretty comprehensive."

"The Provincial Association was very helpful. It's right up to date and includes members who have retired in the last five years."

"I can see that."

"Oh, one minor detail, you'll have to register your firearms. We can issue you with temporary certificates. My advice is to leave them here with us and pick them up on your way out of town."

"That shouldn't be a problem unless we run into any crazed tooth-yankers," Perkins interjected.

"Gun violence is rare here, and most of the troublemakers are off at the front where they can be of some use."

"Yeah, we heard you boys gave 'em hell on the Normandy beaches."

"Likewise, I'm sure. Let's pray for an early Christmas present this year."

"Amen to that."

"Inspector Turcotte," said Shadbolt, adopting a conciliatory tone, "the F.B.I. is happy to comply with the local laws, but our firearms are standard issue and I'd feel a whole lot better knowing it's within reach if I ever needed it. Rest assured, we don't intend to engage in anything of a reckless nature. It's purely a precaution."

Turcotte leaned back in his chair, considering the request. He pulled at his earlobe in an affected gesture and looking Shadbolt in the eyes delivered his response.

"I suppose I'm willing to make an exception. You come highly recommended from the people at the top. I'll have to trust your good judgment."

"Thank you Inspector, it's much appreciated." Shadbolt checked his watch. "If it's all the same to you, we could start now. There are still a couple of hours left till closing."

"As you wish; I'll call for the constable. In the meantime, let's get these registration certificates filled out."

While they were completing the necessary paperwork, a young constable approached and introduced himself.

"Constable Akerman, pleased to meet you." At first glance, Shadbolt doubted he had yet to be acquainted with a razor.

"Special Agents Shadbolt and Perkins, but you can call us Jack and Gene."

"Umm, mm, Myron, if we're going to be on a first name basis."

"So Myron, we thought we'd start at the last known address and work our way from there." Shadbolt held out the paper bearing the address Serge's mother had provided.

"Ah, St. Urbain Street in the heart of Mile End. I can see why Inspector Turcotte asked me to accompany you. Unless you speak Yiddish, you might not have gotten very far.

"Yiddish!" Perkins spat.

"It's the Jewish district, mostly Ashkenazim from Eastern Europe, Poland, Lithuania, Ukraine, you know."

"Great, between French and Yiddish this outta be a cakewalk."

"Don't worry, there are plenty of English speakers and I was brought up right next door in Outremont. I know the lingo."

"Alright then, Myron, lead the way."

* * *

The boarding house was situated in a continuous row of brick and stone tenements lining both sides of the bustling thoroughfare. Everywhere Shadbolt cast his eye was a riot of color and motion: honking automobiles and horse carts competed for space; gaggles of laughing children ran helter skelter while venders hawked their wares from the crowded sidewalks.

From several blocks away the plaintive cry of a rag and bone man announced his impending arrival aboard a creaking wagon drawn by a swaybacked horse, his long sidelocks dangling in greasy tendrils beneath a black, stovepipe hat.

As the clop of hooves receded, Shadbolt exited the car and the trio ascended the metal staircase to the second floor and rang the bell. That the landlady would even remember Tremblay was a long shot, let alone where he may have gone for his dental work, but Akerman showed her the name, and to the best of his ability, translated Shadbolt's description, garnered from the interviews of friends and family. After a five-minute exchange she simply shrugged her shoulders and then unceremoniously shut the door.

They made several more visits on foot before Shadbolt called a halt to the search. His watch read five minutes past six o'clock and offices were closing throughout the district. No one had identified Serge Tremblay as a past patient or recognized the dental plate as their own. Tired and a little dispirited, they dropped Akerman off back at RCMP headquarters and then headed to their hotel for the night.

"Maybe we'll get lucky tomorrow," said Shadbolt.

"I'll drink to that. In fact, make it two. The rye whiskey here is supposed to be pretty damn choice."

"You'll get no objections from me, Gene. We more than earned it today."

"Ain't it the truth."

* * *

The noise from passing traffic roused Shadbolt from a troubling dream. Through sleep-filled eyes he strained to see the alarm clock; only 6:37 a.m. with dawn barely seeping through the curtains. The third day of the sweep had taken them to the outskirts of the City and no closer to a match. Perkin's suggestion of a backroom job was starting to gain traction. They were getting exactly nowhere with their legitimate inquiries. He made up his mind to re-visit Mile End and the shadowy underground network of blackmarket commerce he sensed as soon as he set foot in the Jewish quarter. He outlined his suspicions to Perkins over breakfast and together they confronted Akerman with a change in tactics.

"So who's in the know in Mile End? Who are your prime stoolies and snitches?" Shadbolt asked.

"It's a pretty closed shop, and there's been a change of the old guard since the cross-border bootlegging stopped."

"What about your higher ups, would any of them be tapped in?"

"I could speak with Sergeant Shalansky. He has the longest history in Mile End."

"Okay, let's start there. Can we meet with him this morning?"

Akerman went off in search of the sergeant only to return unaccompanied ten minutes later.

"He was just going off shift, but he gave me a name. I know the gentleman personally. We go to the same synagogue. Saul Yakubov, he's a shochet, a kosher butcher, works out of the alley behind Rue St. Vieteur."

"Good work Myron. This could be the break we've been looking for."

* * *

Shadbolt nosed the car into the back alley, a warren of sheds, shacks and lean-tos, boasting as much activity as was taking place on the street front. He pulled over next to a fenced compound, parking behind a cart piled high with crates of live chickens. A crudely-lettered sign in English and Hebrew advertised Halakha Meats.

Shadbolt opened the gate, entering a small yard as a man in a blood splattered apron sliced the throat of a tethered steer. In one fluid motion he made a single incision across the trachea and esophagus, severing the carotid arteries in the process. The animal gave a shudder and collapsed, bleeding out onto a concrete apron before the carcass was hoisted aloft to be gutted and dressed.

The shochet acknowledged Akerman with a silent gesture of raised eyebrows and exposed palms, and then motioned for them to step into the nearby shed which served as outlet, office, and meat storage locker. Once inside Akerman said a few words in Yiddish and then switched to English.

"Sorry again for interrupting your day, but we're looking for whoever made this." He stepped forward and showed the dental plate to Mr. Yakubov. "They're not in any trouble. We just need to match it to a particular person." He repeated what he had said in Yiddish to which Yakubov replied,

"I understand, just not speak so good English." He wiped his hands on the back of his trousers before taking the item from Akerman. He inspected it carefully, turning it over slowly and focusing particular attention on the underside. "Is good work. See here?" He pointed to a tiny mark on the metal. "I see this before, lots times."

"Do you have any idea who made it?" said Akerman.

"Go see Chaim Lipsky. He tell you."

"Chaim Lipsky?" Akerman's brow furrowed.

"He know."

"You're sure of that?"

"Yes, him for sure know."

"Alright then. Thanks. Thanks a lot."

"Now you do me favor."

"Sure. What would you like?"

"You know Tobias Cohen family?"

"Yes, from synagogue."

"Go sit shiva for me and take package, yes." Before Akerman could answer, Yakubov went over to an ice box, reached in and extracted a package wrapped in butcher's paper. "Keep cool until you go, yes."

"Yes, I will." Akerman tucked the package into his tunic pocket.

"Zay Gezunt."

"Zay Gezunt."

* * *

"You know this Lipsky character?" said Shadbolt once they were back in the alley.

"Yes, not personally or anything, he's an artist, a sculptor actually. He does a lot of work for the synagogues and the Catholic church too, icons, mezuzahs, crucifixes, you know, all that religious paraphernalia. I'm not too sure what that has to do with dental plates though."

"A sculptor works in clay and wax and metal, making molds and such. It's not that far-fetched to think that the dental angle might be a lucrative sideline between commissions, especially if the patient doesn't want to leave a trail."

"Never thought of that. You have a good point. But Yakubov didn't actually say it was Chaim. He said to ask him because he would know."

"Either way, his place is our next port of call. Where to?"

"His studio is a ways east of here on Tannery Road."

From inside the compound came the sound of a cleaver hacking at freshly-killed flesh, as the shochet began the task of butchering the carcass. Shadbolt thought of the single incision and the skill it took to master that deadly stroke. His mind turned to why they had come in the first place and the urgency to do whatever it took to stop the ritual slaughter and bring the killers to justice.

* * *

Through the mid-day traffic Shadbolt followed Akerman's directions eastward to a squalid neighborhood of ramshackle walk-ups and flyblown storefronts. Bums loitered on every street corner, scrounging for discarded butts and whatever spare change they could wheedle from passersby. It reminded Shadbolt of a hundred other neglected places he'd visited over his career, all the sad tales and sad lives, rolling snake eyes at every shake of the dice.

He grew up in such a place, his earlier years at least. He and his sister, Connie. A hard scrabble existence, running errands, hawking newspapers, and scavenging for empty soda bottles. Anything to make a nickel. They were a close-knit family, working hard to improve their lot. After their parents died during the typhoid epidemic of '27, Shadbolt was entrusted with Connie's care. She was independent and headstrong. No way was she going to be shipped off to distant relatives in another state. Not that any offered.

He was home from college when it happened. Right out front in the street. One minute she was exchanging words with a rough-looking character, and the next he was screaming from the shattered, third storey window as the man slashed her face and then sank the blade deep into her abdomen.

Time slowed to a crawl, seconds passing like minutes, the air thick and heavy. He struggled down the apartment stairs, spilling Mrs. Hildebrand's groceries, when they collided at the entry. He fought his way across the crowded boulevard scattering bodies left and right, clawing through the gathering crowd of rubberneckers impeding his progress.

It was worse than he imagined, her face slashed to the bone, gleaming white where it had been severed from the cheek. Both hands were clutched tightly to her gut, attempting to stem the river of blood pooling where she lay.

Their eyes locked and he knew instinctively that this was the end. She died in his arms, her last words to get the dirty bastard.

From somewhere a car backfired, sending a row of starlings perched atop a sagging telephone wire wheeling into the sky, their wings reflecting iridescent in the slanting sunshine. Shadbolt released the memory, allowing it to fade with the flight of the birds for now.

Perkins led the way up a set of rusted iron stairs to the second-floor studio. A note was tacked to the door with a message scrawled in red ink.

"Says he won't be back until 8:30 tonight," Perkins relayed, a scowl animating his features.

"Well at least he's coming back."

"Should we wait for him?" said Akerman.

Shadbolt checked his watch. "Gene, why don't you and Myron drive back to headquarters and meet me back here at 8:15."

"What do you have in mind, Jack?"

"I'd like to nosey around for a while, get the lay of the land."

"You don't want any company?"

"We'll attract too much attention, and Myron's uniform will have 'em buttoned up tighter than a fat man's trousers. No, just meet me back here at 8:15."

Shadbolt watched as they drove away and then set off up the street. Right now they were pinning their hopes on this Lipsky character providing them with a lead. Shadbolt never liked to put all his eggs in one basket. Chances were there would be others in the neighborhood who could point them in the right direction. If they ended up drawing a blank with the artist, he wanted to have a contingency plan ready.

From what he had gathered so far, Tremblay struck him as hard-boiled, a real shady character, operating on the far side of the law. He needed to tap into whatever passed for the underbelly in this neck of the woods and find someone in the know, familiar with working outside the system. Hell, they might even be acquainted with Tremblay and who he did business with. The dental plate was the only piece of evidence that would prove conclusively that the corpse in the lake was Serge Tremblay and that an imposter connected to a string of brutal murders in Iowa in '41 was committing the same kind of atrocities with the 101st.

His gut told him the imposter was Octavius Cadogan, but he needed proof, and the clock was ticking.

"Un peu de monnaie pour un café?" The rubby held out his hand as Shadbolt passed by.

"Sorry, I don't speak French."

"Roas' bif, eh?"

"Pardon?"

"English, non."

"American actually."

"Same t'ing."

"Whatever you say."

"Spare a nickel for a cup of coffee?" The rubby continued holding out his hand. Shadbolt reached into his pocket and handed him a quarter.

"Here, get yourself a sandwich too, on Uncle Sam."

"Merci."

"Say, who's the bull goose around these parts?"

"Bull goose?"

"Yeah, who runs the show?" The rubby's eyes narrowed, suggesting to Shadbolt that he was contemplating how he might parley the quarter into enough for a bottle of rot gut."

"What you want, reefer, goof balls, noir, er a, black tar?"

"Not today. I've got some hot ice, jewelry that needs a good home."

"Is it worth a fin?"

"How about a deuce?"

"Okay, a deuce. See dat pawn shop up de street, right dere," he said, pointing to the sign.

"Uh huh."

"Ask for Ira."

He handed the bum the colorful note and then made his way towards the three golden balls suspended above the entry. The tinkling of a bell announced his arrival into the dusty interior. Goods of all descriptions were stacked on every available surface. He sauntered down a crowded aisle, fingering tags of cameras, musical instruments and all manner of tchochkes. Over at the main counter, a white-haired geezer in a green visor was haggling with a customer.

"I can let you have twenty-five dollars."

"Twenty-five, come on. It's gotta be worth two, three hundred at least. That's real gold, eh."

"There's not much call for these kinds of brooches anymore."

"But what about the gold?"

"By the time you melt it down, you got one, maybe two ounces, if you're lucky. Twenty-five is as high as I can go."

"Come on, Ira, you know I'm good for fifty by the end of the month." The customer glanced about furtively and lowered his voice. "I got a line on a sure thing, a real sweet deal."

"Not here, okay. Your business I don't want to know."

"Sure, sure. I'm just sayin' I've got you covered. Have I ever not come through?"

"Alright already, call me a soft touch, a real meshugana. Thirty-five and that's the limit."

The man blew out his cheeks. He pocketed the cash and, tucking the ticket into his top pocket, walked briskly out of the shop. Shadbolt waited a tick and then approached the counter. The pawnbroker looked up from his ledger.

"So anything catch your fancy?" Ira asked.

"Information is what I'm after and I'm told you're the man in the know."

"Depends on who wants to know and what they want to know."

"This is strictly on the QT you understand."

"Of course."

Shadbolt reached into his pocket and placed the dental plate on the counter in front of the pawnbroker. "I'm trying to match this item with its maker. It's a backroom job, but a first-class piece of work. The person I'm asking for doesn't want to leave anything that's traceable, if you know what I mean, and he'll pay handsomely for that kind of workmanship and discretion."

The pawnbroker picked up the partial plate and examined it closely. He put it down again and reaching into a drawer, extracted a jeweler's loupe. He re-examined its detail, using the loupe, turning it this way and that. He sucked at his teeth, and returning the loupe to the drawer, pushed the plate back toward Shadbolt.

"I'll give you a name and address in the port district. Are you familiar with it? Of course not, you're a stranger in these parts, south of the border if I'm not mistaken. Surely, you could find this kind of service in one of your own cities, Boston or New York?"

"It's a long story and I don't have a whole lot of time to explain."

"You're law enforcement aren't you, and my guess is you don't want to get another of these made, but you're trying to find out who this one belonged to?"

Shadbolt stared hard at the man. "You're a quick study, my friend. If you ever get tired of this gig the F.B.I. is looking for a few good men."

"And once you find out what you need to know, I can have your assurance that there will be no repercussions? The maker will remain anonymous?"

"I swear I'll take his name to my grave."

"You strike me as a man of your word."

"My word is your guarantee."

"Then, take this down and when you see her don't tell her who sent you."

Shadbolt hesitated momentarily, taken aback by this revelation, and then slid a sawbuck across the counter.

* * *

The cab deposited Shadbolt at a bustling pier where gangs of stevedores were unloading the hold of an Australian freighter. The day had turned quite dull and was compressed beneath a squatting sky, the chill wind, blowing in off the river, massing a dark phalanx of angry clouds along the horizon.

In the fading afternoon, streetlights winked on, casting violent shadows as bailing hooks vigorously attacked the bundles of wool in an effort to beat the impending downpour. Shadbolt went off in search of the foreman, finding an individual of impressive girth barking orders above the clatter of machinery and the insistent gulls, wheeling noisily overhead. None too politely he was directed down a long alleyway of numbered sheds, walking several hundred yards before reaching the address provided by the pawnbroker.

He knocked on the man door, and then finding it unlocked, stepped inside the shed, a dark, cavernous space. As his eyes adjusted to the gloom, a stairway leading to a mezzanine appeared at the far end of the building. He picked his way past wooden pallets of ceramics, kilns, and other apparatus scattered in a somewhat haphazard fashion across the floor.

If he wasn't mistaken it was beginning to look like the shed had been ransacked when from out of the shadows several dark figures emerged and in that instant Shadbolt dove to his left and pulled out his pistol.

The intruders froze on the spot.

He counted four of them and drew a bead on the closest one who held a shaft of some sort above his head, poised to strike. They remained stock still, and Shadbolt surmised he had stumbled upon a burglary.

His heartbeat thundering in his ears, the only sound.

The intruders hadn't moved a muscle or uttered so much as a grunt. As the standoff continued, reality struck him. He shook his head in disgust.

"Jack, you fucking idiot," he spat, and holstered his weapon.

The would-be villains were life size sculptures. On closer inspection, cast bronze soldiers destined for some sort of military monument. He flicked on his lighter, running his hand over the smooth, polished surfaces. He examined each one in turn. The detail was exquisite; the expressions on the faces of the combatants captured both the anguish and elation of battle, something that was all too familiar to him.

He called out a hello as he ascended the stairs; his footfalls, matched in metallic reflection, announcing his arrival. Although the mezzanine windows were covered, here and there slivers of light penetrated the gloom, indicating that the occupant, hopefully the sculptor herself, was home.

Shadbolt advanced along a railed catwalk and knocked at the door. It flew back before he even had time to rap a second time and he stood staring down the bore of a large caliber firearm held by a dark-suited greaseball.

"Hey Dino, we got a visitor," he called over his shoulder as he motioned Shadbolt into the room. Shadbolt was caught between reaching for his own piece, or making a lunge, and disarming the man. He wasn't given that chance as two of the man's accomplices quickly grabbed him, one pinning his arms while the other patted him down.

"He's carryin' Dino, big piece."

"Who you with, Mac, Port Authority, R.C.M.P.?" Before Shadbolt had time to answer, he felt a heavy blow to the back of his head. The room started to spin, and he was unable to keep from falling. Time slowed, and a series of images flickered by like a grainy silent film as the floor rose up to meet him: the swarthy gunman still aiming squarely at his chest, and behind him seated on a battered couch, a raven-haired girl, red about the eyes, her hair disheveled like it had been pulled hard. It was the last thing he saw before he blacked out.

* * *

When Shadbolt came to, he was sitting upright, his clothes soaking wet from a dousing with cold water. His head throbbed and he felt a warm trickle of blood roll down his neck. Dominating his field of vision was a bull of a man, barely contained by his waistcoat. A single black curl adorned his brow, which furrowed deeply as his dark eyes bored in on Shadbolt.

"What's a G-man doin' up here?" said the bull. Although groggy, Shadbolt determined it would be to his advantage to improvise a story that might have a chance of eliciting a measure of cooperation. As far as he could see, the actual intent of his inquiries wasn't going to cut any ice with these thugs. He cleared his throat and patted at the back of his head, wincing as his fingers brushed the wound.

"We're working with the Canadian authorities tracking down a German spy ring."

"So what's this got to do with Miss Auffray here?" The bull nodded his head in her direction.

"We believe she may have information on one of the ring."

"What kind of information?"

"We've intercepted coded messages that were carried in ceramic icons that have been traced back to Miss Auffray. We were hoping she could lead us to the buyer."

"Well as you can see, Miss Auffray is indisposed right now."

"Look, this is a situation of National importance. The whole war effort hinges on apprehending these traitors. You'd be doing a great service to your country if you'd let me have some time alone with her. I give you my word, there'll be no repercussions as far as this little incident is concerned. Let's put it down to a simple misunderstanding."

"Save your breath, flatfoot. Right now, Miss Auffray is going for a little ride with us." Just then one of the others came over and whispered in the bull's ear. "Okey doke, looks like you're comin' along too, but don't worry, we'll drop you off along the way."

Shadbolt was pulled to his feet and his hands roughly tied behind his back. Then he and the girl were marched down the stairs and back through the shed, past the bronze infantrymen, forever in conflict, and out into the night. A light rain pattered the alley. Behind Shadbolt, the bull and the remaining button conversed in hushed tones.

"Too risky. He can make us, and when Auffray turns up missing they'll be able to tie it back to us. No, we can't take any chances."

As he was led to a deserted wharf on the opposite side of the building, Shadbolt considered the situation. He'd inadvertently stumbled onto a shakedown that was quickly turning from bad to worse. The girl was in serious trouble, and he had added a further complication to their plans. He wasn't buying the notion of being 'dropped off,' not for a second.

It was going to take a miracle to get his ass out of this wringer, and he'd need two if he was going to save the girl in the process.

Water lapped against the hull of a lone tugboat moored at the end of the wharf. Shadbolt and the girl were pushed up the gangway and then below deck to a cramped cabin reeking of diesel exhaust.

Once inside, he was forced to sit against the wall while the girl was tied to a straight-backed chair. Her feet were bound and then placed into a bucket filled with water. One of the buttons left the room, returning with a bag of cement which he tipped into the bucket along with a bottle of liquid. She started to squirm and cry out, receiving a blow across the head in return. A pitiful whimpering ensued but drew no further rebukes from the thugs. Shadbolt sought to intervene once more.

"Any way I can make a deal for the girl?"

The bull turned to Shadbolt smirking. "You ain't in no position to cut a deal, G-man."

"Like I said before, catching this spy ring is a hell of a lot more important than whatever little domestic dispute you got going on here. Look, we'll pay for the right information and bury whatever you're trying to hide right now. I give you my word."

"We don't need your help to solve our little problem and besides we're looking for a permanent solution."

"But killing the girl is a hanging offence."

"Shut up already will ya. It's been decided."

"By who?"

"By me, that's who and I ain't plannin' on changin' my mind anytime soon." The bull turned away from Shadbolt. "How's that mix comin'?"

"Another ten, fifteen maybe. Plenty of quick dry in there," said the button holding the bottle.

"Good. Let's shove off then."

"I'll go tell the captain."

The button scurried topside. After a few shouted commands the engine roared to life. Shadbolt felt the vessel shudder beneath him as it slipped the hawsers and slowly made its way through the inner harbor.

Upon entering the river a few minutes later, the boat heaved abruptly and then settled into a regular pitching motion as it labored upstream against the strong current. Outside the wind and rain was picking up. He could hear it lashing the porthole above his head. He prayed it would slow their progress enough for him to execute a plan of escape. Overpowering three with weapons in hand was going to be challenging enough without having to consider the girl, whose feet were now encased in a bucket of cement.

He hung his head in a portrayal of resignation while his fingers scrabbled furiously against the coarse twine they used to tie his hands. It was a simple knot the trainees at the Bureau had practiced untying hundreds of times.

As he was finishing slipping the bonds, the bull said something about the other side of Nun's Island, and then headed topside to instruct the captain. When his feet disappeared up the stairs, Shadbolt eased himself into a standing position unseen by the two remaining buttons who were distractedly poking at the hardening mixture. His eyes scanned the cabin floor for a weapon, eventually settling on the discarded bag of cement. There was a call from above and the bull clattered halfway down the stairs.

"Looks like we're gonna have company, Port Authority. Take Auffray and the flatfoot into the engine room and make sure you keep 'em quiet."

Shadbolt watched the buttons drag the girl out of the cabin without even bothering to look back at him, so confident that he was securely tied. He heard the scrape of the metal bucket above the din of the engines and a few minutes later, a lone button returned, his sidearm drawn.

As he reached down to grab Shadbolt's arm, a hand snaked out and locked on to the button's wrist, the thumb and index finger exerting tremendous pressure on the pericardium.

The gun fell to the floor.

Shadbolt extracted his other hand from his coat pocket and hurled a fistful of cement directly into the button's eyes.

Blinded, he staggered backward.

Shadbolt followed up with a knee to the groin and a vicious left hook, sending the button crashing to the deck, unconscious. Shadbolt stooped down, retrieved the gun, and with a judicious blow to the head, rendered the button comatose.

He slipped out of the cabin and made his way to the engine room. The second button, sitting astride the girl with his hand over her mouth, presented an easy target.

Shadbolt crept within striking distance and administered three vicious blows to the back of the head with the butt end of the revolver.

The button went down like a ton of bricks.

Shadbolt untied the girl, and then hog-tied the button with the loose rope. She stared up at him still in shock. Beside him the engines thundered.

"Can you pull your feet out of the bucket?" he mouthed.

"I don't know."

He grabbed her calf with both hands and, placing his foot on the lip of the bucket, started to pull upwards. The mixture, although not yet fully set, was still firm enough to hold her feet in place. After five futile minutes he gave up the struggle, realizing he would need a concrete saw or a sledgehammer to free her.

"If you can find me a hammer and chisel, I can chip my way out," she said.

"Of course, the tools of the sculptor; but right now that may be a bit of a tall order on this scow. Can you use a gun?"

"I've never shot one before."

"Okay, I'm going to show you how."

He picked her up under the arms and placed her behind the starboard engine, facing the stairway to the main deck. He took the second buttons revolver, a Webley 38, checked to see that it was fully loaded, and showed her how to cock and fire it.

"If anyone comes down those stairs, wait until they get past that fuel tank there; then aim for their middle and squeeze. Don't hesitate, your life depends on it."

She nodded and he recognized a steely resolve starting to manifest itself in the set of her jaw.

He hurried back to the cabin to check that the first button remained unconscious and tied him to the fixed leg of the metal bunk as a precaution. Through the porthole he could see the Port Authority patrol boat keeping pace through the swells. They had entered a stretch of rapids, the tug pitching wildly enough to send him careening against the hull.

He steadied himself and watched the patrol boat signal to the tug.

The wheelhouse lamp flashed out a message in Morse code.

A command to return to the harbor.

Shadbolt slid to the cabin light switch beside the door and, using the porthole as a makeshift signal lamp, flashed out an SOS, three short, three long and three short bursts of light. He repeated the message several times before returning to the porthole. The patrol boat was closing on the tug, nosing through the wake.

It continued to signal until a gunshot from the tug shattered the light.

At the same time Shadbolt heard someone come clattering down the stairs.

He crouched on the floor of the cabin getting off a shot as the third button, spitting lead willy-nilly, filled the door frame. He squeezed off another round, catching his assailant square in the chest, sending him hurtling backwards. The button staggered into the engine room, and as Shadbolt rounded the door frame in pursuit, the button's head exploded in a shower of pink mist.

Not exactly the middle of the torso as instructed, but plenty good enough for a first-timer.

He gave a thumbs-up to the girl and then signaled he was going topside. He peered up the stairs to the deck and the back of the wheelhouse beyond. It was partially obscured by the smokestack. His angle of sight didn't allow him a view into the bridge where he assumed the bull and the captain were exchanging gunfire with the patrol boat.

He took a tentative first step and was thrown against the side rail as the tug swung about, abruptly changing course.

He clung to the rail to avoid falling backward as the bow pitched upward. In this position he was a sitting duck, so as the boat righted itself, he stepped back off the stairs and quickly returned to the cabin.

From the porthole view he noted that the tug was now heading across the river, charting a course between stretches of rapids. The patrol boat had not made the adjustment in time and continued to run upstream, no doubt waiting for the next less-turbulent stretch to come about and continue the pursuit.

He couldn't take the chance that the Port Authority would catch up before the tug deposited its human cargo on the other side of the river, or in a pinch, directly into the river.

This lull in hostilities didn't augur well for him and the girl.

It called for drastic action.

He reentered the engine room and located the main fuel supply line, closing the shut off valve to the forward and aft fuel tanks. He gave the valve wheel an extra rotation and then stationed himself behind the port side engine opposite the girl. The thrumming of the motors continued for a spell and then abruptly sputtered out. He felt the boat turn downstream, adrift now and at the mercy of the malevolent currents.

Footfalls sounded on the deck above his head and on the stairs leading to the engine room. He and the girl braced for the assault, training their weapons on the doorway opening. The lights cut out, the engine room becoming as black as night.

A muzzle flash shredded the darkness, while from behind, the rear deck hatch burst open and a spray of bullets ripped into the engine cowlings.

Shadbolt yelled for the girl to keep the stairway covered, and wheeling around, returned fire through the open hatch. Killing the lights had worked against their assailants this time, obscuring the whereabouts of he and the girl amidst the machinery of the engine room.

After the next exchange of shots, he heard the Webley click, once, twice.

She was out of ammo.

He spun around and fired at the bull, who had made it as far as the fuel tanks. All at once there was a thunderous crash as the tug was driven against the rocks. A long gash appeared below the waterline, the spray quickly flooding the floor.

The bull popped his head up and got off one more shot before turning and running back toward the stairway. Leaving the bull for the moment, Shadbolt pivoted back to the hatch in time to see the gunman taking aim at the girl. She was cowering behind the engine, trying to make herself as small a target as possible.

Shadbolt raised his gun and fired.

Brilliant blue sparks scarred the dark hold followed by a cannonading report and cries of pain. The girl slumped over as the gunman toppled through the hatch.

Shadbolt went to her side, turning her over and cradling her head. She gave a low moan. He felt around for the wound. She was hit in the upper back, the bullet entering close to her spine. He raised her up and lifted her onto his shoulders in a fireman's carry, the bucket of cement adding a good 50 lbs. Then he sloshed through the rapidly filling engine room, now tilting drunkenly to starboard.

How long before the patrol boat showed up? He prayed his gamble had paid off, because he wouldn't last long in the strong current with the dead weight of the wounded girl to contend with.

He carried her to the foot of the stairs where he set her down while he made his way to the deck, alert to the slightest sound or motion. The rain eased and the sound of the rapids diminished as the boat was swept downstream.

Venturing higher up the stairway, Shadbolt removed his battered fedora and waved it above the lip of the hatch, a tempting target for whoever might be waiting for him. There was no response, only the sound of the wind and the waves. He waited a few more seconds and then poked his bare head topside.

The bull was nowhere to be seen.

He edged his way to the gunwales, spying an inflatable tender with a sole occupant at the rudder, fleeing toward the near shore. He took aim and discharged the rest of the clip.

The tender veered suddenly and then capsized.

The person at the helm, who Shadbolt presumed to be the bull, never re-surfaced. He wasn't sure whether a bullet had found its mark, or the bull was trapped beneath, entangled in the lines. The tender slowly disappeared from view, claimed by the deadly currents of the river.

Shadbolt went back for the girl, setting her to rest beside the gunwales while he went in search of lifejackets. By the time he returned, the boat was listing precariously, the wheelhouse edging ever closer to the water. He managed to secure two lifebuoys and fixed one around her middle and the other to her legs.

Off in the distance he could see the searchlight of the patrol boat as it sped toward them.

He ditched his topcoat, shoes and jacket and, with water spilling over the gunwales, slipped into the river, carrying the girl like a bride over the threshold. The icy cold took his breath away, but despite the initial shock, he kicked hard, moving steadily away from the sinking vessel to avoid the inevitable undertow when the tug finally plunged below the surface.

The boat capsized, the wheelhouse slapping the water like a breaching whale. He gulped for air, fighting the current, desperate to keep the girl's head above the wake. His grip was loosening, the numbing cold draining the life from his fingers like some blood-sucking creature.

With the patrol boat closing in, he called out, and expending his last reserves of energy, waved his arm above his head. The searchlight flashed back and forth across the black expanse, eventually capturing him in its harsh, white glare. A figure called out and a lifebuoy sailed toward him. Shadbolt grabbed hold and prepared to be reeled in. For some reason the boat was standing off, venturing no closer. Above the noise of the engines another deadly sound assaulted his ears, steadily drowning out the throb of the motors.

The last stretch of rapids, the most treacherous.

Standing waves towered overhead. The line from the boat went slack, the patrol vessel taking a wide berth to avoid the worst of the hazards, shelves of hull-puncturing igneous rocks.

He had to make a split decision, let go of the girl and save himself, or take a chance of perishing with her.

Heroics aside, in his mind he rationalized that she was the key to unlocking the dead man's identity and putting him on the trail of the Iowa killer. But the odds were stacked against them, this realization hitting him hard as his knees slammed against an unyielding outcrop. He cried out then submerged, gagging and spitting out a lung full when his head finally broke the surface again.

He was battered by the waves, at the whim of the river, grimly holding on. By this point he could hardly feel his limbs, which was a blessing of sorts given the beating they were receiving.

Full blown hypothermia couldn't be too far off.

Another wave rose up to engulf him and then another, and another in succession. He hardly had time to draw breath between inundations. Coughing and spluttering, he hung onto the girl through a violently-turbulent stretch that threatened to tear her from his grasp.

When things seemed at their bleakest, he was granted a momentary reprieve, finding a welcome trough between the waves.

It was all he needed.

From some deep well of reserves, he found a second wind and, remembering a long-ago lesson, leaned back into the current, kicking his legs out in front of him so that he was floating supine, feet first. He held the girl across his chest and went limp, letting the current take him through the path of least resistance.

Into the waves once more, but now as flotsam, riding the crests, avoiding the deadly obstructions lurking just beneath the surface. He came out of the downstream end and was snared by a gaff hook wielded by an officer from the patrol boat.

Unceremoniously, he and the girl were hauled onto the boat, battered and bruised, but alive.

* * *

Clearly spent, Shadbolt slumped back into the chair while the medics bandaged the worst of his cuts and scrapes. He had declined a trip to the hospital with the girl, who was in much rougher shape, though thankfully the bullet wound was not life-threatening. The small caliber projectile missed any vital organs. Thank God for small mercies Shadbolt commented before she was whisked away in an ambulance.

In the warmth of the Port Authority building, swaddled in blankets and with a shot of rum, she had revived enough to acknowledge him and whisper a heartfelt thanks. He would follow up with her in a few days, once she had recovered sufficiently to answer his questions.

Shadbolt lit another cigarette and waited for Perkins to show up with a change of clothes and a pair of shoes. One of the officers brought him a freshly perked cup of coffee, liberally spiked with rum. It was a small slice of heaven after the ordeal on the river. He replayed the events, realizing just how lucky he was to escape with his life. He'd been far too casual, naïve really, in seeking out the sculptor, one with known shady connections, hell, underworld connections by the look and actions of the bull and his accomplices. He should've been much better prepared, with back up.

Never again, he muttered to himself. He drained the coffee and stubbed out the butt.

A short while later, Perkins strode down the hallway, hefting a suit bag over his shoulder, Myron Akerman trailing in his wake.

"You're a sight for sore eyes, Gene, you too, Myron."

"Here, freshly pressed. Shoes and smalls are at the bottom."

Shadbolt shed the blanket and stripped off the coveralls the Port Authority had loaned him. He dressed quickly and then sat back down and lit another cigarette.

"What's the low down, Jack? When you didn't show up at Lipsky's, we knew somethin' wasn't right. It's not like you to go A.W.O.L."

"I managed to get the name of our sculptor from the local know it all."

"Lisette Auffray?"

"Right first time."

"Yeah, Lipsky confirmed her as the go to for that kind of thing."

"Well, a funny thing happened on my way to question her. I managed to walk in on a shakedown by local goons, followed by a boat ride under duress, complete with cement shoes, fireworks, a sinking, and finally a death defying plunge into the rapids, the Lachine Rapids so they tell me; a bit like going over Niagara Falls without the barrel. Anyway Ms. Auffray is going to be out of action for a while. I figure we can do the interview in two, maybe three days."

"No need to, we got a match."

"Jesus Christ on a pony," Shadbolt practically shouted. "How in the Sam Hill did you manage that? Lipsky?"

"No, Serge Tremblay, that charge he was facing before he twenty-three skidooed, domestic battery." Perkins paused for effect. "In the heat of the moment he almost bit her arm off. Their crown prosecutor, sorta like a D.A., had the police x-ray his jaw and match it to the bite imprint. He's got the jaw of a caveman. Very distinctive, and a perfect match with what we had from the coroner on our corpse."

"When on earth did you make that connection?"

"It was Myron here. When we got back to H.Q., we got talkin' about the case, the fact that Tremblay was facin' charges. All it took was a call to the crown prosecutor fella, another member of the tribe, right Myron." Myron nodded sheepishly. "Same synagogue, if you can believe it. It's like the local jungle telegraph, only kosher. So anyway, they were happy to share their files and in a couple of hours we had our match."

"Great police work, Gene, Myron. Like I'm fond of saying, more often than not it's right there under your nose. You've just got to look. Maybe next time I'll make a point of following my own advice."

"You gotta admit, these Boy Scout hats are a lot more savvy than they look. No offence, Myron."

"We could've saved ourselves a ton of shoe leather if we had asked a few more questions, or shared a few more details."

"Yeah, but you would've missed all the excitement, not to mention that refreshing dip in the river."

"Okay, enough of the Marx Brother's routine. Let's get back to business, Myron can you get us a secure line to Washington? We've got to get a message to Major Berry; let him know what he's dealing with over there."

"I think we can get one from here. I'll go talk to the duty officer."

"Thanks Myron, and thanks for all your help. I'm going to make sure your superiors get the full details."

Myron was unable to contain the grin, spreading like a Cheshire cat's, from ear to ear.

* * *

"You'll have to speak a little louder," Major Berry yelled into the phone.

"How's that?" said Shadbolt, cupping the handset.

"Better, a lot better. Sorry about the line, Jack; it's the best we can do under the circumstances."

"Hey, you're only fighting a war over there."

"Say again?"

"I said, what do we expect, you're only fighting a war."

"Yeah, and it's tough sleddin', let me tell ya."

"Newspaper says you're making headway on all fronts, Brits and Canadians too."

"If we had a few more Pattons this thing would be over by thanksgiving."

"We live in hope."

"That we do, Jack. That we do."

"Okay, so down to business. Your man, Serge Tremblay isn't who he says he is. He's an imposter. We've just confirmed conclusively that Serge Tremblay died, was murdered, two years ago, give or take."

"So any idea who we've got instead?"

"We think the man claiming to be Serge is a repeat offender, the same individual we were tracking for a string of brutal murders back in Iowa in '41. The M.O. is too similar to be a coincidence."

"Sorry, you're breaking up."

When the line cleared Shadbolt repeated the claim.

"What the hell is he doing with the five-o-deuces?" said Berry, incredulous. "Does he have a death wish as well?"

"We're not sure. That's something we'll have to find out when he's interviewed. What's the arrest protocol?"

"I'll have to consult with the brass to determine what takes precedence, a Court Martial or the charges he's facing Stateside."

"Do you have the forensics for a Court Martial, you know hard evidence, witnesses?"

"Good point. Let me talk to his commanding officer, Captain Brubaker. Funny, I haven't heard from him since the five-o-deuces returned to England. I assumed it was because they we out of the action. As you can imagine, I've been distracted with a few other things and kind of put it out of my mind."

"Jesus, we better put him on ice until we work this out. Who knows what kind of mischief he could be getting up to in the old country?"

"Okay, let me follow up with Brubaker. We can get the imposter detained with a Summary Court Martial and confined for

30 days for the false identification. The more severe offences would be prosecuted under a General Court Marshall, especially if we're seeking the death penalty. That will take longer to arrange."

"Okay, you know where I am. Any idea when you'll get back in touch?"

"Give me at least a week, maybe ten days at the outside."

"Alright, in the meantime keep your head down."

"Will do, Jack."

* * *

In Chilton Foliat the dog days of summer wore on, perhaps even gaining a measure of strength as they advanced toward the equinox. The countryside lay still and languorous under a blanket of heat that threatened to immolate those mad dogs and Englishmen foolish enough to venture out into the noonday sun. Atop the high scaffold, Eddie Longstaff mopped at his brow with the shirt he had gladly shed in the early hours. He was finishing the last of the gable coursing of knapped flint squares, covering the south façade of the rectory house. A tricky piece of work at the best of times let alone in the parching heat, and he needed more 'mud'. Where the hell had his brother gotten to? Now he'd have to descend from his perch and mix it himself, which would add another fifteen minutes to the half hour they had already lost when Benjamin had buggered up the pulley.

"Stupid git"

"'ooh you talkin' to?" His brother stared up at him from beneath the frayed brim of his straw hat.

"Where've you been, you silly-born bugger?"

"There an' back to see 'ow far it was."

"Enough of your cheek. Mix us up some more mud will ya."

"Not until you say please."

"Stop playin' about. I told you I wanted to finish early today."

"What, so you could see your fancy woman?"

"None of your business, and she's got a name you know. Now 'urry up before I come down there and sort you out."

"Keep calm and carry on brutha, Rome wasn't built in a day."

"And if you keep skivin' off this'll never get finished today."

"It's too bleedin' 'ot to be rushin' about."

"You call that rushin'? You don't know you were born, you."

"So you're fond of tellin' us."

"Alright, let's 'ave some lunch and rest your weary bones then. What did you get us from the baker's?"

"Couple of pasties and empire biscuits for afters."

"Good lad."

Eddie clambered down and wandered to the opposite side of the house, joining his petulant sibling in the shade of an ancient Wych elm that occupied a verdant stretch of north lawn. Resting back against the trunk he sat quietly for a spell before tucking into the pastie.

"I 'eard some 'orrible news just now in the baker's."

"Is that what was keepin' you?"

"Yes, if you must know."

"'orrible, 'ow?"

"You remember that girl what went missin' from 'round 'ungerford way this past July?"

"Yeah, I remember."

"Well, Mr. Wooten says they found her over in Savernake forest."

"I take it she wasn't found alive?"

"No, she were butchered an' 'angin' from a tree. They reckon she'd been strung up there for a month or so, pecked to bits by the crows an' all."

"That's just morbid, that is."

"I'll say. 'ooh d'ya think would do som'at like that?"

"A wicked person, that's 'ooh."

"Mr. Wooten reckons it's one of them Yanks from the base."

"Mr. Wooten's an old woman. Them Yanks are over 'ere 'elpin' us beat the Jerries for a start, and I've gotten to know some of them. They're alright in my books."

"Still, makes you think."

"Well don't go thinkin' too 'ard, or spreadin' rumors before you know anythin' for certain. Alright then, you ready to finish the job?"

"'ang about, we just sat down."

"I've got a lady to see tonight and I don't plan on bein' late." He stood up and brushed the crumbs off his pants. "Clear up 'ere and I'll get the mud goin'. There's an extra ten bob in it for you if we can be done by four o'clock."

The rest of the afternoon passed swiftly, Benjamin driven by the prospect of the fattened pay packet. Eddie's mind was on his date with Vivian, although from time to time it came back to the tale of the murdered girl. He knew her by name, Norma Woodgate, and had seen her earlier that summer in the Blue Boar, flirting with some of the Yanks. He wondered if Cathy remembered her and if she had heard the news.

* * *

Cathy was surprised to see the lights on in the greenhouse as she pedaled up the lane that evening. It had been a quiet night at the Blue Boar and so Mr. Evans had let her go early. She was unnerved by the news of Norma Woodgate's murder, making the rounds in the pub, and quickly putting a damper on the usual boisterous atmosphere.

"Da, what are you doing fussing with those blasted orchids at this hour?" she said aloud, chiding his obsession with yet another trophy at this year's fall fete. She dismounted and wheeled her bike to the back shed. She was meeting with Mike tomorrow and thought she would have an early night and catch up on her beauty sleep, maybe read a chapter of the latest Agatha Christie she had just borrowed from the library. She crossed to the back door and went into the kitchen to make a cup of tea before bed. Mittens, her ginger tom, meowed a greeting. She bent down and gave his ears a scratch before letting him outside. Soon the kettle was whistling, and she decided to take a cup out to her father who would no doubt be gagging for one by now.

Two sugars and a good pour of milk, just how he liked it. She carried the tray across the yard to the main greenhouse, entering the potting room where she expected him to be. The work bench was clear.

"Da," she called out, "I've brought you a nice cuppa. Should I leave it here?" There was no response, only a sigh of wind high up in the trees. The slightest prickle of fear arose at the base of her skull and shivered its way down her spine.

"Don't be silly," she admonished and called out again, louder this time, "It's going to go cold." Still nothing. She put the tray down and pushed through the swinging doors to the seedling beds, traversing the long aisle between the rows of raised planters to the adjoining greenhouse. The complex was configured in a quadrangle, with four greenhouses surrounding a large rectangle of open area for storage of soil, compost, gravel and clay pots. It was beginning to resemble a bomb site, and she made a note to hire one of the local workmen to clean it up, not that her father would take any notice.

Inside greenhouse number two the air was redolent with the nectared bouquet of Encyclia, Gonjora and Jumellea, along with a dozen other fragrant orchids, overwhelming her senses with their pungency. She strode on to the next greenhouse. Now another scent emerged, a distinctive mélange of floral and citrus with an exotic spicy note. She followed its tendriled trail into the last greenhouse.

There on the floor, midway down the aisle, her father lay face down in a scattering of pot shards.

"Da!" she cried out and rushed to his side. She felt for a pulse, still there, but weak. An ugly contusion glared from the back of his balding pate. It looked like he had taken a bad tumble. Gingerly, she turned him over and cradled his head. The scent that had drawn her, intensified suddenly, and a gloved hand reached around, cupping her nose and mouth with a damp cloth. Another odor, stronger and medicinal filled her nostrils. She gagged and started to flail, momentarily breaking free. Then she turned sharply and clawed at the bandana-ed face of her assailant. Her nails sunk deep into his eyes. He yelped in pain and lashed out, sending her tumbling backward.

A row of pots crashed to the floor. She lay there stunned, watching as he clutched at his wounded face. Blood oozed between his fingers. As her head cleared, she scrambled beneath the row of planters, flattening her body against the wall. She saw her assailant stoop down and wave an arm in her direction. She kicked out like a mule. The arm flashed toward her again. Out shot her leg, catching his wrist and causing him to draw back. His head reappeared below the planter. Blood dripped from the bandana. He kneeled down and lay flat on his stomach and started to inch his way toward her.

She cocked her leg, raising it to her chest, ready to deal another blow. Cobra-like she struck out, aiming for his head. This time a hand locked tight around her ankle. She grabbed the metal leg of the planter and held on for all she was worth. In the next instant she was ripped from her mooring, leaving several bloody fingernails behind. She let out a sharp cry as she was hoisted into the air feet first and swung around like a sack of potatoes before being thrown hard against the concrete floor. The room spun crazily, and she felt the gag covering her mouth. He sat astride her, pinning her arms, his weight forcing the air from her lungs while she felt the cloth being pressed down on her face with both hands. She lay there helpless, quickly slipping into oblivion.

* * *

It was late by the time Vivian returned to Braestead Cottage, balancing on the crossbar of Eddie Longstaff's bicycle. She was feeling a little guilty having kept him out till the Blue Boar closed, and then, being the perfect English gentleman, he insisted on taking her all the way home. She contemplated an appropriate reward for his chivalry, provided they arrived back to a slumbering household. Unfortunately, the place was lit up like a Christmas tree. Even the lights in the greenhouse were on. She experienced a second twinge of guilt, thinking that Cathy had stayed up on her account, making sure she arrived safe and sound before turning in.

"Ay up, looks like the 'ole place is still awake."

"Sorry Eddie. I was hoping we'd have a little time to ourselves before you headed home."

"Not to worry. Save your blushes for the next time."

"Come 'ere ya big lug." Wrapping her arms around him, she planted a wet kiss on his lips.

"Don't get me started. I'll go off like a firework, so I will."

"Yeah, you're a regular Roman candle, too hot to handle."

"I can't 'elp it with you. You'd put Jezabel to shame, so you would."

"I'll take that as a compliment. Okay, just wait here. I'll go and show my face to put their minds at ease and then I'll come back out and give you a proper send off."

"What 'ave you got in mind?"

"It's called a midnight surprise."

"Well jus' as long as I don't 'ave to wait until midnight to get it. It'll be tomorra' mornin' before you know it."

As Eddie went to lean his bike against the fence, Vivian made her way around the side of the house to the kitchen. The door was ajar, and she could see the tea makings sitting on the counter. She called out a hello and wandered through into the living room. Finding it empty, she walked to the foot of the stairs and shouted up, louder this time. There was no response.

"Huh, must be in the greenhouse," she muttered.

She went back through the kitchen and walked over to where Eddie stood stroking Mittens.

"'e's very friendly tonight."

"Mustn't be getting enough attention." She gave him a coy look. "Like someone else I know." She bent down and patted the mewling tom. "Looks like Cathy and the professor are in the greenhouse. I should go in and say hello in case they're worried."

"Do you want me to come with you?"

"No, I've kept you late enough as it is."

"I don't mind, in for a penny, in for a pound."

She reached up and embraced him, her lips yielding to his searching tongue. She felt him stir, inciting her own simmering passions. They remained entwined, consumed by mutual lust for several minutes until reluctantly, she disengaged.

"Hold that thought for tomorrow and I promise I'll make good on the midnight surprise."

"Can you make it a nine o'clock one instead?"

"Consider it done. Now be off home with you, Eddie Longstaff or you'll be good for nothing tomorrow."

"You sure?"

"I'll convey your best wishes. Now skedaddle."

She watched as Eddie rode off down the long drive and then started to walk toward the greenhouse. In the sky a platoon of dark clouds scudded across a fingernail of moon while overhead the wind huffed, scuttling leaves along the pathway. She entered the potting room, spying a cup left on the work bench. A thin film of milk scummed the surface. She felt the cup.

Stone cold to the touch.

She called out, her voice too loud in the deafening silence. She pushed open the doors and traversed the rows of seedling beds. As she entered the second greenhouse, she was immediately assaulted by the rich scent of the orchids, an overwhelming concoction of vanilla, lemon, rose, citrus, chocolate, coconut, and spicy cinnamon.

"So this is what all the fuss is about." She stopped to admire the blooms, long trumpets and deep bells, showy bibs and delicate petals vying for attention, attracting and captivating, infinitely seductive. She fondled several in turn, caught up in the allure before returning to the reason for her being there in the first place.

"Cathy, Professor Yates, I'm home … Hello, it's Vivian … I'm home … Professor?"

Still nothing.

She could only guess that they were hard at work on some or other tricky transplanting procedure, although for the life of her she couldn't imagine what that might be. She pushed on to the third greenhouse. Partway down the centre aisle she heard a loud bang, stopping her in her tracks.

"Cathy, is that you? Professor Yates, are you alright?"

In that instant the lights went out. Up ahead she heard the door open and footsteps, slow and steady, advancing. She gave a shudder, spun on her heels and ran in the opposite direction.

* * *

"Oh buggery!" Eddie swore loudly. A puncture. A good half mile down the main road his front tire went flat, leaving him betwixt and between. Should he push the bike all the way into the village and home, or quickly leg it back to Braestead Cottage and borrow one from Cathy's shed? She had at least two spares she'd managed to borrow for the previous outing with Mike and Vivian. He could do it without disturbing them and cycle it back tomorrow evening. He pushed his bike off to the side of the road and then broke into a trot back in the direction of the cottage, wondering what else could possibly go wrong tonight.

* * *

She barged through the doors into the second green house, her heart thundering in her ears. As she sped through the darkened interior, she realized that the chasing footfalls had ceased. When she reached the doors at the far end of the greenhouse, she came to a halt. Had her pursuer doubled back to intercept her in the potting room? It was the shorter route. What now? She crouched down, holding her breath. Pitch black engulfed the building, high clouds blocking what little light the insipid moon cast. She remembered a door to the outside from greenhouse number three, on the north side of the quadrangle. If he was waiting for her in the potting room in the southeast corner, she could get to the door by backtracking, a risky proposition, or by cutting through the yard in the middle of the quadrangle. Ever so slowly she felt her way along the central aisle to the row of planters which led to the door accessing the yard.

The hinges squealed in protest as she slithered out.

She flattened against the low side wall of the greenhouse and on hands and knees crawled past hillocks of dirt and debris. She was rounding a small mountain of manure when she heard a door on the opposite side of the yard open. Gravel crunched underfoot. She froze. As the footsteps came closer, she eased herself into the stinking mound, willing it to swallow her up.

* * *

When she failed to show up in the potting room, Octavius quickly concluded that she had twigged to his deception. Now he'd have to track her in the greenhouse complex before she made it to the outside and went for help. There were only two means of escape, through the potting room, or the outside exit door from greenhouse number three. Given that he had chased her out of greenhouse number three, it was unlikely that she would return via that route. If he could flush her out in the next few minutes and dispose of her on the spot, he could continue with his intentions for the main prize, the Nell Madisson doppelganger. His mind was afire with the imagined debauchery, the smoke and flames clouding his judgment. The plan, so carefully laid, was unraveling before his eyes, but he was blind to the implications, his appetites trumping discretion.

He heard the sound of a door opening on the other side of the quadrangle. Leaving his hiding place in the potting room, he stepped out into the yard. Gravel crunched underfoot as he made his way toward the source of the noise.

* * *

As the footsteps drew closer, she hunkered further into the stinking mound, suppressing the urge to retch. Her heart hammered like a barrage of Howitzers. Should she make a break for it, or await the inevitable? She sensed him on the other side of the manure pile. Tensing, she readied herself for flight. The gravel crunched not a foot from where she lay, and there he stood, towering above her, a behemoth dressed in black from head to foot, his face covered by a bandana. Her resolve weakened as she stared up at him, but his gaze was fixed on something straight ahead. He seemed unaware that she lay quivering below him. He took another step forward then turned abruptly, skirting the mound and heading away from her, in the direction of greenhouse number two. She heard the familiar screech of the door and sprang up, running as fast as she could toward the wall of glass enclosing greenhouse number three.

* * *

Octavius had no sooner re-entered the greenhouse than he heard her scrambling across the yard. He turned back to see her careen into the side of the building. Glass shattered and he watched as she pawed the wall in search of the entry. He barreled out the door, and in a dozen ravenous strides ate up the distance between them. Too late, she found the elusive handle and disappeared into the dark maw of the portal.

* * *

She crashed through the entrance just in advance of the footsteps thundering fast behind her and made a sharp turn to her left away from the doorway to the outside. She would've never made it in time. She flew down the center aisle and dove for cover beneath a row of planters.

Her hand was throbbing from the deep cut on her palm.

Blood trickled down her wrist.

She crawled to the wall, putting as much distance as she could between herself and the edge of the planter. They were arranged in back to back beds, measuring eight feet across and sixteen feet from the aisle to the inside wall. He'd have to crawl in after her, which was going to be a difficult task for someone as big as her assailant. She heard him come to a stop at the head of the row. Something brushed the ground behind her. Fingers scrabbled across the concrete.

Nails clicked percussively.

She drew her knees in tighter, clutching them to her chest. She heard a grunt as he dropped to the floor. Fingertips brushed the fabric of her skirt. In that instant she wriggled away, rolled across the adjacent opening, and curled into a fetal position under the next row of planters. She heard him swear before extricating himself from the cramped space and stamping off down the center aisle in the direction of the outside doorway. As his footsteps receded, she scootched out from beneath the planters and removed her jacket and skirt, which she balled up and stuffed back under the beds.

Quickly and quietly she crawled across the center aisle and hid as before. She heard rattling, followed by a metallic clanging as the footsteps returned, stopping several rows beyond where she lay. There were more grunts and then the sound of metal scraping the floor and hitting the wall. She guessed he was using a garden spade to prod the space under the beds and that way drive her out into the open. Several more piercing blows rang out in advance of a muffled thud when the sharp blade of the shovel contacted the wadded-up clothing. A dozen vicious swings preceded an explosion of swearing. She detected an American accent, Louisiana if she wasn't mistaken.

From the base? A serviceman in the 101st?

The scraping resumed a little further away this time. Scrape, scrape, clang, scrape, scrape, clang. She bought herself a little time, but sooner or later he would switch to her side of the aisle and then what? Could she risk crawling toward the door? She had to try.

She unfurled her limbs and in serpentine fashion inched out from under the planter. Without her skirt and jacket, she was more mobile, and less prone to announce her whereabouts with the telltale rasping of belts and buttons. She timed her movements to coincide with the shovel blows, now a good number of rows behind her. Only another one or two to go and she would make a break for it. She eased herself out from beneath the planter closest to the doorway. At the other end of the greenhouse the clanging stopped suddenly, and the sound of stamping boots rushed toward her.

She ducked down and crawled back under the planting bed. She felt him round the row, making straight for the door. In the darkness she felt a draft of cold air and then the door slammed shut. Had he left for good or was this a ploy to flush her from her hiding place? She couldn't tell if he had stepped out or was standing right there by the door ready to strike. Although her eyes were adjusting to the inky blackness, there was still too little light leaking from the sky to make anything out, not even a throbbing hand in front of her own face. Blood continued to trickle down her forearm.

She lay there in a cold sweat, taking tiny breaths of air, straining to hear anything to give away the presence of her attacker. Several minutes passed, and then a new sound pricked at her ears.

The meowing of a cat.

She wasn't sure how Mittens had gotten into the greenhouse, but he was definitely coming towards her. Closer, insistent, a long, pleading cry. Her heart thumped louder still. What if Mittens discovered her hiding place? Gave her away? The cat was only a few rows away. Now at her feet, purring contentedly.

A sharp scraping sound was followed by a vicious blow, barely missing her head and sending a shower of blue-tinged sparks out into the night. Mittens let out a banshee yowl and shot, as if from a cannon, out from beneath the planter, momentarily disrupting the attack and allowing her to roll away and under the next row of beds. She curled into a tight ball and prepared for the worst.

* * *

Walking up the drive, Eddie saw that the lights were on in Braestead Cottage. Funny that they should still be up at this hour, he thought, wondering if he should knock and let them know what he had in mind. Better left till the morning, he decided, and went around to the shed to retrieve the bike. Wheeling in onto the drive he heard a thumping noise coming from the greenhouses. He glanced over. Dark, the lights extinguished. Surely, the professor wouldn't be fussing with his orchids in the dark. There was another muffled bang and then another. He lay the bike down and jogged the short distance through the serried ranks of chestnut trees standing sentinel along the approach.

He entered the potting room, feeling for the light switch. His fingers brushed the control, which he toggled up and down to no effect. "Fuse must 'ave gone," he said aloud, searching along the wall for the fuse box. The banging continued. It seemed to be coming from his left, the west arm of the quadrangle, greenhouse number two. He abandoned the search for the fuse box and walked through into greenhouse number one, calling out as he traversed the rows of seed beds.

* * *

Octavius was startled by a new voice, a man's basso rumble, catching him in mid-swing. Yet another obstacle to overcome. He had spent far too much time already dispensing with the first interloper. There was something about her that triggered a mist-shrouded memory, but he was too engrossed in the matter at hand to follow it any further down the rabbit hole of his once impeccable mind. He ditched the spade and ran in the opposite direction, back to greenhouse number three and his intended prey. Fleeing down the long aisle, he heard a loud cry from behind.

"Eddie!"

The shouted response was lost in the clatter of his footfalls. As swiftly as his legs would carry him he made it back to where he left the girl, but when he arrived she wasn't there. In the darkness, had he misjudged the row where her body lay hidden? His eyes scanned the floor. Mentally, he counted down the rows, suddenly realizing that the man's body, the professor, wasn't there either. Had the latest intruder moved them? Frantically, he pawed beneath the planter beds, seeking the reassurance that his prize was still secure, and that he was confused in this murky, unfamiliar space. He felt a rush of air as something heavy came down hard across his back, knocking the breath clean out of his lungs. A second blow followed in close succession, digging painfully into his right shoulder. He rose up and held his arms in front of him to fend off the next blow. It came in low, unexpected, a thrusting motion, spearing him in the groin and forcing him back down to his knees. Without warning, the greenhouse flooded with light, temporarily blinding him. When he regained focus, there she stood, towering above him poised to strike a final blow. She was bloodied and disheveled, her features blurred. With clarity's return her hair grew in inches, cascading in ringlets of spun gold to rest upon her ample bosom. Her piercing, all-seeing eyes. Her brutal mouth, chastising and belittling. Her lips full and wet. The recognition undeniable. She was every woman he'd ever brutalized and the one who had made him what he was.

Nell Madisson no longer.

But instead another female, the true object of his twisted fantasies.

His mother.

Elsinore Cadogan.

Born of Beauchamp blood and breeding.

This time as the iron bar descended, he deflected the blow and ripped it from her hands with the force of a lifetime of rage, tossing it aside. She let out a plaintive wail, drawing a rush of footfalls in their direction. He turned and fled back through the potting room and out into the dark night, the image of his mother trailing like a tattered vestment.

* * *

With Cathy waving the smelling salts under his nose, the professor slowly regained consciousness, and other than the ugly bump on the back of his head seemed none the worse for wear. Even so, she was intent on getting him to the infirmary in Hungerford to be on the safe side. Her own head was throbbing and her back aching where she had been hurled to the floor. Vivian too was a mass of cuts and bruises, stockings laddered and uniform in tatters. Only Eddie had escaped unscathed. She convinced him not to go after the attacker, but to stay put in case he returned. His timely puncture and subsequent intervention saved them all from a fate she dared not imagine.

"What in blazes?" croaked the professor.

"Easy da, you've taken a nasty bump."

"How's my zygopetalum doing?"

"Don't worry about that now."

"But, I ... "

"We're taking you to the infirmary."

"Whatever for? I'm as right as rain." He attempted to get up but didn't resist when she gently restrained him. "I'll be alright, just give me a minute." He squinted up at her. "You don't look so good yourself. Did you fall as well?"

"No, we had an intruder."

"Intruder?"

"I'll explain later. Right now, we're driving over to Hungerford." She turned to Eddie, who was applying a bandage to Vivian's cut. "Eddie, can you bring the car around? The keys are on the hook by the front door." He gave Vivian a pat on the arm and went to retrieve the family automobile. "We'll need to see the police," Cathy stated matter-of-factly.

"Yes definitely, and the base too. That was a genuine American accent, Louisiana if I'm not mistaken," said Vivian.

"You think it was a soldier?"

"Positive."

"I didn't want to jump to conclusions. I was under the impression that the 101st had been confined to base. According to Mike the billets have been cleared for a few days now."

"There are still plenty of administrative staff and stores people around. Let's see what the MP's can turn up."

They got the professor into the car, and Eddie drove the short distance to Hungerford where the night nurses took over, ministering to his contusion and convincing Cathy to keep him in overnight for observation. The professor resisted at first, but relented, too tired to put up a fight. As Cathy returned to the waiting room, and Eddie went to retrieve the car to take them to the police station, Vivian motioned for her to sit down.

"I didn't want to say anything before but there's something very familiar about this whole episode."

"What do you mean?"

"The same thing happened to my sister Helen just before the war, well just before we got involved."

"She was attacked?"

"Yes and kidnapped, and her attacker used a chloroform-soaked rag like yours did. And he was a big brute like this one. And from the south. My boyfriend, Gene and the other FBI special agents were closing in on him and his accomplices. My sister was the last victim in a string of killings."

"But she's still alive isn't she?"

"Yes, by a stroke of luck. She was rescued, but not before being shot."

"Oh my God."

"It was touch and go for a while. She spent a long time convalescing and she's never really gotten over it. She's not the same person anymore. But there's something else you should know. Before she was rescued, she was raped, and the kidnappers were about to butcher her, like they had the other victims. And now you, and that girl they found in the forest. It's too much of a coincidence."

"You think it's the same person?"

"I'm not sure. I mean I thought I'd left it all behind me in Kansas City, but now this. I just don't know. I've got to get in touch with Gene and tell him what's happened. Look, don't say anything to Eddie. I don't want him to get all worked up and do something crazy. We'll report it to the police and the base commander, and I'll get a wire off first thing in the morning. Gene will know what to do."

"What about Mike?"

"Tell him what happened, but leave out what I've said about Helen until Gene gets back to me."

"Alright." Cathy put on a brave voice, but her legs were shaking as she stood up, Vivian's revelation unnerving her. She gathered herself and walked out of the infirmary to the awaiting automobile.

* * *

Colonel Atkins, commander of the five-o-deuces, closed the door and returned to his desk. He checked the sentry's log once more. No one was reported going into or out of the base after curfew, so it couldn't have been anyone from the regiment, although the physical description provided by the witness did match a few of the Raging Redskins, and one in particular, Sergeant Serge Tremblay. It was the second time his name had come up in the past few days. A Major Berry from Fourth Division had requested that he be detained pending a Summary Court Marshall for providing false information about his identity. He hadn't heard all the details as they had a bad connection, which kept breaking up, and the following wire did precious little to clarify the charge. Didn't they know he was in the midst of a critical mission, probably the most important offensive since D-Day? It had been conveyed to the men, and Tremblay, along with the rest of the Raging Redskins played a key role in Operation Market Garden. Their opportunity to break through German lines and seize a number of key bridges in the occupied Netherlands. The 101st was responsible for a fifteen-mile segment of narrow concrete and macadam stretching northward from Eindhoven to Grave.

Responsibilities had been assigned. It was too late to issue alternate instructions, besides Tremblay was the type of soldier they desperately needed for a successful operation. He had distinguished himself at Carentan, been recommended for a purple heart by his former Captain, and his new company commander, Major Briggs, spoke glowingly of the newly-promoted sergeant. For the sake of the mission, he had to make an executive decision. Besides, his own career and legacy hung in the balance. He couldn't risk a wrong move now. No, it was settled in his mind. Damn the torpedoes and full steam ahead. He balled up the wire and tossed it into the wastepaper basket.

* * *

"Bad news, Jack. Captain Brubaker went A.W.O.L. in Cherbourg. He never returned to England with the 101st, disappeared it seems." Ed Berry's voice echoed on the other end of the line.

"No body, no witnesses?"

"No, he was last seen leaving a bar in the City, and listen to this, a woman was reported missing around the same time, and she hasn't shown up yet either."

"Jesus Christ on a pony."

"It gets worse, and you can't breathe a word of this to anyone. The 101st are due out again real soon. More than that I can't say. They're locked down on the base as we speak."

"What about the Summary Court Martial to get him detained, stop him from leaving at least?"

"I'm not getting much support from the regimental commander, Colonel Atkins. It doesn't help that he's been recommended for a purple heart, and get this, they promoted him to sergeant. It wouldn't look good on the brass, and besides, we've got no real evidence on the war crimes. It's all conjecture right now. Look, get your ass over to this side of the Atlantic and make the criminal case on behalf of the FBI, charge him with the Iowa killings and transport him back for trial. We can always bring in the military side of things later, for good measure. It's not like we can execute him twice."

"That's a tall order, Ed. I'll need to clear this with the brass here in Washington, and I'll need you to make the request with enough urgency to get immediate action if what you say about his imminent departure is true. How the hell do we get him back once he's in the field?"

"Let's cross that bridge when we get to it. In the meantime, I'll see what I can do on my end."

"Alright, do your best. I'll start working on this end."

Shadbolt replaced the receiver and reached for his cigarettes. He lit up and leaned back, propping his feet up on the desk. He blew a smoke ring and watched it rise to the ceiling, already yellowed from his two pack a day habit. In his mind he composed the request to apprehend Octavius, methodically sifting through facts, constructing a solid foundation of circumstantial evidence, implicating the brutal killer in the Iowa murders. The leap to Serge Tremblay, however, was over a deep chasm of speculation. In effect, a leap of faith; faith in a gut reaction that had served him well over the years.

But was it enough to convince J. Edgar?

This is when he could've used a little input from Special Agent Will, whose powers of deductive reasoning would be a huge benefit in formulating the arguments. He could call him back from Mexico if necessary. Leaning forward, he drummed his fingers on the desktop and crushed out the butt. No, they were too close to the twins now. He'd manage this himself, relying on his own counsel. He picked up his fountain pen and began composing in longhand. His secretary, Miss Penhaligan, 'Penny' for short, would type it up tomorrow.

He needed this collar, for the victims, for Musgrave, for his long dead sister. Of late her death was festering in his mind like a boil that needed to be lanced. He had an idea that required a touch of prevarication, an ever so subtle bending of the truth. Call it a sleight of hand.

But would it hold up at trial?

He'd cross that bridge when he got to it.

* * *

Shadbolt finished editing his request when Perkins burst into his office waving a telegram.

"Jack, you'll never believe the message I just got from Vivian."

"Whoa, slow down Gene."

"It's him, it's gotta be."

"Him who?"

"Octavius Cadogan, who do you think?"

"Here, let me see." Shadbolt read the telegram and then sat back, expelling a long breath. "I had a hunch about this the minute I received the initial inquiry from Berry."

"First Helen and now Vivian. I never made the connection between her medical unit and the 101st. Everything is so damn hush, hush. Until now I never even knew where she was stationed. What are the chances she'd end up in the same stinkin' neck of the woods?"

"Fate, pure and simple. Sounds like her friend was the preferred target, no doubt blonde and bountiful. Vivian just happened to be in the wrong place at the wrong time. But as things turned out, maybe the right time. They managed to foil our killer and give us the ammunition we need to plug his ass. This should get us over the line. I'll attach it to my request, which I'll amend right now. I've got a meeting with the chief tomorrow. Let's see if I can move it up to this afternoon and then get ready to haul ass."

"Us?"

"You and me pardner, Berry says it's the only way."

"What about the Court Marshall?"

"Too much brass jamming up the works. We've got to do it our way and we've got to hurry before we lose him again."

* * *

That night Shadbolt and Perkins lined up with assorted military personnel ready to board a converted C-54 Skymaster headed for Bermuda.

"So what's the low down, Jack, Bermuda sounds more like a vacation in the wrong direction."

"It's the Atlantic Wing of the Army-Air Transport, Washington to Bermuda, to the Azores and on to Exeter in the south of England. Then we drive to the base, a little place with a double-barreled name, Chilton Foliat. Berry has wired his commander to hold him there until we arrive."

Shadbolt handed a letter signed by J. Edgar himself to the flight orderly and then flashed his badge. He walked up the stairs and an attendant directed him to a seat near the back of the plane. Perkins followed, easing into the seat beside him.

"Let's hope this oversized sardine can gets us there in one piece." Perkins pulled his fedora down over his eyes and settled back for the first leg of the thirty-hour flight ahead.

The engines came to life, propellers windmilling port and starboard. With a shudder the plane lumbered up the runway, picking up speed as it made a final turn and raced past the tower. It seemed to take forever to lift off and Shadbolt held on to his seat wondering how this bucket of bolts was ever going to clear the onrushing buildings at the current trajectory. At the last possible instant, the nose inclined and the Skymaster began a steep ascent into the night. Shadbolt watched as the lights of the capital receded. With a final dip of the wing, as if waving goodbye to the slumbering nation, the aircraft climbed higher into the clouds. Beside him Perkins snored, wrapped in the sleep of the innocent. Shadbolt would have gladly joined him, but he was a nervous flyer. The weightless sensation he felt, along with the constant chop and motion of the fuselage, kept him alert and a perpetual insomniac. From the window, he saw they'd broken through the uppermost layer of clouds, now lying below like a blanket of freshly fallen snow. Above, a fingernail of moon shone brightly, and a million stars dazzled in the firmament. He started to relax a little and finally closed his eyes.

Three hours later the plane touched down in Bermuda to change pilots and refuel. Shadbolt got off to stretch his legs and reacquaint himself with terra firma. Reaching the bottom of the boarding stairs, someone called his name. He let Perkins and the others pass and then turned to see a figure in a flight jacket, presumably the pilot or co-pilot, coming down the gangway to meet him. Red hair spilled in waves as she removed her helmet.

"Jack Shadbolt, what are you doing on my flight?"

"Stella!" He recognized his old college flame right away. "If I had an inkling you were flying this bucket I would've come up front to say hello. How long have you been playing Icarus?"

"Since forever, well graduation anyway. Which reminds me, you never showed up for the ceremony, or our last date for that matter."

"Well I'm here now. Can I buy you a drink?"

"Yeah, ten years too late."

"Better late than never."

"I'll be the judge of that."

"So where to?"

"There's a swell little beach joint not five minutes from here."

While Perkins and the others filed into the base PX, she led the way past a row of corrugated Quonsets to a well-worn pathway traversing the green foothills to the water. They walked along the shore to where a palm-fringed cabana festooned with twinkling lights occupied a long stretch of white sand. As they sidled up to the bar a couple of patrons sitting at the other end called out.

"Stella by Starlight."

"Boys." She nodded in their direction.

"When did you acquire that handle?" Shadbolt asked.

"It's from some Ray Milland film. Haven't seen it yet."

From behind the bar, a loud Hawaiian shirt approached, placing two coasters in front of them. "What'll it be Stella by Starlight?"

"Whatever concoction you're passing off as alcohol," she answered.

"Want to try a hurricane? Straight from Pat O'Brien's in New Orleans."

"What's in it?"

"More rum than you can shake a stick at, and a whole lotta love."

"Keep the rum, ditch the love and we'll take two apiece for the road."

"Comin' right up."

"Now that I think of it, should you be drinking when you're flying?" said Shadbolt.

"I only go as far as here and then back to Washington tomorrow. They don't let us dames fly trans-Atlantic, or fighter missions, being the weaker sex an' all."

"Guess they don't know you too well."

"Obviously not." With drinks in hand, she motioned him down the beach, away from the bar, drawing a barrage of good-natured cat calls from the boys on the stools. Shadbolt followed in her wake to a clutch of waving palms. Here they settled into the sand, leaning back against the trunks.

"Wow," she exclaimed after a long swallow, "this sure ain't your usual girlie drink."

"Easy there, fella, I don't wanna have to carry you back to the base."

She looked him straight in the eye. "Still the love 'em and leave 'em type, huh?"

"If you only knew." He looked away.

"Jack, why didn't you answer my letters?"

"Oh Stella, we've been through this before. I was too broken up over Connie's death and the trial to do much of anything, least of all burden you with my guilt."

"I thought we were in love. Headed for new adventures together, like we talked about?"

"We were, I swear. Leaving you was the hardest decision of my life, but it was the right decision at the time given my frame of mind. I thought you understood that."

"Maybe I've had a change of heart. Girls like me aren't used to getting jilted."

"It turned out okay didn't it, you and Bobby Albright? He was in your league. Me, I always thought I was punching above my weight."

"Still the same old Jack, modest to a fault." She took another long swallow, draining the first glass.

"By the way, how is old money bags?"

"I guess the jungle drums don't make it all the way out to Kansas City. We split up back in '41."

"Sorry to hear that."

"Don't be sorry, 'cause I'm not. What about you, no Mrs. Shadbolt?"

"No Mrs. Shadbolt."

"Sweethearts?"

"Few and far between, and none at the moment."

"And what if the urge strikes?"

"I take a cold shower until it passes."

"That's not the Jack Shadbolt I remember." She tipped her head back to let out a throaty laugh. "You remind me of that time you convinced me to go skinny-dipping at the lake. God, the water was like ice. Didn't seem to dampen your enthusiasm though."

The memory conjured a vision of Stella naked in the moonlight. The slope of her breasts and the dark, puckered nipples bathed in the bright lunar glow.

"I was drunk with passion."

"And what about now? We're both free agents. Fancy another dip?" She stood up and unzipped the jump suit, stepping out of the garment to reveal long, shorts-clad gams. She quickly doffed the rest of her clothing and stood before him, an auburn-haired goddess in the full bloom of womanhood.

He was beguiled.

"Come on, catch me if you can." She took off into the breakers.

He caught her in the surf, pulling her under, limbs entwining like they had never been apart. Afterward they walked back arm in arm. He escorted her to where she was bunking for the evening and bid her goodbye.

"Jack, look me up when this is over. I'll make an honest man out of you yet." Then she was gone, but her image was permanently stamped on more than his psyche.

* * *

The warm on-shore breezes caressed his face and he lingered outside until the last possible moment. When he returned to his seat, he observed Perkins in conversation with a marine colonel across the aisle. They were jawing away like long lost buddies and Perkins was offering to spike his coffee with the good stuff from his hip flask.

Once again, the plane taxied to the runway, engines throbbing. Shadbolt steadied himself for the rush to the ocean and the long haul to Portuguese territory on the other side of the Atlantic. When the plane reached cruising altitude, Perkins turned to Shadbolt and, lowering his voice, asked, "Now we've established that Tremblay is Octavius Cadogan, have you figured out what the hell he's doing with the 101st?"

"I've been wrestling with that very question. Although the more logical starting point is how and why he appropriated Tremblay's identity in the first place. My guess is it was an opportunistic set of circumstances. His cover was blown, and he was being pursued by us and Joey Lasorda's Kansas City mob. Call it serendipity, he comes across Serge Tremblay, himself fleeing prosecution, does away with him and assumes his identity. Along the way he changes his appearance, habits, and avoids contact with family and past associates. It's hard to say whether or not he remained in contact with the terrible twins. As to the 101st, it's unlikely that Tremblay received an induction notice given the outstanding charges against him, which means Cadogan, using Tremblay's identity, enlisted voluntarily, and the draft board either missed the warrants or someone was bribed to lose the incriminating paperwork. Concerning motive …" Shadbolt looked squarely at Perkins. "He's a natural born killer, combat gives him license to kill and maim the enemy along with the means to pursue his own heinous agenda. Which, according to Berry, includes at least four civilians in France and now another who knows how many in England, not to mention the missing Captain Brubaker. In short, he's got a free hand."

"Yeah, but he's on the front lines with the advance guard, drawing the most dangerous assignments. What, has he got a death wish as well?"

"I assume he's addicted to the adrenaline rush. He's been living on a knife's edge for the better part of his existence, if you'll pardon the pun. According to what Will found out, it's been bred in the bone and honed to its most brutal form."

"Well at least the hunt is over. Let's hope he draws a hanging judge when we get him back Stateside." Perkins pulled out his hip flask and offered it to him. "You want a nip of this. It'll help you sleep."

Shadbolt took a long swallow and then another. From behind a stentorian voice inquired if either one of them was interested in joining a game of poker.

"Don't mind if I do." Perkins got up and sauntered to the back of the plane where a raucous group was seated around tables on either side of the aisle. Several hours later he returned.

"So how did you fare?" said Shadbolt.

Perkins patted at his breast pocket. "Like shootin' fish in a barrel. I was raised on five card stud back in Hoboken."

* * *

Sunset burnished the evening sky as they descended onto the main island of the Portuguese Azores. Here they'd refuel and refresh in anticipation of the final leg of the trans Atlantic flight. Shadbolt hired a taxi and went off in search of a hot towel and a shave while Perkins headed for the nearest bar to refill his flask. By 9:00 p.m. they were on the runway again, taking a northeast heading to Exeter and USAAF station 463.

* * *

Shadbolt was fuming as he returned to the hangar from the Exeter airbase headquarters.

"What the hell happened, Jack?"

"You're not going to believe this." Shadbolt paced back and forth unable to curb his anger. "He isn't there."

"What?" Perkins sat bolt upright.

"The base commander is totally in the dark. He doesn't know a thing about it."

"I thought they were holding him."

"So did I, Gene, so did I." He lashed out, kicking an empty bucket clear across the hangar.

"What do we do now?"

"We stay put and wait for his call. He's looking into it right now. In the meantime, I'm going to try and get hold of Berry. What a SNAFU."

"You can say that again."

"I thought we had him dead to rights. Jesus Christ on a pony, this guy 's got more lives that a black cat with a lucky rabbit's foot." With nothing else to kick at, Shadbolt drove his fist into his palm with a resounding splat.

"That ain't the half of it. I was set on paying Vivian a surprise visit before she ships out."

"Yeah sorry, I wasn't even thinking about that little side benefit. Don't worry we'll try and get you there one way or the other. Okay, sit tight while I go and see what's what."

Shadbolt returned after a long interval to find Perkins snoozing atop a bomb carrier, oblivious to the hubbub going on around him. Shadbolt let him slumber for a while longer before they retired to a small office to plot their next move.

"I got hold of Berry. He's resending the original order. It was delivered to Colonel Atkins, but he chose to disregard it. The base commander has assured Berry that it'll be carried out when the mission is over and the 101st returns."

"A fat lot of good that does us in the meantime."

"I'm with you there, Gene. Anything could happen in the field. The brass could decide to send them off on another mission, or he could go A.W.O.L. It's too risky. If you're game, we'll go after him now. War or no war, Hoover's letter gives us full authorization to apprehend him and transport him back to the States."

"In for a dime, in for a dollar."

"I knew I could count on you. Berry is going to call back with an update. I'll tell him what we plan to do and get him to make the necessary arrangements. Let's go see about some chow. We've got another two hours to kill before his call."

* * *

"That's pretty unorthodox, Jack and you'd be risking life and limb," said Berry after Shadbolt outlined his request.

"First we need to get a message to this Colonel Atkins and his superior to remove Serge Tremblay from active duty and hold him pending our arrival. We'll also need the coordinates of the proposed rendezvous. How do we get within' spittin' distance of this melee anyway?"

"From what I know there's a British armored column, XXX Corps advancing from the south. We could maybe drop you where the five-o-deuces went in. The drop zones are secure."

"Parachute?"

"Afraid so."

"Can we get a fast lesson beforehand?"

"It's your neck, Jack. I'd strongly advise against it."

"Look, come hell or high water, we're determined to do this."

"Now that I think of it, there is another option."

"Spill it."

"Glider. The various offensives are being re-supplied by glider, ammunition, heavy equipment, provisions, and reinforcements. That's probably your best bet."

"We'll take it. Now how do we hitch a ride?" Shadbolt asked.

"Let me see what I can do."

"Just do it fast. We're burning daylight here."

"Understood Jack. You're a man on a mission."

* * *

In a squall of virginal white silk, parachutes rained down upon the Dutch countryside. Octavius and the Raging Redskins were the first of the five-o-deuces to shroud the drop zone. Flak was light on the approach, and the mission thought to be an easy one, but within minutes they were engaged in combat moving through the fields towards the bridge at Best. Octavius used the church steeple as a reference point, directing his squad to the intended target. The incoming fire was intense. They soon lost orientation and became separated from the other platoons of the company. He hunkered down behind a haystack and returned fire, strafing a German machine gun emplacement. They looked to be dug in up and down the highway leading to the bridge and were supported by 88mm guns by the sound of the shellfire.

There was movement on his right flank as paratroopers charged into the gaping maw of the conflict. Octavius waved his men across the highway, hot lead coming fast and furious. They were in the thick of it along with the rest of the platoon and taking heavy casualties. A deafening explosion shook the ground, instantly vaporizing the lieutenant leading the assault. Machine gun fire quickly eliminated several other senior officers, leaving Octavius in charge. He signaled the remnants back across the highway, where he organized a defensive line along the edge of a large tract of woodland. Here they dug in, returning fire while they awaited further instructions.

From the north in the direction of Boxtel, a convoy of German reinforcements advanced down the highway unaware of the 101st concealed in the woods. Led by a motorcyclist, they consisted of a dozen troop trucks and artillery in the form of two 20mm cannons. Octavius drew a bead on the motorcyclist and instructed the others to concentrate their fire on the troop trucks. The convoy continued to advance into certain annihilation at the hands of him and his men. Whether nerves or stupidity, one of the paratroopers opened fire on the motorcyclist, sending him skidding off the road and causing the convoy to come to an abrupt halt. The element of surprise, lost. The panzergrenadiers poured from the vehicles, forming a shooting line that unleashed even more firepower on the undermanned platoon. They retreated a little further into the woods and Octavius instructed the radio operator to send for help.

While the rest of the battalion slowly moved in to reinforce their beleaguered colleagues, Colonel Atkins ordered Octavius to take his platoon and push through the forest to the bridge. With the skirmish swirling all around, he led them south through dense tree cover, subdivided by fire lanes at one quarter mile intervals. They came across the first opening, a straight line to the highway, some fifty yards wide. As they moved across, machine gun fire broke the stillness and sent them scuttling back into cover. Octavius kept on running, firing one-handed, legs pumping like a high-stepping fullback. He dove to the ground and rolled into the brush in advance of a fusillade that re-contoured the earth behind him. Signaling across the break for covering fire, he circled the machine gun nest, a sand-bagged emplacement situated where two fire lanes intersected. Octavius crept within sight of the position, advancing until he had an unobstructed view of the coal-scuttle helmets. They were completely oblivious to his presence, looks of wonderment etching their haggard faces when he rose up, like the grim reaper, to dispatch them from point blank range. Then he unsheathed his blade and moved in to satiate his blood lust.

* * *

In order to avoid further encounters, Octavius moved the platoon further into the forest, away from the highway. He was down to fifteen men and a handful of engineers moving resolutely through the dense undergrowth. They wasted an inordinate amount of time crossing the fire breaks one by one, never knowing if the next one would contain a hidden nest of ordnance-spewing vipers. A laborious process, and by dusk they still hadn't reached the forest edge and the Wilhelmina Canal beyond. Octavius ordered the men to dig in for the night, shallow foxholes and slit trenches, and then he called for the radioman.

"Can you contact Colonel Atkins. We need to let him know where we are."

"I haven't been able to raise anybody for a while. The radio must have been hit."

"You've got to be kidding. Here, let me take a look." He turned it this way and that. "See, right there, grenade shrapnel by the looks of it."

"That's what I thought."

"You've got to keep trying, otherwise we won't be able to call for support once we get to the bridge."

He posted watch, and then with two scouts in tow, traversed the remaining distance to the edge of the forest. Octavius crawled through open ground to the earthen dyke bracketing the canal and reconnoitered from the top of the grassy incline. There was a widening to the west and what looked like loading docks for the fleet of canal barges moored alongside. Beyond was the bridge, the object of their mission, to be taken and held at all costs.

He signaled for the scouts to hold while he advanced to the bridge. He needed to get a better handle on the situation before ordering the rest of the platoon to attack. Impossible at this distance in the dark. He crept forward using the warehouse sheds to screen his movement. Closer now, he spotted a single guard posted on the north side of the bridge, the orange glow from his cigarette hovering like a firefly in the dark.

Suddenly from the sheds behind him came a shout, "Auchtung!" A warehouse guard he somehow missed appeared in silhouette pointing directly at him. Shots rang out from the bridge, followed by the thump of boots moving swiftly. He froze and held his fire, guessing from where the bullets were landing that they hadn't actually spotted him yet. The silhouette advanced, and from above a torch beam swept the surrounding bushes. Octavius slowed his heart rate and breathing, attaining a state of calm in the vortex of the turmoil. In his camouflage and war paint he became part of his surroundings, transmogrified from a sentient being into an inanimate piece of the landscape. The silhouette waved his rifle at the bushes. There was an immediate flash of movement as a large Hare sprang from its hiding place, followed by a girlish shriek as the guard toppled backwards. This in turn drew shouts of derision from the soldiers watching him from the bridge.

"Es ist nur ein Hase, dummkopf!"

The silhouette muttered an apology and slunk back to the sheds. Octavius let ten minutes pass and then crept back along the darkened facades of the buildings. Cupping his hands to his mouth, he imitated the call of a night owl, the response guiding him to where the scouts lay in the deep grass covering the dyke.

"Good to see you, Sarge. When we heard the shootin', we thought you were dead meat for sure."

"Not this time, I was saved by a Hare."

"A Hare?"

"A rabbit if you will."

"A bunny rabbit?"

"Of sorts."

"So Bugs Bunny saved your bacon? Wait till the guys get a load of this."

"Okay, enough of the chit chat, let's vamoose before Elmer Fudd makes another appearance."

"What's the bridge situation?" asked the other scout after they had re-entered the forest.

"Couple of guards, but no gun emplacements that I could make out. We'll get some shut eye and then hit 'em before sun-up."

* * *

Octavius and his men slept fitfully through the night punctuated by a cold, penetrating rain, the distant sound of guns and mortar fire disturbing dreams of hearth and home and places untouched by the dogs of war. They arose before dawn, Octavius and the scouts leading three groups towards the canal. Octavius' group would attack from the north side of the waterway, supported by the second group, who'd skirt the warehouses and launch a frontal attack on the bridge, while the third group would cross the canal in a stolen barge, catching the sentries in a pincer movement.

Soundlessly, they made their way through the forest, phantoms plying the mist suffusing the cool morning air. Reaching the perimeter, more by touch than by sight, Octavius crawled to the face of the dyke and moved westward to the sheds in search of the night watchman. He spied him slumbering by the docks and drew his blade, executing a deadly stroke across the carotid. Cupping the man's mouth, he held him fast while he bled out, wide-eyed in disbelief.

Creeping to within fifty feet of the bridge abutment, Octavius peered through the haze, scanning for his initial target. He checked his watch. Two minutes to zero hour. He was still looking for the sentry when machine gun fire broke the stillness. German troops on the far side of the dyke had spotted the barge crossing the dark ribbon of water. The sentries were immediately alerted, calling back and forth from opposite ends of the bridge. That was all he needed. He aimed for the guttural voice closest to him and squeezed the trigger, bullets tracing streaks of red in the crepuscular light.

He heard the soft thud of something landing behind him. Potato masher hand grenade! He pivoted, picked it up and hurled it back across the dyke, the explosion lighting up the pre-dawn sky. In succession he retrieved several more, exposing himself to the Germans now massing on the bridge. How many enemy troops were entrenched on the other side? They certainly weren't evident when he had reconnoitered last night. A volley of concentrated fire from the group staging the frontal attack hit the panzergrenadiers on the bridge. Bodies fell like bowling pins with the remnants fleeing to the opposite end in the ensuing chaos. Octavius and his men lay down a steady stream of covering fire while the second group pressed their advantage, swarming onto the bridge. With bayonets fixed they hacked at the wounded until the carriageway ran crimson. The Raging Redskins were earning their epithet in spades.

Octavius and his squad ascended the bank, joining the second group and keeping up the barrage, moving inexorably across the bridge. Here the beleaguered sentries made a last-ditch effort before falling back under the withering fusillade. Those fleeing were mowed down as they ran.

From his vantage, Octavius had a clear view of the enemy positions along the south side of the dyke, ordering the machine gunners to establish enfilading fire and the mortar team to set up behind a wall of sand bags.

"Get your range right before you waste any shells." While the men took up positions, Octavius catalogued their firepower, which consisted of individual carbines, several sub-machine guns, a single heavy machine gun with one thousand rounds, two mortars with eight rounds each, a bazooka with a dozen rockets and two dozen hand grenades amongst the twelve men on the bridge, two of whom were wounded.

"Johnston, Peters, collect whatever you can from the dead Germans, guns, ammo, mashers."

"Will do, Sarge."

He posted snipers at strategic points along the overpass and then hurried back to rendezvous with the barge group dug in on the north side of the canal. Only three of the squad were battle-hardened veterans, the rest engineers with limited firearms training for the most part. Luckily two were from the backwoods of Kentucky and seasoned hunters. These he assigned sniper duty from a protected vantage atop the dyke.

They had taken the bridge as ordered. Now all they had to do was hold it until reinforcements arrived.

* * *

Shadbolt, didn't like the look of the approach. The glider had come in too high. Trees at the end of the landing zone loomed ahead. The craft hung as if suspended by a phantom puppeteer, the angle of descent unchanged. Anxious voices could be heard from the cockpit. His guts plummeted as the craft dropped suddenly, slewing into the canopy. The starboard wing was sheared clean off, followed by a tremendous crash. He braced himself for the impact of hurtling cargo. Something brushed past his shoulder and then he was lying spread-eagled, men and materiel in heaps all around him.

"Gene!" he called out. "Gene, are you alright?" There was no response, just groans from the injured. "Okay, let's go." He picked himself up, and climbing over the debris, staggered to the front exit and kicked the door open. He clambered out as the first of the rescuers arrived, and glancing at the cockpit, witnessed the pilot draped over the yoke, blood streaming from his head. He was woozy, fighting nausea when he realized that Gene wasn't there beside him. He spun around and joined the crush of bodies carrying the dead and wounded from the wreckage.

"Gene!" Fighting panic, he scanned the faces of the victims.

"Jack," came the strangled reply. The voice he recognized, but the face belonged to a stranger, the jaw skewed to the side and the front teeth smashed out.

"Stand back, we've got him." Perkins was being carried by a medic and another soldier. Shadbolt followed them out of the trees and into the field beyond where they lay him down next to the other men. A small convoy of jeeps and open trucks flooded the area, raising a cloud of brick-red dust. Perkins was stretchered off to a makeshift field hospital on the far side of the landing zone.

Shadbolt wandered aimlessly amidst the hurly burly of the re-supply operation, trying to clear his head. Gliders landed in rapid succession, disgorging men and machinery. Often, they came to a halt in a vertical rather than horizontal attitude, noses buried in mounds of dirt. He aimed for the hospital tent but got sidetracked when someone offered him a cup of tea. As he sat on the ground outside a hastily assembled mess tent, he remembered that he hadn't retrieved his duffel bag, sidearm, and most importantly the letters of authorization from the Bureau and the war office. He started walking back in the direction of the crash when someone called his name. He turned around, coming face to face with his old college roommate, Ed Berry.

"Jack, thank God you're alright." A wave of emotion swept over him as he found himself in the warm embrace of a once good friend and confidant. Images kaleidoscoped in his mind, battles of another sort, played out on the gridiron in the crisp fall air, the rustle of pom poms, the blare of the marching band and the roar of the crowd driving them on; late nights combing the library stacks, sweating over case law and back in the dorm quizzing each other on the finer points of arguments; cold beer and swapped fishing stories at the Berry family cabin out in the wilds of Montana, Flathead Lake reflecting the end of the day in hues of vermilion and gold. He'd lived a lifetime in those four years, the sunniest of times until the gathering clouds of family tragedy cast a dark shadow over his world.

He stepped back, shaking off the cobwebs.

"I took a bit of a knock and my partner looks like he went ten rounds with Joe Louis, but we're here now."

"Have you seen the medics yet?"

"I don't think so. I was pretty woozy after we cracked up. They carried Perkins over that way." He pointed across the field.

"Okay, first things first, let's go get you checked out." Berry laid a comforting hand on his shoulder and walked him to the hospital tent.

* * *

Shadbolt sat for a long spell after being attended to by the harried medical staff who diagnosed a mild concussion before rushing on to the more serious cases. Perkins was transferred to a liberated hospital in the nearby town of Zon to have his broken jaw set. Otherwise he was in good spirits, cracking wise through the pain and shattered teeth that gave him a decidedly ghoulish appearance. As far as Shadbolt was concerned, he was out of commission for the duration of the assignment to the extent that it could be completed in the next couple of days. He was anxious for Berry to return from his meeting with the brass to determine the whereabouts of Serge Tremblay and secure permission to remove him from the field and transport him to England and then back home for trial.

Berry walked in and handed Shadbolt his duffel bag. "I hope you don't mind, Jack but I took the liberty of retrieving your letters of authorization. I can't say General Cuthbert was thrilled about the whole idea, but he got on the blower to Atkins pronto and turned the air several shades of blue. Swears worse than a sailor."

"That's a relief. So, what's the plan?"

"Now here's the bad news."

"Why did I know there'd be a catch."

"His platoon is out of radio contact. They were up against stiff resistance. The whole battalion was sent in to support the three companies under fire. Octavius and the Raging Redskins were ordered on ahead through the Zonsche forest to secure the bridge at Best. They haven't been heard from since yesterday afternoon and the patrols sent out looking for them haven't reported back yet. Right now, they don't know if they've been captured or wiped out. Enemy strength is about three times greater than what they originally bargained for. What I'm telling you is that it would be extremely dangerous to try and make the arrest now. It jeopardizes this part of the operation, not to mention your own safety. That being said, the General has given his full consent. It's entirely up to you, Jack. Your call."

"What about back-up? With Perkins gone I'm a little short-handed." Shadbolt leaned forward, stubbing out his butt in a makeshift ashtray.

"I could request a couple of MPs, and my driver and I are at your disposal."

"You don't have to do this, Ed."

"I'm in it too far now to be getting cold feet. Like they say, in for a dime, in for a dollar."

"Could be your last dollar, buddy."

"I like the pot odds."

"You always were a lucky son of a bitch at poker."

"It's all in the way you play your hand, Jack."

"So you tell me."

"Get a little shut-eye while I make the necessary arrangements. We'll need to get you a tin pot and fatigues. You don't want to be mistaken for a spy if we run afoul of the Krauts." He looked at his watch. "If we set off by eighteen hundred hours we should make the front line by sunset."

* * *

Octavius and his platoon managed to keep the enemy pinned down behind the dyke for the better part of the day with disciplined enfilading fire and a well-placed mortar strike. They hit a munitions dump causing a series of explosions and mass panic in the ranks. Panzergrenadiers fled their protected positions, presenting easy targets for the shooters on the bridge. As the light began to fade, he sensed renewed activity in the area to the south of the canal, trucks arriving and the faint patter of boots as reinforcements were disgorged. His ears pricked up at a new sound, the fretted clank of tank treads coming their way. He rushed over to the machine gun emplacement.

"Pull back to the other side, quick. O'Hearn, Karpovich bring your bazooka, hurry. Izzy, Santori, six grenades now. The rest of you fall back to the other side."

Stuffing the grenades into his jacket pockets, Octavius placed the bazooka team below the bridge, behind the abutment. "You know where to aim? The base of the turret at the rear. Let it get by. I'll take care of the escorting panzers." He scrambled under the bridge to the abutment on the opposite side. The tank rumbled into view, a Tiger Mark IV belching diesel and hot lead in equal measure. It approached the bridge, trailing a contingent of panzergrenadiers who crouched behind the treads. The big 88 mm gun swung into position, aiming for the barricades at the far end of the viaduct. Octavius yanked the pins, waited two seconds and then tossed three grenades amongst the massed infantrymen. A heartbeat later the turret exploded into flame, but not before the big gun roared. Octavius mounted the treads, opened the top hatch and dropped another live grenade into the bowels of the Tiger. He jumped down in advance of a thunderous detonation with flames spewing from every orifice before opening fire on the disoriented survivors of the first grenade strike.

A second wave of German infantry rushed the disabled tank, forcing Octavius to duck down behind the treads. O'Hearn was hit as he scrambled for cover, falling to his knees. He swung the loaded bazooka around, but before he could unleash another rocket, he was shot dead. With nowhere to hide, Karpovich dove from the bridge and struck out for the north bank. As the bazookaman hit the water, Octavius lobbed his remaining grenades at the swarming reinforcements and then turned and ran for his life, tracing a zig-zag course through a hail of bullets to the barricades at the other end.

* * *

With Sergeant Mankofsky at the wheel and Berry navigating, the jeep left the landing zone destined for the defensive lines on the west flank of the Zonsche Forest. Their first port of call was the field HQ and the regimental commander of the five-o-deuces, Colonel Atkins, in Shadbolt's mind the culprit behind the unauthorized release of Octavius Cadogan a.k.a Serge Tremblay, and the indirect cause of Perkin's injuries and their current precarious situation. He couldn't imagine what had possessed him to disregard the order and release the murderer into the theatre of battle with access to a vulnerable civilian population. He was itching to haul the bastard off and give him a hiding he wouldn't soon forget.

The distant boom of artillery echoed in the direction of Best, and as they reached the outskirts, they found themselves in the middle of a firefight with the 101st falling back to take up positions south of the road on which they were travelling. Mankofsky took the next turn left and followed the troops south and into the fringe of the forest. Berry went off in search of someone in the know, coming across a lieutenant marshalling the retreating troops.

"I'm looking for the field HQ," Berry shouted.

"They're dug in about two miles southwest of here on the flank of the Zonsche," the lieutenant called over his shoulder as he continued waving the troops further into the woods. When the last man had run by, he turned to face Berry. "The Krauts are thick along the highway, plenty of 88's and mortars and SS divisions. So much for the old men and teenagers we were going to sweep aside like so much straw."

"Where's the Brit armor? I thought XXX Corps was supposed to be leading this parade."

"They're a day behind schedule as usual so we're up against it until they get here."

"Do you know anything about Q Company, the Raging Redskins?"

"Couldn't tell you. One of their platoons headed south to the canal yesterday. Haven't heard anything since."

Berry walked back to the jeep. He checked his watch. Only forty-five minutes till sundown and the fire lane was already in deep shadow.

"We can risk getting shot at by our own guys or bunk down here for the night."

"We've come this far. Let's push on.'

"Okay Mankofsky, you heard the G-man, onward to HQ and don't spare the horses."

* * *

Mankofsky drove eastward for a quarter mile and then swung southwest, criss-crossing the uneven ground of the clear cut to avoid the worst of the mud holes from the previous night's rain, and piles of deadfall waiting to be burned. They made little headway before night fell.

"Watch out for the stump!" Berry yelled. At the last instant Mankofsky swerved to miss the obstruction, skidding into the quagmire he'd been trying to steer clear of in the first place. Water sprayed up into the jeep. The wheels sunk axle-deep in mud. Shadbolt clambered out and, with the others, pushed, pulled and lifted in vain to extricate the vehicle from the muck. When they failed to dislodge it after fifteen minutes of Herculean effort, Berry signaled them to give it up. All five were covered from head to foot in fetid black sludge.

"I guess we're legging it from here. Stick to the right flank so we're not exposed," Berry instructed.

They retrieved their weapons and packs from the jeep and followed Berry to the edge of the fire break, Shadbolt in second position, followed by the two MPs with Mankofsky bringing up the rear. After several hundred yards they came across another fire lane running perpendicular to their path. Berry signaled a halt before sighting northward to where the highway paralleled the forest edge. Berry crossed the break with Shadbolt close on his heels. They were halfway to the other side when the shooting started. Shadbolt hit the deck as the ground in front of him erupted. He heard the others behind him scramble back into cover. He lost sight of Berry and realized that he was stranded in the middle of no man's land, redfire scarring the dark night all around him.

Carbines barked from the forest edge to his right, drawing an immediate response from the machine gun emplacement. This was his chance. He was up and running in a heartbeat, his ravenous strides chewing up the ground as he closed in on pay dirt. He leapt into the stand a split second ahead of a round of slugs that ravaged the trunks like a buzz saw.

"Glad you could make it," came Berry's disembodied voice from the underbrush. "I see you haven't lost anything from your glory days scoring touchdowns for our beloved Cyclones."

Shadbolt took a moment to catch his breath. "I thought we owned this neck of the woods?"

"Apparently not."

"How can you tell those aren't our boys doing the shooting?"

"MG 42, 'Hitler's Zipper,' nothing else sounds quite like that, or has the range."

"Jesus Christ on a pony."

"Hang tight, I'm going to signal the others to cross further down, out of range, and hook up with us here."

Berry took out his flashlight and, using a trunk for cover, sent a lighted message in Morse code to Mankofsky and the MPs. The 'Zipper' fired several more rounds into the forest and then went quiet. Shadbolt and Berry tucked a little further into the trees and sat back against a trunk to await the others.

"So what do you think happened to Brubaker?" Shadbolt asked as they passed a cigarette back and forth between them.

"Why, what's your theory?"

"I think our boy knocked him off and got rid of the body, and I think someone else must know, and is keeping 'schtum'. He can't be operating solo."

"The Raging Redskins seem like a pretty tight bunch. Maybe he's playing on platoon loyalty to cover his tracks. Loyalty is often unquestioning. I doubt whether they have the faintest notion what he's been up to."

"Possibly, but Brubaker can't have been alone in his suspicions."

"You could be right, and we'll see how far that loyalty extends when we try and take him away."

Twenty minutes later he and Berry were joined by the others. They set off again in search of the field command unit, arriving at the sentry post after an uneventful crossing of the next fire lane.

* * *

To say that Colonel Atkins was displeased with the unwelcome intrusion was a monumental understatement. His face turned scarlet and he glared at Shadbolt when he was presented with the orders for the removal of Serge Tremblay from the field.

"Gentlemen these orders are academic at this point. Tremblay's platoon has been out of radio contact since yesterday afternoon and two patrols have failed to find them." He spoke with eyes cast down on the map before him.

"What was their intended target?" Shadbolt persisted.

"The bridge over the Wilhelmina Canal, but as you no doubt saw for yourselves the Germans are dug in up and down the highway with heavy artillery and three times the strength we anticipated. It's doubtful they made it to the bridge."

"Give us the coordinates and your best scout and we'll be on our way."

"We're undermanned as it is," he huffed. "And I don't recommend it in the dark."

Shadbolt took a step forward and leaned across the table. "We wouldn't be in this jackpot now if you'd done what you were supposed to."

"My priority is winning the war, not hounding my men over trifles."

"The brutal murder of American citizens, and the people we came here to save are hardly trifles. Don't think for a moment we won't be taking further action against anyone who aided and abetted this butcher, regardless of rank."

"Are you threatening me?"

"It's not a threat, it's a God damn promise." Atkins rounded the table and stood nose to nose with Shadbolt. Two powder kegs ready to explode at any second. Berry jumped between them.

"Alright Jack, you've made your point. Colonel Atkins if you'd be so kind as to point us in the right direction, we'll be out of your hair tout suite."

Atkins called for an orderly, muttering under his breath as they were escorted out of the tent, and after a short briefing, to the perimeter. Shadbolt was still fuming over the encounter when they arrived at the main fire lane ten minutes later. Major Berry led the group southwesterly in the direction of the canal. They defiled as before, moving steadily into the heart of the night, but soon the forest closed in around them. Berry halted and gathered the group together.

"I've gotten off track in the dark. We should've come across another break by now, the one that leads to the canal."

From deep within the woods Shadbolt heard a noise, voices carrying on the wind. If he wasn't mistaken, German commands.

Soon the tramping of boots filled his ears. Patrol, or a whole platoon, it was hard to tell. Berry whispered for them to take cover and hold their fire until he gave the command. If there were too many, they'd avoid a conflict and let them pass unhindered.

Shadbolt drew his sidearm and slunk off to take position in the low crotch of a gemel oak tree. Sweat beaded his upper lip. He tasted salt and realized how thirsty he was. The tramping boots came closer. He guessed a dozen or so, skirting the lines, probing for areas of weakness. He realized how much of warfare was down to blind luck, and although a far cry from the more predictable tactics of the past, largely trial and error, move and counter move, weather and terrain, and a hundred other circumstances. In the end, serendipity dictating the outcome.

He heard the signal and, from behind the tree, took aim at the dark shapes animating the gloom.

* * *

Under cover of darkness, the Germans continued to move reinforcements into position behind the tank. Octavius observed their maneuvers from a protected salient at the midpoint of the crash barriers that ran the length of the structure. The platoon had kept the enemy pinned down through the course of the day, but now they were desperately low on ammunition. The mortar and heavy machine gun ordnance long since expended. Their defense was down to a handful of crack shots with carbines along with one of the Raging Redskins, an ex Ivy League quarterback, in possession of a rocket launcher for an arm, capable of dispatching grenades with pinpoint precision.

Octavius was intent on re-taking the far end of the bridge but needed additional men and materiel to succeed. He couldn't understand why they hadn't been re-supplied yet. Where the hell were those British tanks? XXX Corps was a good twenty-four hours behind schedule. He crouched down and ran back to where the grenade chucker was stationed.

"What have you got left?" he asked.

"I'm down to my last two grenades and half a dozen potato mashers." The QB patted the grenades, dangling like miniature pineapples from his belt.

"I can hear them moving around behind the tank. Probably constructing fortifications for a 'Zipper' or twenty-millimeter emplacement. What are the chances of dropping a long bomb right in behind?"

"I make that about seventy-five yards to the end zone. No sweat."

"Okay, let's give 'em another ten minutes to get nice and cozy and then air mail them another little present. What time have you got?"

"Twenty one hundred and thirty-two on the dot."

"Good, we're synched. I'll alert the sharpshooters and give you a flare at exactly twenty-one, forty-two." He signaled the men stationed along the bridge and then hurried back to his position.

* * *

Shadbolt didn't have time to stop and catch his breath; he was badly winded, but kept running, weaving through the trees, panzergrenadiers in close pursuit.

"Holt, holt!" A shot rang out, splintering a tree trunk over his left shoulder. He took two steps to his right, pivoted, and fired the last shot in his clip, before barrel-rolling behind a coppice clump. He snatched a replacement clip from his belt, snapped it in place, and fired several more rounds in the direction of the onrushing Germans. The initial shot found its mark, catching the lead man square in the chest. He brushed at the tear in his uniform, as if shoeing away a troublesome insect, before crumpling to the ground. The other two stopped short and scrambled for protection in the underbrush.

On hands and knees Shadbolt eased himself backwards, putting as much distance as possible between pursuers and prey. From the surrounding woods the fire fights continued, combatants partnered in a deadly dance. He couldn't recall if he had actually heard Berry give the signal or had reacted once the shooting started. Confusion had descended pell-mell with the first bark of a carbine.

A twig snapped off to his right. He held his breath, arm extended, pointing his weapon in the direction of the noise. He kept his arm in this position until it ached terribly, the pain running from shoulder to fingertips. When he could no longer bear it, he let the arm relax, but kept the sidearm cocked. Were they still out there, just beyond the clump of tress? There were no other sounds save for the rustle of leaves in the treetops. After a while he heard them again, moving off, footfalls receding in the distance.

Despite the fear-fueled adrenaline coursing through his veins, a profound tiredness descended upon him like a great weight. He could sleep for an eternity of days. He let his head come to rest in the crook of his arm, and against his will, his eyelids closed.

The crack of a rifle roused him from slumber. How long had he been adrift? There was another shot followed by a guttural cry, and then something came crashing towards him, leaping between the boles of the coppice and straight over his head. The undulating shape jerked and fell, flopping like a fish out of water as it tried to escape the steady stream of fire from the muzzle protruding through the branches.

He called out as the firing stopped.

A familiar voice spoke back. "Is that you, Jack?" It was Berry at the other end of the carbine.

"In the flesh. How are we doing?"

"Not so good. Looks like it's down to you and me old Buddy."

"What about Mankofsky and the MPs?" Shadbolt asked.

"Both Bradshaw and Collins were hit. Mankofsky is heading back to the field HQ to bring back the medics. I think they're gonna make it okay."

"Jesus Christ on a pony, if I had known it was going to cost us this much blood I never would've come."

"Hey, it was me who got you involved in the first place. I'll take full responsibility."

"Like hell you will. This was my show and I've cocked it up." Shadbolt was adamant.

"We're in a warzone for God's sake, doing our jobs. Nobody was forced to take the assignment. We all knew the risks and we all volunteered in spite of them. Now we've come this far, what say we make like the Mounties and go get our man."

"What about the rest of the Krauts?"

"Those we didn't waste ran like rabbits back to where they came from."

"You're sure?"

I counted an even dozen. There's eight dead with this one, and four who scampered away."

"Do you think they'd double back?"

"Highly unlikely."

"Okay, let me get my bearings." Shadbolt put his canteen to his lips and took a long swallow. Then he poured some water into his hand and splashed it over his face.

"Ready?"

"Lead on MacDuff ."

* * *

Taking aim, Octavius discharged the flare, a momentary sunburst lighting up the night sky above the German position behind the gutted tank. A split second later, the grenade chucker, under a barrage of covering fire, hurled the deadly projectile. It traced a parabolic arc into the heart of the partially constructed emplacement. Octavius watched as the subsequent detonation set off a firestorm when the stockpile of twenty-millimeter ordnance ignited in a chain reaction of cannonading explosions. With the flames raging at the far end of the bridge, Octavius was satisfied that the platoon's position was secure for the time being. The moment was fleeting, for in the next instant the entire western half of the bridge lifted off before his eyes, as if in the grasp of a colossus. It was accompanied by a deafening report. He hit the deck, covering his head as chunks of iron and concrete descended in a lethal rain.

* * *

When the shower of debris subsided, Octavius raised his head to observe the damage. The smoke and dust from the explosion hung like morning mist above the naked abutments, and he came to the realization that the activity he had sensed was in actuality sappers dynamiting the underside of the bridge. Once the Germans had determined the intent of the allied mission, demolition of the bridge crossings became the logical response to halt their advance. The sacrifices of the platoon had been for naught. He contemplated their next move, fall back and rejoin the battalion, or continue to hold the now derelict and somewhat useless structure.

He heard the slap of boots on pavement coming up behind him.

"Sarge, you alright?" Two of the men began brushing the rubble from his back.

"We thought you went up with the bridge."

Octavius looked around to see whole slabs of bone-crushing concrete inches from where he lay. He stood and hunching over, led the men back to the barricades.

* * *

As daylight approached, the call of a meadowlark broke the stillness. It was like a symphony, almost too sweet for his ears after the discordant clamor of battle. The notes transported Octavius to another world, one of music and art and intellectual pursuits; cotillion balls staged in opulent surroundings, operas and ballet and sumptuous cuisine. A world of grandeur and refinement, cultured, urbane, sophisticated, far removed for the mundane, quotidian existence of the masses. How had he come to this place in time? What forces had compelled him to tread this wretched path? Something in him was changing. As if a hideous caul had been removed from his face. He felt different, divorced from his past, but mostly unsure of himself, his future, and how he should proceed.

He was roused from the reverie when one of the engineers from the squad on the dyke ran up to him.

"Looks like they're pulling back from their side of the canal. We've heard vehicles leaving for over an hour now."

"You're certain of that?"

"Absolutely, sir."

"Okay, go back and stay on your guard. It could be a ruse. Let me know if anything changes."

* * *

Dawn met the day along a squat horizon, hemmed by a ceiling of slate grey clouds, portending rain. Octavius sighted through his field glasses. Nothing stirred on the other side save for gasps of smoke from the guttering fires. He waited for a while longer and then satisfied that the enemy had vacated the field, called the platoon together.

"Gentlemen, it looks like our mission here is over. Karpovich, take the platoon back the way we came through the forest and assemble back at HQ."

"What about you, sarge?"

"I need a volunteer to accompany me to the other side. We're going to reconnoiter, gauge the Kraut strength and positions and rejoin you at HQ afterwards." In truth his mind was set on one last conquest, one last frenzied bout of debauchery to the extent that he could find what he was looking for amongst the remaining civilians in the ravaged town.

"I'll come with ya, sarge." 'Izzy' Israelson, a big Swede from Minnesota stepped forward.

"Okay, let's move out." He led the platoon back along the canal to the commandeered barge and, waving them off, piloted the craft to the opposite side. Disembarking, he crept along the top of the dyke and sighted to the bridge. The sandbagged emplacements were deserted, dead and wounded removed. The entire position had been abandoned. He waved Israelson over, and skirting the main highway, they made their way to the outskirts of Best.

They moved from house to deserted house. By the looks of it the residents left in a hurry. Through the windows, Octavius noted a general dishevelment, partially cleared tables and items strewn about the floors. There was no sign of the Germans yet, so they pressed onward. As they ventured further into the deserted town, the scars of the conflict were laid bare. Blackened and shell-gutted buildings, ruptured earth, and the acrid pungency of gunpowder and death.

Without warning, Israelson's head snapped back, a sniper's bullet taking out his right eye. He collapsed at Octavius' feet, a grimacing Cyclops, pawing the air. Octavius flattened himself against the wall. A second shot rippled Israelson's chest. He jerked spasmodically and then froze as if posing for a sculptor, arm extended skyward. A shot whistled by Octavius' cheek, fragmenting the bricks behind him. He slid backward and squeezed his bulk into a narrow doorway. The next shot rang off the stone lintel inches above his head. His fingers scrabbled spiderlike for the doorknob.

Locked.

He ducked down, pivoted and started for the other side of the street. Halfway across, his boot caught a cobble and he was sent sprawling, landing spread-eagled, his weapon clattering out of reach. For the first time that he could remember since childhood, he felt vulnerable and afraid.

* * *

Shadbolt and Berry arrived at the forest edge in advance of the retreating platoon. They heard the tramp of boots and froze until the whistling of a familiar refrain identified the troops as friendly.

"They're ours," said Berry. He called out, "Q Company, Major Berry here from Fourth Division."

The platoon halted weapons drawn. He and Shadbolt stepped out from the trees.

"About time ya got here," said Karpovich. "Where the hell are the rest?"

"Just us for now."

"Well you're about two days too late. They blew the bridge."

Shadbolt surveyed the men. They looked like they'd been in the field for a month. They were dirty and unshaven, eyes rimmed red from lack of sleep. Several were heavily bandaged and being helped by others.

"Is Sergeant Tremblay with you?" Berry asked.

"He went into Best to scout out Kraut positions."

"When?"

"About twenty minutes ago."

"How'd he get across with the bridge down?"

"Barge, why?"

"We need to speak with him."

"He's gonna meet us at HQ when he's done. We'll escort you back."

Berry conferred with Shadbolt out of earshot of the platoon. "What do you think, Jack? Do we press on, or wait for him back at HQ?"

"Seems like we can't catch a break. He's always one step ahead no matter what. Between you and me, I don't fancy our chances with Atkins and the rest of the company back at HQ."

"What are you saying?"

"It might be easier if we apprehend him now and go directly back to the landing zone and then make arrangements from there."

"That's a bit of a haul, but I take your point."

Karpovich was growing impatient. "So you coming with us, Major?"

"No, we'll see if we can catch up to him before he gets too far."

Karpovich's eyebrows registered surprise. "Suit yourselves." He turned on his heels, signaling the remnants of the platoon to follow him back into the forest.

* * *

Finding a skiff upended on one of the barges, Shadbolt and Berry rowed across the canal, upstream of what remained of the bridge, and followed the road into town. They wound their way through the streets, moving inexorably to the center where the recent fighting had taken place. To Shadbolt's eyes the shattered landscape of the once thriving burg resembled the worst kind of dystopian nightmare. Buildings indiscriminately pulverized lay in smoldering ruin. Streets were littered with corpses from both camps, bloating in the heat. They came upon a mangy dog tearing at the innards of a carcass, its muzzle matted with blood. With teeth bared it prepared to defend the kill against all intruders. They gave the snarling beast a wide birth.

Further on their passage was blocked by a number of burned-out tanks, Shermans and Tigers. The charred remains of the occupants lay scattered about in a hideous tableau. Trapped while escaping the flames, a blackened body protruded through a top hatch, arms outstretched to the heavens above, beseeching his maker for mercy that never came. Outside a shell-scarred hospital, the dead were stacked for burial, and here and there the lifeless bodies of collaborators, or members of the Dutch underground, impossible to distinguish between the two, hung limply from iron lampposts.

Amidst the carnage an unfamiliar sound issued from a nearby doorway. A newborn crying. There on the step sat an emaciated young woman, a girl really, holding a baby to her shriveled breast. She was gently rocking the child, her lips moving to some comforting lullaby, unvoiced. Stepping around the rubble, Shadbolt offered his canteen. She stared vacantly and continued to rock the child. He put the spout to her cracked lips and poured. She clutched the crying child closer while the water dribbled down her chin. Then he took out a bar of chocolate from his rations, and breaking off a small piece, placed it in the woman's mouth. She sucked on the sweet morsel which he washed down with more water from the canteen. He continued feeding her a piece at a time until half the bar was consumed, and the canteen drained.

Ever so slowly she revived, her eyes cleared somewhat, and she removed some of the chocolate residue from her lips and stuck her finger in the baby's mouth. After a while the crying turned to a mewling as the baby suckled. In the midst of death life was still ascendant.

"Let's see if we can get them somewhere safe."

"What about our man?"

"Right now this is more important. There's got to be someone else around who can take care of her and the child. Let's go back to that hospital we passed."

"Alright, Jack."

Shadbolt helped the woman to her feet, and with Berry holding the other arm they trudged back in the direction they had come from.

* * *

The first bullet hit him up high, sending him reeling. It felt like he'd been kicked by a mule, but he kept his footing, and while the sniper re-sighted, launched his frame into the doorway across the narrow street. He hit the ancient door with full force, sheering it from its rusty hinges. Before he crashed through, a second bullet entered his lower back, metal tearing flesh above the hip bone. He crawled along the hallway and into the scullery at the back of the dwelling and sank to the floor. He rested his head on the cool stone slabs until he recovered his breathing, and then gingerly fingered the wounds on his shoulder and back.

He was in luck; the lower wound had missed any vitals, despite the blood soaking his tunic and trousers. The upper wound was a little more troubling. It exited through his pectoral muscle, puncturing his left lung. If the wound was small enough, it would clot without the lung collapsing or filling with blood. He removed his fatigues, and entering the adjacent bedroom, stripped the sheets from the bed, and attended to both punctures, applying pressure to staunch the worst of the bleeding. When he was satisfied that it had subsided sufficiently, he opened the first aid package attached to his utility belt. He sprinkled 'sulfa' powder on the shoulder wound and covered it with the Carlisle bandage. For the lower wound, he applied the rest of the powder and then wound a length of bed sheet, tightly around his waist. He returned to the kitchen, and drawing a cup of water, swallowed four of the eight sulfanilamide pills from the kit. He decided to save the syrette of morphine for later, when the pain was sure to kick in.

He rinsed the blood from his undershirt and tunic and set them on the draining board to dry. Then he removed his trousers and underwear and repeated the procedure. He re-entered the bedroom and searched a battered armoire for articles of clothing that might suffice in the meantime. Fortunately, the occupant was a capacious individual and Octavius was able to find a bulky, wool sweater, and suit trousers, the pant legs dangling at mid-calf. With knife and sidearm in hand, he sat back against the wall to contemplate his next move when he heard footsteps on the pavement outside, and then someone entered the house.

* * *

Shadbolt stopped dead in his tracks at the sound of rifle fire. He counted four shots. He looked over in the direction of the reports and then glanced at Berry.

"That's got to be our guy, one street over."

"Just our luck."

"Look, you carry on. Get them to the hospital and then come and find me. I'll give you a whistle."

"Jack, you're not thinking clearly. It could be anybody and probably the Krauts."

"I've got a feeling in my gut."

"That feeling is gonna get you in a whole mess of trouble."

"We don't have time to argue. Do as I ask, please."

He un-holstered his pistol and ran back in the direction of the shooting.

* * *

Berry stood open-mouthed, watching Shadbolt disappear around a corner. He was in two minds, give chase, or get the girl and her baby to safety and follow on. He chose the latter, picking up the pace, practically carrying the pair past the stacked corpses and up the front steps to the hospital entrance. He pushed open the door to witness the main floor ravaged beyond repair. Windows were shot out, walls had collapsed from shell fire, and everywhere he looked, rubble littered the floor. He skirted the piles of debris, drawn by an ominous sound emanating from below.

Berry and the girl descended the stairs leading to the basement level. There he found the source of the strange noise. The collective groans of the wounded, lying in serried rows of cots covering the entire floor. He gasped in the rank atmosphere, an overpowering mélange of festering wounds, blood, sweat and excrement. Doctors and nurses shuffled zombie-like along the rows, attending to casualties from both camps along with civilians who had been caught in the crossfire.

Men in the throes of combat fatigue babbled incoherently, some calling for their mothers, while others shouted inanities at specters inhabiting the ether. A nurse rushed by, her clothes soaked with the blood of the wounded men. Berry saw a discarded limb lying in a corner. The entire scene more closely resembled Bosch's grotesque vision of the underworld than a place of healing.

He drew the attention of a nun and waved her over, inquiring if she could look after the girl and her baby. She spoke no English but understood what he was getting at. With a kindly smile she laid a comforting hand on the girl's shoulder and led her away, presumably to another less hectic area of the hospital where she'd receive the help she so desperately needed.

As he turned to leave, Berry heard one of the Dutch doctors speaking English to an American casualty and hurried over to him.

"Major Berry, US Army Fourth Division, what's the situation here, Doc?"

"Not very good, I'm afraid. We're, how do you say, 'wanhopig', ah, desperate low on supplies: bandages, morphine, plasma."

"I see you've got German and American casualties."

"Yes and our own who didn't ah, 'evacueren' in time. This part of the town has changed hands, 'drie', three, four times now. We are being shelled from both sides."

"We're sorry about that."

"It is war, what can you do?"

"Do you know where the Americans are, here in Best?"

"When they brought in the last of the wounded, the medic he say they withdrawing to the highway."

"When was that?"

"Four," he looked down at his watch, "Ja, four hours ago."

"Thanks, I'll let our medics know you need supplies."

Berry hurried back to the stairway. He had to find Shadbolt before the Germans retook the town.

* * *

Octavius eased over to the iron bedstead, sitting in the middle of the small bedroom. The door was ajar giving him an unobstructed view of the narrow hallway and a clear shot at anyone passing by to the scullery at the back of the dwelling. Footsteps advanced, the intruder treading cautiously. He raised his pistol to where he gauged chest height would be. On the corridor wall opposite, shadows danced as a momentary sunburst streamed through the scullery window, infusing the gloom with a gayety at odds with the tension-charged atmosphere.

The footsteps moved agonizingly slow. His wounds throbbed, and he had a strong urge to cough as blood continued to pool in his injured lung. The footsteps halted before the open doorway. Sweat dripped into his eyes, stinging and momentarily blurring his vision. He shook the drops from his brow, and as he did, he noticed the trail of blood and water leading from the scullery to his hiding place.

Too late!

There was a harsh intake of breath and a body clothed in German 'feldgrau' filled the doorframe, the lightning flashes on his collar identifying him as Waffen SS. The weapons spit fire, the sniper's bullet finding the wall behind Octavius' head as he ducked. His own pistol shot shattered the trigger hand of the sniper, causing his weapon to fall to the floor. Before Octavius could get off a second round, the sniper hurled himself across the mattress, knocking him backward and pinned his knife-wielding arm, already weakened by the shoulder wound. The sniper grabbed for the pistol as Octavius brought it up to fire. Plaster showered down from the ceiling while they wrestled on the floor like two titans in a feat of strength. Locked in the struggle, equally matched, neither gave an inch. Octavius' left arm shook with the exertion, every hardened fiber at maximum intensity despite the searing pain. His wounds screamed out and he felt his strength ebbing after three days of combat with little sustenance and no sleep.

From his dominant position, the sniper slowly gained the upper hand. He sat astride Octavius, sliding higher up his chest to pin both arms with his knees.

At the same time, he wrenched at the gun, leveraging it from Octavius' grasp, his efforts hindered by his blood-slicked right hand.

With his final reserves of energy, Octavius arched his body, fighting to buck the sniper off. The pain from his wound was excruciating. Blood started to flow again, spreading across his back.

Like the seasoned horseman he must have been before the onset of the war, the sniper rode the undulations and stripped the pistol from Octavius' failing hand. Octavius felt the handle strike his face, and then the barrel against his forehead. There was a fearful explosion and a warm spatter of blood and brains caressed his grimacing countenance. The sniper pitched forward, toppling to the floor beside him like a spent lover.

Wiping the blood from his eyes, Octavius looked up to see a G I standing over him. There was something familiar about the face, the eyes in particular, and the cleft chin. He loomed tall, with wide shoulders and a barrel chest. Where had he encountered him before? Images swirled in his brain; a rooming house back in Kansas City, eons ago now, a tip off and a swarm of agents descending on the premises, a flight to safety and a new partnership with his cousins. The face, it fit in there somewhere. Then the face began to talk.

"Octavius Cadogan, I'm arresting you in connection with the murders of Iris Billings, Gloria Shepperton ..."

Now he remembered, the face belonged to an FBI agent from Kansas City, but what was he doing here?

"... of Cedar Rapids, Iowa. You have the right to remain silent. Anything you say can and will be used against you in a court of law ..."

Then another face appeared next to the first one. He was sure he recognized that one as well, but from a more-recent encounter. Was this really happening, or had delirium taken hold? The first face continued talking, sonorous waves washing over him, but the actual words and their meaning were lost somewhere in the swell. He closed his eyes and drifted into oblivion.

* * *

At first Shadbolt couldn't fathom the unorthodox attire of the big paratrooper, in fact he wasn't even certain it was him until he came across the drying fatigues in the scullery.

"You don't think he was disguising himself as a local do you?" asked Berry. "Blend in with the natives and disappear into the background."

"I don't think so. Why would he be rinsing out his battle dress? And he had no way of knowing we were on our way."

"I suppose, but he must've known that the killing spree was going to have to come to an end eventually, that he was going to get caught."

"Well, when he regains consciousness you can ask him."

"That better happen soon, or we'll be spending the rest of this outing in a Kraut stalag."

"Let's get him stabilized before we move him."

Shadbolt took a long drink from the scullery faucet and then returned to the bedroom to determine the extent of Octavius' injuries. Blood was pooling on the floor where he lay, and a crimson stain was spreading across the front of the sweater. He reached for the knife lying beside him and sliced through the soaking wet wool. He replaced the Carlisle bandage with one from his own kit after stemming the blood flow. Then he cut off the trousers, removed the bed sheet dressing and applied steady pressure to the gaping wound before dousing it with another packet of sulfa powder and rebinding it with freshly torn linen Berry scavenged from an upstairs bedroom.

Octavius remained comatose, his breathing labored. Taking the syrette from Octavius' kit along with his own, Shadbolt administered two shots of morphine. Then he and Berry lifted Octavius onto the bed, afterward dragging the sniper's body out of the room and depositing it in the small yard outside the scullery. Shadbolt fired up a cigarette and sat down at the table. Off in the distance the boom of artillery broke the silence of the waning afternoon.

"I don't think he'll be coming to anytime soon. We need to find a way to transport him out of here; jeep, truck, hell I'll settle for a cart if push comes to shove." Shadbolt leaned back and blew a smoke ring, watching it rise to the ceiling.

Berry thought for a while. "There was a hand cart they were using to move the wounded over at the hospital. If we could lay our hands on a couple of Red Cross patches, we might just be able to make it back to our lines without getting shot up too badly."

"Well that's a whole lot better than trying to carry that big son of a bitch out of here."

"Give me twenty minutes or so."

"Just be careful. Don't take any chances."

"From the man who ran into the gunfire."

"It was a calculated risk."

"No, it was reckless, but let's not quibble about it now." Berry retrieved his carbine, and stepping over the splintered door, sighted up and down the street before sprinting off to the hospital.

* * *

Berry was leaving the hospital yard pushing the borrowed cart when he heard the rumble of an approaching half track. He didn't wait around to see what colors it was flying. He disappeared down an alley, the harsh clanging of the metal wheels on the cobbles marking his passage. For an instant he considered abandoning the noisy conveyance. He could hardly remain inconspicuous with the bellwether announcing his whereabouts to anyone within earshot.

He wound through the streets, taking a circuitous route back to Shadbolt. Up ahead he heard the thrum of approaching trucks and the distinctive rumble of a tank bruising the cobbles. The lead vehicle, an open-canopied staff car, turned down the street toward him. He abandoned the cart and ducked down a nearby passageway. Voices called out after him. The chase was on.

He sprinted past a dozen doorways, arriving at an alley where he veered right and clambered over a high stone wall enclosing a cooper's yard. Wooden casks and barrels were stacked in rows to one side with bundles of staves and metal hoops of different sizes piled on the other. The workshop door was locked, and he didn't want to risk breaking the transom window for fear of the noise alerting his pursuers. Footsteps approached, he scrambled inside an upright hogshead. They ran past and he breathed a sigh of relief, raising his head above the rim of the cask. The footfalls stopped partway down the alley and returned, coming to a halt outside the yard. He ducked back down as a padlock rattled, and he heard the hollow thumping of a rifle butt striking the door. After several heavy blows, the fastener fell to the ground. With a dissonant creak, like the opening of a coffin lid, the door swung inward, and they entered the enclosure. He heard them start to poke about, rapping each empty barrel in turn as they moved along the rows. The knocking came closer to the hogshead, half a dozen casks away. He drew his sidearm. Now they were within three casks. He cocked the hammer, his heart racing a mile a minute. His legs tensed ready to spring. It was now or never.

A voice called from the doorway,

"Hast du ihn gefunden?"

"Er ist nicht hier."

"Schau in den nachsten hof. Macht Schnell."

From his rudimentary knowledge of German, Berry gathered that they were being directed to the next yard. His chin dropped to his chest. If he had been a religious man he would've cried hallelujah. He heard the door pulled to and the footsteps retreat up the alley. He was dying for a cigarette but held off, waiting a full fifteen minutes before climbing out of the hogshead. He stepped over to the door, and opening it partway, stuck his head out to see if the coast was clear. Instead, he stared down the barrel of a Luger, held by a cadaverous figure in a long, black trench coat, the skull and crossbones insignia on his service cap identifying him as SS, the oak leaf pairing on his collar identifying him as a high-ranking officer, an Oberfuhrer. He addressed Berry in English.

"I would gladly shoot you even with those Red Cross armbands, but I need information and by your rank," he eyed Berry's golden oak leaf collar patch, "I believe you may have what I am looking for."

"Edward Berry, major, O16647."

"Yes, name, rank and serial number, a very good start." A dyspeptic smile curled his lips and eyes set in the deep wells of his cranium conveyed a malevolence unbounded by the strictures of conventional warfare, a diabolical force that had wrought untold suffering in the ghettos of Holland and France and beyond. He stripped Berry of his sidearm and motioned him back down the alley.

* * *

When Berry hadn't returned after a nervous hour passed, Shadbolt became concerned about his friend's well-being along with their plans for spiriting Octavius out of the town. The sound of heavy vehicles was growing closer by the minute. He ascended the narrow staircase to the second floor and made his way to a bedroom window overlooking the street. Drawing the curtain to one side, he peered down the road to witness a convoy of troop trucks, led by a battle-scarred Tiger tank approaching from the west.

He raced back down the stairs to the front hallway and set the fallen door back in its frame, propping it closed with an overstuffed chair he wrestled from the sitting room. Next, he entered the scullery and discarded the empty sulfa packets and bloody bandages before retrieving Octavius' drying fatigues. Crossing the threshold to his bedside, he lowered Octavius to the floor and laid him against the wall. A low moan issued from his lips, but he didn't awaken. Shadbolt lifted the bed, setting in over top of the sleeping figure. He straightened up what remained of the bed clothes and then draped the duvet over the side of the bed facing the doorway so that it concealed the paratrooper. He tucked his fatigues under the mattress and did his best to hide the blood stains on the floor with a rag rug.

Satisfied that their occupation of the dwelling wouldn't be immediately obvious to scrutiny, he ascended the stairs, moving past the second floor to the very top of the house, the front half of which was occupied by an attic bedroom with a tiny gabled window affording a view of the street below. From here he was able to observe the movement of the convoy.

He watched as soldiers in pairs entered dwellings up and down the street. Where the doors were locked, they shouldered or kicked them open, calling out for the surrender of any occupants before barging in with weapons raised. As they moved steadily down the block toward his hideaway, he considered his next move, visiting each room in turn before deciding none were suitable for his purposes. In the end he came back up to the attic and crossed the landing to the small room at the rear of the house. He squeezed through the window and scrabbled crab-like up the steeply-pitched roof to the chimney chase, cresting the peak. Here he had a good view of the comings and goings of the panzergrenadiers along the opposite side of the street. He kept his fingers crossed that Octavius remained well-hidden and that the morphine injections would keep him sedated as the search progressed.

From the far end of the block he heard the muffled report of rifle fire and shouting, praying the resistance came from stubborn locals and not Airborne troops who were trapped in the town, or heaven forbid, Berry making his way back. His thoughts returned to his friend. Berry had gone way out on a limb and gotten them this far. He couldn't let him down now, no matter what.

A heavy rapping came from directly below and he heard the door being forced open, and the sounds of surprise from the intruders as it toppled clean out of the frame. Twenty minutes later a helmeted head emerged from the attic window and peered into the yards lining the alleyway. Shadbolt flattened himself against the roof, his heart pounding. He stayed that way until dusk dulled the sky to pewter. Only then did he venture back to the peak. He watched as the house to house searches continued. He didn't want to risk re-entering the dwelling until the convoy had moved off. He hadn't heard the intruders leave and wondered if they were settling in for the night, and what might happen if they stumbled on Octavius.

* * *

Octavius awoke from the morphine stupor, pain gnashing at his chest and side like a rabid canine. The back of his throat felt like it had been flayed. He opened his eyes to find himself entombed, the oppressive cavity closing in on him from all sides. He reached out with his good hand. His fingers traced a thickness of rope, a knotted web. He was lying beneath a bed. But how had he gotten there? As his head cleared, he assembled a series of images to construct a face.

The face must've hidden him there. To what end he was unsure. He continued exploring the underside of the bed, feeling a bulge of material, damp to the touch, and then a button. There under the mattress were his clothes. He was confused and his mind too cobwebbed to make sense of the disparate threads.

He crawled out of his sanctum and raised himself to his knees. Then he stood. The room spun. So much so that he was forced to his knees again. He lay back down and waited for the revolutions to slow and eventually stop. Slithering on his belly, he made his way to the scullery. At the sink, he forced himself to stand, and lowering his head, drank directly from the spigot. The water was sweet and cold, extinguishing the fire in his throat. He dunked his head under the steady stream, holding it there for several minutes. As he revived, the intensity of the pain notched up. He needed morphine. He went back to the bedroom and retrieved his fatigues. The first aid kit wasn't attached to his belt and a further search of the lower floor failed to turn up the syrette or his sidearm and knife.

He remembered passing a pharmacie along the way. The town would've been evacuated in a hurry. There was a chance some of the drug might still be found about the premises. He dressed as quickly as pain would allow and then rummaged through the scullery drawers in search of a suitable weapon, extracting a paring knife, which he tucked into his utility belt. He walked down the hallway to find the front door leaning back against a chair. He clambered around the obstruction and stepped out into the approaching dawn.

* * *

From his perch on the rooftop, Shadbolt was roused by the sound of stamping boots and shouted commands. It was still dark, the air chill. He heard a cock crow three times. Down below the trucks fired up. Without hesitation the convoy moved off. He waited until the last vehicle had departed and then crawled back down the roof to the dormer housing the window from which he had exited the attic. When he tried forcing it open, he realized that it had been locked. He shattered the glass with the butt of the sniper's rifle he had carried with him, reached in and unlatched the closure. He made his way to the second floor and, peering inside the bedrooms, noted that they had been slept in, stuffy and smelling of sweat and foul breath.

Descending to the lower level, he walked to the scullery at back of the house. Water glistened on the stone floor. The door to the small bedroom was ajar. He looked in to see the mattress upended against the wall and Octavius gone. He cursed out loud and ran to the front of the house. The convoy had only this minute left. Octavius couldn't be too far ahead of him. He stepped out into the street. Streaks of carmine portended a sailor's warning about the coming day. There on the pavement in front of him wet footprints reflected the dawn light. He followed the trail until it petered out at the entrance of a dusty alleyway. On hands and knees with his nose inches from the dirt, in the posture of a tracking bloodhound, he discerned the faint imprint of a boot.

"Come on, show me the way," he hissed.

The alley led to a street of shops, some shuttered, while others invited entry beneath gaily-striped canopies. Off in the distance the growl of artillery, like a pack of distempered mongrels, broke the stillness. Passing a smashed storefront window, he noted the disarray of the interior, ravaged no doubt by looters. He was about to move on, when through the miasma of cordite and death a familiar scent drifted into his nostrils, the merest whiff of citrus and spice. He breathed deeply, letting the fragrance awaken his olfactory memory. The bouquet was unmistakable.

Fougere Royale.

Stepping over the broken glass, he walked past the ransacked aisles to the back of the pharmacie. There on the dispensary counter sat an open bottle of the distinctive perfume. He picked up the sculpted glass, letting his fingers explore the sensuous curves of the extravagant decanter. He set it back down and followed the aromatic trail through the storeroom to a rear staircase. He raised the rifle to his waist and slowly placed his foot on the riser, testing to see if it would bear his weight without revealing his presence. Satisfied, he ascended, his finger poised on the trigger.

* * *

Up in one of the second-floor apartments, Octavius swallowed a handful of sulfanilamide pills and then prepared to inject a syringe of morphine. While the dispensary shelves were cleared of medicine, he had come across the pharmacist's personal stash of drugs in a locked cabinet in the adjoining office. He inserted the needle into the vial and drew back the plunger. Tapping the cylinder to dislodge any air bubbles, he ejected a small spurt of the precious liquid into the air. The anticipation of relief from the pain licking at his wounds was palpable. The needle was poised above his thigh when he heard the sharp crunch of glass from below. Without hesitation, he gathered up his things and tiptoed to the door of the apartment. He let himself out into the hallway, and traversing the threadbare carpet to the staircase, climbed to the next floor. To his right an apartment door stood ajar. He entered, locking the door behind him.

The apartment was well-appointed, at odds with the deteriorating hallway, and obviously occupied by a person of means. A generous entry opened onto two reception rooms decorated with Louis XIV furniture, the brocaded walls adorned with classical art in gilded frames. In another life, he would've been quite comfortable in these surroundings. He made his way through the apartment, navigating a string of smaller bedrooms overlooking a rooftop terrace festooned with tropical blooms: bougainvillea, hibiscus and oleander. He surveyed the kitchen and pantry before returning to the main hallway where he entered what appeared to be the master bedroom, stationing himself so that he had a clear view of the entry from the doorjamb.

He needed to be clear-headed to confront the intruder, but the pain was quickly sapping his strength, emptying the deep reservoir of resistance. Had someone seen him enter the building, or was this a random search by the Wehrmacht, or worse, an SS division intent on re-taking the town? And then another thought entered his head, engendered by snippets of conversation that floated to the surface, about Iowa murders, and Miranda Rights. Could it be the all too obvious Major from Cherbourg, or the Kansas City G-man 'comin' for to carry me home'? He recalled their faces now as if in a dream, ethereal, hovering in the ether. Had he hallucinated the pair, or had they actually been there?

He heard movement at the front door, and then it flew back on its hinges with a heavy crash. He saw the long muzzle of the sniper's Mauser and instinctively reached for the paring knife. It preceded a broad-shouldered apparition in G I camouflage filling the doorframe. And the face, dark-eyed and ruggedly handsome. The same face that had stood over him and tended to his wounds after killing the sniper. The face he recognized from another time and place altogether.

"I'm in here, Sergeant Serge Tremblay of the five-o-deuces."

The face raised the rifle. "Come out with your hands out front where I can see them."

"I've got a shot of morphine I need to inject first. I've been hit." So he wasn't hallucinating after all. The vision was real. They had finally come for him. Now he needed to play for time, let the morphine do its job and shake off the side-effects, pretend to go along until an opportunity for escape presented itself.

"I'm aware of your condition, Sergeant. Now show yourself."

"It's done. I need to rest for a few minutes."

"We don't have any time. The place is crawling with Germans."

Octavius took three steps back and settled himself on the silk duvet covering the ornate four-poster that dominated the room. He was enveloped in the cooling folds. His head swam. The air was suffused with color, vivid magentas and deep purples. He heard the rustle of silver-backed leaves and the call of a thrush from deep in the woods. Along a distant shore the tide rolled pebbles up a cobbled beach. Further out, a great whale breached, spume-tinged waves of bottle-green rising into the air. Whole galaxies of starfish sparkled like diamonds in the deep. He felt the tectonic vibrations of shifting plates as the earth pulsed, spinning into infinity.

* * *

Shadbolt nosed the door open with the rifle barrel to witness Octavius supine upon an archaic four poster bed. The empty syringe lay on the floor beside him. He was staring up into the canopy over his head.

"You've already been read your rights. Now I need you to get up and accompany me back to Drop Zone C."

Octavius swatted away the request with a wave of his hand as if shoeing a troublesome bluebottle. "Give me a few minutes to clear my head."

"How much morphine have you taken?"

"Enough to settle the pain."

"Can you stand?"

He looked over at Shadbolt. "I'll be able to in another five minutes. Give me ten and I'll run a marathon for you." He lay back and closed his eyes. After a brief interlude, he raised himself up on his elbow. "You haven't told me what this is all about yet."

"Don't play coy. It doesn't suit you, Octavius, or would you prefer Caddy? You and your cousins, Morgan and Carter Beauchamp are wanted in connection with the murders of four women and at least two others in Iowa, not to mention your involvement with the death and identity theft of one Serge Tremblay."

"If you insist, and what exactly have you got in store for us if we manage to make it out of this little bear trap?"

"You're going back to the States to stand trial."

"I'm not sure the military will be too thrilled about that."

"The orders have been signed, sealed, and delivered."

"And how do you plan on making these outrageous charges stick?"

"Don't worry your head about that, we have enough evidence for you and your partners to swing a dozen times."

"All circumstantial, no witnesses, no weapons, and besides I have it on good authority that those murders were committed by one Casper Littlejohn."

"A handy stooge for your planted evidence."

"Your word against mine, I'm afraid."

"We'll let judge and jury decide that. Now let's get a move on." Shadbolt motioned with the rifle. He could tell Octavius was stalling for time, looking for an opening, waiting for the debilitating side effects of the morphine to subside. Unfortunately, he had little to no leeway. He could hardly shoot him if he resisted, not if he wanted to get him back in one piece to stand trial.

* * *

Octavius could tell the G-man wasn't going to shoot him if he didn't comply. That would defeat the purpose of the mission, and go against his sense of justice, his strict moral code.

"If you're so convinced it was my dear, misunderstood cousins and I, can you guess the roles we assumed?"

"I'm not interested and I'm not going to tell you again. Move your ass."

"Just another minute I swear. The pain is almost bearable. As I was saying, like actors in a play, we all had our assigned roles: the procurer and butcher; the enabler and confessor, spiritual counselor if you will; and the rapist and torturer. Or perhaps all took part in the brutalizations. The possibilities would make Descartes' head spin. And now members of the jury we turn to the influences, the domineering mother still suckling the overfed boy into his teens. Would it shock you to learn that the mother and her wicked brother were incestuous, that they relished abusing the servants, drawing immense pleasure from the suffering they caused, and passing on these heinous proclivities to their progeny. Instructing them, as it were, in the sadistic arts, the exhilaration, the frisson of inflicting pain, degradation and death."

Music burst forth from one of the apartments below, thunderous chords hammering from a grand piano. Octavius saw the face turn towards the source of the noise and leapt for the Mauser, now angled away from the bed. He sent the G-man sprawling across the floor, but the gun remained in his grasp. The distance was too great to close in time, so he turned and fled from the bedroom, through the hallway and out the front door, aiming for the staircase. Grasping the balustrade, he made the top floor landing in three ravenous strides. He aimed for the rear of the building, his hastily concocted plan to scramble to the deck below, and from there the back alley.

When he heard no following footsteps, he slowed his run. Maybe he had stunned the G-man and could've pressed his advantage. Too late now. He traversed the hallway, noticing that the entire top level was being renovated. Drop sheets covered the floor, and the walls had been stripped to bare plaster, the lath exposed in several locations. He turned into an open doorway and crouched down against a badly deteriorating panel where he could see right through the weave of the lath. In spite of the morphine, the exertion had caused his wounds to flare up. He didn't trust his luck at shimmying down the outside wall to the floor below. He'd have to disable the G-man if he had any hope of 'slipping the surly bonds.' From further below the piano concerto continued uninterrupted. Another reluctant evacuee emboldened by the temporary flight of the occupiers.

After a few minutes he heard footfalls above a passage of melancholy chords, and the creak of a loose riser on the stairs. An ascending arpeggio mirrored the upward trajectory of the stalker. The volume of the music rose. His heart beat faster. A rivulet of sweat traced a meandering course through the deep valley of his chest. He clenched and unclenched his fists, straining to hear above the approaching crescendo. His muscles twitched, thighs tensed ready to spring.

A noise to his right.

Exhalation of air.

Another step.

And one more, soft as the padding of a stalking tiger.

A shadow darkened the spaces between the slats of lath.

Octavius drew back his fist and struck the wall with all his might.

* * *

The wall exploded in front of Shadbolt's face. A serpentine form emerged from the cavity and latched onto the arm holding the barrel of the Mauser. His arm was yanked through the opening and bent at an impossible angle. He cried out and dropped the weapon, twisting his body around to use his right hand to extract his trapped limb. His fingers were wrenched apart with a sickening snap. Then, the swish of steel against leather. A blade sliced deep into his wrist. With only one hand restraining him, he threw himself backward, his full weight coming to bear on breaking the death grip. Warm blood coursed down his forearm. The slickness causing the tenuous hold to slip to the meat of his palm, and then his broken fingers, the pain shooting all the way up his arm. Using his legs for leverage, he gave a final tug and fell back against the wall. He reached for his sidearm and fired into the hole. There was an explosion further down the landing as Octavius crashed through the wall and thundered down the stairs in a chalky cloud of dust. A ghost taking flight.

Shadbolt got off another shot, before turning his attention to his ravaged forearm, spurting blood. He leapt to his feet, holstered his sidearm, and grabbing a length of drop sheet, wound it tightly around the gaping wound. He ran along the landing to the apartment at the front of the building. He hit the bank of windows overlooking the street in time to witness an open staff car flying the swastika parked outside. An SS commandant in a long, black leather trench coat stood beside the idling vehicle, watching as two troopers dragged a white-haired gentleman down the front steps of the building.

Shadbolt hadn't noticed that the music had stopped.

He observed the officer reaching for his Luger as another white-haired figure came down the steps waving a sheet. The officer motioned the trio aside and went down on one knee, covering the specter as it slowly descended to the sidewalk. Shadbolt heard a shouted exchange between the two, and then the officer stood up and approached, his Luger still trained on the man.

Was Octavius surrendering to the Germans? Risking the lesser of two evils by becoming a prisoner of war. No God damn way was he assuming another identity and melting back into the masses once the conflict was over. Not this time.

Out of the corner of his eye Shadbolt saw the pianist bolt. In that briefest of moments with all heads turned toward the fleeing man, Octavius lashed out with his knife, in one vicious stroke slitting the throat of the SS officer. He dropped his gun and clutched at the gush of blood. Octavius stooped to retrieve the Luger and fired at the stunned panzers, their rifles still hanging on their shoulders. The shot obliterated the eye of the first grenadier. The second held up his hands in surrender. Octavius unloaded three slugs into the cowering soldier, and then turned his attention to the figure writhing on the ground beside him, stomping his head to a pulpy mass. He tucked the Luger into his belt and climbed into the driver's seat, slamming the idling vehicle into gear.

Shadbolt's heart hammered in protest, a lifetime's rage coursing through his veins, assailing the bulwarks of the status quo, due process, morality and justice.

He thought of Perkins mangled, Berry captured or dead, and Will alone, skulking the backwaters of Mexico.

He thought of Connie. Entrusted to his care after the death of his parents.

Watching the law fail and her killer walk free when all he wanted to do was rip him limb from limb. This was different. Now he was the law and he wouldn't fail.

He raised the apartment window with his good arm, and kneeling, took aim, using the sill to steady his pistol hand.

Two explosions peeled like thunder, sending a murder of crows wheeling noisily above the rooftops.

The speeding automobile veered, and with a deafening crash of twisting metal, wrapped around a lamppost. The horn blaring, and no one to silence it.

* * *

Later that evening a lone figure crossed the Wilhelmina canal and entered the Zonsche forest. His movements were labored, unsteady, a trail of blood marking the haphazard passage through the darkening wood. A match flared, scattering jagged shadows amongst the boles. It revealed eyes set deep within a haggard countenance, unshaven, streaked with dirt. Smoke drifted upwards into the canopy, and as his gaze followed the transient coils, he sought out the constellations of the Perseus family: Andromeda, Cassiopeia, Pegasus, Cetus and Cepheus. He noted each in turn along with their mythological provenance. When the cigarette had burned down to a stub, he rose from his haunches and, gathering himself, moved with renewed determination through the underbrush.

* * *

Perkins sat up in bed when Berry entered the room.

"Good to see you, Ed," he slurred through clenched teeth, a tangle of wires holding his broken jaw in place.

"How they treatin' you?"

"Can't complain, but who'd listen anyway? Say, tell this Abercrombie over here how you single-handedly captured twenty Germans."

Berry turned to the soldier in the next bed. "Take everything this G-man says with a grain of salt. I'm no Sergeant York. Once the Waffen SS Commandant was killed, the panzers surrendered en masse."

"From what I hoid, they'd re-captured the town." The soldier looked far from convinced.

"Not for long. Once the Brit armor showed up and they saw they'd be fighting to the death, they voted with their feet. We walked 'em directly to our front lines. I took twenty of 'em from the hospital myself. Easiest assignment so far despite the earlier setbacks. We're pushing on up the corridor. Ain't nothin' stoppin' this juggernaut no how."

"You tell 'im, Ed. Say, wasn't Jack supposed to be comin' with you?"

"That's Shadbolt for you, no time for sentimentalities."

"Don't I know it."

"Here, he asked me to give you this." He handed Perkins an envelope. "Now if you don't mind, I must be running along. We've got a war to win." Berry gave Perkins a wink, nodded to the soldier next to him, and disappeared out the door. Perkins settled back into the pillows, tearing at the envelope. He extracted a single, hand-written page, and read:

Dear Gene,
sorry not to show up in the flesh, but I grabbed the first transport back to England. I'm headed Stateside and then south of the border. I've got a feeling Felix might be in a spot of trouble. I'll fill you in later. Say hi to Vivian for me. The command unit of the 326th are right behind the 101st. We've arranged for a visit when she gets to Zon.

One down and two to go, my friend. Get better soon and I'll see you on the flip side.

Regards, Jack Shadbolt

About The Author

Born on father's 27th birthday, pints all around. Quickly falls in with gang of junior teddy boys where he earns the nick-name "Sureshot Shawcross" due to accuracy with a catapult. Burns down abandoned army camp after starting largest grass fire ever witnessed in British Isles including Jersey and Guernsey. Subsequently flees to Canada. Takes up ice hockey and fighting (oftentimes indistinguishable). In 1965, joins rock group "The Knack", playing first gig for the princely sum of $8. Dance shuts down early on account of brawl with town hoods. Graduates high school in 1969 after five year running battle with principal over length of hair. Enters York University, wreaking havoc with various subversive organizations including Jewish Defense League, Black Panthers and Weather Underground, Toronto Chapter. Attempt to blow up Maple Leaf Gardens fails when fuse man sets off sprinkler system. Gets married and takes year off studies, working as "wedge man" on tree-felling crew in dead of Canadian winter. Did he learn nothing in school? Graduates University in 1973, Magna Cum Laude (kidding). Tours Europe in British ambulance with glam-rock band "Ginger Muff". Quickly tires of wearing makeup so gets real job. Quickly loses real job but creates major headlines after exposing corrupt bureaucracy. Quickly learns that you can't eat headlines. Takes 1979 off to tour Europe and North Africa with wife (same one). Starts water fight with gullible Australians (aren't they all?) in sacred fountain in Morocco. Subsequently flees continent. For next 41 years attempts to juggle career, wife, kids, assorted jazz gigs, painting, killer squash game, and the odd night of high stakes poker. Takes sabbatical in '04. Finishes writing first novel in Venice. Runaway Summer tops Calgary Herald best seller list for 32 weeks in 2007.

In his spare time, Stephen Shawcross is an urban planner and partner in Canada's number one and the world's third largest architectural practice, the IBI Group.

39 KEYS TO MONEY SUCCESS

For The 39 Forever Mom

39 Keys to Money Success for The 39 Forever Mom

LYNDSIE BARRIE

Published by Barrie Financial Consulting Inc.

Edited by Karla Barrie, Margaret Davey, Margaret West, Rhonda Cockwill and Laurie Lakeman and Yvonne Winkler

Cover photos by Roz Edge

Book cover and layout designed by Dragan Bilic

Proudly printed in Canada

Contents

About the author

After graduating high school in Dawson Creek, British Columbia, I knew only three things about money; you work for it, you spend it and you save some. Growing up in an outdoorsy family, we spent lots of time quadding, horseback riding, moose hunting and boating and very little time talking about how money works. I used to think "saving" meant burying money in a coffee can in the back forty or hiding it under my mattress!! The concept of putting money to work instead of just trading hours for dollars wasn't introduced to me until I was a 20-year-old hairstylist.

One day, as I was cutting a business owner's hair, he asked me if I wanted to own a salon in the future. I informed him that managing employees didn't appeal to me. He said if I wasn't planning on being a business owner myself, I should learn about investing in other people's businesses to make money. He recommended a book called Smart Couples Finish Rich, and my passion for investing began while reading that book.

Soon after arriving in Cochrane, Alberta, my career as an investment and life insurance broker began. My title was "Financial Advisor". About half of my clients were looking for investment ideas only. The other half wanted help with cash flow management and planning for their futures. The investment firm's "Financial Advisor" training was focused on building and protecting investment portfolios - not cash flow management. I was struggling with the ups and downs of my commission income combined with my poor money management skills. Each time a client would ask for help with "budgeting", I'd think *"I can't teach something I don't know!!!"*

Luckily, Junior Achievement asked me to teach middle school students about topics we wish we were taught in grade eight:

1. Cash flow management
2. Saving
3. Starting and growing your own business
4. Investing

> (Find out more about Junior Achievement volunteer opportunities at **jacan.org**. $1 from each book sale will be donated to Junior Achievement.)

FINALLY! The basic financial keys my clients and I had been looking for, presented in a fun, easy to understand format. The focus of my client conversations shifted from topic 4 (investing) to topics 1, 2 & 3 - *how to manage money like a successful business owner*. My life began making an impact on those who needed help getting to the point where they could invest - not just those who already had loads of money to invest.

Inevitably, the investment firm and I parted ways. Barrie Financial Consulting was born. I discovered more and more keys in books, Ted Talks, podcasts and live mentors, which I turned into presentations, articles and videos. The financial challenges and successes of many, many 39 Forever Moms are in the pages you are about to read.

This book is dedicated to my son

I knew I ***could*** and ***should*** write a book to help Canadian women manage their money better. Even though I knew that if I turned my best information into a book, it could have a huge impact on many lives, these aren't the reasons why this book exists. This book is dedicated to the reason you are reading this book, my son.

Son,
The day I wrote on my goal board "I will write my first book by June, 2016", you came home from school, quickly noticed it and read it out loud. Thank you for doing that. Thank you for asking "What will it be about?" and "Will it be like 200-300 pages?" You taking my goal seriously is the reason I took my goal seriously. This book is your proof that you can accomplish anything you put your mind to.

Introduction

If you're 39 and holding, and have children, this book is the turning point you've been craving. Say goodbye to money uncertainty.

If you're under 39, this book *probably* isn't for you. The knowledge I've gained from working with women age 39 and up is contained in these pages. You'll definitely get some good information if you're under 39, but I'd bet there are better books out there for you.

If you are 39+ without children, this book definitely isn't for you. Every one of my 39+ female clients has children. This book is a collection of lessons I've learned alongside 39+ moms during my career. Besides, you will likely get annoyed with how much I talk about children. Imagine you're at a birthday party and you realize every person there is consumed with their children's lives...while you're thinking about the next art show you're going to. Annoying.

What do you want?

No matter what your age, I'm sure you'll agree that very few people know what they actually want. I don't know exactly what I want to achieve with my life. I wanted to write a book. I wanted the book to help others and bring me fulfillment. I don't know what specific things I want to have accomplished five or ten years from now. All I know is I want to be happy and healthy. I spent many years worrying about money, and I know I don't want to do that ever again. What about you? I bet you're like most 39 Forever Moms; you may not know what you want but you definitely know you don't want to constantly worry about money any longer. Every mother I've ever met worries about one or both of these **what ifs**:

"What if I end up poor and destitute?"

"What if my kids end up poor and destitute?"

Get off the hamster wheel. It's time to replace your worry with knowledge & action.

Stop Worrying!

Key 1

Worry is the #1 cause of health problems and health problems are the #1 cause of ending up poor and destitute. Worry causes all sorts of mental and physical health problems. If you don't believe me, Google "worry cause health problems study" and do some reading. Make sure to include this one in your research: **webmd.com/balance/guide/how-worrying-affects-your-body**

If your talents and abilities which you use to earn income are prohibited by illness, you are in trouble. Whether you work in the city or you are a stay at home mom, your talents and abilities produce income. What would it cost to replace a stay at home mom? Exactly. *Cha-ching.* You must protect your health, talents and abilities in order to protect your loved ones. *You really do have to take care of YOU first.* No, it's not selfish. It's a simple fact. The first thing you have to do to take care of yourself is this:

Replace worry with knowledge & action.

Worrying about what went wrong yesterday is as pointless as worrying about what could go wrong tomorrow. Worry, like being broke, is a bad habit which can be broken.

"...we must equip ourselves to deal with different kinds of worries by learning the three basic steps of problem analysis. The three steps are:

1. *Get the facts.*
2. *Analyze the facts.*
3. *Arrive at a decision – and then act on that decision."*

~ *How to Stop Worrying & Start Living by Dale Carnegie*

Dale Carnegie goes on to explain *"When we are worried, our emotions are riding high".* If you pretend to be someone other than yourself as you gather the facts, you skip over the emotions and take action straight away. Throughout this book you will use the "three step problem solver" to help you replace your worries with knowledge & action.

Congrats on taking the first action step by reading this book!!!

You want your kids to know the difference between needs and wants, yes? Thought so. Show them how it's done. If being broke is your main money issue, you must identify which bad habits are at the root of your issue. **Your kids don't deserve to have you snapping on them because you're broke.**

If you find you run out of money before payday often, it's time to put pen to paper as you take Dale Carnegie's advice.

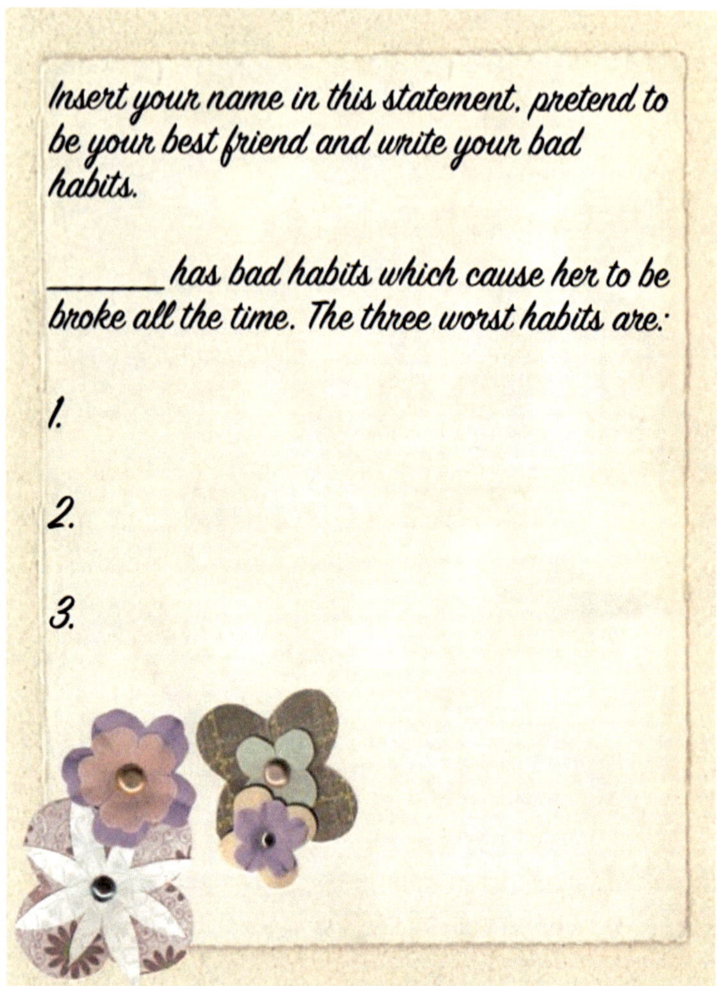
Insert your name in this statement, pretend to be your best friend and write your bad habits.

_______ has bad habits which cause her to be broke all the time. The three worst habits are:

1.

2.

3.

This and all other "writing pages" can be printed at **barriefinancialconsulting.ca/resources**

There are the facts (1). Now analyze the facts (2) then arrive at the decision (3) of what action you need to take.

Here's what I tell myself when I'm in "best friend mode": *"Your income allows for a certain amount of spending on non-essentials. After you reach that amount, you are trading needs for wants. You NEED nutritious food and fuel for your vehicle. You WANT a new purse. You can't have everything all at once, Princess."*

If you're like me - sometimes oblivious to the needs and wants scale tipping - **mint.com** can bring you back to reality. A **Mint account** is a huge part of my tried & true cash flow management system, which is coming in **Part Two of the book**.

If I asked you right now *"What do you want to be better at when it comes to your money?"* you'd say something like **"I want to learn more about investing."** I'd ask *"Why?"* Your response would be something like **"To have more money."** Then I'd ask *"Why do you want to have more money?"*

Why do we all want more money? Because we think having more money will reduce our stress and make us happier.

Happiness = Emotion

The flip-side of the emotion coin is, of course, unhappiness/discomfort/**pain**.

Humans run faster from pain than they run towards pleasure.

This fact is why your fears are my #1 concern. Your wants are secondary. **Fear drives the bus.** We will identify what you are running from soon.

Who will hold you accountable?

This is usually my role, but since I can't be everybody's live accountability partner, you will need to keep each other accountable. Holding yourself accountable may be easy for you - *WAIT! What's that shiney thing over there!?!?* As I was saying - if you're not easily distracted - good for you. For the rest of us, this experience will be much more fun and effective if you join forces with 1, 2 or 7 like-minded people. Suggest to your book club, Bible study, best girlfriends or family that you embark on the journey to money success together with the help of a great new book.

"What about my spouse?"

Your spouse, if you have one, may be your ideal accountability partner. If you have your doubts about working together on bettering your money success skills together, master the skills presented in this book yourself THEN invite your spouse to join you. If yours is one of the many marriages on the rocks due to money disagreements, all the more reason to share in a life-changing learning experience with your life partner.

Part One: My Journey

Money always frustrated me. I was frustrated when I was out of money. I was frustrated when I had to babysit and deliver newspapers to make money. I was frustrated with the buyers' remorse roller coaster: *you finally get those jeans you really want and have been fantasizing about for a month only to find they don't make your butt look as great as you'd expected.*

It wasn't until age 30 that the true causes of my money troubles became clear. What a revelation it was to see the numbers on paper showing that I could afford to live comfortably on what I was making! My frustration with my lack of cash flow management skills was replaced with a passion to figure out how to manage my money successfully.

My childhood included the usual babysitting and newspaper delivery jobs. Saving money wasn't my forte. As soon as I made money, I wanted to spend it. There were always opportunities to buy stuff, mostly at garage sales; garage sales were and still are my Dad's favourite! When we shopped at malls, we only bought things that were on sale. Oh, the rush I got when I found a great deal! Nine out of ten purchases were followed by buyers' remorse because I didn't really need or want the item. It felt good to spend money. It didn't feel good, hours or days later, to look at the item and wish I could exchange it for the money spent on it. The true source of the rush I felt that always caused me to fork over my hard earned cash was a mystery to me until I reached my early 30's.

My first job began at age 13 at the gas station my Mom and step-dad owned. They were always stressed out from teenaged employees ripping them off and customers charging to their accounts and not paying on time, or sometimes at all. Mom taught me how to get over my shyness by greeting customers, washing windshields and offering to check engine oil. She also may have asked me to pay close attention to a few of my co-workers whom she suspected were stealing!! As I got used to dealing with people, my smiling personality helped me earn tips! After a few years, I decided to use my expert gas station attendant skills at the restaurant where my girlfriend worked as a waitress. It wasn't the work that appealed to me. It was the huge tips she earned during Saturday and Sunday breakfast shifts. It turned out I made better tips at age 14 as a gas jockey than I did at age 16 as a waitress! This fact is probably due to my high level of passion for vehicles and my minimal passion for whether or not to hold the onions on a customer's omelette.

Dad (my folks divorced when I was seven) had been an RCMP officer until I was born, then he began working for the government. My step-mom was also a government employee. In addition to owning the gas station, Mom had a part-time job working for the provincial government. All three worked remotely as much as in their offices. To me, being allowed to work remotely was the most appealing part of their government jobs. They talked about their "pensions" with great enthusiasm (I had no idea what a pension was but I knew it had something to do with retirement) as the key reason why my siblings and I should aim to get government jobs. *I eventually concluded that a pension pays for trips to Hawaii which is the government's way of thanking its workers once they are too old to be of use to the government anymore.* This childish assumption turned out to be somewhat accurate.

It wasn't until grade 10 that I had a clear savings goal and managed to save some money. Mom agreed to pay half the price tag on my first horse, which was $2500. I saved the money, and bought my very own Quarter Horse mare, Jade.

Buying Jade was just the beginning of the horse expenses. Luckily my best friend was a farm girl. She hooked me up with her old saddle and her parents allowed me to board Jade at their farm for only $1 per day including feed plus farm labour whenever possible. Farm labour happened less and less once we teenaged girls had our driver's licences! During my high school years, I enjoyed many hours on that farm trying to earn my keep and of course, trying to be a cowgirl. I even showed my horse twice one summer. I loved being a part-time wannabe cowgirl: cattle drives, checking fences, working Jade in the arena (she worked me, actually) and rides to the swimming hole.

I joined a 4-H Beef Club one year. I viewed my 4-H steer, whose name was Big Mac, as a financial investment, which he was not. 4-H is more about the investment of time in personal growth than it is about the investment of money. Unfortunately, I realized that many years later. If I had to choose between a Saturday shift at Turbo or participating in a 4-H public speaking event, I thought I'd be losing money if I didn't choose Turbo. I was also terrified of public speaking, and didn't care that I might need that skill later on in life. It sure would have been nice to get over being scared to death of public speaking in front of a bunch of Dawson Creek farm kids rather than a room full of women I was trying to turn into clients. Hindsight is 20/20.

Since I didn't have my own wheels, Mom usually drove me to work at Turbo in the winter. In the summer, rollerblades were my favourite transportation. I took the school bus (45 minutes each way) to the farm and back twice each week.

The months leading up to my 16th birthday, saving was once again on my mind. A fantastic deal on a vehicle came my way a few weeks before I had my drivers licence: a beautiful, rust-free, green 1985 Dodge 4x4. The asking price was $3000 but

I got the seller down to $2500 thanks to *Dad's Garage Sale Dickering Lessons*. Dad taught my brother, sister and I NOT to pay the asking price for used items. Ever. "If they won't come down in price, walk away" he'd say. I had saved only $1000 for a vehicle, so my mom took me to the Dawson Creek Credit Union for my first loan. Mom of course had to cosign the $1500 loan. She threatened me with my life if I missed a payment.

After a few trips in my new truck to the farm where I kept my horse, I realized I'd still have to ride the school bus to the farm most of the time if I wanted to be able to afford my truck payment. My truck *guzzled* gas!!!

Back then, propane was 16-18 cents per litre compared to gasoline which was around 50 cents. Conveniently, there happened to be a very pretty 1985 Chevy short box pick-up, lifted with 35 inch tires, sitting at the used car lot in town. The pretty Chevy also had a dual-fuel system. She ran on propane or gas at the flick of a switch. Bonus. Sold.

Here we are, my true-cowgirl bestie,
my dream truck and I on graduation day.

Money was rolling in faster than I could spend it, even with my truck and horse to pay for.

My new boss at Turbo called me "rich" because I would pick up my bi-weekly pay cheques 2 at a time. This blissful period of my life lasted about a year and ended around the time in grade 11 when my girlfriend and I flew to Vancouver for May long weekend. She had lots of savings from her job at Smitty's and was far better at saving than me. We stayed with my relatives, shopped on Robson Street, got our hair done and ate sushi for the first time (we thought it was gross!), and had a blast. I ended up running out of money on the trip and since I knew my girlfriend had loads of savings, I asked her for a loan so I could keep buying stuff. I can't remember how long it took me to pay her back, but it wasn't fast enough because it put some stress on our friendship. I promised myself I'd never borrow money from a friend again.

Here we are upon arrival in Vancouver, feeling like big deals in front of the limo we hired at the airport.

As graduation approached, Dad began encouraging me to move to Vancouver. He insisted it would be good for me to get away from the "Northern Mentality", as he and my step-mom called it, and try the big city life. (They moved from "The North" to Vancouver Island the summer I turned 13.) Having no career path in mind and zero desire to attend post-secondary school, I decided to attempt becoming a big city girl in order to learn some life lessons. I thought of myself as the star in one of those movies where the small town girl moves to the big city and learns a few valuable life lessons which she wouldn't have learned in her home town. Dad lined up my room and board with relatives for $300 per month and agreed to pay my room and board for the first three months.

Mom was sure I'd hate living in Vancouver, but she wished me well, and reminded me of what would happen if I missed a payment on the now bigger truck loan she'd cosigned for: certain death. She also agreed to take my sister out to ride my horse once or twice a week while I was trying to be a city girl. She also informed me that the only way she would allow me to move home, now that I had graduated, was if I agreed to pay her $500 per month rent. Tough love is still love. After all, no one wants to be 30 and still living with their parents!

My Pretty Chevy (Dad hated her - called her a *"gas guzzling pig"!!*) stayed in Dawson Creek and I flew to Vancouver on a one-way ticket. My first city girl job was a receptionist in a hair and nail salon, which I landed without any effort because one of my relatives worked there as a nail technician. Wanting a second job, I applied at every pub and bar on Robson Street.

Meanwhile, I learned lots about life and work at the salon and made tons of mistakes. Those ladies were great to me. A few took me under their wings, taught me everything from how to dress ("NOT like you're going to the beach") to how to keep the salon running smoothly. They specifically told me the things I did that angered them. For instance, filing my nails at the front desk when the magazines in the waiting area weren't tidy and the floor needed to be swept was a great way to get some dirty looks and probably fired. I smartened up and didn't get fired.

A month later, still without a second job, I took advice to apply at the big downtown hotels in banquets. I was told a job with one of the big hotel chains could lead to working on cruise ships. I was also keen on becoming a hairdresser, and one of the "mother salon hens" pointed out to me that if I possessed skills in both banquet serving and hairdressing, I would be even more likely to get hired to work on cruise ships. This became my goal.

After not hearing back from any hotels or restaurants, I began to apply at retail shops on Robson Street. Indeed, I had a thing for Robson Street.

I ended up landing jobs at Hotel Vancouver and Banana Republic. I also kept my job at the salon. I left my "family deal" of $300 per month room and board in Port Coquitlam to live downtown on Beach Ave in a $900 per month apartment with a co-worker.

My life in Vancouver went from feeling like a test to feeling like the place I wanted to live *for a while*. I wasn't sure if it would be a little while or a long while. I flew back to Dawson Creek, loaded up my truck with more of my belongings and made Vancouver my home, *for a while.* After all, I was finally feeling like I was mastering the city girl challenge. Plus no one likes to hear "I told you so." I persevered mostly out of stubbornness.

During my time in Vancouver, my relatives introduced me to the idea of owning my own business and being my own boss by helping others succeed. These new friends seemed so eager to help me succeed. I wanted to know more. I was told to read "How To Win Friends & Influence People" by Dale Carnegie. They said if I didn't read the book, I wasn't serious about becoming a successful entrepreneur. I read that book at age 17 and it changed my life.

If you are serious about becoming successful at ANYTHING,

Read How To Win Friends & Influence People by Dale Carnegie.

Key 2

Dentists, restaurant owners and folks who seemed successful taught me that working long hours and babysitting employees day after day is no way to live. They taught me the same things I'd heard over and over again in church all my life: *do unto others as you'd have others do unto you*. It sunk in more coming from people who had the success I wanted; the careers, fancy homes and cars. It shocked me that these people STILL weren't fulfilled! They said they didn't have the one thing they wanted - FREEDOM.

"Be your own boss" wasn't the theme of many conversations with any of my three government employee parents. They taught me to get a good job with a pension. My new perspectives on work and money concerned them. The Kool-Aid I was drinking was growing a part of my brain I didn't know existed, and I was loving it. At the same time, I was frustrated that no one believed it was possible to have the type of freedom I was talking about. I also didn't have any proof in the pudding.

The hairdressers encouraged me to combine my new entrepreneurial spirit with my desire to learn how to do hair. My boss said I could apprentice at his salon for two years to get my British Columbia Hairdresser Certificate.

While all of these epiphanies were coming to me, my three jobs were paying the bills. My job at Banana Republic began with a big discount on five pieces of clothing to help me look the part. Eating five-star hotel food at a discount and getting my hair done for free at the salon helped keep costs down too. Life was simple with only myself to care about. My days of having savings, however, were over. I couldn't manage to save money because I didn't have a specific savings goal. Seeing expensive clothing, shoes and purses everywhere made me want them more. I stuck to my bargain shopper roots but just like in high school, 9 times out of 10, when I bought a new item, the pleasure it gave me was gone within days. I found myself looking around at all the people with their fancy-looking clothing and accessories, feeling like I was in a rat race. I began to feel homesick. It was fall in Vancouver, and it rained continually. By November, I was looking for a way to end the *city girl* chapter of my life.

I found a hairdressing school close to my home town in Grande Prairie, Alberta. I knew my mom had a RESP (registered education savings plan) to pay for my first year of post-secondary schooling. Once my plan was Mom-approved, my beauty school tuition was paid. I gave my Vancouver roommate notice and began counting down the days until I'd see my high school besties.

I left Vancouver in the middle of December on my jacked up truck's 35-inch mud tires which were now 34-inch slicks. The tires were beyond worn out. There had been a few near-crashes in Vancouver. I figured if I drove all the way home in four wheel drive and didn't speed, I'd be able to keep her shiney side up. On the drive back up north, I had one terrifying near-death experience thanks to my bald tires. I pulled over to sleep in my truck for a few hours, still doing that shudder breathing thing that happens after a good cry, and made a deal with God that if He got me into the next phase of my life in one piece, I'd accomplish big things with my life. Thankfully, He obliged, and I white-knuckled it to Dawson Creek after my nap.

Upon my safe arrival, the first thing on my to do list was GET NEW TIRES. I took Dad's advice and didn't go with 35-inch mud tires. Not my folks, or anyone, knew the terrifying details behind my sudden change of priorities (from looking cool to staying alive). I didn't want to confess that I had tried to pass a slow truck in the dark before realizing how slick the road was and ended up sliding almost sideways in the wrong lane towards an oncoming semi then, somehow, slid back to facing forward and barely got back behind the slow truck in time for the semi to pass. I also wasn't going to admit to bursting out in tears, my heart beating so hard that I thought

I might be having a heart attack, as I passed a bad accident a few minutes later. That was the closest call of my entire life. It taught me that my safety is much more valuable than looking cool in a jacked up truck. It taught me that safety is not a want; ***safety, like food and water, is a NEED.***

Invest in safety by saving for emergencies.

Key 3

If your car breaks down, bad things can happen. If you blow a tire or your brakes fail, death or paralyzation can happen. Don't sacrifice safety when it comes to your vehicle's tires and brakes. Safe tires and brakes on your vehicle are a NEED - not a want.

I'm not sure anyone could have convinced me to prioritize being alive above looking cool when I was 18. It took a literally *terrifying* experience to snap me out of this immature mindset. Before you buy clothing, accessories and pay your kids' sports fees, prioritize your health and safety by:

1. investing in tires and brakes for your vehicle before they wear out.
2. saving an emergency fund equivalent to at least three months' expenses.
3. investing in disability and critical illness insurance.

While I was living in Vancouver, a credit card with $1000 limit found its way into my wallet. I told my folks about my new plastic friend. Their advice was:

1. *"Using a credit card will help you build credit score."*
2. *"Make sure you pay it off before the end of the month, or your credit card will hurt your credit score."*

These statements seemed conflicting, plus I didn't know what a credit score is.

Fortunately, I was aware of the financial mess that could come from credit card misuse. One of my relatives in Vancouver had shared with me his credit card story. When he and his wife were newlyweds in their early twenties (in the mid-90's), they applied for a $5000 credit card and were approved. No sooner had they received the card in the mail did they begin to receive applications in the mail from other credit card companies. They applied for another, were approved, then another and another. They went on shopping sprees until their multiple cards were maxed out, then used ATMs to make cash withdrawals from the cards to make the minimum payments. My jaw dropped as he told me his story. Before their bad credit had caught up to them, "just looking" in furniture and electronics stores turned into sales people convincing them to buy that TV/sofa/dresser they wanted on a store credit card. They loved buying whatever they wanted and having nice, new things. It felt amazing to "seem wealthy". They chose to push the consequences of their credit card misuse out of their minds and "live in the moment". They ended up owing about $25,000 to credit card companies and the amount owing kept climbing as the interest compounded each month. At the time I moved to Vancouver, they had been on a strict debt repayment plan for about a year. They were chipping away at the debt, keeping track on a "Debt Free" chart on their fridge. I couldn't believe it. *"How can people be so irresponsible as to think they can continue to use someone else's money and never have to pay it back?"* I thought. Their awful experience could have been avoided if they had been taught by their parents or high school teachers or SOMEONE - ANYONE - how credit cards work. If he hadn't shared his credit card story with me, I may have ended up feeling the pain of **credit card compound interest** myself.

Understand how credit cards work.

Key 4

A credit card can make or break one's credit.

Immediately after moving to Grande Prairie Alberta, a new set of less sexy, more responsible tires were my first credit card purchase. As far as I was concerned, my first credit card purchase was helping me two-fold. A few people had told me that in order to buy my first home, I had to build credit by having and using my very own credit card. *"Own a home!"* was the only type of investment advice I ever received from my folks. *"Renting is not smart, because your money pays for your landlord's house. Put the money in your own pocket by buying a house."* My goal evolved from working on cruise ships to buying a house in Grande Prairie. Oh, to be 18. *Look! Over there! Something shiney!*

First, I had to complete hairdresser training followed by an apprenticeship, preferably not leaving me with a debt-free fridge chart. Living in Grande Prairie also allowed me to reunite with my high school friends, whom I had missed very much while living in Vancouver. Just like we'd planned in grade 12, we all moved to Grande Prairie and lived together, to our parents' dismay, even though it was quite inexpensive to do so. The savings we enjoyed from living together like sardines was not actually SAVED, rather, it was spent at the bar.

Dad was not sold on my choice to become a hairdresser, but if you ask him now if he agrees that becoming a "hair engineer" enabled me to pay my bills for the next 10+ years, be my own boss, work anywhere and spend the utmost time raising my son, he'd concur.

Back to credit cards and credit reporting...

whether or not you are looking to build or repair your credit, you must:

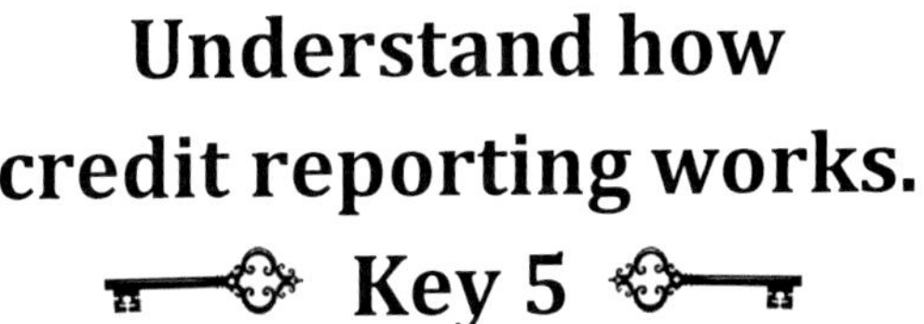

1. Your credit rating has two components: your credit score and your credit report. In Canada, there are two companies that manage credit databases: Equifax and Transunion.
2. Your CREDIT SCORE is a number between 300 and 900. Higher scores are viewed more favorably.
3. Your CREDIT REPORT lists your debts, past and present, and whether or not the accounts are in good standing. The report also lists how many companies have inquired about your credit recently. An unusual increase in the number of inquiries can have a negative impact on your credit.
4. Each and every year, request your credit report from both sources by going to **transunion.com** and **equifax.com**. Request they mail you your **free** copy or if you don't want to wait, you can pay to have your credit report emailed to you.
5. Once you have your credit report, ensure your information is accurate. Look at all the companies and dollar amounts listed under "credit history" and make sure they are accurate.
6. By law, negative information can only be kept on your credit report for a certain length of time. For most information, the maximum is 6-7 years. The exact amount of time varies by category and by province or territory. Positive information, such as accounts that you paid on time, may be kept longer.

7. Go to **barriefinancialconsulting.ca/resources > How credit reporting works** to view a sample credit score and credit report.

Looking to build or repair your credit?

If so, a **Secured Credit Card** can help. Some secured cards are like a reloadable calling card. These "reloadable"/ "prepaid" credit cards won't help you build credit, as they are simply a gift card you can use for purchases anywhere, including online. To build credit, you need a Secured Credit Card which is like a reloadable phone calling card, except if you go over your deposit amount, the card keeps working, but the fees get super high. Most secured cards require a minimum deposit of $500 and, depending on your credit rating, you may have a spending limit of 2-5x the amount of your deposit. The goal is to spend less than the amount of your deposit each month, and of course, pay it back before the fees kick in so you're actually building credit.

I discussed building credit using a prepaid credit card with a mortgage broker friend of mine. She gave me the following tips to pass along to you:

"Here is what I would want to know before picking a Secured Credit Card:

A) Do they report to Equifax and/or Transunion?

B) How often do they report to the Equifax and/or Transunion? You want to build your credit as quickly as possible, so look for a card that reports monthly. Before applying, call the credit card company and ask them to email you a copy of the cardholder agreement or some sort of written proof that they report monthly.

C) Do they send credit info to both Equifax and Transunion, or just one? You want a card that sends your credit info to both credit bureaus.

D) What is the annual fee? Some cards have no annual fee.

E) What interest rate will you be charged if you spend more than your deposit amount? Some credit cards have introductory offers of 9%, then move to 29% after 6 months.

Once you have your secured credit card, use it ONLY for planned purchases, such as vehicle fuel 4x a month. And pay that exact amount back before the monthly payment due date."

~ Courtesy of Stacey Scott, Alberta Mortgage Specialist

If you get approved for a $500 deposit Secured MasterCard with a balance of $2000, you must pretend the $1500 of true credit doesn't exist. It's not bad for your credit to dip into this $1500, but most of the cards I researched charge 20-35% on every dollar you borrow. You won't get into trouble if you don't spend above your deposit amount.

Here's a snapshot of my first few years as a hair engineer...

- I fell in love and began my first serious relationship, luckily with a mechanic because...
- the Pretty Chevy's engine blew up and I had to borrow $1000 from my mom to buy the parts (thanks to my mechanic boyfriend, the labour was free).
- I moved my horse to my boyfriend's parents' farm.
- I passed both the Alberta and inter-provincial hairdressing exams.
- I worked at a hair salon just long enough to complete my apprenticeship and build the foundation of my clientele.
- I began my own mobile hair and nails company.
- I paid my mom back.
- my first love and I bought our first house.
- he proposed; I said "yes!"
- we didn't save any money.
- we argued lots about money.
- we broke up.
- I sold the Pretty Chevy to my brother and put the money towards a down payment on my own house.
- *Mom cosigned my mortgage.*

Banks don't always get paid back.

Key 6

(If you lend money or cosign a loan, you're a bank.)

If you lend money, be prepared to lose all the money you lent. If you cosign a loan, be prepared to make 100% of the loan payments.

When it comes to lending money and cosigning loans for friends and family, stick to these rules:

- Don't lend more money than you can afford to lose.
- Don't lend more than the amount that could ruin your relationship with that person if they don't pay you back.
- Don't lend money to the same friend more than once. Tell him/her it is a ONE TIME LOAN and you will absolutely never lend to them again.
- I wish I didn't have to say this, but since some of you are terrible at saying **NO**: **don't add to an existing loan. One loan at a time, or, even better, ONE TIME LOAN (the previous rule!) Explain to your friends that you value their friendship more than money, and you would rather they borrow from someone else to keep the worst type of stress away from your friendship: money stress.**

- If your friend ditches you because you won't lend him/her money, they aren't really your friend.
- Be a friend, not a loan shark. If you want to loan money to people as a way to make money, you are a loan shark and a jerk, not a friend.
- Don't make your friend feel awkward for asking. The friendship is most important. If you know they are really hurting, buy them a few bags of groceries and make sure this book is in one of the bags.

A relationship damaged by money is difficult if not impossible to mend. A family dinner or your friend's child's birthday party gets pretty awkward when *that person who stiffed you on a loan* shows up. What's worse is when your friend is paying you back in small installments and they show up at the birthday party with an over-the-top $100 gift.

My first loan experience on my trip to Vancouver with my girlfriend in grade 11 could have turned out a lot worse. I know when she reads this she will laugh about the lesson she helped me learn. Had that same scenario happened in our thirties, I could have lost her as a friend.

I'm not saying don't lend or co-sign for your friends and family. I'm saying you must understand the risk you are placing on your financial well being and on the relationship. Mom co-signed my first mortgage. I owned that house for six years. If I had defaulted on that mortgage, or become disabled, the house would have had to be sold. That's not too terribly scary until you factor in the volatile housing prices in Northern Alberta due to oil and gas being its main economic driver. I also didn't have disability or critical illness insurance in my twenties because I was not aware I could protect my income against disability or critical illness. It could have turned into a scary situation.

If you find yourself in a financial bind, and you're considering asking a friend or family member for a loan, look at all your options before asking for the loan. I bet there are other solutions you haven't thought of, and I'd be glad to help you discover them. Email your situation to me:

info@barriefinancialconsulting.ca

Back to my life as a self employed mobile hair and nails engineer in the early 2000's. I...

- spent loads of money at Winners.
- opened a RRSP and saved $50 per month.
- asked my bank for a loan to pay for new windows, shingles and a new furnace for my 1960's shack and was approved for a HELOC (home equity line of credit). Thanks to a Grande Prairie boom, my house had increased in value!
- began dating the eventual father of my son, who we'll call Tom.
- invited Tom to move in with me.
- re-mortgaged so Tom and his dad could turn "my shack" into "our home" because we were **expecting a baby**!!!!!

- brought my perfect, bald, blue-eyed baby boy to his "like new" home.
- began doing hair right away - what else was I going to do? Babies sleep LOTS!
- argued with Tom more and more about...guess what? Yep. Money.

Around my son's first birthday, I made an appointment at my bank to open a RESP (registered education savings plan) and get help figuring out how much I should be putting away for retirement. Surely the $50 per month wasn't enough, I thought. At the bank appointment, the lady wasn't keen to help me with retirement planning. She was, however, keen to encourage me to save more than $50/month. I didn't increase my retirement savings because she didn't help me determine how much I should be saving. I realized her lack of interest in helping me with retirement planning was due to the fact that I didn't have a lot of money. It didn't cross my mind to ask her how she got paid nor did she offer to explain. It was frustrating. Thinking back to the book **Smart Couples Finish Rich**, realizing I had forgotten much of the information, I decided to reread the book. My frustrating bank appointment wasn't a total waste of time because it did push me to read that book again.

Tom came home from work one day and told me about an investment opportunity he'd been hearing about during coffee breaks. He excitedly talked about a boat manufacturing company in the Caribbean in which his supervisor had invested. Tom's supervisor said he had met the owners of this company, saw the patented glass-bottomed boats they were building, and the company would be a gold mine when it went public. I had no idea what "going public" meant. Tom's supervisor also happened to be married to one of my nail clients. My client and her husband were really nice people and seemed financially savvy, so Tom and I decided to invest some money into the glass-bottomed boat endeavour. We converted about $3000 into a US dollar money order and mailed it to the US address my client's husband provided. He advised us to put the investment in my name, since the investment's income would be taxed at my lower rate. After a year of waiting for my "share certificate", or ANY sort of documentation to come in the mail, we began asking questions. It turned out many other people were also asking questions. Eventually I chalked it up as a lesson learned; a lesson better learned at 24 with a $3000 investment than at 54 with a $300,000 investment.

Understand the basics of investing before you invest.

Key 7

The basics of investing are coming your way in **Part Three**:

Key 30	Investment risks
Key 31	Types of investments
Key 32	Diversify! Diversify! Diversify!

Shortly after our son's first birthday, Tom and I decided to separate permanently. Our completely different backgrounds and our differences in opinion about almost everything drove us apart. Being a single mom didn't scare me financially or otherwise, and I knew Tom would always be a great dad to our son. Emotionally, however, I was a mess. Thanks to my fantastic friends in Grande Prairie and having my mom close by in Dawson Creek, I held it together.

For the next few years, my mobile beauty company met my needs. Money was always tight because I didn't keep track of my spending nor did I save an emergency fund. Every time a house or vehicle repair was needed, I paid for it with my credit card. My credit card was my emergency fund.

I knew I could and should do more with my life, but was too comfortable to explore other career paths. I couldn't imagine leaving my amazing friends and clients, or no longer having the freedom to choose how, when and where I make money. I didn't want to have to put my son in full-time daycare to go back to school.

I thought about the lady at the bank who I felt had done a poor job in her role as "financial advisor". I went back and forth between wondering which courses she completed before becoming a financial advisor, and dismissing the idea since it probably involved working 9-5 at a bank, which didn't seem fun. No 9-5 for me, thanks. I was spoiled, and proud of the fact that I had spoiled myself. "Work" rarely felt like work. If I'd known I could have a career very similar to my hair styling business, *beautifying financial situations*, I wouldn't have hung out in the comfort zone as long as I did.

While I was enjoying my comfort zone, I often prayed for one or the other of the following:

1. a career that offered me the freedom I currently enjoyed, or
2. my very own Prince Charming.

I thought, *"Falling in love with a kind, fun, ambitious, talented (preferably gorgeous) man and cheering him on to success seems like the easiest, least scary way to join the real world."*

Cinderella Syndrome is real. So is its antidote.

Key 8

Early on in my financial coaching career, one of my mentors referred to this Prince Charming Prayer as "Cinderella

Syndrome". Throughout my career, I've heard many Cinderella Syndrome stories; some of which had happy endings.

If you were like me when I was in my twenties, my next statement will ring true for you:

I craved financial security and a fulfilling career. Cinderella Syndrome gave me a similar sense of security without all the work.

If this sounds like a struggle you are having, or perhaps your daughter, granddaughter or girlfriend is having, **here's the antidote:**

Focus on fulfilling your own life rather than looking for a Prince Charming to do it for you.

While wishing Prince Charming and/or a great career would land in my lap, one of my girlfriends, another single mom, accepted a promotion and transfer to Calgary, Alberta. Her willingness to take risks and move away from her comfortable life in Grande Prairie inspired me. I visited her a few times after she moved and decided I wanted to move there too.

After arriving home from house shopping in the Calgary area, I put my house up for sale. Grande Prairie had just begun an economic downturn. My house remained on the market for two years. People kept asking me *"Why do you want to move?"* and *"What will you do for work when you move?".* I tried to explain my need for a fresh start although I wasn't sure exactly what I was looking for. I was willing to take a leap of faith. It felt right. After all, working in a salon was always an option. I made two lists to solidify my motives for why I was moving: 1. Pros & Cons of staying in Grande Prairie and 2. Pros & Cons of moving to the Calgary area.

While I waited for my house to sell, the pride I felt from my "home owner" status was replaced with frustration. The list of renos and upgrades I invested in that house was long. My 1960's shack was purchased for only $85,000, sold 6 years later for $172,000 and left me with about $25,000. The equity was my "bank account" for renos and debt consolidation which worked until the price of the house dropped. Thank God it didn't drop further before I sold it!! That said, my folks were right. My home had been a great investment. However, after I sold my house, and obtained "renter" status, life became much simpler. There was no longer fear of an appliance or hot water tank blowing up, or the annual property tax bill.

To rent or to buy?

Renting doesn't have to mean not building equity. In fact, renting can allow you to build a diversified portfolio of equity. How? Rent a place that costs half to three-quarters of what you can afford and save the difference. Invest your savings in real estate and companies all around the world. A diversified portfolio won't follow your area's real estate market. One of the "house poor" symptoms is not having money to invest in assets other than your home. If your home is your only investment, all your eggs are in your town/city's real estate market basket.

As my life story progresses, you'll understand why I am not opposed to renting when one's life is in transition and/or when saving is impossible due to being house poor. If you are currently feeling house poor, you'll find ways to solve this problem as you continue reading this book.

If you haven't bought a home yet, **don't borrow 100% of the amount for which you are approved.** Analyze your cash flow numbers from the last 4-6 months to determine the mortgage payment that's right for you, or go with 80-85% of the amount the lender is offering. ***Knowing your cash flow numbers is one of the most important keys to money success, which is coming in Part Two.***

If you're sure buying a house is right for you, you need a down payment. If I were you, I wouldn't save for my down payment in my RRSP. On the contrary, if I was working for a company that has a RRSP contribution match plan (example, they match your RRSP contribution up to 5%), I would contribute the FULL match amount. How it works is you put in 5% of your pay and they match it with another 5% from the company. The 5% from the company is **free money**. If for some silly reason, I chose to contribute only 4%, I'd miss out on 1% free money.

Say "Yes!" to free money!

Contribute the full match amount so you can receive all the free money your company is offering. If you are eligible for the Home Buyers' Plan, you can borrow this "company RRSP money" for the down payment on a house.

Borrowing from your RRSP to purchase a home is called the Home Buyers' Plan. For more info on how long your RRSP money has to stay in your RRSP before you can use it for a down payment, how much you can borrow, and other Canada Revenue Agency stipulations, go to:
cra-arc.gc.ca/hbp/

The second situation in which you might want to save for your down payment in a RRSP is if you have zero willpower when it comes to saving money, but **be warned: it can be a huge pain in the rear to access your RRSP money if you need it in a hurry to buy your dream home.**

If you are successfully using your Mint account or another tried & true cash flow management plan - by "successfully" I mean you are watching every dollar coming in and every dollar going out AND sticking to your savings goals - put your down payment money in a high interest savings account. This way, you can earn some interest and your money's easily accessible when you find the house you want. One more time: money in a RRSP will take longer to turn into a down payment.

"Should my house down payment be in a TFSA (tax-free savings account) instead of a RRSP (registered retirement savings plan)?"

Nope. Your TFSA should hold long-term savings. I'll explain why in **Part Three**. For now, trust me that a high-interest savings account and some will power (**mint.com** helps!) is all you need to save your down payment.

When it comes time to buy the home, first-time buyers should NOT sign a five-year fixed rate mortgage. Here are two common situations when an open-ended or shorter term mortgage is best:

1. Prepayment penalty fees on a five-year fixed rate mortgage could stop a first-time home owner from saying yes to a fantastic career opportunity in another city or part of the world.
2. First-time home owners with a baby on the way often want to upgrade from their starter home to a home with a bigger yard in a better neighbourhood. Or they might want to renovate their old 1960's shack before bringing the baby home. Take it from me, babies aren't always planned. You can, however, plan on avoiding prepayment penalties by having an open-ended/floating rate mortgage.

In addition to your down payment, you'll also need to have roughly $2500 cash saved for closing costs, which include a home inspection, legal fees, and title insurance.

Before signing an offer to purchase, know the costs involved in buying and owning a home. Don't be HOUSE POOR.

Key 9

My house had been on the market about a year when I found my very own Prince Charming. He was driven, successful, charismatic, handsome, tons of fun and we shared a passion for the outdoors. After a few months of dating, my son also fell in love with him. The Prince knew my move to the Calgary area was on the horizon, with or without him. Conveniently, he received a job offer in Calgary, asked me to move away with him, and I said yes. My fingers were crossed that Tom (my son's dad) wouldn't flip out and drag me into a court battle. Thankfully, the only thing Tom and I had ever agreed on was that Grande Prairie wasn't our forever home. My move resulted in Tom following a few years later.

The first six months of living with the Prince went like this:

- the Prince and I both found renters for our houses up north.
- we rented a great house in Cochrane, Alberta.
- I travelled back to Grande Prairie every 2-3 weeks so my son could be with his dad and I could do hair and nails.
- the Prince paid most of the bills.

- we had tons of fun river boating and camping.
- since the Prince was working downtown Calgary, I decided to look for a job at a hair salon downtown and commute with him a few days each week.
- I began working at a medi-spa in downtown Calgary.

The medi-spa was the first time I'd had co-workers since my job at the salon in Grande Prairie eight years prior. I'll skip the explanation of the many reasons why working at the medi-spa was terrible and get to the good part. I made a key connection near the end of my three months of employment there: a lady from Cochrane who lived down the street from us invited the Prince and me to her husband's birthday party.

At the party, the Prince and I met some nice people. We noticed from their conversations that they were all affiliated with the same company. When we inquired about this company, we were invited to find out what it was all about at their next "meeting". They said they didn't want to talk business at the party, so we should attend the meeting to find out about their business. We sensed it was some sort of get rich quick scheme, but we went to the meeting anyway, in the spirit of being open to new ideas and meeting new people. As you'd expect, the business opportunity was geared towards people who dislike their day jobs and want to get rich doing part-time sales. It was a MLM (multi-level marketing) life insurance and investment sales company.

As I met more kind, supportive people like the ones I met at the party, they all encouraged me to gain understanding of financial products by completing the LLQP (life licence qualification program). This way I could make an informed decision as to whether or not this business was right for me.

It was during that spring, while I was working hard to learn and study in preparation for my LLQP exams, that I began to feel like the Prince didn't want me to succeed. I couldn't pinpoint why he wasn't cheering me on. Either he liked me relying on him, which didn't make sense because I knew he was sick and tired of paying my bills, or he missed having me on hunting and boating excursions. I'd go to the office to study and 15 minutes later, he'd stroll in and start chatting about what we should cook for supper or where we should go boating or hunting next. No matter how many times I asked him to leave me alone so I could focus, he didn't respect my need for peace and quiet while I studied.

Some of you think I sound like a whiny, unappreciative baby. A few people told me to leave this part out of my book completely. The reason I didn't heed this advice is because I know that some of you reading this can relate to where I was at at this point of my life: "Grow up" had been added to my to-do list. It wasn't just about being a mom and having fun anymore. The Prince's lack of support turned out to be due to the latter reason - he missed me. It wasn't that he didn't want me to succeed. My wish had been granted: a great career opportunity had found me. It was time to do some hard work and although I didn't want to, it looked like I'd have to do it on my own. Although the arguing and resentment intensified, we held it together because neither of us were ready for the good times to stop rolling.

A few days after my successful completion of the LLQP (life licence qualification program), I struck up a conversation with one of the moms at my son's preschool picnic. She asked what I did for a living and I told her about completing the LLQP. She asked about my career plans in the financial services industry and informed me there was a vacant office in town with the same investment firm her husband worked for. She raved about the company and said I should go talk to her husband. So I did.

During the meeting with her husband, I explained my concerns about working for the multi-level marketing company which had so kindly helped me get my foot in the financial advising door:

- *I didn't want to have to recruit part-time financial advisors in order to achieve success. I wanted to focus 100% on becoming a great financial advisor.*
- *I wanted my income to reflect only my own productivity - not the productivity of the advisors "below me".*

He agreed and said I'd be a great fit for the company, and I could have my own office in less than a year if I got to work straight away on completing the Canadian Securities Course (CSC). So I did.

The Prince wasn't excited about me taking another course. He had a growing business to manage and he needed support. He deserved support, but I couldn't give it to him. I had to invest my time and energy into building security for my son and I and I'd found an opportunity to do so.

The *"support a successful man"* route might have worked out for me had I not matured and realized that supporting my successful man meant selling myself short. He'd be selling himself short too by settling for a woman whose self-focus left little support for him. No matter how much I wanted it to work with him, I couldn't have and be everything.

After a particularly heated argument, I knew it was time for life with my fun, charismatic, adventurous Prince to end.

It was sink or swim. The beginning of my career brought a sea of challenges, successes and tons of learning about financial products and services. Thankfully I'm a fantastic swimmer. I:

- found a tiny, very affordable walk-out basement suite that was perfect for my son, dog and me.
- borrowed the first month's rent and damage deposit from my mom.
- borrowed money from my mom to pay down my credit card so I could register for the Canadian Securities Course (CSC).
- sold my house.
- passed the CSC exams.
- learned the art of "door knocking" by getting 25 names and phone numbers (mandatory for getting hired), which was relatively easy thanks to my hairdresser's gift of gab.
- landed the job
- knocked on many doors in Cochrane introducing myself and my new business, which is where I met many of the clients I still have today.
- received the best training in the financial services industry.
- continued to utilize my hairdressing talent a few hours each week.

It feels great to finally tell my "hairdresser single mom to financial coach" story. I've heard many other stories similar to mine. Those of us who have found fulfilling careers which we didn't know existed are proof that being open to new opportunities works.

Love & excel at what you do for money. Key 10

In order to **love** and **excel** at what you do for money, your career must stem from *your true passion.* Some call it ***"finding your true calling".*** Don't fret if you haven't yet found your path. Volunteer roles, activities, sports and career opportunities you didn't know existed will appear if you are open to letting them find you. You don't need to search. You simply need to open your life so there's room amongst all the busyness. *How can you be open to new opportunities when your calendar is filled up with the same old tasks?* Driving kids around. Going to the same gym you've gone to for years. Having coffee with the same girlfriends. I'm not saying your kids should walk to and from hockey 10km each way in the winter so you can take up boxing or serve dinner at your local shelter. What about carpooling? Free up some time. Try a new gym or boot camp. Invite the new ladies you meet at the new gym to coffee. Replace some of the same old tasks with new ways to meet new people. I promise you'll discover new talents and passions within yourself.

Be open to being found

Whether you are a stay at home mom, have your own business or a job outside your home, you must open yourself up so exciting opportunities can find you. I'm not saying you should say "YES!" to every invitation/opportunity that comes your way, but I do recommend you say "YES!" to opportunities which are in line with your goals. I'll remind you to **be open to being found** at the end of the book when you have a clear picture of your goals.

Try new things.

Key 11

Your routines may add up to organization but *do your routines add up to exciting opportunities*? Nope. Boring. Mundane. Same old. A certain amount of structure/"time blocking" is helpful but if too much of your time is "blocked", you are blocking opportunities. Leave gaps in your schedule. Trying new things will help you find **Key 10** (love & excel at what you do for money), if you haven't found it already.

A note on "time blocking": 50% of my calendar is blocked with MUST DOs. That leaves 50% of my time available for who knows what. Those who know me well will attest to the fact that I do what I say I'll do while remaining flexible. I remain flexible by ditching or rearranging tasks occasionally - only tasks which don't involve obligations to my friends or clients. Do you hate getting stood up or ditched at the last minute? Me too. I do my best to avoid doing that to others.

It simply isn't true that you need to block your entire day in order to run a successful business. As I've learned to weed out unnecessary distractions in the form of media, email and meetings, my MUST DOs are completed within less than 5 hours per day, 4 days per week. How did I remove most of the time sucking distractions from my life? I haven't had cable for over 6 years. I watch less than an hour of TV/YouTube each week. I cancelled my Netflix in the spring of 2016 and I don't miss it. My son misses Netflix a bit, but we both began listening to podcasts and reading more since Netflix left our home. I don't watch news online. I don't read newspapers. When it comes to social media, I check Facebook twice daily and LinkedIn once every 2-3 days. I'm currently neglecting my Twitter, Instagram and Pinterest accounts for the most part. Hopefully by the time you read this I have addressed this issue!

> *If you analyzed the media you allowed into your brain yesterday, could you honestly tell me it was positive and will help you reach your goals?*

Media is mostly negative and/or irrelevant to my goals.

Use your limited time wisely. If anything potentially life changing happens, we'll find out about it on Facebook.

Four days per week, these are my time blocks:

7-9

Exercise and eat breakfast.

9-10

Create content. Write a new article, presentation or a video script.

10-11

Respond to and delegate urgent email and voicemail. My assistant checks my voicemail at 9am, labels urgent email and emails me about urgent voicemail.

11-12

Customize content for one audience (39 Forever Moms, youth or clients). Post/email an article/video/survey at 2pm daily.

12-1

Eat lunch and walk dogs.

1-2

Make money/close business.

2-3

Check email for any urgent requests that can't wait until 10am. My assistant posts/emails an article/video/survey on TWO platforms: LinkedIn, Twitter, Facebook, MailChimp, Instagram and/or Pinterest.

before 3

Send a social text or email to at least one client and one prospect.

I have one meeting max per day at 9am or 1pm. If a meeting is scheduled, I move "create content" or "make money" to 8-9am or 9-10pm.

Bonus Keys for Business Owners

1. Never check email first thing in the morning!!! Email is a huge time sucker if it is not structured!!! Remember, **email is not instant-messaging. It's mail.** Since I first began experimenting with and implementing **delegation**, less and less of my time is sucked by non-urgent email and phone requests. My assistants deal with them. Why would I pay someone to do something I can do myself, you ask? Because I can make more **money**. I can't make more **time**.
2. It can be difficult to allow someone other than yourself to deal with your hard-earned, precious clients, but you have to get over it. Stop micro-managing. If you haven't done this already, it's time to find the right person to do the things you don't need to be doing and TRUST them to do their job. Here's how I figure out which of the people who want to work for me have the required skills and personality: the **Kolbe A Index**. Here's how it works:

...the Kolbe A Index measures your instinctive way of doing things and the Result is called your M.O. (method of operation). It is the only validated assessment that measures a person's conative strengths. It gives you greater understanding of your own human nature and allows you to begin the process of maximizing your potential both personally and professionally. Research on the Kolbe A indicates no significant differences in outcome by age, race, gender or physical handicap.

Source: **kolbe.com/assessments/kolbe-a-index**

Here's my Kolbe A Index:

You are uniquely able to take on future-oriented challenges. You lead the way to visionary possibilities and create what others said couldn't be done. You'll say "Yes" before you even know the end of the question – then turn it into a productive adventure.

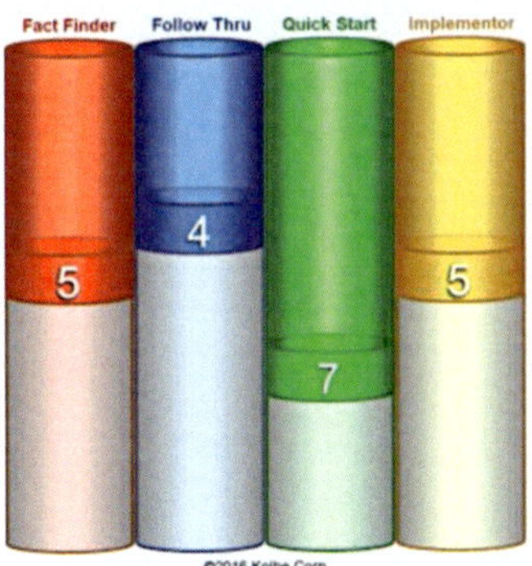

I was lucky enough to find the following two people to help run my business...

Assistant 1:

Your Kolbe A™ Index result shows you are excellent in situations that require strategic organization of information. You set priorities and put them into appropriate sequences.

Assistant 2:

You are excellent in situations that require strategic organization of information. You set priorities and put them into appropriate sequences. Your talent with both strategies and tactics makes you essential to any massive effort.

Notice neither of my assistants have the same lowest score or highest score as myself. It's fabulous. These two gems have allowed me to…

Delegate! Delegate! Delegate!

Key 12

The delegation mindset begins with realizing every human's time is worth money and there are people on earth who **want** to do the stuff you aren't good at, don't want to become good at and dislike doing. Your ideal "assistant" could be a family member, friend, local business or someone you hire on a site like **upwork.com**. It's not just about hiring someone at $10 per hour to do stuff you don't want to do because your time is worth $25 per hour. More importantly, it's about freeing up time to do the things you love to do and excel at. Things that make the world a better place. Things that fulfill you.

Why delegate? Because time is worth more than money. Time is priceless.

Invest money in creating more time to do the things you love and are good at. If done correctly, this investment will pay you great returns!

What would you do with a few extra hours each week? Maybe you'd learn a new skill or sport or explore a new hobby. Maybe you'd take a course.

It's time to put pen to paper again...

Write five things you want to learn how to do well:

Write your six favorite and six least-favorite household/personal tasks. Career tasks will go on the next list. Write only critical tasks which, if not done, would result in very, very bad things happening. These tasks are ones which would have to be done by someone else if you stopped doing them.

Personal tasks

I'm good at & love doing these tasks:	I'm terrible at & don't love doing these tasks:
1.	1.
2.	2.
3.	3.
4.	4.
5.	5.
6.	6.

Write your six favorite and six least-favorite career tasks. Write only critical tasks which, if not done, would result in you losing your job or business.

Career tasks

I'm good at & love doing these tasks:	I'm terrible at & don't love doing these tasks:
1.	1.
2.	2.
3.	3.
4.	4.
5.	5.
6.	6.

Which of the tasks on the right side of the last two lists could you delegate to your children, a local business or someone else? Put a star beside the tasks you want to delegate.

What do you ACTUALLY get paid to do?

How much money do you ACTUALLY get paid?

When it comes to delegating, you need to know what your time is worth so you can be sure you are not over-paying your assistants. This can be tricky to calculate for business owners, but it is quite simple for those who get paid a set amount per month or per hour.

Ask yourself:

"If I removed all the distracting emails, chatty phone calls, texting, Facebook and pointless meetings from my day, and just did what I ACTUALLY get paid to do, how many hours would it take me each day to get my work done?"

Write how many hours per month you are actually making money:

____

Now calculate your actual hourly income. Divide your monthly net income by the number above.

Write your actual income per hour:

$ ______________________

We'll use the last number in a few minutes.

What are you really, really good at which makes you money?

This was the focus of my first session with my business coach. My homework was to dwell on this question to the point where I knew the answer so clearly that it would forever be at the center of everything I invested my time, money and energy into.

I'm really, REALLY good at helping 39 Forever Moms save and invest better. Sure, I'm OK at playing the piano, colouring and cutting hair, designing and sewing my own clothes, graphic design and a few other things. I could make money at so many things but I know, without a doubt, that I am meant to help mothers and their children by sharing what I know about saving and investing. I'll always enjoy doing hair and sewing but I don't intend to use those skills to change the world.

When I needed a website, I hired a web designer named Tynan. I had designed a few websites in the past, and even thought about making that my career at one point, but I didn't love designing websites. Tynan loves designing websites and he's fantastic at it. While he was getting my website up and running, I created a survey for women. I needed the survey PDF turned into an online survey using **surveymonkey.com**, so I jumped on **upwork.com** and posted the job. The lady I hired set up my survey then offered to set up my **mailchimp.com** account. Then she offered to integrate my MailChimp account with **eventbrite.com**. She loves doing that stuff and she's really good at it. Sure, I could become good at all that contact management stuff too but why would I bother? It would have taken me at least six hours to do what she did in an hour and a half. Then, I put her in touch with Tynan and they worked together to link my new survey and contact management accounts to my website. They were literally solving my problems in a fraction of the time it would have taken me while I was eating dinner with my son.

Did I mention virtual assistants are game changers?!?!?!

"Which tasks should I delegate?"

Look at your lists on page 63 and 64. Use the **three step problem solver**. Remove the emotion of delegating the tasks you starred by looking at them from your best friend's perspective. Maybe even text a photo of your lists to your three best friends and ask for their help finding people to whom you can delegate these tasks.

For advice on delegating all sorts of life's tasks, I highly recommend **The 4-Hour Workweek by Tim Ferriss**. This book will change your life if you adopt even a few of Tim's many perspectives.

When it comes to hiring local help, aim to hire entrepreneurs. If they don't have experience managing their own business, but you still want to hire them, you can often teach the "business owner" mindset to someone with an "employee" mindset. The books I recommend in this book are great training material for budding entrepreneurs.

As my Kolbe A Index proved, I lack follow through. As I've become better at delegating, I've found help with seeing my ideas through to completed projects. I've also found time and the ability to be my flexible self without the chaos.

When you learn how to turn some of your new free time into income, the delegation key will unlock more money success than you can imagine.

Keep these tips in mind when delegating:

1. Read The 4-Hour Workweek by Tim Ferriss.
2. Don't delegate things you should eliminate. If the task you want to delegate isn't clearly defined and important, aim to eliminate it.
3. Delegate one thing at a time/one task per email to avoid confusion.
4. Delegate your "To Delegate" list in priority order. Don't dump too much on one person at once. You may need multiple assistants at times.
5. Set a clear deadline for each task.
6. Use **upwork.com**. Need a better LinkedIn profile or resume? Need your daughter's 8th birthday party planned and EventBrite invitations sent out? Need

your vacation to San Francisco planned complete with Giants game tickets and hotel reservation? Need a presentation for work created? Upwork.com.

7. Attach a price tag and bonus to each task.

   Example A) I hire a guy on upwork.com to format my book for printing. I agree to pay him $300 in three increments; $100 for each of the three sections of my book.

   Example B) I ask my son to wash the dishes for $2 plus a $1 bonus if I don't find any food stuck to the dishes.

When it comes to **simple physical tasks** like scanning documents, shredding paper, prepping dinner and emptying the dishwasher, ask yourself, *"How long would it take me to do that task?"* Then ask yourself, *"How much is my child's time worth?"* Here's how I calculate this:

> Say you are worth $30/hour net of taxes, and it takes you five minutes to empty the dishwasher. Offer to pay your child half of what you earn in five minutes working at your career. If you are worth $30/hour, pay your child $1.25 to empty the dishwasher. Make sure to offer a bonus to ensure your child puts every item in its place: seventy-five cents to empty the dishwasher and a bonus fifty cents if everything is put away correctly. This of course only peaks their interest if you aren't giving

them money constantly/paying for most of their wants.

I know what you're thinking. *"I'm not paying my children to do everyday chores! That's why I pay them an allowance! Besides, it's unrealistic for them to believe they should get paid to empty the dishwasher!"* Agreed. However, there will be times when your child has already taken out the garbage, cleaned the bathroom, folded and put away the laundry and been an all-around gem. In these rare situations, you can offer them an optional bonus job to make extra money, which may or may not be a household chore. It could be shredding documents in your office or vacuuming the vehicle or weeding the flower beds. Maybe picking up dog poop. Use your number from page 65 to calculate values for bonus jobs you can delegate to your kids.

Spoiled Brat Syndrome

We've all felt the horror that comes along with the realization that our children are unappreciative of their optimal lives. They always want more. Our kids aren't the only ones suffering from **spoiled brat syndrome**. Adults are worse because the price tags on the things we want are much, much higher. Can you imagine if children could have credit cards? That's basically why so many Canadians are in loads of debt: most Canadian adults haven't learned how to win the battle with their inner child screaming ***"I want it now!!!"***

In addition to being born in one of the best countries in the world, Canadian kids have the best of the best - sports equipment, tablets, clothing and vacations. I'm all for keeping kids busy and giving them the opportunity to learn every sport and develop their creative talents, but how often does your child jump up after dinner to wash and put away the dishes while saying wonderful, appreciative things like *"I'm so glad I'm able to play soccer. Thanks for paying my soccer fees and for buying me new cleats every year. Doing the dishes doesn't even come close to paying you back but I hope you know how thankful I really am. I'm so lucky to have you for a Mom."? Probably just as often as my 10 year old son - NEVER.* Although he is quite helpful around the house and does know the value of a dollar, my son, like most Canadian children, displays symptoms of spoiled brat syndrome from time to time. At these times, I lovingly remind him that he will have to pay for his children's sports and drive them to tournaments and pay for hotel rooms someday. I am simply paying it forward because my parents did the same for me.

Want your children to be more appreciative and quit expecting to get everything they want? Quit giving them everything they want. Teach them **they need their own money** and they can have it if they work for it. The last thing you want is a child who doesn't know how to manage money. Give your child $5-10 each week depending on their age. When they have their own money, it is easier and more justifiable to say no to their wants. They need to learn that when they spend all their money, the only way to get more is to work for it. Make sure your children have money to manage NOW!

Put your kid(s) to work!

Believe it or not, children as young as age three can put away silverware, fold towels and they can most definitely fold and put away their own clothing. Put them to work!! Pay them per task in addition to their base rate. It's not about whether or not they get paid to do a task that you know you don't get paid to do. I realize they won't always get a loonie when they put away the silverware but why not give them some incentive to get their earning level higher so they can afford to delegate tasks too? If one of your children hates dishes more than vacuuming and the other hates vacuuming more than dishes, teach them to trade tasks. Depending on the price tags you've attached to each task, maybe they will have to trade 2 for 1 or add their own money to make the trade fair.

Next time your kids are being lazy and won't help out with their standard household chores, ask them:

"Would you rather:

a) I clean up messes mostly made by you which makes me grumpy and doesn't make our family money to enjoy vacations and new hockey equipment for you, or

b) I work on my laptop for an hour <u>making money</u> - some of which I will share with you - while you tidy up the kitchen and do the dishes after supper?"

My son began receiving a $5 weekly allowance at age five. Each year, his allowance increases with his age; $1 per year. My 10 year old son currently receives $10 per week. This is because the amount and complexity of his tasks has increased each year. He pays for his wants with his own money, except on occasion when I pitch in up to half.

My son and I went on vacation to Orlando Florida a few months after his 10th birthday. He had about six months to save for the trip. He knew he was saving for half of his Universal Studios ticket and ALL of his "wants". He went to Orlando with about $200USD. The condo was stocked with groceries but he wanted to buy himself chicken fingers and fries at the poolside restaurant a few times. So he did. When he complained about having to spend his own money I reminded him how much I had spent on flights and accommodations. Soon he will figure out that many kids don't have to pay for anything themselves. At this point, he will probably say that I'm mean. Then I'll tell him that the kids who don't have to earn and manage their own money won't grow into successful, happy adults as soon as he does, or maybe at all.

The 6 Keys to Money Success for Kids.

Key 13

1. Each child receives a set amount of money each and every week. I recommend the dollar amount matches their age, if you can afford it.
2. Children don't get paid for everyday chores (unless you offer a "bonus job").
3. Children buy their own non-essentials.
4. Children dictate how their money is spent NO MATTER WHAT. ***DO ENCOURAGE*** them to use the SMART steps (coming in **Part Two**) - but ***DON'T FORCE*** them to. They will make mistakes and experience buyers' remorse. That's OK. It's part of learning.
5. You can advise (not force) them to save half their money in a bank account for a larger purchase, and divide the other half between fun money and giving. For example, my son gets $10 per week so he usually asks me to put $5 into his bank account and he wants the other $5 in cash. He puts a loonie in the offering plate at church most Sundays. If your child is in aggressive saving mode, **remind him/her that when it comes to giving, time and talents are more valuable than money**. Encourage him/her to help out an elderly neighbor

by raking leaves, mowing grass or shoveling snow. Invite him/her to join you for an afternoon at your local long term care center to play cards with the residents.

6. Money is NEVER taken away from a child as a punishment. Ever. I learned this from Barbara Coloroso's book "Kids are Worth it!".

Not only will The 6 Keys to Money Success for Kids benefit your little darlings now and in the future, you will enjoy more free time as they ask to take on more tasks to earn more money. Woop! Woop!

At first, your kids won't be excited about your focus shift and their now longer list of chores. Soon, they'll get used to you spending a few hours each week learning a new skill or sport. I promise the new things you try out (tennis, fishing, archery, carpentry, book club, etc) and the conversations you have with new people about your new adventures will lead you to discovering a new passion or talent. Don't be one of those moms who has nothing to talk about other than her kids. Get a hobby or two. Play a sport. Write a book. Be interesting. Do something to grow yourself that has nothing to do with being a mom. The best part is, when you take the focus off being a mom in order to learn and grow as an individual, *you become a better mom.*

If you're a mom who believes it's extremely important to soak up every moment with your 5/7/11 year old because *"they're only (insert age) once!"*, I challenge you to consider the other side of that perspective. I have met many moms who spent 10-12 years out of touch with their friends, sports and hobbies. They didn't make many new friends during that 10-12 years because everything they did involved their kids. Each time I meet a mom like this, a look of concern takes over my face (I'm told) as I ask "*Why???*" I've heard all sorts of responses that all boil down to guilt. They feel guilty when they even consider spending time away from their sweet little darlings.

Don't shut out everything unrelated to your children. My son has spent many hours on the sidelines of my basketball and touch rugby games. Books, snacks, coloring books and of course an iPad with age appropriate, mom-approved apps will diminish your child's excruciating torture of being with mom during her hour of "me time".

As your children get older and become less dependent on you, they will respect and admire your ability to accept a challenge and stick with it.

When it comes to filling the time you've created by delegating:

Live The Golden Rule.

Key 14

(Do unto others as you'd have others do unto you.)

One of the key reasons I aim to eliminate and/or delegate tasks to create more time is to increase my acts of service. I am living proof that when you focus on serving others rather than yourself, your income rises and, most importantly, your feeling of fulfillment rises. When I removed the mundane tasks from my life, my creativity sky-rocketed and I found my true calling.

I know you're not reading this book to help you find your true calling. You're reading this book because you want to get your finances in order. Then why so much focus on analyzing whether or not your daily routine is in line with your true calling? Because once you have finished reading this book and have developed new money success habits, you will no longer be consumed by the desire to get your finances under control.

You will be amazed at the opportunities and ideas that fill the void left by money worries!!

As soon as you've finished reading this book, read from page 54 to here again. Much will have changed by then.

Skip the next page if you're reading this for the first time. If this is your second time around...

Write your top three money success stories:

I'd love to hear your money success stories and share them with other moms. If you'd like to share, email your story to me at

SuccessStories@The39ForeverMom.com

Before I share the next chapter of my life story, let's look at why we work to make money.

Why do you work to make money?

Write the first five reasons that come to mind:

If **retirement** is one of the reasons you work to make money, here's another perspective for you to explore...

Retirement isn't all it's cracked up to be.

As a teenager, I observed my family members longing for retirement. They couldn't wait to get off the weekly grind merry-go-round. They weren't loving their careers.

During my time in Vancouver, I discovered neither ***financial freedom*** nor ***retirement*** are defined by trips to Hawaii. Striving for financial freedom is striving for the ability to choose whether or not to work. Striving for retirement is striving to end your job completely - probably because you hate it.

If you find yourself running away from career pain towards retirement – after you read How To Win Friends & Influence People AND have begun volunteering for a cause you are passionate about – it's time for a career change. Retirement isn't a desire for those who love & excel at what they do for money. I bet you don't like golf or sleeping as much as you think you do.

Make money doing what you love & excel at FOREVER.

Key 15

Remove the word "retirement" from your financial goals. I could go on and on quoting hundreds of studies proving that when people who love what they do retire/stop working, they are miserable. Why waste your talent by leaving your field of expertise because the government or a large corporation says you are "retirement age"? Keep working if you love what you do and are healthy enough to do it - whether or not you need the money. ***There is nothing more fun and fulfilling than giving money away.***

The Seamstress & the Stock Broker

A stockbroker named Wendy was grocery shopping. She passed a woman wearing a beautiful summer dress. Wendy had been looking everywhere for a dress just like it - simple and summery with lace detail. Perfect for the cottage. She turned her shopping cart around and caught up to the dress.

"I must say, that is a lovely dress! Do you mind telling me where you bought it?"

"Oh, thank you! I sewed it myself."

"Really?!? How long did it take you?"

"About an hour. This is a really simple design. Plus I've been sewing for many years."

Seeing the dress up close, Wendy was even more impressed with its expensive-looking quality. "With your talent, you could make dresses and sell them in local stores and online!"

"Thank you! I do sell some of my creations. I sew for a few ladies. Mostly mending and alterations, but they do send me photos of dresses they want me to make from time to time. Mostly I make my own clothes and clothes for my family. I sew for an hour or two each day."

"Is sewing your only job?" Wendy couldn't believe that someone with such talent was only working at it so little. If she loved it, why not work more? Make more money?

"Well, it depends on what you call a 'job'. We live on a farm. We raise our own beef and chicken, grow our own vegetables and crops to feed the animals. We grow most of our own food so we rarely have to buy groceries. My husband has a business fixing vehicles and machinery. What do you do for a living?"

"I'm a stockbroker in the city. I invest in companies. I also have my MBA, which is why I'm curious about your sewing business. I'm Wendy, by the way. What's your name?"

The ladies shook hands. "I'm Suzanne. And this is one of my two sons." Suzanne gestured to the teenager coming up the aisle towards them carrying big bag of flour.

Suzanne continued "It's been lovely chatting with you Wendy. Thank you for the compliments on my dress. I'm not sure what kind of business idea you have regarding my sewing skills, but I'm quite content with the little bit of money I make from my sewing business. We love the farm life..." Suzanne looked at her son. "Taking care of a farm and growing your own food is a lot of work, but it doesn't feel like work, right Luke?"

The boy laughed. “Sure Mom! Feeding cows at 6:00 every morning doesn't feel like work at all!” They all laughed at his expression of pretend-fatigue. “It ain't that bad. I'd much rather live in the country than in the city. You know, my mom gets compliments on her dresses all the time! Do you think we could get rich if she sold her designs or somethin’?”

The ladies laughed. Wendy said “I was just asking your mom about that. I think if she invested 4-6 hours a day in her business - designing dresses - I could help her make lots of money.”

“How could you help her do that?” Luke asked Wendy.

“I have an MBA and I'm a stockbroker. I’ve also helped grow a few small, private businesses into large publicly traded companies.” answered Wendy.

Luke and his mom looked at Wendy, awaiting further explanation.

“When a company goes public, and people buy shares, the company has more money to grow their business. In your mom’s case, she could use the money to travel overseas and find workers to manufacture the clothing, pay for advertising and hire more staff. Anything that will grow the company. In exchange for the money, shareholders would get voting rights.”

“So we’d use other people’s money to grow mom’s business so we - I mean - she could get rich?” asked Luke, as his mother shook her head and smiled.

"Exactly. And when other stockbrokers like me research Designs by Wendy and find the company looks profitable, they'd invest their clients' money in her company by buying shares, in hopes that the shares will increase in value. If the shares do increase in value, the shareholders could sell some or all of their shares and make a profit. It would be a win-win for everyone."

Wendy paused. "Suzanne, what do you do in your spare time, when you aren't sewing or farming, if you don't mind me asking?"

"Not at all. When my husband needs my help in the shop fixing an engine, I lend a hand. We saddle up the horses and check fences. Every weekend, we get together with friends to play guitars and sing. In the summer, we harness the team and load up the wagon with food and guitars and go camping on our property. My girlfriends and I get together most Sundays after church for crafting and visiting. I love my life. I wouldn't change a thing for all the money in the world. Have you ever spent any time on a farm?"

"Not really." Wendy said, as a pang of jealousy hit her. *Would I trade my 60 hour work weeks and greedy clients for the farm life? Maybe I would…*

"Have you ever been camping?" Suzanne asked Wendy.

"I think I prefer my cottage on the lake. I have to have cell service at all times. I went on vacation in Europe for 10 days two years ago. I desperately needed a break so I decided I would turn my phone off and leave my assistant and associate in charge. Long story short, all hell broke loose. I lost two of my best clients. It was a nightmare!"

Suzanne and Luke looked at each other, then at the stock broker. Luke broke the silence "Have you ever rode a horse?"

Wendy laughed. "No! I'd be terrified!"

"You'd be fine. You'd need to take horseback riding lessons is all. I bet you'd love it!"

Wendy smiled "Maybe you're right." The more she thought about riding a horse, the less terrifying it seemed. It actually did sound quite exciting. *I need to get their phone number* she thought. "You know, I'd love to talk more with you about your son's question-"

Luke jumped in "About whether or not mom could get rich?"

"Precisely! I know talent and hard work when I see it. I could help you make millions and retire!" beamed Wendy.

Suzanne thought for a moment, as a smile slowly spread across her face. She looked at her son, who was looking back at her intently.

"So?!? What do you think?" beamed Wendy.

Suzanne, still smiling, spoke slowly "I'm thinking, if I had millions of dollars, and I were retired, I would still take naps with my husband, ride my horses, go camping and sew. Nothing would change."

Wendy looked at Suzanne, dumbfounded by the realization that retirement isn't the dream of those who love what they do for a living. Luke broke the silence "You should come to our farm for a horseback riding lesson sometime. And maybe you can help me get rich!" They all laughed.

"Yes, Wendy, we would love to introduce you to the farm life..." Suzanne said as she pulled a piece of paper and pen from her purse and wrote down her phone number. "What are your plans next weekend?"

"How sweet of you. I'd love to come out to your farm –" Wendy paused. "...on one condition: as long as your farm doesn't have cell service!"

The original version of this story is about a fisherman and a stockbroker. Google "Mexican Fisherman Stockbroker" if you'd like to share it with the gents in your life.

My "hairdresser single mom to financial coach" story continues

In our own little basement suite, my son, dog and me were quite happy. I got to work completing financial courses with fewer distractions. As soon as I passed the Canadian Securities Course, my salary started rolling in. I would receive a salary for 13 months which would decline after the sixth month. By the 14th month, my income would be commission only. A scary thought, but far enough away to push out of my mind.

My rusty 1998 Toyota 4Runner wasn't going to cut it anymore. A new vehicle is important when you're a salesperson. My prospects and clients would see my vehicle. They wouldn't see the tiny basement suite I lived in. It's unfortunate, but true, that people judge your success based on your appearance. A shiny new vehicle tends to move a person up the appearance scale. Thanks to thrift stores, I faked the clothing part of my appearance. I couldn't fake the vehicle part. It was time for a shiny new vehicle.

I posted my rusty old friend on **kijiji.com** and hours later, I found myself in the Cochrane Toyota show room. Of course "I'm just looking, thanks" turned into a test drive. I fell in love with a new 4Runner.

I didn't believe in buying brand new vehicles. I understood "depreciation". I hadn't had a vehicle payment since my Pretty Chevy which I bought in grade 11 for $8500. Five years and a new engine later, I sold her to my brother for $8000. I didn't want to sell that truck. I sacrificed **Automobile Attraction** for practicality. It was a wise move.

OK! OK! I promise, no more pictures or stories about my Pretty Chevy… after this last one: A few years after my brother bought her from me, my little sister bought her from him. It was comforting to know my baby was still in the family.

Back to the Cochrane Toyota show room, I managed to leave without buying. It was time to do some research. After calling two other dealerships and finding their prices to be higher, I called my sales guy and offered him $5000 less than the asking price. He only came down by $1500 but it was the best deal I could find on my dream vehicle. My old 4Runner sold for $5000. That money was the down payment on my brand-spanky-new 4Runner. My payments would be $740 per month for five years at 3.9% interest. Right after I signed the paperwork, still sitting in the financing office, I opened the calculator in my cell phone and looked at how much this Automobile Attraction was actually going to cost me:

12 x $740 = $8880 x 5 = $44,400 plus my $5000 down payment = **$49,400!!!**

YIKES!!!

After posing for this picture, I drove away half beaming with joy and half terrified of the huge financial commitment I had just made.

A few weeks before my house money landed in my bank account, I had replaced my "Responsible Home Owner" status with my new "Faking it 'til I Make it" status. If I hadn't paid thousands of dollars in interest in exchange for my one-and-only new vehicle experience, I wouldn't have this fascinating true story to share with all of you. You're welcome.

The thing is, I had another option. You see, by the time my house sold, I owed Mom about $2000. She had helped me out financially until my salary began. The $2000 hadn't covered all my expenses, so I also had a credit card to pay off. I was really looking forward to getting my house money to pay Mom back and pay off my credit card. I was so anxious to remove these measly debts from my mind that that I chose to spend fifty grand on a vehicle. Stupid! Stupid! Stupid! Emotions were riding high. I hadn't yet discovered the three step problem solver. Rather than explore other options, I went with Option 1.

Option 2, which I should have chose, was:

1. Wait until I receive my house money.
2. DO NOT pay back Mother just yet.
3. Go to a bank with my $7000 ($2000 I owed Mom plus $5000 proceeds from old 4Runner sale) and borrow another $10,000-15,000.
4. Ask Mom to cosign the loan, if needed.
5. Buy a reliable, 4-5 year old vehicle.

Why did I choose Option 1 rather than Option 2?

- I wanted to stop the damage the loan was doing to my relationship with Mom ASAP.
- I was a sucker for Automobile Attraction.
- I lost the battle with my inner child yelling "I want it now!!!".

I had borrowed money from Mom before and paid her back every time. The last time I had borrowed money from her was to put the new engine in my Pretty Chevy. It took a few months to pay her back, and boy, was that painful. The pain was caused by Mom's apparent worry about not getting paid back and her disappointment that I didn't have an emergency fund. Her lack of faith in getting her money back upset me. We always talked less when I owed her money. While I owed her money, a simple non-essential purchase like going out for dinner or a new pair of jeans were a risk to my relationship with her - if she found out. That's part of why I'm so hooked on thrift shopping - I got good at it when I owed her money. She would see me wearing a pair of jeans she didn't recognize and say "Those are nice jeans" but the look on her face said "I'm never lending you money again you spoiled brat." I'd awkwardly exclaim with great joy which thrift shop I'd purchased them at for only $10. I usually wasn't lying.

I'm thankful she was hard on me but even more thankful she didn't deny me the loans that enabled me to begin my dream career. Before I had built up my trailer commissions - you'll learn about trailers and how financial advisors get paid near the end of this book - my income fluctuated big time. There were months when I asked her for help with my bills. Years later, with the help of **mint.com**, I realized many of those relationship-damaging loans and uncomfortable periods of my life could have been avoided. Had I been keeping track of every dollar in and every dollar out, I wouldn't have needed her help as often or maybe at all.

My plan to stop the damage to my relationship with Mom failed. Once I was on straight commission, there were months when my 4Runner payment was too much to handle and she bailed me out. Thanks Mommy. I love you.

Want to lose 19% on a bad investment? Neither do I, but I did it once and I won't do it again.

Don't buy or lease a brand new vehicle. Ever. Buy a 2-3 year old vehicle. A brand new vehicle is worth about 19% less one year after you drive it off the lot. Read any of the best-selling books on accumulating and preserving wealth, and you'll find that the people with the most money and brains buy 1-2 year old vehicles. Those with money and brains know that buying or leasing a brand new vehicle means a 19% loss (or so) on investment.

Take the SLIGHT UPGRADE route

If you can't get a vehicle loan due to bad credit, put your would-be new vehicle payments in a savings account until you have enough for a *slight upgrade*. Do this a few times, and get more aggressive with your saving, and you can pay cash for that "like new" vehicle in a few years, while rebuilding your credit.

Example: Tara is currently driving a 10 year old car worth $10,000. She could probably be approved to finance a brand new vehicle for $40,000 at her local dealership. If she sells her current vehicle for $10,000 and uses the money for her down-payment, her payments would be $539 for five years.

Tara's Automobile Attraction Option 1:

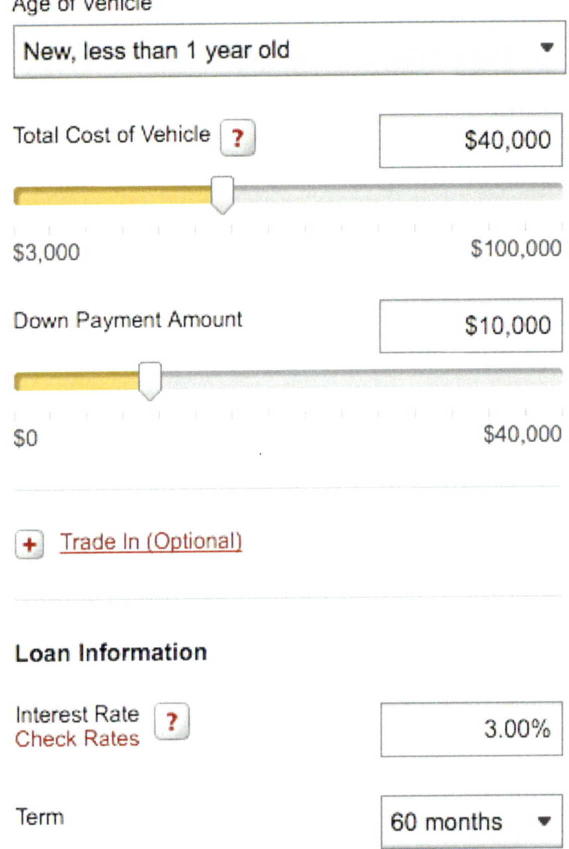

Source:

cibc.com/ca/loans/calculators/car-loan-calculator

Tara's Automobile Attraction Option 2:

a) Buy the two year old model of the same vehicle she has her eye on for $25,000. How long will it take her to save up $15,000 (she will sell her current vehicle to buy the new one) if she saves her would-be car payment of $539 per month?

2 years and 4 months

b) If Tara really, **really** wants that new vehicle sooner, she could save $1000 for 15 months.

Tara's Automobile Attraction Option 3:

Take the *slight upgrade* route by saving aggressively for about six months, buy a newer vehicle, and repeat once or twice. **Voilà**. Paid for 2-3 year old vehicle.

Tara's Automobile Attraction Option 4:

If Tara is in the same position I was in (clients see what I drive! Need a newer, rust-free car STAT!) and could get approved for a bank loan, she could take her $10,000 down payment to a bank and get a $15,000 loan to buy a "like new" vehicle.

Don't buy on Automobile Attraction impulse. Know all the options available to you before you buy.

Key 16

(Don't choose Option 1 until you have explored Options 2, 3 & 4.)

Don't buy new when you can buy used.

Key 17

A 19% investment loss hurts. You know how to avoid this now. **Moving on from vehicles...**

People gain weight. People lose weight. People realize there are too many pictures of them on Facebook in the same, fantastic dress. These are some of the many reasons why high quality clothing ends up at your local thrift store - ripe for the picking.

Smokin' hot deals on everything from appliances to work out gear to furniture can be found on the many "online garage sale" sites. There are seldom situations where one should buy any item brand new.

I faked it 'til I made it wearing second hand clothes while living in a 600 square foot basement suite. This doesn't mean I don't buy second hand clothes anymore. I will always be a thrift shopper - and not just when it comes to clothes. Whenever my son and I take a bag of our used clothes and household items to the second hand store, we usually score an item we need worth $20-40 for $3-5.

Back to my story...

How to build a financial coaching business

Once I was approved by IIROC (Investment Industry Regulatory Organization of Canada) to do business, it was time to turn prospects into clients. I followed the blueprint to success I had been taught during the firm's "New Financial Advisor Training". It truly was the blueprint to success.

As rapport was built during the meetings with my prospects, I'd offer one of two things:

1. a portfolio analysis report, or
2. a retirement income projection report,

...depending on their answer to *"What keeps you up at night when it comes to your money?"*.

While knocking on doors, I came across many people who told me they were impressed with my ability to build rapport with strangers. This compliment was usually followed by confessing they were unhappy with their current advisor. These two factors alone turned them into clients. They didn't require any fancy reports to get them to transfer their accounts.

Those who were keen to have me prepare a financial report were asked to provide copies of their investment statements. Seven out of ten times, this resulted in a new client.

Once I had a new client, meaning their accounts were in the process of being transferred to me, ***Step 1* was: dig deeper into his/her financial picture** by asking questions like,

- what would happen if you lost your job tomorrow?
- what would happen if you died tomorrow?

- what would happen if you needed long term care for the rest of your life beginning tomorrow?
- what would happen if you went blind or lost a leg tomorrow?

These questions were followed by ***Step 2**: an education session on the different types of personal risk insurance: disability, critical illness, long term care, and life.* I explained that people are much more likely to become critically ill or disabled than they are to die, and if their level of concern about these **what ifs** was high, we'd look at insurance quotes.

Step 3** was: invest their money, and/or apply for the personal risk insurance policy of their choice.* Once the transactions were under way, I'd offer to complete one of the other financial reports. This was ***Step 4; the final step of the "new client on-boarding process".

These four steps covered all the bases, or so I thought, until clients began asking for help with ***budgeting***. Wondering how the heck I could fake Budgeting 101, I called my favourite mentor, a senior advisor at the firm. He recommended a few books about money management which he said really helped him in his early years as a financial advisor. I started with David Chilton's book, ***The Wealthy Barber Returns***. That book was the course correction that put me back on ***the path towards the Keys to Money Success***; the direction I was meant to travel.

My mentors taught me that seminars are a great way to turn prospects into clients. One of my mutual fund reps, a fantastic lady named Julie, offered to help me with my first seminar. She recommended we hold a seminar for women. I got to work inviting ladies to my "Women & Investing" seminar and ended up with 21 confirmed guests. A snow storm hit the night of the seminar and only 12 ladies showed up. In my disappointment, Julie pointed out that 12 ladies at my very first seminar was an incredible turn out. During the seminar, all I did was introduce Julie and explain a little bit about why I became a financial advisor and I just about passed out. I was extremely nervous. My first ever attempt at public speaking felt like piano recital butterflies times 100. Feeling dizzy 30 seconds in, I paused to catch my breath and made a joke about wishing I hadn't skipped my 4-H club's public speaking events. Everyone laughed. I calmed down a bit and got through the last 30 seconds of my one minute introduction. The seminar was a hit. Julie did an amazing job. Most of the women in that room became clients and some of them are still my clients and great friends today. Thank you Julie for braving the snow storm and showing me how to share nerdy financial knowledge in a fun, easy to understand way.

It was around this time I was asked to volunteer with **Junior Achievement**, teaching grade eight students the *Investment Strategies Program*. This was the second time I wished I hadn't opted for shifts at Turbo over 4-H public speaking events!! I was terrified the first time I stood in front of a class full of grade eight students!! It was way more scary than talking to the 12 adult women at my seminar!! Eventually I also began teaching grade seven students the *Dollars with Sense Program.* Both programs contain excellent money lessons and videos. You can find links to my favourite Junior Achievement videos at **barriefinancialconsulting.ca/videos**

The day I realized I could reduce people's money stress by teaching money management first and investing second was the day I found my passion. Chasing wealthy prospects who had already mastered most of the money success strategies wasn't fulfilling. Of course it's profitable to have only "high net worth" clients from an income perspective, but from a fulfillment perspective, I know for a fact that helping people earn their "high net worth" status is most profitable. I am proof that when you switch your number one focus from growing your income to serving others, money finds you, and more importantly, fulfillment finds you.

Being an entrepreneur stuck in the confines of a JOB made it difficult to develop my passion for teaching money basics. By confines I mean commission targets. And by targets I mean ultimatums. I was grateful for the opportunity the firm had given me and the training had been top-notch, but the stress was getting ridiculous. I didn't always hit the monthly commission target, which increased month after month. Still, I was pleased with my own progress and tried not to worry.

I am proud to say, I successfully resisted the pressure of putting my needs ahead of my client's needs when it came to selling. Although I was struggling and more stressed than I had ever been before, sticking to my guns ultimately landed me in my dream career. Barrie Financial Consulting was born.

When you take care of others, the world takes care of you.

Key 18

With the inception of my own financial coaching business came improvements in every aspect of my life, however, **making** more money didn't mean **netting** more money. To start a business, I needed a great website, an assistant and a business coach. My business was operating without the key it needed to become successful: **Keep track of every dollar in and every dollar out**. Without watching the numbers, I wasn't aware of when I could and couldn't afford to make purchases. My career pain was gone, but my money pain hadn't improved.

Part Two:
Know your numbers.

Numbers impact every aspect of life from investments to cognitive abilities to how we look in a bathing suit.

Look back on last month's numbers and write your answers to the following questions:

1. *How many hours did you invest in working out? ___*
2. *How many dollars went under your expense category "restaurants & bars"? ___*
3. *How many alcoholic beverages did you consume? ___*
4. *What was the return on your investments? ___*
5. *What was your net income? ___*
6. *How many grams of sugar did you consume daily, on average? ___*
7. *How many hours of sleep did you get every night, on average? ___*

If you can't answer all of these, you will be able to soon.

The numbers are always right there – plain and simple – attached to every action and every result. Similarly, there are numbers attached to everything we DON'T do. Spend more than you make for a month and watch the debt number increase. Eat a higher number of calories than you burn for a month and watch the number on the scale rise. We each have a balance we are all striving for to ultimately be the happiest, healthiest people we can be. There are of course numbers associated with this "balance". It's impossible to find this balance without knowing the numbers associated with where we are RIGHT NOW.

Physical fitness parallels financial fitness

My dear friend and fellow financial nerd, Rhonda Cockwill (CPA, CGA), introduced me to **Audible.com**. Audiobooks became one of my key sources of valuable information from that day on, beginning with **Thinner Leaner Stronger by Michael Matthews**. This book for women taught me the importance of knowing my food numbers: **macronutrients, micronutrients and calories**. It also taught me that classic exercises like the squat, deadlift and military press are all you need to build and maintain an optimal body when combined with the right numbers. 70-80% of one rep max (one repetition max = the amount of weight you can lift/push only once). 8-10 reps (example 8-10 push ups). 4-5 sets (how many times you complete your 8-10 reps). Cardiovascular training is great too - especially HIIT (high intensity interval training) - but cardio alone won't build a lean, muscular body. ***You must know your numbers to achieve success both financially and physically.***

My church led me to my second audiobook: **The Total Money Makeover by Dave Ramsey**. In just 3 hours and 41 minutes, Dave brought me back to reality through simple explanations of money dos & don'ts. The knowledge I'd gained from the book Thinner Leaner Stronger was paying off; I was seeing results in the mirror. I realized I could apply my new ability to "know my numbers" to my money. I discovered **mint.com** (insert audio of angels singing) which enabled me to keep an eye on every dollar in and every dollar out.

You probably think the answer to the following question will not be fun. My promise to you is that managing your money is a lot more fun than having your money manage you.

"How do I keep track of every dollar in and every dollar out?"

Dollars are just like grams of fat/carbohydrate/protein. You have to know where you're at right now before you can get to where you want to be. Mastering the simple art of keeping track of my macronutrient and caloric intake proved to me that knowing the numbers works. I repeated the process with my money.

Keeping track of the numbers seems overwhelming at first. Here's my tried & true **five step process** to discovering and keeping track of **your numbers.**

> *The good news is you don't have to keep track of the numbers forever. You do need to keep track of your numbers until you've created the habit of staying within your limits.*

The Five Step Blueprint to Cash Flow Management Success.

1. Write your cash flow numbers:

PRINCIPAL RESIDENCE **(PR)** MORTGAGE/HELOC/RENT	VACATION HOME EXPENSES
PR MAINTENANCE	HOME FURNISHINGS
PR UTILITIES	HOUSEKEEPING
PR INSURANCE	GIFTS
PR PROPERTY TAXES	TOILETRIES/ PERSONAL CARE
PR WATER, GARBAGE & RECYCLING	ALCOHOL & BARS
GROCERIES	RESTAURANTS & FAST FOOD
TV, INTERNET & PHONE(S)	MUSIC, BOOKS & MOVIES
CLOTHING	GYM/SPORTS/ FITNESS
CHARITABLE DONATIONS	ALLOWANCE FOR CHILD(REN)
LIFE INSURANCE	MOM'S FUN
DISABILITY INSURANCE	DAD'S FUN
CRITICAL ILLNESS INSURANCE	FAMILY FUN
LONG TERM CARE INSURANCE	TRANSPORTATION/ VEHICLE MAINTENANCE, INSURANCE & FUEL
* (GROUP) HEALTH INSURANCE	DEBT PAYMENT(S)
HEALTH EXPENSES (massage, chiro, meds)	**TOTAL CASH OUTFLOW**
COMPANY RRSP/ TFSA SAVINGS	**NET INCOME**
** PERSONAL SAVINGS INCLUDING RRSP & TFSA	**SURPLUS/ DEFICIT**

This worksheet is available at

barriefinancialconsulting.ca/resources

* If you have pay deductions like group benefits and/or a group RRSP/TFSA, make sure to add the amounts which are deducted from your pay to your net income.

** Include both short-term and long-term savings.

Congrats if you have a surplus, but it's unlikely you know your exact numbers. You need at least 30 days of money tracking data in order to know your numbers. If you have a deficit, don't freak out. Once again, it's unlikely you know your exact numbers. Even if the numbers are right, you can and will fix them.

2. Schedule a one hour time block to set up your Mint account on your computer

Enter every bank account, debt and asset so you can see your entire financial picture in one place. Don't set up your spending goals just yet. After downloading the Mint app on your phone and paying close attention to where your money is actually going for 30 days, it will be time to set some limits.

Step 2 is a must in order to...

3. Label every purchase as a <u>need</u> or a <u>want</u>

Want to stop worrying about ending up poor and destitute? Save for the future. Stop spending more than you make. How? Start by labelling every purchase as a need or a want. Your Mint account will show you how much you are spending on needs vs wants.

Present You vs. Future You

Before we talk about needs vs. wants, imagine the most adorable, sweet old lady you've ever met. Multiply your adoration for her by 100. That's how much you actually care about Future You, but you are distracted from this fact by TV ads and the Jones' down the street. Turn off the TV. Snap yourself back to reality. You have to take care of **Future You** too.

On the other hand, don't miss out on all the fun in case you don't live to be 65. This doesn't mean you should completely skip the next 10 pages of this book because I just told you to live like there's no tomorrow. Aim for the right balance of needs and wants. Like most Canadians, you usually feel like you're spending too much on wants. Nobody's perfect. The goal is to improve, not to be perfect. The first step to shifting some of your dollars from WANT$ to SAVING$ is simply knowing your current numbers. Pay close attention to your numbers on your phone's Mint app.

Both *Present & Future You* need **food, water, shelter, heat** and (thrift shop) **clothing**. If you currently have to leave your home in order to earn money, add **transportation** to the list.

Know your monthly basic needs price tag.

Key 19

Write your list of BASIC NEEDS:

Basic need	Monthly cost
Food	$
Shelter	$
Heat	$
Clothing	$
Transportation	$
	$
	$
	$

Now it's time to fill in a second cash flow worksheet while prioritizing your NEEDS.

Write your needs with a bright green marker in their respective categories:

PRINCIPAL RESIDENCE **(PR)** MORTGAGE/HELOC/RENT	VACATION HOME EXPENSES
PR MAINTENANCE	HOME FURNISHINGS
PR UTILITIES	HOUSEKEEPING
PR INSURANCE	GIFTS
PR PROPERTY TAXES	TOILETRIES/ PERSONAL CARE
PR WATER, GARBAGE & RECYCLING	ALCOHOL & BARS
GROCERIES	RESTAURANTS & FAST FOOD
TV, INTERNET & PHONE(S)	MUSIC, BOOKS & MOVIES
CLOTHING	GYM/SPORTS/ FITNESS
CHARITABLE DONATIONS	ALLOWANCE FOR CHILD(REN)
LIFE INSURANCE	MOM'S FUN
DISABILITY INSURANCE	DAD'S FUN
CRITICAL ILLNESS INSURANCE	FAMILY FUN
LONG TERM CARE INSURANCE	TRANSPORTATION/ VEHICLE MAINTENANCE, INSURANCE & FUEL
* (GROUP) HEALTH INSURANCE	DEBT PAYMENT(S)
HEALTH EXPENSES (massage, chiro, meds)	**TOTAL CASH OUTFLOW**
COMPANY RRSP/ TFSA SAVINGS	**NET INCOME**
** PERSONAL SAVINGS INCLUDING RRSP & TFSA	**SURPLUS/ DEFICIT**

In my opinion, disability and critical illness insurance for your family's highest income earner are **NEEDS.** You'll understand why by the end of the book.

"Mom's fun" is a NEED.

Key 20

Everyone needs fun - even you. If mom's not having a little bit of fun every day - ***watch out!*** We tend to put our fun on the back burner when time and/or money is tight so our kids can continue to enjoy their fun. Prioritizing your fun equally to everyone else's doesn't make you selfish. Smiles and feel-good moments are a huge part of maintaining health, and often require a financial investment; that new pair of running shoes you desperately need or hiring a babysitter for an afternoon so you can go hiking with your friends. Sometimes, fun can be free, but let's be honest - there aren't a lot of things in life that bring happiness and also happen to be free. Even a marshmallow roast over a fire costs the price of the marshmallows and a pocket knife to make the roasting sticks. Swimming in a lake on a hot day costs the price of your bathing suit (maybe not? Haha!), towel, flip flops and possibly fuel to get to the beach.

When it comes to fun with your kids, there are many games you can play that are fun and free. Mom grew up in a rural area near Dawson Creek, BC. She says that although her family struggled financially, she and her siblings didn't know they were poor. Being resourceful, self-sufficient and able to get by with very little was their way of life as it was for most of the folks they knew. She and her siblings played all sorts of games that involved items they had on hand. Money was not required for their "Farm Fun." Outside, they played tag, hide-and-go-seek, raced each other jumping in potato sacks and walking on rolling barrels. Indoors they played hangman and card games.

These days, unless you live in the country or have friends who do, fun usually isn't cheap or free. Fun money is a must, but I challenge you to enjoy ***free fun*** as often as you enjoy fun that costs money!

Write about the fun people, places and activities that make up your best memories:

Write about three not-so-fun experiences. Why do you feel the experience was a waste of your time and/or money? Who were you with? Where were you?

Switch gears from not fun times to the most fun experience you can imagine. Picture the one thing you want the most. It could be a boat, new car, vacation, owning a zoo, becoming a pilot, opening an art studio - ANYTHING. Imagine you're experiencing whatever it is right now.

I bet if you were able to own it or experience it tomorrow, it would take only a few days to a few weeks before you would find yourself wanting the next big thing.

The new wears off.

That's why you need to be very careful how you invest your time and money. Your ultimate goal for every minute and dollar must be fulfillment.

Look at the last two lists. What <u>are</u> the sources of your fulfillment? What <u>aren't</u> the sources of your fulfillment? Take a few minutes now to analyze your upcoming plans and goals to ensure they're in line with your best memories. Recognize if you tend to chase things which you remember as "not fun times".

Write three experiences or big purchases you often fantasize about:

Unlike money, time is priceless. Both money and time are never spent; they are invested or wasted. Financial success isn't measured only by how much money someone has. It's also measured by how his/her money makes them feel.

Owning the latest and greatest toys often results in lack of time to enjoy the toys. A purchase will result in dissatisfaction when it isn't in line with the owner's true passion.

Growing up, my parents owned boats, quads/ATVs (all-terrain vehicles), and a holiday trailer, all of which were far from new or fancy. I'm all for toys - as long as toy purchases are combined with **Key 17** (don't buy new when you can buy used). Some of my best childhood memories involve those old quads. We used them tons. Too often, people buy holiday trailers and toys in hopes the financial investment will magically result in time to use them. Like buying a gym membership. Sometimes this works, but remember, you can **rent** a motorhome and boat once or twice each year. You don't have to **buy** them.

The same goes for your home. Just because you can afford an above-average home doesn't mean you should attach yourself to an above-average mortgage. The above-average home probably won't make you happier. How much living space do you actually NEED, anyway? I bet you'd be happier if you invested the surplus income in life-changing experiences rather than a bigger home.

Money always involves risk. Every time you trade money for an experience or a physical item, you run the risk of being disappointed, especially when purchases are made on impulse. This disappointment is called **buyers' remorse**.

WHEN IT COMES TO IMPULSIVE BEHAVIOUR...

STUDIES SHOW STRESS IS CAUSED BY THE DESIRE ITSELF. GETTING THE CHEESECAKE, VIDEO GAME, NEW JEANS - ANY TYPE OF IMMEDIATE GRATIFICATION ITEM - WILL NOT GIVE YOUR LIFE MORE MEANING. YOU WILL NOT BE HAPPIER ONCE YOU HAVE THE "STUFF" YOU DESIRE.

THE PERSON WHO DIES WITH THE MOST STUFF STILL DIES.

A brain chemical called **dopamine**, which we'll talk about in a few minutes, is often to blame for buyers' remorse. Other culprits are bad habits and lack of clear financial goals.

There are two types of buyers' remorse:

1. **Experience buyers' remorse**
2. **Item buyers' remorse**

Let's say you invest $100 in a girls' night out. While eating your too-well-done steak, you realize the dinner service is poor, the beer is flat and the new woman your friend brought along is less than charming. You love meeting new people but this woman is grating on your nerves. Maybe a live band and some dancing will improve help. It doesn't. The band's lead singer couldn't carry a tune in a bucket. By 11:00, you have $20 left for a cab ride home. The night probably won't improve so you decide to go home. The next day, and in the coming weeks, you wish you had stayed home that night. **Experience Buyers' Remorse** is less avoidable than **Item Buyers' Remorse** because there are more variables involved in a night out on the town than with buying a new pair of shoes. Plus you can't return a night out if your feet start to hurt or you break a heel.

Item buyers' remorse can often be avoided by researching purchases. This is an extremely important lesson not only for adults but children as well. Here's a lesson based on **Junior Achievement's Dollars With Sense Program** to help you lead by example when it comes to avoiding impulse purchases:

Are you a **SMART** consumer?

Stop and think!

This step needs to take an increasing amount of time as the price tag increases. Some of the questions you should be asking yourself are:

- Is this an item I've wanted/needed for a long time and I know for a fact I will use often?
- Is it wise to buy it now or should I wait 48 hours/1 week to purchase this item so I can be sure it won't be a waste of my money?
- Is there a high-priority item on my NEED list that I should be purchasing instead?

Make a plan!

My plan usually includes waiting at least 48 hours before purchasing any item over $20. Sometimes I apply my "wait 48 hours rule" to invitations to concerts, dining out, events and parties. I'm less likely to turn down an invitation and more likely to walk away from a purchase.

Plan where the money will come from. Look at your cash flow numbers. Understand the effect, if any, this purchase will have on your goals.

Ask questions!

Find a friend who owns the item or has experienced the vacation/restaurant/Broadway show you have your eye on and ask them a few questions, such as:

- is there a better product/item than this one?
- do you use it as often as you thought you would?
- what was your favourite and least favourite part of your vacation/new toy?

Review information!

Take a few days to a few weeks, depending on the price tag, to review the information you've gathered. Present your findings to a friend and ask what he/she would do if in your shoes.

Take action!

Choose to invest in your desired item or experience, or choose to say no. Don't let that feeling of anxiousness push you to finalize the purchase. That feeling of *"I want it now!"* is often not that at all. It's simply your brain telling you to *"Make a decision already!"*. If you are undecided, remember that you will feel as much relief from walking away as you will from forking over the dough, except when you walk away, you have a 100% guarantee of no buyers' remorse!

Hopefully your child will be or was taught this information by a Junior Achievement volunteer in grade seven. If not, it's that much more important that you utilize online learning tools designed to teach youth about money. I'm working on an online video series for youth. Sign up to be notified when the videos become available at **barriefinancialconsulting.ca**

In the meantime, introduce your kids to the SMART steps and lead by example. You can print/share the steps at **barriefinancialconsulting.ca/resources**

Avoid buyers' remorse by being a SMART consumer.

Key 21

I surveyed 50 women in my community and asked for their best, tried & true money saving tip. The best one was this: "Don't go to the mall."

"Don't go to the mall? Are you serious???"

Yes. I'm very serious. Why, you ask? Because of ***dopamine***.

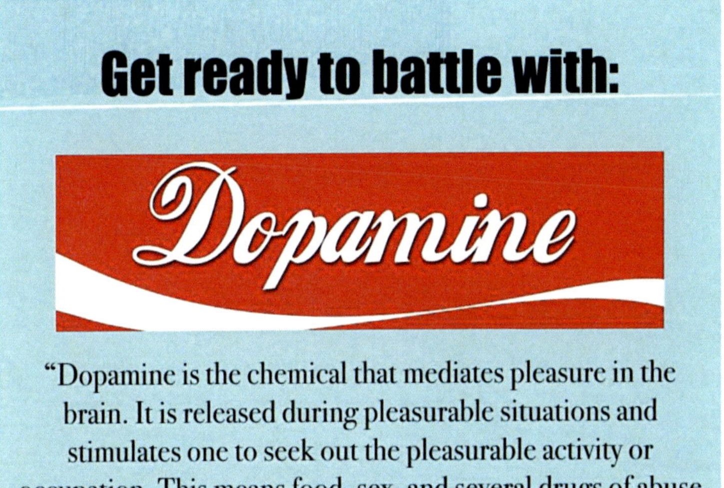

Source: **news-medical.net/health/Dopamine-Functions.aspx**

After learning about dopamine from **Thinner Leaner Stronger by Michael Matthews**, I decided to do my own research to find out just how much this brain chemical is to blame for people not achieving their goals. Turns out, Michael Matthews was right: we must win the daily battles with dopamine if we want to achieve our goals.

Dopamine isn't all bad. In fact, it could save your life. If you found yourself in a dangerous situation, this brain chemical would give you the bravery/ACT NOW push you need to get yourself or someone else away from danger. That's why we have this brain chemical in the first place - we used to need it for survival. Nowadays, we usually don't have to kill our food with a spear or escape grizzly bears. Today's threats come in the form of a pair of hot leather boots which get our hearts racing. In order to keep these threats from emptying our bank accounts - or worse - maxing out our credit cards, we have to take deep breaths and convince our brains that fashion is not a life or death situation.

I know you won't be shocked to hear this, but **malls are designed to take your money.** Retailers invest millions of dollars every year in discovering and utilizing the best colours, scents, images, words and music to drive you to spend in their stores. Malls also have food courts, which are HUGE challenges to your fitness goals. STAY AWAY LADIES!

Eventually, you'll have to go to a mall. Even I have to go to a mall a few times a year, and if you ask any of my friends, they'll tell you I avoid malls at all costs when possible. Prepare to beat dopamine by making sure you are rested and have eaten nutritious food (stay away from processed food) within the hour before you step into the mall. When blood sugar levels are low, stress can easily beat us down. An insulin crash in a mall usually results in buyers' remorse.

Even when you step into a mall with a specific purchase in mind and a price tag limit, you will see things that will spike your dopamine levels to the point where you are ready to give in and buy. This is less likely to happen if you are ready for the surge of anxiety caused by dopamine.

Stop mistaking that feeling of excitement as a signal to INDULGE, SPEND or CHEAT. Excitement doesn't always end in fulfillment. When you're feeling excited, ask yourself:

What's the source of this excitement? Is this event/person/purchase in line with what I truly want to achieve?

If not, say **"Beat it dopamine!"** and walk away fast.

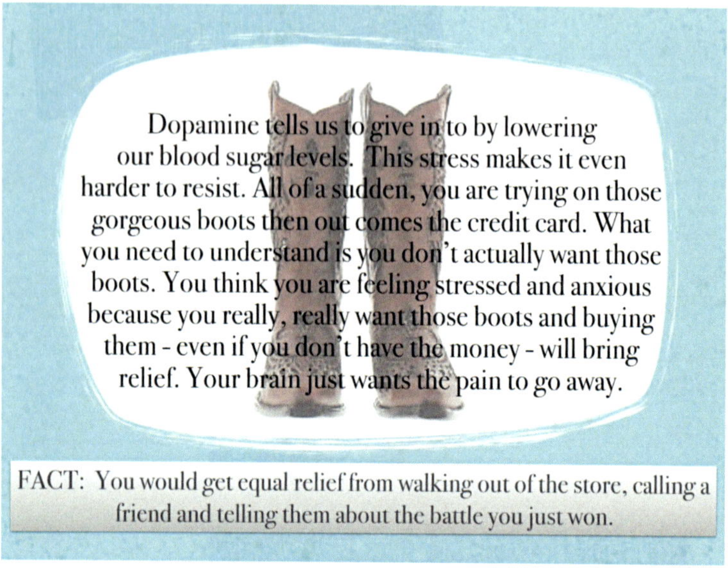

Dopamine tells us to give in to by lowering our blood sugar levels. This stress makes it even harder to resist. All of a sudden, you are trying on those gorgeous boots then out comes the credit card. What you need to understand is you don't actually want those boots. You think you are feeling stressed and anxious because you really, really want those boots and buying them - even if you don't have the money - will bring relief. Your brain just wants the pain to go away.

FACT: You would get equal relief from walking out of the store, calling a friend and telling them about the battle you just won.

Beat dopamine.

Key 22

There's no grizzly bear to escape. No bison to kill. Combine the knowledge of what dopamine is with your goals, and **you have the ammo you need to achieve your goals.**

Now that we've identified the #1 threat to your goals, let's move on to step 4 of **The 5 Step Blueprint to Cash Flow Management Success**.

- ✓ **Enter your numbers in the cash flow categories.**
- ✓ **Set up and use your Mint account.**
- ✓ **Label every purchase as a <u>need</u> or a <u>want.</u>**
- ☐ **Know what you are running from.**

What are you afraid of?

Each of my financial consultations starts with me asking *"What do you want to get out of working with me?"* She describes her money trials, fears and what she wants to achieve. I write it all down. Throughout that initial meeting and, if she becomes a client, throughout our relationship, I am her accountability partner. I remind her of her fears and goals.

Know exactly what you are running from.

Key 23

You must focus on your greatest fears more than your goals because humans, like animals, run faster from pain than towards pleasure.

Debt is scary

If you have debt, and you don't have a 30 year old son or daughter living in your basement, ask yourself,

"How did I get myself into this much debt???"

Probably the same way I did. Spoiled brat syndrome.

You've heard financial gurus say that it's OK to carry debt into your 60's. Well, it's not OK. It's dangerous and irresponsible. I found this in one of Canada's top money magazines: "Today's low interest rates have changed the game - as long as you borrow smart. Make sure your payments are much lower than your capacity to cover them." Really? Wow! OK! Let me get out my crystal ball and see what the future holds... exactly. Absurd. The only way to ensure debt payments are lower than our capacity to cover them is to calculate what EI (employment insurance) would be if laid off and keep debt payments at an amount less than that number minus basic expenses. If you have an emergency fund for these situations, fantastic. If you don't have an emergency fund, then you are like the many Albertans who have quads, boats, sleds and jacked up trucks for sale. Not fun. **Debt = Risk. Period**.

Some people don't mind living payday to payday. The thought of "What if I lose my job?" either doesn't pop into their head, or doesn't scare them enough to save an emergency fund. If this is you, it's OK. You know how I feel about worrying; it's an unhealthy habit that stems from lack of knowledge. Blissful ignorance is better than worrying. Those who are enjoying blissful ignorance are going to get a wake up call one day that will leave them worried about their money.

As you know, I enjoyed blissful ignorance throughout most of my twenties. I didn't listen to my folks when they told me not to spend every penny I made in case of an emergency. When the pain of being broke got bad enough, I knew I had to fix my bad habits. Problem was, I didn't know how!

Money problems are the most difficult problems to have for three reasons:

1. many people don't even realize they have money problems! *(BLISSFUL IGNORANCE!)*

2. people with money problems are scared to expose their bad financial condition.

3. people with money problems are scared to ask "stupid questions". *(There are no stupid questions when it comes to money!)*

Thus, financial success is often FAKED. It's a lot like wearing those tight bodysuits that rhyme with THANX instead of actually working out.

The question isn't *"Will a financial storm hit?"*. The questions are *"When?"* and *"What?"*. Job loss? Illness? Injury? Next month? Next year? In ten years?

Take off that super-tight bodysuit that rhymes with THANX, look in the mirror and do what it takes to be ready for a financial fitness test.

Key 24

The question isn't "Will my financial fitness be tested?". The questions are "When?" and "What?". Job loss? Illness? Injury? Next month? Next year? In ten years?

1. Save an emergency fund. You know how much money you need to survive each month. Save at least three times that amount STAT. Six months' living expenses is even better.
2. Make a list of what you OWN and what you OWE. The OWE list should start with the smaller debts and end with your mortgage. If a portion of your mortgage is debt consolidation or you have a HELOC or "All-in-one" account, treat the portion that isn't from your initial mortgage or maintenance on your home as though it is credit card debt as it probably was once upon a time. As I've shared with you, embarrassing as it is to admit, I know how people get caught up in using their home like a bank account. Trust me, it's risky.
3. Eliminate debt one debt at a time.

Write your numbers:

OWN	OWE
CASH	CREDIT CARD
NON-REGISTERED INVESTMENTS	OVERDUE BILL
REGISTERED SAVINGS RRSP TFSA LIRA	VEHICLE LOAN
VEHICLE	STUDENT LOAN
HOME	MORTGAGE
RENTAL PROPERTY	HELOC
COTTAGE/SECOND HOME	
OTHER	OTHER

Look at your **OWE** list. If the list doesn't include credit cards or loans for toys, furniture, 60 inch TVs, or pets (yes - PETS! I've heard people are doing this - I know, right?), congratulations on being less of a financial mess than most.

The rest of you need to **write your debts from smallest to largest:**

You will eliminate the smallest debt first. Trust me, you will achieve more when you focus on one goal at a time. **There's something inspirational about making those individual wins.** Put your "My debt" page on your cork board. Don't rip the last page out of this book; print one at **barriefinancialconsulting.ca/ resources**

Dave Ramsey's book "The Total Money Makeover" taught me why debt consolidation loans don't work for most people. Mainly it's because we like seeing the list of debts get shorter. Don't pay a little bit on all of your debts each month. Put the hammer down on one debt until it's gone, then move on to the next.

Most importantly, don't put money on debt #1 until you've saved your emergency fund. Otherwise, every time you have an emergency, your debt will come back. Keep making your minimum payments until you have the emergency fund saved, then it's time to crush debt #1.

Be debt-free other than your mortgage.

Key 25

*No investing until all *personal* debt is paid off!*

If you are currently investing and have personal debt, pause all investments other than group retirement savings matching programs. Redirect the money to debt. If you're a business owner, I'll address "personal debt vs. business debt" soon.

Now back to your fears.

Write your top five fears:

Remember, humans run faster from pain than they do towards pleasure. The problem is, we don't always see the ferocious beast creeping up on us...

Mint.com helped me see what I should be afraid of. Like most people, I'm a visual learner and emails like this from Mint helped me tons with paying off debt:

Here's how you're doing.

Your activity, budgets and goals for last 7 days

WHERE YOUR MONEY WENT

You spent $560.07 in the last week.

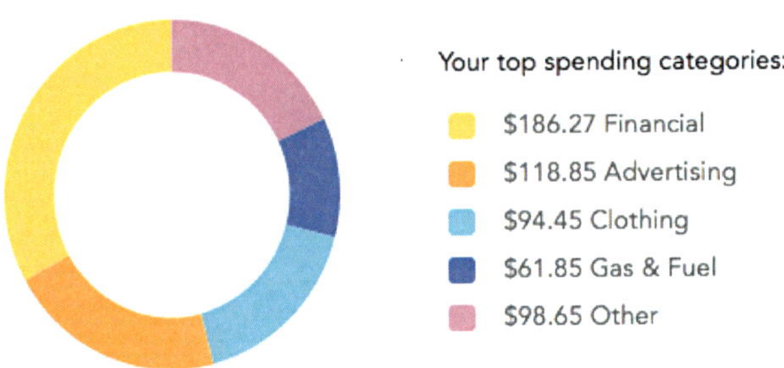

COMPARE TO PREVIOUS SPENDING

During my first few weeks as a Mint user, seeing the amount I was spending on restaurants, beer and credit card interest made me feel sick. The fear of continuing on this downward spiral hit me hard, and I ran away. Fast. I don't know how I would have done it without this clever little app called Mint.

After about a month of Mint showing me where every dollar went, and feeling sick and angry a few times from what I saw, I entered my spending goal amounts. Not only did Mint send me emails, like the one you just saw, with my actual spending numbers, Mint also warned me on my phone (from the app) when I got close to reaching my spending limit and gave me heck when I paid interest on credit cards. Mint provides the "all-in-one" account look & feel without the potential for failure of a real "all-in-one" account. If you don't know what I mean by "all-in-one" account, Google "all in one banking YouTube" and watch the video. In a nutshell, all-in-one accounts can work well if you are super duper diligent, but I've also seen many people pay only the interest on their debt; spinning their tires. This happens frequently with HELOC (home equity line of credit) accounts too.

Back to paying off debt.

There are many ways to free up cash to pay off debt. What worked for me was:

- write debt #1 (start with smallest debt and work towards largest) on cork board + completion date + reward.
- weigh every purchase against that single goal. For me, paying off the credit card usually won, and I wouldn't buy the item I wanted, or I'd have one pint of beer instead of three!
- use mint.com's charts, graphs and numbers to stay on track.

If your cash flow surplus number isn't very high, or if you don't have a cash flow surplus, consider the following ideas for paying off debt #1:

- downsize your home whether you rent or own.
- get a second job or start a business. Preferrably a dog walking service in my neighbourhood, or look on upwork.com for jobs you can do.
- sell the fancy brand-new car and pay cash for a 4-5 year old car.
- tell your kids they will have to work part time while in college or university. Parents shouldn't be wallowing in debt to give their kids luxuries.
- sell valuable stuff you don't need or use, like that professional camera you haven't touched in two years. You aren't going to be a photographer anyway so put the $300 towards debt #1. You could easily get $100 for those really nice boots you bought in Vegas last year that you've worn twice. Sell the Wii since your kids only play the X-Box.

Again, don't invest until you're debt-free. Put every dollar of your cash flow surplus into an emergency fund, then pay off debt #1, then debt #2, 3, 4, ...and so on. Just hurry up and get debt free because the exciting world of investing is waiting for you.

I've coached people who put inheritance money on their "OWN" list. **Future** inheritance money! Money a relative has either promised to them or money he/she is confident he/she will receive upon a relative's death!!! It actually made me laugh! Yes, it is extremely unprofessional to laugh at someone about an aspect of his/her money when he/she does not find it funny, but I could not help it!!!

Whether or not you are sure you will receive SOME inheritance money, your "potential inheritance" is exactly that. A potential inheritance. You can't possibly estimate how much it will be. Your relative could have more debt than assets, or wind up requiring expensive medical treatments, or go off his/her medication and blow it all. A potential inheritance does not affect your current financial picture and should not be included in any of your financial planning.

Pay off your own debt rather than hoping an inheritance will do it for you.

Clearly you are one of us who has to actually work for our own money. Otherwise, you wouldn't have invested your hard-earned money in this book.

Free money can kill talent and passion

The gift of talent, when combined with a fierce passion to succeed, can result in a person earning loads of money for themselves and more importantly, for those who need it more than they do. Unfortunately, some talented people become lazy. *"Why work hard when my parents let me live in their basement for free?"* Sometimes when parents and grandparents want to help their son/daughter "get on his/her feet", they are killing talent and passion.

Just the same, an inheritance (or the promise of an inheritance) can be the killer of passion to succeed rather than a gift.

If you suspect a family member might leave your children/grandchildren a lump sum of cash that could potentially kill their drive, **talk to him/her about it.** To make this conversation less awkward, you'll begin it by sharing with them a true story about Joe.

I was recently venting my aggravation to another financial coach about life insurance salespersons who push the idea of buying life insurance for inheritances in place of leaving a true legacy, or what I believe is a true legacy. I was about a minute into my rant about trust fund brats and how free money kills talent when he began looking a bit uncomfortable with the topic. I paused for a moment, wondering why this normally outspoken guy wasn't saying anything, and asked him for his thoughts about free money killing talent. We'll call him Joe. Joe's story went like this:

Joe's step-brother's half-brother, Fred, left Joe's son $300,000. Joe's son was 21 when he inherited the money.

It all began about five years before Fred passed away. Fred asked Joe to be the executor of his will. Joe's financial coaching career had just begun, so he didn't think too much of it or ask for a copy of the will. I'll repeat: **Joe didn't ask for a copy of the will.** BIG mistake.

When Fred passed away, Joe had to dig through Fred's apartment to find the will. When Joe finally found Fred's will, you can imagine his reaction when he read that **his 21 year old son Teddy was about to inherit $300,000.**

Fred's half brother and sister, Ken and Sara, were furious with Joe. They blamed Joe for cutting them out of the will. Teddy wasn't a blood relative, but he was the only "young person" close to Fred. Neither Ken nor Sara had children. They were sure that, since Joe was the executor of the will, Joe knew his son would inherit the money. **Ken and Sara vowed they would go to their graves without speaking to Joe.** And that's exactly what they did.

Teddy, at 21, became $300,000 richer all at once. Do you think Teddy listened to his dad, the financial coach, about what to do with that money? Nope. He spent it all. Other than a paid-for house, **he has nothing to show for it.** He didn't take courses. He didn't open a business. He didn't travel. He basically sat around until the money ran out, which of course infuriated his father. The disagreements between Joe and his son over the inheritance caused them to not speak to each other for almost 10 years.

No wonder Joe felt uncomfortable during my rant.

In my opinion, the family's relationships would not have been damaged and Teddy would have accomplished more with his life during those 10 years if:

1. Joe had read the will as soon as he agreed to be the executor.

2. Joe had recommended to Fred that the estate be divided equally between his loved ones and/or charities.

Start your "will inquiry" with that story. He/she will understand why you want to know if your child will inherit any of his/her assets.

Leave a lasting legacy

Many insurance and investment salespeople would like you to believe "leaving a legacy" involves leaving money behind for family, friends and charities when you die.

Every person's definition of "a lasting legacy" is unique. Here's mine:

> **Each and every year, I will work to change the world for the better. My life's accomplishments will continue to positively impact the world for many years after I'm gone.**

Everyone wants to leave a legacy, but don't buy excess life insurance in order to leave money for your children and grandchildren (or someone else's children or grandchildren) when you die. If you simply must buy excess life insurance to leave "gifts" when you die, cap each gift at $50,000, and make sure each loved one receives the SAME AMOUNT. This way your gift won't damage relationships.

What's your definition of "A Lasting Legacy"? Write it here:

____

____

____

____

Do you want to know the #1 way to ruin the chances of leaving that legacy?

Don't update your will regularly.

Do you want to minimize the chances of your loved ones fighting about your estate after you're gone?

Have a "will conversation" with your loved ones every year; share the details of your will with every person affected by your will and ask them to do the same.

If you're asking a loved one to share the details of their will because he/she is fond of your minor child, ask:

> *"Does your will state that my child will inherit any money or assets when you pass away?"*

If yes, ask for a copy of the will. If they provide this to you, read the will and ask yourself:

> *"Does his/her will present potential conflict between my family members?"*

If you can come up with a more fair way to divide the assets, present your recommendations openly. Don't wait. Be assertive. Ask questions and make suggestions **now.**

There are many, many aspects to estate planning which I won't get into in this book. There are many great books out there on this topic. Estate planning is completely different from one person to the next; seek professional help with preparing and updating your will.

Have conversations about "When I die..." and "When you die..." with your loved ones.

Key 26

If a live conversation isn't possible, simply give/mail them a copy of your will.

The family cottage

The most common family legacy is the family cottage. Talk to your parents about what they plan to do with the cottage when they pass away, or even before they pass away. Don't be shy. Have these conversations now and make sure you and all siblings/relatives involved in the inevitable transaction are aware of how it will go down.

Most cottages were purchased years ago and have large unrealized capital gains. Unfortunately, there is no way to avoid the income tax bill when a family cottage is passed from the last surviving parent to the children. Whether the cottage is transferred while the parent(s) is/are still alive or upon death, taxes have to be paid.

When a cottage is inherited by someone who is unable to pay this bill, the inheritor is forced to sell or mortgage the cottage. If the "cottage conversation" would have happened years prior to the death of the cottage owner, a plan could have been put in place involving charitable donations and/or life insurance or another strategy to remove the inheritor's tax burden at death of the cottage owner.

Canada Revenue Agency rules are always changing. At the time you are reading this, the information written here may no longer be accurate. Consult a tax professional regarding what will happen with your assets upon your death.

It took me a while, but you have finally arrived at the final step of The Blueprint to Cash Flow Management Success!

- ✓ **Enter your numbers in the cash flow categories.**
- ✓ **Set up and use your Mint account.**
- ✓ **Label every purchase as a need or a want.**
- ✓ **Know what you are running from.**
- ☐ **Present your goals for all to see on a cork board.**

Build a "Goal Board" to display the pictures, words and dates for which you are striving. You read at the beginning of this book about when I put my goal to write my first book on my cork board. My son waiting for me to achieve my goal was the main driver. I ran from the fear of disappointing him.

My cork board is on display for all to see. It's not hidden behind a closed door. The more people who see my cork board, the more people I can impress or disappoint. The choice is mine.

Your cork board needs more than pictures of sunny beaches with palm trees (or in my case, log cabins and off-road upgrades for my 4Runner) – it needs the steps you will take to reach each goal and each step must have a date. Once you display your goals on a wall in a high-traffic area of your home, you may want to make a second goal board for your office. Each time you add or check off something, take a picture of the board and set it as the background for your tablet, computer and TV screens.

Know exactly what you are running towards and don't keep it a secret.

Key 27

Forget commercials and billboards. Put pictures and words that describe *YOUR* ideal life on your goal board. Look at it every day and ask yourself *"If I don't reach that goal by that date, how will I feel? What will my friends and family who saw my cork board think of me if I fail?"*. Run from that pain.

By the way, I have missed and will miss a few of the deadlines I set for myself. Knowing I've missed the mark adds pressure, but I work best under pressure. These two facts stop me from beating myself up when I'm a few days or weeks late on one of my goals:

1. **I have accomplished much more than I would have without setting goals at all.**

2. **I know I will reach the goal/hit the target ASAP.**

Push hard to achieve each goal before the date you set, but remember: the **fulfillment** will come whether you achieve the goal on time or a few days/weeks late. Don't quit if you realize you will miss the deadline. Love yourself for trying to achieve the goal, and be proud of yourself for each little win on the way to checking the box next to that big goal.

> To succeed in this world that is full of traps like TV shows, ice cream, social media and credit cards, we must learn to distinguish between the temporary rewards and the real rewards that bring fulfillment and meaning to our lives.
>
> (The cheeseburger can't cram itself down your throat. It needs your cooperation.)

No more blaming handsome car salesmen or boat shows for your money problems. Set goals and look at them daily. Don't allow anything to get in your way.

Reward yourself

You've got to make that feeling of accomplishment last as long as possible. Otherwise, your thrill of the chase instinct will allow you to enjoy your sweet success for a day or two, and then you will be back to longing for the next big thing.

Attach a reward to each goal. Write each reward next to each goal achievement date. Involve friends and family in your rewards so they can help drive you towards success. Train yourself to feel maximum fulfillment from your accomplishments by rewarding yourself.

Where do you find maximum fulfillment?

Sure, rewarding yourself for a job well done feels great, but I bet you could find more fulfillment if you focused less on having the latest and greatest things and more on helping others.

Allow me to explain.

Amidst the camping, quadding and hunting, my childhood weekends involved attending church, youth group and one week each summer at Bible camp. Pastors, youth group leaders and camp counselors introduced me to the source of true fulfillment: helping others. Much more than their words, their selfless giving to bratty, selfish kids like my friends and me had a huge impact on my life. These lessons unfortunately didn't turn me into a teenaged philanthropist; rather I was like most of my peers, caught up in the thrills of chasing boys and looking cool.

As I struggled through my twenties, I gave measly amounts of my money and time to charity and my church. I dealt with my guilt by making a deal with God that once He had made me the successful person I knew He would make me, I'd do my part to make the world a better place. I figured I'd know when this had happened.

> ***Soon after my 30th birthday, I was literally SHOVED over and over towards understanding why I am on this earth.***

Finding my place

Soon after moving to Cochrane, I found "my church"; Cochrane Alliance. Pastors Jason Koleba and Larry Charter gave me gentle pushes for the first few years, reminding me that no matter how much I have or don't have, I will always want more. As the years went by, the pushes turned to shoves. At the peak of my stress and worry, months before the inception of Barrie Financial Consulting, words spoken by these 2 incredibly gifted men helped me realize how fortunate I am and how much of my precious time and energy was being wasted worrying about things that may or may not happen. As months went by and I shifted gears in my career, Jason and Larry's shoves (in the form of sermons) helped me realize that the reason I was not giving was not because I hadn't yet achieved a certain degree of financial comfort, it was because I was a selfish control freak. It was time to trust and think of others first.

Around the same time I attended a conference. The keynote speaker was Mike Skrypnek, a Calgary entrepreneur whose accomplishments were my aspirations; financial coach, author, charitable donation advisor and business coach. I knew I was in the right place at the right time. I wanted to learn more about Mike's passion to change the world for the better and his proven ability to put the rubber to the road. In the months to come, while reading two of Mike's books, I couldn't ignore the push to hire this successful entrepreneur who would provide me with his proven blueprint and drive me to success. I knew I'd work harder than ever to ensure maximum return on investment. What I didn't know was how I'd afford to pay Mike. My leap of faith turned out to be one of my best decisions, because without Mike's pushing and shoving (a.k.a. coaching), my philanthropic vision may not have become reality. I wouldn't have written this book.

A book, a Ted Talk and a speed skater with MS

There were more shoves to come, and they hit me in the form of a book, a Ted Talk and a speed skater with MS (Multiple Sclerosis). I came across the book immediately after the conference where I met my future business coach. The book is a collection of stories about the challenges facing women around the world. Some of the stories ended with folks forming charities around the causes. There were also some stories which didn't end well. **Half the Sky** is written by husband-and-wife journalist team, Nicholas Kristof & Sheryl WuDunn. Since I'm usually guilty of sticking my head in the sand, I would NOT have chosen to read this book had I known what I was in for. Having joined a book club earlier that year, it came around to my turn to choose the book of the month. I texted an avid-reader friend asking her what the best book she's read lately that would be suitable for my book club. She responded with "Half the Sky". Without question, I forwarded the title to the 10 ladies in my book club and began reading the book myself. That same week, I listened to my first **Ted Talk**, found by typing "Ted Talk Philanthropy" in a Google search. The perspectives presented by Dan Pallotta's Ted Talk were immensely fascinating and inspiring. **The Way We Think About Charity is Dead Wrong** excited me beyond words. These new perspectives, combined with the books I was reading, pushed me to create a video to spread the word about my discoveries. Despite the fact that my book pick was not popular, all 10 ladies were impressed when I told them I was working on a video that was inspired by Half the Sky. Here's the email I sent to my book club ladies when the video was complete:

> Here it is ladies!! I know many of you didn't read the book but I strongly recommend you do read it someday. I believe it is our duty as women to read Half the Sky. This book, along with other books, people and a Ted Talk that I came across this past 6 months, has changed my life. Here's how it all came together for me:
>
> Check out this video I made: Double the Impact of Your Charitable Donations

I posted my video on Facebook, and soon, it grabbed the attention of Crystal Phillips, co-founder of Calgary's **Branch Out Neurological Foundation**. After meeting with Crystal, I updated my video to include this great photo of her and her inspirational story.

Crystal Phillips began speed skating as a young girl growing up on an acreage south of Beaumont, AB. You'll notice her farm gloves in the picture and believe it or not, that skin suit was home made!! Crystal's speed skating talent brought her to Calgary and by age 19, she became a hopeful for the 2010 Olympics. Shortly after this, she woke up one morning with no feeling in her lower abdomen or legs. She was diagnosed with MS and was told she would probably never speed skate again. The next five years of Crystal's life were tough. She worked hard to rehabilitate her body while learning everything she could about the links between neurological disorders, nutrition and herbal medicine. Her hard work paid off. She made a full recovery and in 2009 she qualified for the 2010 Olympic trials! But her triumph was short lived.

She woke up blind in her left eye. She was told her disease was progressing and there was a good chance she'd be in a wheelchair in two years. Aggressive drug therapies were recommended, but this time, she chose to treat her disease 100% *naturally.* Eight months later, she came six places away from the Canadian Olympic speed skating team and 2016 marked her sixth year both drug free and relapse free. Through this personal experience, a gap in the medical and research system was highlighted, and Crystal was determined to help fill it. Crystal's drive has led her to help develop an academic field of study now known as **neuroCAM**, which is funded exclusively by **Branch Out Neurological Foundation**, a charity which Crystal and her friends began in 2010. Each year they have organized a bike tour and a snowshoe tour. These events raised over $1 million in their first four years. Branch Out has funded over 40 neuroCAM research projects at universities, mostly in Alberta and Saskatchewan. Branch Out is on track to achieving its ultimate goal of establishing a neuroCAM research center in 2020 in Calgary, and is attracting the world's top neuroscience minds along the way.

Find out more at **branchoutfoundation.com**

These are the other two charities I featured in my video:

Kiva is an international nonprofit, founded in 2005 and based in San Francisco, with a mission to connect people through lending to alleviate poverty. Kiva celebrates and supports people looking to create a better future for themselves, their families and their communities. By lending as little as $25 on Kiva, anyone can help a borrower start or grow a business, go to school, access clean energy or realize their potential. For some, it's a matter of survival, for others it's the fuel for a life-long ambition. 100% of every dollar you lend on Kiva goes to funding loans. Kiva covers costs primarily through optional donations, as well as through support from grants and sponsors.

Find out more at **kiva.org**

Kidsport is a national not-for-profit organization that provides financial assistance for registration fees and equipment to kids aged 18 and under. Through a confidential application process, Kidsport provides grants so kids can play a sport for a season. Nationally, KidSport is comprised of a network of 11 provincial/territorial KidSport chapters and 178 community KidSport chapters. Since its creation in 1993, over 530,000 kids across the country have been given the chance to play a sport through KidSport grants and sport introduction programming.

Find out more at **kidsportcanada.ca**

When it comes to loving others, it's not just about donating money and time. It's also about sharing what you know. We all have a moral obligation to share our gifts, talents and what we know.

I decided to share what I know through articles, books, videos and presentations. I encourage you to do the same.

Give some of your time, money and talent every month.

Key 28

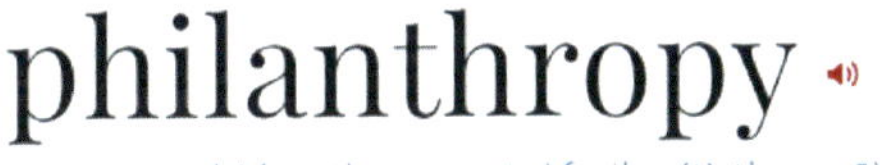

noun | phi·lan·thro·py | \fə-ˈlan(t)-thrə-pē\

Simple Definition of PHILANTHROPY Popularity: Top 10% of words

: the practice of giving money and time to help make life better for other people

Source: Merriam-Webster's Learner's Dictionary

Origin and Etymology of
PHILANTHROPY

Late Latin *philanthropia,* from Greek *philanthrōpia,* from *philanthrōpos* loving people, from *phil-* + *anthrōpos* human being

First Known Use: circa 1623

Teaching kids about loving others

An important lesson for kids to learn about money is that it's really fun to give it away. A great way to help them understand this is to get them involved in developing a philanthropic vision for your family. Ask them what comes to mind when they hear the word "suffering". They might say "mistreated and abandoned animals" or "parents who can't afford to pay for their kids to play hockey". Help them develop a plan to commit 10% of every dollar they earn to the cause of their choice. Teach them how to love others by giving their time. Encourage them to participate in fundraising events or simply help the people in your community who they think need it. Teach them this just like anything else: lead by example. Show your children how to find fulfillment from their money; by giving some of it to those who need it more than they do.

Part Three:
Put Your Money to Work

"I need a team in my corner who have dedicated their professional lives to helping people like me invest wisely. I want at least one of "my team" members to be in charge of knowing me well. This means I want to have a conversation with my "relationship manager" at least once a year; twice preferably. Other than my relationship manager, I want the rest of my team to focus on the markets and my investments. Am I asking for too much?"

This is most definitely not too much to ask.

The investment service I just described is what most 39 Forever Moms want based on my research. That's the type of service you should strive to find. Use the above when interviewing investment firms, or email the above to your current investment advisor if you aren't getting the service you want and deserve. Your career, your family and the things you love to do are what you want to focus on. You want to have a basic understanding of the types of investments available to you and what's going on with your own investments. You don't want to be an expert. The same goes for your life insurance. It can be difficult to select your team of experts without understanding the basics of what they are paid to do. I'll begin with sharing my knowledge of investments and later on, I'll share what I know about life insurance.

Types of Accounts vs. Types of Investments

For starters, **Tax-Free Savings Accounts (TFSAs) and Registered Retirement Savings Plans (RRSPs) are <u>not</u> investments. TFSAs and RRSPs are accounts** in which you can hold investments. Radio and TV ads say things like *"Invest in a 2% TFSA!"* which is actually referring to two separate things:

a 2% GIC (guaranteed investment certificate)

▷▷▷ INSIDE ▷▷▷

a TFSA (tax-free savings account).

These confusing, inaccurate ads are everywhere during "RRSP season".

"How do I earn tax-free income in my TFSA?"

A TFSA, like a RRSP, can save you money on income tax in a different way than an RRSP can. Basically, a RRSP is a deferral of tax whereas a TFSA starts out with you putting in your after-tax dollars. Once your money is in your TFSA, you will never pay tax again on that money! Even if your $10,000 TFSA is invested and grows to $20,000! YOu would have made $10,000 tax-free!

After you put money in your tax-free savings account, the most important step is **investing** it. Without this step, you won't pay less income tax if your investments make a profit (compared to owning the same investments in a non-registered account). This is a very, very important key, so I'll repeat it obnoxiously.

IF YOU DO NOT INVEST THE MONEY IN YOUR TFSA, YOUR "T-F-S-A" BECOMES JUST ANOTHER "S-A" - SAVINGS ACCOUNT. YOUR POTENTIAL TAX PERK IS BEING WASTED. DON'T DO THIS.

Since there are no guarantees you will make money on the investments in your TFSA, paying less income tax by investing in a TFSA is not a guarantee. There are, however ways to mitigate investment risks. We'll talk about the types of investments you can hold in your TFSA soon.

Why I think TFSAs shouldn't be used for short-term savings

I hear things like this all the time:

Them: ***"I'm saving up for my vacation in my TFSA."***

Me: ***"WHAAAAAAAAT?!?!?! WHYEEEEEEEEE?!?!?!"*** Usually this is just in my head, but sometimes it slips out. Then, if time allows, I explain how the TFSA works.

This is the only semi-legitimate reason I've heard to save CASH in a TFSA for short-term goals:

> *"If I put money in my TFSA, I can't get it out easily. I have to actually go into the bank to take it out. I can't just transfer money in and out of my TFSA online like my chequing account."*

Fair enough. However, I suspect that if these people were using mint.com or another cash flow management tool, they'd have more financial will-power. Plus, if your TFSA is maxed out, you can't withdraw then reuse TFSA room in the same year. Kind of a pain.

Know the differences between the RRSP (registered retirement savings plan) and the TFSA (tax-free savings account)

Key 29

To help you with this, I wrote a little song called The RRSP Promise. There's a video of me singing it to you on YouTube.

When you contribute to a RRSP, the income tax you paid on that money is *LOANED* back to you.

The RRSP portion of your tax refund is not actually a refund.

Sing with me! *"It's a loan!"*

You will have to pay this "tax loan" back. The goal is to have the loan amount be less than what you will have to pay back to the government in the future, but this is tricky. Who can be 100% certain that they will be in a lower tax bracket at age 71? No one.

Withdrawals from your RRSP are taxed at your Marginal Tax Rate in the year you make the withdrawal.

RRSP contribution room depends on your income and can be found on your most recent Notice of Assessment.

Read the complete list of RRSP rules online at **cra-arc.gc.ca/rrsp**

Just for fun, and to hopefully prove my point, fill in the following cash flow numbers according to what you think they will be when you are 70, in today's dollars.

PRINCIPAL RESIDENCE **(PR)** MORTGAGE/HELOC/RENT	VACATION HOME EXPENSES
PR MAINTENANCE	HOME FURNISHINGS
PR UTILITIES	HOUSEKEEPING
PR INSURANCE	GIFTS
PR PROPERTY TAXES	TOILETRIES/ PERSONAL CARE
PR WATER, GARBAGE & RECYCLING	ALCOHOL & BARS
GROCERIES	RESTAURANTS & FAST FOOD
TV, INTERNET & PHONE(S)	MUSIC, BOOKS & MOVIES
CLOTHING	GYM/SPORTS/ FITNESS
CHARITABLE DONATIONS	ALLOWANCE FOR CHILD(REN)
LIFE INSURANCE	MOM'S FUN
DISABILITY INSURANCE	DAD'S FUN
CRITICAL ILLNESS INSURANCE	FAMILY FUN
LONG TERM CARE INSURANCE	TRANSPORTATION/ VEHICLE MAINTENANCE, INSURANCE & FUEL
* (GROUP) HEALTH INSURANCE	DEBT PAYMENT(S)
HEALTH EXPENSES (massage, chiro, meds)	**TOTAL CASH OUTFLOW**
COMPANY RRSP/ TFSA SAVINGS	**NET INCOME**
** PERSONAL SAVINGS INCLUDING RRSP & TFSA	**SURPLUS/ DEFICIT**

"Of course I'll have less expenses when I'm in my 70's than I do now! I won't have a mortgage, or kids' hockey fees, or huge grocery bills!"

Really? I bet mortgage money will become travel money. Kids' hockey money will become hobby money. The money your kids used to eat in groceries will become medical expenses. Your total cash outflow number will be the same as it is now, unless you work really hard at keeping it lower. Sitting at home watching lots of TV is one way to accomplish this/prove me wrong.

Look at your present and future cash flow numbers. Are they much different? Probably not. If it looks like you'll need the same amount of income to cover your expenses in retirement, you'll likely be in the same tax bracket unless you're getting some of this income from your non-registered savings and/or TFSA.

Maybe you don't agree with me about the last part, but no one can argue with the fact that the RRSP is extremely inflexible compared to the TFSA. A TFSA doesn't have to be converted to a RRIF at age 71. With a TFSA, the government doesn't give you your tax money to "hold onto" for 20-40 years then demand it back, whether or not you need to take the money out of the account.

Now that I've beat it down, I'll bring the RRSP back up a little.

Here are some RRSP tips courtesy of my dear friend and accountant, Rhonda:

1. ***"A great way to utilize the RRSP tax perk is to move money into the RRSP in years when your taxable income is high, then move money out when your taxable income is lower.***

2. ***For couples in which one spouse is in a higher tax bracket, a Spousal RRSP can save money on tax by equalizing income when the RRSPs are taken out later.***

3. ***A RRSP is a great tool to teach teens about delayed gratification. Although one can't open a TFSA until age 18, encourage your children to save for their first home throughout their teens with the goal of depositing, say, $5000 into their RRSP on their 18th birthday. Then they can utilize the Home Buyers' Plan (HBP)...***

4. ***Although utilizing the HBP can be a slow process when it comes time to signing an offer to purchase, I'm still a fan of the HBP. The money borrowed from the RRSP must be paid back within 15 years or be brought into income. This requirement provides an incentive to replace the funds as compared to relying on willpower alone."***

Source: Rhonda Cockwill CPA, CGA in Cochrane, Alberta.

"What's a LIRA?" (locked-in retirement account)

A LIRA is a locked-in RRSP. When someone transfers a pension, it goes into a LIRA. Money cannot be withdrawn from a LIRA except for in specific circumstances, which vary by province. The minimum age at which one can withdraw funds from their LIRA depends on the province in which the original pension was issued.

Did you know that if you have children, or a disabled dependant, the government is offering you ***FREE MONEY!!

If you haven't heard of the RESP (registered education savings plan) or the RDSP (registered disability savings plan), you need to do a little more reading than what's in this book. RESPs are a great way to finance children's post-secondary education and RDSPs are a great way to finance the future of disabled children.

*****FREE MONEY** in the form of **grants** (contingent on contribution amounts) and **savings bonds** (contingent on family income).

Answers to both of the following questions can be found at **barriefinancialconsulting.ca/resources**

"How does the RESP (registered retirement savings plan) work?"

"How does the RDSP (registered disability savings plan) work?"

As you're beginning to see, there are many exciting ways to put your dollars to work. As we continue, I'll share about different types of investments along with, as promised, some basic investment lingo. Lingo and translations are written in red.

In pursuit of our goal to earn passive income from investments, our money is exposed to different types of risk.

Understand the risks involved with investing.

Key 30

Why do you want to expose your hard earned cash to risk? Because:

1. You will sleep better knowing you are earning income from sources other than your job/career.
2. Investing in companies is exciting, can be very profitable, and is great for the economy.

Before we go any further, you simply must watch two of my favorite investment videos. Go to **barriefinancialconsulting.ca/videos** and watch **Investing Series: Different Investment Vehicles**. Then watch **How The Stock Exchange Works (For Dummies)**. If you don't watch these videos, there's a chance you won't understand all of what you're about to read so go watch them right now!

Understanding the potential risks and which risks freak you out the most enables you to build an investment **portfolio** you're comfortable with.

Portfolio = all the different types of investments owned by one person

Risk #1 - Liquidity

If your money is "locked in" an investment at a time when you need cash for an emergency, you will have to find money elsewhere. Some investments lock your money in for a number of months or years. Before investing, know the answer to *"Would I be able to get my hands on this money in an emergency?".*

Risk #2 - Market

If the value of your portfolio of publicly traded stocks and bonds is low at a time when you need the money the most, you may have to sell at a loss on your investments if you can't find money elsewhere. Media, politics, natural disasters, war, and many other uncontrollable events cause market volatility. Because such factors can affect the stock or bond market as a whole, diversification does not reduce market risk. Maybe you need to quit your horrible job because your boss is abusive and you are on the brink of losing your marbles, or you need to put a roof on your house. You have to accept the risk that an emergency could arise at a time when your investments aren't performing well. The goal is to buy low and sell high, but an emergency is an emergency. Adding private investments to your portfolio can minimize market risk because private investments aren't traded on public stock and bond exchanges. More on private investments coming up.

Risk #3 - Management

The humans running the company can make or break the company. That's why it's important to research the names of the owners and controllers of a company before you invest. Search online for information about their accomplishments and keep an eye out for shady business transactions. Read reputable websites only.

Risk #4 - Business

Generally speaking, all businesses in the same industry have similar types of business risk. Business risk is driven by economic and political factors as well as industry/product supply and demand.

Risk #5 - Concentration

If your investments aren't spread across many sectors and geographical locations, you are riding high on the concentration risk scale. Not good.

EXAMPLE:

Portfolio A

$50,000 invested in each company

Calgary, Alberta

Portfolio B

$15,000 invested in each company

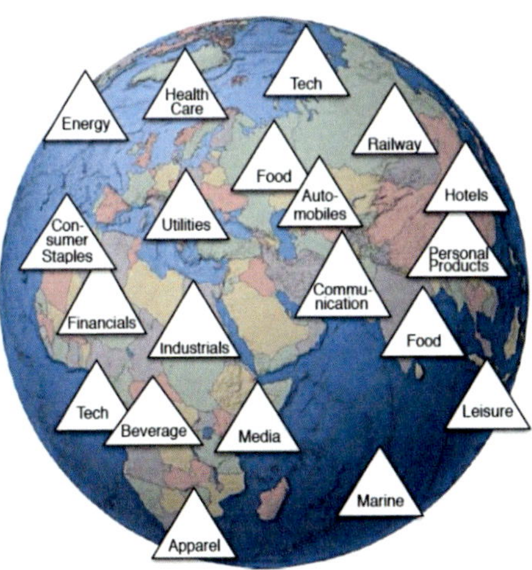

Planet Earth

If you owned investment **Portfolio A**, and one of your "Oil & Gas" companies went bankrupt, yeah. Ouch.

Investment **Portfolio B** wouldn't feel as much pain if one of the companies went bankrupt. Why? **Diversification.**

Diversification = the opposite of having all your eggs in one basket

A portfolio of 20+ companies in different sectors and geographical locations is at **Diversification Level 1** of 3.

Here are the **North American Stock Sectors**:

Consumer Discretionary

Consumer Staples

Energy

Financials

Health Care

Industrials

Information Technology

Materials

Telecommunication Services

Utilities

Each sector consists of multiple industries.

Example 1

The **Telecommunication Services Sector** consists of three industries:

1. Diversified Telecommunication Services (approx. 29 companies)
2. Telecommunication Services (approx. 33 companies)
3. Wireless Telecommunication Services (approx. 19 companies)

Example 2

The **Health Care Sector** consists of eight industries:

1. Biotechnology (approx. 118 companies)
2. Health Care Equipment & Services (approx. 180 companies)
3. Health Care Equipment & Supplies (approx. 110 companies)
4. Health Care Providers & Services (approx. 94 companies)
5. Health Care Technology (approx. 15 companies)
6. Life Sciences Tools & Services (approx. 37 companies)

7. Pharmaceuticals
   (approx. 63 companies)
8. Pharmaceuticals, Biotechnology & Life Sciences
   (approx. 266 companies)

Source:
bloomberg.com/research/sectorandindustry/overview/sectorlanding.asp?region=US

A portfolio consisting of 20+ companies which are spread across different industries is at **Diversification Level 2** of 3.

If the portfolio includes 20% PRIVATE INVESTMENTS, the portfolio is at **Diversification Level 3**.

"What are private investments?"

Back to my life story, the investment firm where I began my career gave me access to only **publicly traded** investments.

Publicly traded = bought and sold on a public exchange, such as the TSX (Toronto Stock Exchange) and the NYSE (New York Stock Exchange)

When the markets went up, my clients' portfolio values increased. If the markets went down (which they did not, thankfully, during the years I spent at that firm) my clients' portfolio values would have decreased.

The first time a prospect gave me a statement for an account that held a private investment, I forwarded it to my mentors and asked *"What the heck is this?"*. The answer was something like, *"It's a private investment. Private investments are extremely illiquid and often fail. You probably won't be able to get your hands on it, but phone the investment company with the client present and see if you can. If they can cash it in, find out what the fees and/or penalties would be to do so."*.

This sort of thing happened a couple other times and I was left believing that private investments are bad. Very, very bad.

Back before Barrie Financial Consulting was even on my radar, I was introduced to a co-owner of a private investment brokerage. Months later, when I began looking at what else was out there, I let him know I was searching for brokerage partners. (Thank you, LinkedIn!!) He explained how their brokerage operated. Most of what he said was scary because it revolved around private investments. I told him about my encounters with private investments, including my first one at age 24 with the $3000 glass-bottomed boat rip off (mentioned in Part One). He agreed my concerns were valid and shared with me how the Canadian and Provincial Securities Commissions had made changes in recent years to increase regulatory oversight of private market investments, dealerships and the dealers themselves. Once I researched his statements and found them to be accurate, I felt a bit more at ease with the idea of partnering with his brokerage, and I liked the idea of being part of something "up & coming".

Barrie Financial Consulting was formed when I entered into partnerships with three companies. We'll call these partnerships the three "puzzle pieces", and they looked like this:

Puzzle Piece #1.

A private investment brokerage. In the beginning, I was nervous about linking myself to these "too risky" endeavours, so the main reason for this puzzle piece was the fact that it provided the link to the next puzzle piece...

Puzzle Piece #2.

A portfolio management firm which builds custom portfolios for clients with at least $100,000 of ***liquid **investable assets**. This was a comfy fit. This firm was similar to the one I had worked at. Nothing new or scary here:

Liquid = cash or assets that can be turned to cash quickly

(Example: A five-year **GIC** isn't liquid until the maturity date at the end of the five years.)

GIC = guaranteed investment certificate

*****Investable assets = cash or investments***

I still needed one more puzzle piece; one that would enable me to provide investment management for those with less than $100,000.

Puzzle Piece #3.

My life insurance licence which enabled me to contract to up to 18 life insurance companies and banks.

In addition to personal risk insurance, life insurance companies offer investments - investments without a $100,000 minimum!

That's how Barrie Financial Consulting began.

Back to these investments which are offered by life insurance companies. Basically how it works is life insurance companies partner with investment managers in order to create **segregated funds.**

Segregated funds = mutual funds with added features. These added features are guarantees backed by life insurance companies

We'll come back to segregated funds in a few minutes.

Understand the basic types of investments.

Key 31

"What are bonds?"

When a company or government wants to borrow money for a specific project, they issue a bond. When you "buy a bond", you're the lender. Just like a bank, you get paid interest for lending the money unless the company or government you lent to goes bankrupt. Bonds are considered less risky than stocks for a few reasons. The key reason being, in the event of bankruptcy, bondholders get paid back before shareholders because bonds rank higher on the capital structure. If you're a business owner, you know what I'm talking about. If your company doesn't pay its bills, everyone you owe money to has first legal right to your assets. Company owners/shareholders get what's left, if anything.

When a new bond is issued, it is attached to a fixed interest rate, called the *coupon*, which investors receive for a set number of years. A new bond is sold in increments of $1000, known as the "***par*** price", or simply "par". If the bondholder chooses to sell their bond before the bond maturity date, they will receive a price above or below par because like stocks, bond prices fluctuate. Bond price fluctuate when interest rates change. Interest rates are impacted by the same economic and governmental factors as share prices.

Say, for example, that Energy Co XYZ wants to raise money to build a new plant. They issue a $1 million 15-year 5% corporate bond. You buy $10,000 of this bond issue. Energy Co XYZ will pay you and all the other bond buyers 5% interest on your investment each year. Your hypothetical profit from this investment would be $500 annually for 15 years = $7500, as long as XYZ doesn't go bankrupt.

At the end of 15 years, the bond matures. XYZ repays the bondholders their initial investments, a total of $1 million. During the 15 year life span of the XYZ bond, anyone who bought the bond in the primary market could do one of two things with the bond:

1. Sell the bond in the secondary market at a price that probably won't be the same as their initial investment. This option would be possible only if XYZ bonds are publicly traded.

2. Hold the bond until maturity.

Non-traditional debt investments

There are other types of "non-traditional" debt investments which are often referred to as "mezzanine" or "bridge" lending. These short-term loans (usually 6-18 months) are sought out by companies experiencing cash flow timing issues. Example:

Shine Shampoo Company has an order for $500,000 profit on a shampoo order which will cost them $500,000 to fulfill. That's a huge return on investment, right?!? The problem is, Shine Shampoo needs the initial capital to make, package and ship the shampoo, which they don't have. They're a small company and this is the largest order they've ever received. If *they don't fulfill the order on time, they will lose their contract with this drug store chain. Since banks are slow when it comes to lending money, and often won't lend if you don't check all the boxes on their list of criteria, Shine Shampoo's owner seeks out a company whose specialty is lending in situations like these, Taylor Capital Corp. Shine's owner works directly with the lending team at Taylor Capital and just two weeks later, Taylor Capital has approved the loan on a six month contract at 20% interest. Taylor Capital's investment fund now owns another loan from which its investors will earn approximately 9% and Shine has successfully expanded its business. Shine's owner doesn't mind reducing her 100% profit to 80%, since it means landing a great new customer. Besides, she won't have cash flow issues like this again...*

Or will she? Here's another way bridge lending can alleviate cash flow timing issues:

Shine Shampoo fulfills their order to the drug stores and is now waiting to be paid. The contract states the invoice must be paid within 90 days of fulfilment. Shine Shampoo's owner is really hoping the drug store doesn't wait until day 90 to pay, but this has happened to her before. In the meantime, Shine receives an even larger order from a different drug store chain - a larger drug store chain. If Shine can pull this off, it will mean $1 million in profit. Shine's owner goes back to Taylor Capital and presents her issue. Taylor's team checks out the invoice, which is due to be paid in 60 days or less. After Taylor's team carefully researches the ability of both drug store companies to pay for their orders, and other important *financial matters which I won't pretend to know about, they agree to loan Shine more money. Except this time, it's actually two separate transactions. In the* ***first transaction****, Taylor Capital agrees to purchase the invoice from Shine and wait up to 60 days to be paid. The drug store will pay the money owed directly to Taylor. Taylor will pay 80% of the profit to Shine and keep 20%. The* **second transaction** *is another bridge loan like the first example.*

Imagine an investment similar to a mutual fund (pool of investors money invested in stocks and bonds), where the investments inside aren't stocks and bonds; they are privately negotiated loans. These types of investments exist and are available in both public and private markets. Exciting, right?!?!

"Why would a company choose to issue bonds/take on debt rather than sell shares?"

Great question! I'll answer that in a few minutes. First, let's talk about shares.

"What are shares/stocks?"

When you buy stocks, you are buying a piece of a company. If you don't recall this from watching the videos earlier because you didn't watch the videos, go to **barriefinancialconsulting.ca/videos** and watch **Investing Series: Different Investment Vehicles** and **How The Stock Exchange Works (For Dummies).**

There are two ways stocks can make you money:

1. **Increase in share price.**

2. **Dividends.**

Back to the question,

"Why would a company choose to issue bonds rather than shares?"

If you own a company and need money to grow your business, do you want to borrow money from people or sell them a piece of your company?

Exactly. Loan please! *But what would you choose as an investor:* loaning money at 4%, or owning shares that could profit you a lot more than 4%? Most would choose the latter. There are never guarantees with investing, but there is potential to make more money from stocks than bonds. With bonds, there is a ceiling, and today's low interest rates mean high quality bonds aren't paying much. With stocks, you have no idea what you will make (or lose). Companies need to keep as many people happy as possible if they want to raise money to grow their businesses.

I'll address what might seem like a huge contradiction when it comes to my opinion on <u>debt</u>...

Let's clarify the difference between Person A borrowing money to invest in other people's businesses and Person B borrowing money to invest in his/her own business. Person A's core income is his/her career, which is why he/she wants to invest in other people's businesses: potential "extra" income. On the other hand, Person B wants to invest in growing his/her core income. If you're an entrepreneur like Person B, you understand your business model and earning potential because it's YOUR BUSINESS. If your business has grown to a point where it simply can't grow further without a cash injection, consider getting a bank loan or rallying your friends and family to invest in your business.

Investing in your business is just like investing in other people's businesses: know your risks and take steps to mitigate your risks before investing. This is the easy part when it comes to investing in your own business. What's not easy is removing the emotion from your decision of whether or not to borrow money to help "your baby"/your business grow. Don't risk more than you can afford to lose. Get help with making this decision from those who don't have emotion invested in the business, such as a professional business valuator and/or accountant.

When it comes to debt in general, I'm not saying "don't do it". I'm just saying be cautious and take on debt only if you really, REALLY need to.

Back to investing in other people's businesses with your OWN money...

"What is a mutual fund?"

A mutual fund is like multi-colour wire. Each colour represents a different company's stock/bond. The whole wire is the mutual fund. Each investor buys a "slice" of the wire so they get some of each colour/company. Although there are only 10 colours of wire in this photo, a typical mutual fund contains 25-50 companies.

A mutual fund management team decides which stocks/bonds to trade (buy/sell) and when to trade. Like segregated funds, mutual funds are ideal for those with less than $100,000 to invest. Unlike segregated funds, however, mutual funds don't come with guarantees. One can invest in most mutual funds for as little as zero initial investment and $100 per month. A popular mutual fund can have thousands of investors and its value can be billions of dollars.

Like stocks, mutual funds are sold in units called shares. Also like stocks, the price of a share bought for $10 will fluctuate daily.

If you own a mutual fund, you probably own bonds, unless it is an aggressive growth mutual fund, which is likely comprised of 100% stocks. "Balanced" mutual funds are considered "medium risk" because they contain some bonds.

Owning **Exchange Traded Funds (ETFs)** can be a great way to add diversification to one's portfolio instead of or in addition to owning mutual funds.

ETF (exchange traded fund) = a "slice" of multi-colour wires. This "slice" of companies, however, is not managed by humans like mutual funds are. ETFs are not managed by humans at all. A common ETF is a slice of the S&P 500.

If you're wondering *"What's a stock index?"*, Google "North American stock index".

Because ETFs aren't actively managed, they are cheaper to own than mutual funds.

"What is a segregated fund?"

A segregated fund is identical to a mutual fund except segregated funds have guarantees. For example, you can invest in "plain vanilla" mutual funds or "maple walnut" segregated funds. The underlying ingredients - *er, investments* - are the same, except the maple and walnuts, which cost a little bit more money but are worth it to those who find them beneficial. Here's an example of this:

You invest $10,000 in the Plain Vanilla Fund (mutual fund) which has an annual management fee of 2%. Ten years from now, you have an emergency and really need that money. Unfortunately, it's value has dropped to $7000.

Alternatively, you could have invested in the Maple Walnut Fund (segregated fund) which has a slightly higher fee. You would have signed an insurance contract stating 75-100% of your $10,000 is guaranteed after 10 years. You decide the guarantee percentage - of course the higher the number the higher the fee. This is why after ten years, when its value has dropped to $7000, you are guaranteed to still have at least $7500.

Segregated funds offer other types of ingredients - I mean, guarantees - as well. This is where terms like "annuity" and "GMWB" (guaranteed minimum withdrawal benefit) come into play. You can find out more about these types of investments which are available only through life-licenced advisors online at Canadian Life and Health Association Inc (**clhia.ca**). The PDF you want to read is called "Key Facts About Segregated Funds Contracts".

"Should I invest in both public companies and private companies?"

Once you understand the differences between these types of investments, you can answer this question for yourself.

Remember how nervous I felt about investments that aren't publicly traded? Well, private investments haven't made me nervous for quite a while now. Quite the contrary, actually. Turns out, the private market doesn't raise money for "newer" and/or "smaller" companies only. This is known as "raising venture capital" and is of course quite risky. My increased comfort with private investing came with the knowledge that many companies with sparkly 15+ year track records and/or large companies choose to remain private. "Going public" isn't the dream of many successful companies because it comes with unnecessary costs and limitations.

When it comes to private investments, "private" doesn't mean the general public can't invest. Years ago, you would have had to know someone who knew someone who could get you invested in a private company, but like most things, technology has changed this. Some say increased regulatory oversight has reduced the risks involved with certain private investments. Prior to 2013, the Canadian and provincial securities commissions weren't monitoring private investment companies as closely as they are today. As more and more money poured into private investments leading up to 2013, the securities commissions began to pay more attention.

"Why the sudden popularity of private investments?"

Popularity of private investments grew as many of the largest pension and **endowment fund** managers began seeking investments that weren't tied to the volatile stock and bond markets. Pension and endowment fund holdings are public knowledge. The increasing allocation to private investments by managers of these billion-dollar funds hasn't gone unnoticed by individual investors.

Endowment fund = an investment account owned by a charity, university, hospital or church funded by donations. These donations are tax deductible for donors.

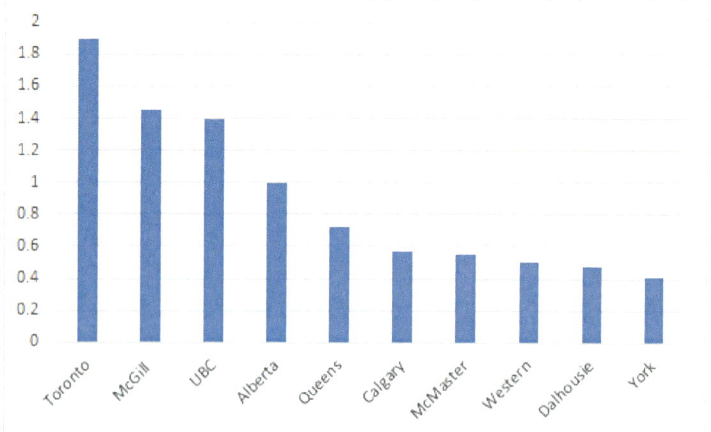

Source: **higheredstrategy.com/university-endowments-in-a-global-context**

If you'd like to see an example, check out The University of British Columbia's endowment fund: **ubcimant.ca/investments/endowment-fund.php**

Nonprofits aren't the only institutions looking to private investments for diversification; even the Canada Pension Plan Investment Board has gradually increased the CPP's exposure to assets such as private equity, infrastructure, and real estate.

Private investments used to be available only to organizations who could write six-figure cheques. Not the case any more.

Once my private market misconceptions were replaced with the above information, I began to familiarize myself with the private investments available through my new brokerage partner. How did I familiarize myself? Much the same way I'd familiarize myself with a new summer camp or sports coach for my son - **Google the names of all the top dogs.** My research led me to a handful of private investments I really liked. I also found a few I didn't trust. All but one of the private investments I chose to partner with were, and still are, fantastic additions to my clients' portfolios. I said "all but one" because I recently had my first ever experience with this. The reality is you can't win all the time. Any company can lose money or go bankrupt whether it's a public or private company. We can do our best to weed out the bad ones, but a few will surface from time to time. As I write this, it is still unclear what percentage of my clients' money has been lost on this one investment. It could be 100%. The good new is, not one of my clients who invested in this now-impaired company will feel severe pain from this loss, even if it does end up being 100%. Why? **Diversification.**

I've met many financial professionals (current and former) who lost some of their clients' money once. Some had it happen more than once. For some, it ruined their career, either because they didn't prepare their clients for the possibility of losing money or because they didn't properly diversify their clients' investments. I've now felt the sickness of knowing I had a hand in losing someone else's money. Upon hearing the bad news, I managed to remove myself from the hamster wheel of worry and thought through Dale Carnegie's three step problem solver.

1. Get the facts.

2. Analyze the facts.

3. Arrive at a decision – and then act on that decision.

In my situation, the facts were, and still are:

1. Investing involves risk.

2. I researched this investment to the best of my ability and believed it would succeed.

3. I was wrong about this one company, and I will be wrong again.

4. My clients' investments are sufficiently diversified and not one of them can be financially ruined from losing 100% of their investment in any one company.

5. I still believe in investing.

6. I won't hide under my desk and hope it blows over. I will provide details and be available to discuss the situation with my affected clients as it progresses.

7. I won't quit.

After analyzing the facts, I decided to make a list of facts and a list of questions in regards to how bad the loss was. I took action by talking to each of my affected clients on the phone or face to face to share my lists. A week later, once I had a few answers, I recorded a video and sent it to each of them. As the weeks and months went by I remained in contact with all of them and prepared them for the worst - that they could lose all of the money they invested in that one company.

Sometimes investments fail.

If you can't accept this fact, you might be better off hiding your money in a coffee can in the back forty.

My five rules of investing:

1. Understand the risks involved with investing. (Key **30**)
2. Understand the basic types of investments. (Key **31**)
3. Trust your gut. Don't invest in it if it seems too risky or too good to be true. (Key **32**)
4. Diversify! Diversify! Diversify! Own many **eggs**/ investments in many **baskets**/sectors and locations. (Key **33**)
5. Use extreme caution when borrowing to invest. (Key **34**)

Playing by these rules doesn't guarantee success 100% of the time. I'm living proof of that. On the contrary, I am winning. I wouldn't step out on the basketball court in a high-stakes game without skills and an understanding of my opponents and my team's plays. I believe my five rules of investing can pull off investment wins most of the time.

"What's wrong with borrowing to invest?"

There are many financial professionals who disagree with me when it comes to borrowing to invest. You'll hear reasons like, *"The interest on your investment loan is only 3% and I can earn you around 8%. Plus you can write-off interest on investment loans! It's a win-win!"* No, it's not. It's a gamble. There is no guarantee that you'll make any money on any investment. Losing money that's yours would be bad enough. Losing money that's not yours would be awful. Investment risks are multiplied when you invest borrowed money. As I said before, use extreme caution when borrowing money in ANY situation.

When it comes to borrowing against one's home to invest, my opinion changes case by case. It also depends on whether he/she is a Person A (has a job) or a Person B (owns a business). When someone asks me to help them borrow against their home to invest, I will consider facilitating the transaction ONLY if I can check these three boxes:

- ☐ Person is extremely financially savvy.
- ☐ No debt other than his/her mortgage.
- ☐ Investment loan won't raise debt above 60% of home's value.

From here, I require all investment statements and insurance policies. If upon reviewing their entire financial picture I know all their bases are covered (meaning if the investment doesn't produce income, or worse, goes to zero, or even worse, goes to zero and illness/injury/job loss strikes, their lifestyle will not be affected), we will proceed.

In a few minutes, I'll share with you how financial advisors are compensated. If someone like myself, for example, facilitated the above transactions, I'd be paid two commissions; one for the loan and one for the investment. It's important to know how "financial advisors" are compensated. It's also important to ask multiple advisors the same questions to compare options, just as you would if a doctor diagnosed your injury and prescribed a treatment plan. You don't have to rush into anything. You can shop around for the option that makes the most sense to you. Whether your questions are about money or health, a little online research from reputable websites never hurts. Sometimes learning from folks who have been in your shoes is better than searching for a local financial guru to talk to.

Back to investing...

During the online research I've encouraged you to do, you've probably come across information about how to invest your own money without the help of a broker/"financial advisor". Some of you have been quite intrigued by the idea of managing some of your own money in an online trading account. I'm more of a "set it and forget it" investor because it removes the emotion from investing. Emotion can cause frequent trading which can turn investing into "gambling". That said, I find it fun and exciting to play the stock market with 10% of my portfolio. I "set and forget" 90% of my investments.

If you're like me and you want to manage 10% (or less) of your money in an online trading account, ask yourself:

"Is the sum of my liquid investable assets at least $50,000?" **Y/N**

"Can I afford to lose $5,000?" **Y/N**

"Am I willing to invest two hours a day for seven consecutive days in studying how to analyze stocks?" **Y/N**

"Am I willing to spend 2-4 hours per week FOREVER watching my stocks and researching new companies to invest in?" **Y/N**

If you answered YES to all three questions, block your calendar for two hours per day for seven consecutive days as soon as you have finished reading this book. "**Seven Days of Stocks**" is waiting for you at

barriefinancialconsulting.ca/resources

I designed this resource to help you research ways to invest your own money. I said "help you research" because this is not a course. I will simply point you in the direction of online resources which I've found helpful.

If you feel excited and ready to open your own online trading account once you've completed *Seven Days of Stocks*, go for it. Just make sure the value of this "*play account*" is never more than 10% of your liquid investable assets, and remember: YOU COULD LOSE ALL THE MONEY YOU INVEST.

You can do a lot with only the basics, but don't get too confident. Leave the majority of your portfolio in the hands of professionals.

If you answered NO to even one of the questions, continue "setting and forgetting" 100% of your investments.

"But I hate paying investment fees!"

Some people try to learn to manage their own investments because they don't want to pay fees. I use a document during the interview process with a potential new client called "Should we work together?" to discover his/her motives for working with me and to open the conversation about my compensation. This is what it says:

We have many questions for each other. Let's start with the one we're both asking ourselves right now, "Should we work together?"

I have identified Seven Key Characteristics present in my most enduring relationships. "They" refers to my best friends, clients and mentors.

<u>They live their lives by principles</u>

Principles like honesty, integrity and hard work - to name a few - are the foundation of everything they do. They do not sacrifice principles for results.

<u>They know the value of a dollar</u>

Whether they are an entrepreneur who risked everything to start their business or someone who earns sweat equity, every dollar they have is valuable to them. They don't want to pay one more dollar in taxes than required. They diligently spend less than they earn, save for future needs and know how to avoid buyers' remorse.

They believe wealth is more than money

They know that true wealth has many dimensions, including social and spiritual. They believe in preserving wealth to secure their lifestyle and to positively impact their family, community and world.

They are open to new ideas

When it comes to managing their business, parenting, cooking, looking for a new job, working out or buying a vehicle, they are open to being coached. They want to move to the next level in everything they do and are keen to learn new ways to reach their goals.

They know what they do well

They also know what they don't do well. They have tried the do-it-yourself route with their money or know someone who has. The results were not good. They know it pays to delegate the things they don't get paid to do plus they find their spare time is better spent with friends and family.

They care about value and quality

They agree with John Ruskin when he said,

"There is hardly anything in the world that some man cannot make a little worse and sell a little cheaper, and the people who consider price only are this man's lawful prey."

They know that hiring a coach who is talented and respected in their field renders a win-win relationship.

<u>They enjoy my company</u>

...and I enjoy theirs.

You know how much your time is worth, so why not **delegate** your investment management along with all the other things you don't want or need to do? If you're a nerd like me, you'll have fun investing some of your money. What won't be fun is trying to manage more than 10% of your investments when you don't love doing it - all because you want to save money on fees!

"How much should I pay my financial advisor in fees?"

Whether it's a new investment or the disability insurance policy you are planning to buy, you want to know what the agent/broker/advisor you buy it from will be paid BEFORE you buy.

Why?

And before you ask, no. It's not nosey or impolite to ask. It's your right to know what your advisor will be compensated before you buy a financial product from him/her because:

1. Most investments have **fee options from which you are allowed to choose**. If this option isn't presented to you, ask *"What are the fees for this*

investment?". If fee options weren't part of the answer, ask *"What are my options for paying the fees?"*

2. Advisors/brokers/agents are paid two types of commissions; **up-front** (lump sum upon sale) and **trailer** (small percentage of sale amount paid monthly or annually). Financial products pay one or both.

Know how your financial advisor/planner/coach is compensated.

Key 35

Your **investment statements** likely do tell you what you pay in fees. I'm not saying they're easy to comprehend, but during the years I've been investing clients' money, I find investment statements have become easier to understand. Investment fees are complicated, unfortunately. I'd love to help you figure out exactly what you are paying, but there are simply too many types of investments and too many ways people like me can be compensated. Just ask questions and do your research.

Some advisors/planners/coaches, like myself, can charge a consulting fee to review your financial picture. This type of compensation is called "fee for service", which means the financial professional is being compensated without any products being purchased. It's simply a service with a price tag attached. This price tag varies depending on the complexity of the financial picture and may include the cost of bringing in a lawyer and accountant to do their parts. ***Find out if your advisor is able to charge for their time or if they are only able to earn income from commissions.***

Here are some great financial advisor interview questions when it comes to **products**:

1. Can you sell me individual stocks and ETFs or are you licenced to sell mutual funds only?

2. Are you life-licenced?

3. Do you sell private debt and equity?

4. Do you have to sell a certain company's proprietary products or are you a broker?

Here are some great financial advisor interview questions when it comes to **services**:

1. How often do you meet your clients face to face to review their financial picture?

2. Do you call or email your clients to check in on a regular basis? If so, how often?

3. Do you provide seminars/webinars for clients? If so, how often and what are some topics you've covered in your past seminars/webinars?

4. Do you provide free financial coaching for your clients' teenaged and young adult children?

The relationship is a huge part of working with an advisor. For more on this, check out this video on my YouTube channel: **"Lyndsie Barrie & Stacey Scott discuss saving, debt, and how to find great financial advice"**.

Moving on to the question I know you've been asking since you picked up this book.

"How much should I be saving?"

Before we look at your numbers, allow me to slam the word "retirement" a bit more.

The grade seven and eight students I've got to know through Junior Achievement mirror what their folks say about retirement; most believe one of the top reasons to save and invest their money is to fund their inevitable retirement. When I ask them what retirement is and why it appeals to them, they respond with something like "retirement is when you stop working" and "retired people can sleep in, play golf and travel lots." Then I ask them to think about their favourite thing to do. I say,

"Imagine you can make money at your favourite thing to do. For example, imagine you can make loads of money wake surfing or designing wakesurfing boards or manufacturing wake

boats because you are really, really good at it. If you are making money at something you love and excel at, which allows you time and money to sleep in, golf and travel too, would you still want to retire?"

Of course not. That's why we're not talking about retirement here. We're talking about financial freedom: **one who is "financially free" has the option to stop working.**

"What if I can't work? What if my health fails or my industry disappears due to technology? What if I hate my job and can't wait for it to end?"

It's wise to know approximately how much savings it would take to replace your income if you became unable to work.

Know your financial freedom numbers.

Unfortunately, it's impossible to determine exactly how much money you need in order to be financially free. There are simply too many variables. That's why I won't recommend specific savings numbers like "10% debt repayment, 10% short term savings, 10% long-term savings,

10% giving and the rest for living expenses", for example. Your situation is unique. I would need to know all of your financial details in order to recommend specific numbers for you. After using your Mint account for a month, you'll have an idea of your spending habits and where you need to rein yourself in. Come up with your own spending limit goals using the categories in Mint and use the following steps to help you come up with your monthly savings goal. Once again, we can't get exact numbers because there are too many variables, but we can **get an idea of whether or not you're on the right savings track** based on:

- How much you have saved.
- How much you intend to contribute to your RRSP and TFSA in the future.
- How many years are left until your ideal financial freedom date.
- A reasonable rate of return (I use 8% until the financial freedom year and 5% thereafter).
- Your current and future (estimated) tax rate.
- Your living benefits and life insurance coverage.
- How much your **CPP (Canada Pension Plan)** income will be.

Your **CPP** income amount is one of your financial freedom numbers. If you don't know what your CPP income will be, I explain how to get your number here: **barriefinancialconsulting.ca/resources** > **"What will I get from CPP?"**

You'll also need to know what your OAS (Old Age Security) will be, if any, as the OAS clawback applies to those whose income is above a certain amount. Find out more about OAS at **barriefinancialconsulting.ca/resources** > **"What will I get from OAS?"**

You will create separate financial freedom income reports for your RRSP and TFSA. RRSP numbers must be kept separate from TFSA numbers because of the different tax treatment of each account type.

Step 1

Open the online calculator at **barriefinancialconsulting.ca/resources > What are my financial freedom numbers?**

This link also takes you to Canada Revenue Agency's website to figure out your tax rate.

Step 2

Once you have your pre-and post retirement tax rates "guesstimated", enter your RRSP numbers in the online calculator. You may choose to enter different numbers than what I have here for Suzy Sample's investment returns and inflation.

Suzy Sample is 39 year old Albertan whose annual taxable income is $50,000:

Starting balance	$50000
Current age	39
Rate of return before retirement	8%
Current tax rate	25%
Inflation rate	2.5%
Annual contributions	$3600
Age at retirement	65
Rate of return during retirement	5%
Retirement tax rate	25%
Years of retirement	35
Savings tax deferred	✓
Increase deposits with inflation	no

Make sure the "Savings tax deferred" box is checked.

For the second box, "increase deposits with inflation", Suzy hopes she will do this but can't be 100% sure so she's planning for the worst.

Step 3

Print or take a screenshot of the input page before you click the "Report" button. Save as/write at the top "**RRSP Income Input**" with today's date.

Step 4

Print or take a screenshot of the report page. Save as/write at the top "**RRSP Income Report**" with today's date.

Go back to Step 1 and **repeat using your TFSA numbers, except this time, you will enter "0" for current and retirement tax rate**. This is because your TFSA holds after-tax dollars and you won't pay tax on the withdrawals.

If you have any **non-registered investment accounts, complete the steps for each account. Don't check the box beside "savings tax deferred" for non-registered accounts**.

Write your financial freedom numbers <u>in today's dollars</u> here:

<u>My financial freedom numbers</u>

RRSP after taxes: $________

TFSA: $________

CPP (Canada Pension Plan): $________

OAS (Old Age Security): $________

From age ____ to age ____, my total monthly income will be approximately:

$__________

Print this page at **<u>barriefinancialconsulting.ca/resources</u>** **> What are my financial freedom numbers?**

Put it on your goal board *<u>beside your list of fears.</u>*

Financial freedom can be snuffed out in a matter of weeks or months if a financial storm hits and you're not prepared. If you aren't prepared, what's the first place you'll draw money from to pay household and medical bills? Bingo. Liquid investable assets. Your ticket to financial freedom.

Protect your future!!

A portion of your income currently goes towards various insurance policies to protect your future: vehicle, home, health, life, etc.

What about protecting your savings? What about protecting your ability to earn income? What about protecting your loved ones against financial loss if you were to become a financial burden on them? There are three types of insurance which are designed to do this, and it's important you understand them.

Understand what "living benefits" are.
Key 37

(Critical illness, disability and long-term care insurance.)

During your peak income earning years, you are more likely to become critically ill or disabled than you are to die. That's why critical illness, disability and long term care insurance are more expensive than life insurance, and just as (if not more) important to have. The alternative to owning the policies I'm about to describe is worrying about having to liquidate assets to pay for medical and living expenses. If you don't find yourself worrying, you may not understand the risk or you are really good at sticking your head in the sand so you can sleep at night.

Critical Illness Insurance

Critical illness insurance **pays a lump sum of cash** if the insured is diagnosed with one of the covered conditions. A policy may cover anywhere from 4-24 conditions. These conditions often include cancer, heart attack, stroke, paralysis and kidney failure. The amount of critical illness insurance that can be purchased depends mostly on the health and medical history of the applicant and their blood relatives. The decision of whether to buy $50,000 critical illness insurance or $500,000 also depends of course on how large of a premium they can afford.

It is important to understand what your policy does and does not cover by reading the description of your coverage with your own eyes before buying! Don't count on the words of a salesperson!

Disability Insurance

Basically, disability insurance **pays a monthly income** to the insured if they become disabled. The many types of disability insurance vary depending on the insured's occupation and whether or not they would retrain to work in a different field. Disability insurance policies also vary in price depending on how soon the premiums would kick in, how long the disability income would be paid, medical history of the applicant and their blood relatives.

Long Term Care Insurance

Many Canadians mistakenly believe that full-time care in a long-term care facility will be fully paid by government health care programs. The truth is that government health care programs may cover only a small part of the costs for a nursing home or other specialized residential care facility, or perhaps none at all depending on the circumstances. This means that individuals (or their families) will have to pay for a significant portion of the costs associated with long-term care out of their own pockets. Yet, most Canadians haven't contemplated the need for long-term care in their financial planning process.

Often, when we think of the need for long-term care, we think of elderly folks living full-time in a nursing home. **Remember that a debilitating illness or accident can result in the need for around-the-clock care at any age.**

An insured person qualifies to receive benefits if he/she can't perform two or more of the acts of daily living, which are:

- bathing
- dressing
- toileting
- transferring (example: moving from a chair or out of bed)
- maintaining continence
- eating

There are many types of plans. Most plans are a variation of one of these two types:

1. Reimbursement for eligible expenses such as homemaking or private nursing services up to a maximum benefit amount
2. Pre-determined monthly benefit amount payable for the number of years specified on your plan or indefinitely

Living benefits "Return of Premium Rider" optional feature

For an added cost, many insurance companies offer a "return of premium rider" which will reimburse you a percentage of the premiums you paid.

For example, if I were approved for a long term care policy with a return of premium rider, the policy contract would state that upon my death, if I had not made any claims on the policy, my estate would receive 50% of the premiums I paid during the life of my policy.

For another example, if I were approved for a disability policy with a return of premium rider, the policy contract would state that if I haven't made any claims by age 65, I will receive 50% of the premiums I paid during the life of my policy.

As you can see, life insurance is just one of the four important types of insurance everyone with financial responsibilities should have. Life insurance money can provide much needed income for your dependents after you're gone, but remember that you are more likely to become disabled or critically ill than you are to die during your peak earning years. In order to protect your family's future, which type of insurance should you designate your surplus income to first, second, third and fourth?

The answer depends on your list of fears. What are you most afraid of? If buying an insurance policy also buys peace of mind, why not look into your insurance options?

Here's a great place to start:
barriefinancialconsulting.ca/resources > What's your risk?

"Should I insure my children?"

When my son was about two, a life insurance agent convinced me to buy life insurance from her and cancel my mortgage insurance at the bank. This made sense, since I'd have a $200,000 policy no matter what, rather than a policy with coverage that reduces as my mortgage decreases. For those of you who don't know this about mortgage insurance, I'll point out that this is a bad deal because the premium doesn't reduce as the amount of insurance reduces. The premium stays the same. I opted to cancel my mortgage insurance and get my own policy.

Then she tried to convince me to add my son's life to the policy as a "rider". The idea of buying life insurance on my son's life appalled me at first. Why on earth would I want to benefit financially from my son passing away? Ridiculous. Then she said to me *"You would want to take some time off work. The money would relieve financial stress and pay for the funeral."* This made sense. Besides, adding my son as a "rider" was going to cost me only another $2.50 per month for $10,000 of insurance on his life. I did it.

A couple years later, a different life insurance agent wanted to show me some insurance options. She, too, stressed the importance of insuring my son, only this time it was on the basis that he would need insurance of his own one day, and by insuring him now, I was removing the risk that he could become uninsurable later in life. I didn't fully understand this at the time, but I did like the idea that I'd be helping out my son in the future by buying him this policy when he was 4 that can help him buy his first house in his twenties. What I realized later was the policy I bought for him could be converted into his own policy in the year he turns 25, without proof of insurability. I know right?!? *Best. Mom. Ever.*

The third reason people insure their children involves whole life insurance. I'll explain the difference between term life and whole life in a moment. In addition to the first two reasons why parents insure their children, whole life insurance offers the potential for the child to borrow money against the policy in the form of a policy loan.

Group insurance coverage

Group coverage often includes a little of each of the three key types of insurance: life, disability and critical illness. Know what your group policy covers, if you have one. Don't assume your group plan coverage is enough to meet your needs.

Think of insurance like a meal: insurance you own is the meat and potatoes. Group coverage is the gravy. It's nice to have, but it can't be relied on. You need meat and potatoes.

Your own coverage follows you wherever you go. Group coverage on the other hand allows you 30 days (usually) to opt for continued coverage if your employment ends. People are often too overwhelmed with their recent job loss to realize this or they aren't informed. That said, continuing coverage on one's own means paying higher premiums than when he/she was a member of the group policy.

Just as home and auto insurance are part of your basic expenses, so should be YOUR OWN critical illness, disability, long-term care and life insurance.

If you have dependents, living benefits and life insurance can ensure your dependents' basic needs will be met if your health fails or you pass away.

"What type of life insurance do I need?"

First, let's look at the different types of life insurance. Before we look at "plain vanilla" term life insurance, I'll try to answer one of the most common questions I get when it comes to life insurance:

"What is whole life insurance?"

Whole life insurance is one of three types of permanent insurance, or T-100 (term to age 100) insurance. Permanent insurance costs more to own than term insurance. Despite all the folks who say *"Buy term and invest the difference!"*, whole life sales are increasing year after year in Canada according to my research. I also get asked about whole life the most, so I'll focus on it the most over the other two types of permanent insurance.

Here's a simple explanation of the three types of T-100/permanent insurance:

- T-100 with guaranteed cash values is WHOLE LIFE.
- T-100 with variable cash values is UNIVERSAL LIFE.
- T-100 with guaranteed cash values and dividends is PARTICIPATING WHOLE LIFE.

Whole life pays a death benefit, just like term life/"plain vanilla" insurance, but here's where whole life is different:

1. Whole life accumulates cash value in an "account". This cash account is separate from the life insurance death benefit and has two key purposes: first to assist the insurance company in making sure it has the money to do what it says it will do in the whole life insurance contract: insure you for your WHOLE LIFE. Second, the cash account is a security feature for the insured in case they can't pay premiums in the future but need to continue coverage.

2. Instead of paying lower premiums in years when you're statistically less likely to die and higher premiums in later years, the premium doesn't change during the life of the policy. One can choose a specific number of years to pay premiums for. **Example:** *39 year old Brenda buys a $50,000 whole life policy which will be "paid up" after 20 years. She will pay $100 per month for 20 years and her coverage will continue for her whole life.*

3. One can choose to "pay up" the policy sooner than the original contract states by using the cash account or use the cash account to buy additional insurance.

4. If a person's financial situation changed to needing less insurance, or if a person became unable to pay premiums, he/she could choose a reduced death benefit. Depending on how much the death benefit is reduced, the premium could be reduced or eliminated and, yep - you guessed it, coverage would continue for life.

There are many misconceptions about this mysterious-seeming "cash account". Here's what you need to know:

1. The "cash account" isn't actually cash; it's investments. It's your money invested by the insurance company. Your money accumulates from over-payment of insurance premiums. This "over-payment" can add up to HUGE tax savings for an incorporated business owner and/or a person donating to charity. The cash account can also remove a few of those pesky **what ifs** from one's list of worries.

2. Each month when cash goes into the account, it is invested and managed by the life insurance company. The account is basically a segregated fund. There are no guarantees as to whether or not the investments will grow, however, life insurance companies do provide guarantees similar to that of segregated funds. Also similar to segregated funds,

the higher the fee the higher the guaranteed cash account value at certain increments, such as year 10, 15 and 20.

3. You can't actually borrow from the cash account. You can borrow against the cash account in the form of a **policy loan**. Interest is charged on these loans. Yes, you would have to pay interest to borrow your own money. The nice thing about borrowing against the cash account instead of actually taking out money is the investment growth remains tax sheltered.

4. If the policyholder stops paying premiums, the policyholder would have two choices: 1) surrender the policy/forego the death benefit and receive the cash value net of any surrender charges, or 2) use the cash value to purchase a paid-up policy. If the policyholder chose option 2, the amount of insurance they can buy will depend on the amount of cash in the account.

5. Cash value interest and/or dividends accumulate <u>tax-free or tax deferred</u>, depending on whether gains are distributed at death or during lifetime.

6. Much like a mutual fund, the **fees to take your cash**, whether you want to borrow from or

surrender the policy, **are often hefty in the first seven years.**

There are many, many more features to whole life insurance than the ones I just shared with you. In my opinion, those are the most important.

Term insurance - the "plain vanilla" of life insurance

1. A term insurance contract is in effect for a term of 10-35 years.

2. T-10 (term 10) is the least expensive because premiums are guaranteed for only 10 years. At the 10 year anniversary of the policy, the premiums go up to a higher amount, which is stated in the original contract, because the older we are the more likely we are to die. Premiums remain at the new higher amount for the next 10 years.

3. There is no cash account. Just a death benefit.

4. Term insurance can be converted to permanent insurance in many cases without medical tests or proof of health. There are, however, medical questions which if not answered in a way that reflects good health, could result in a conversion application being denied.

My permanent insurance rant

I'm not a fan of people being sold expensive insurance that has fancy tax features they don't need. Of course, most of you reading this could probably benefit from the tax perks of a whole life policy someday, and by "someday" I mean when you are debt-free, have accumulated substantial savings and want your estate to pass to charities and loved ones without a huge tax bill. Convincing people who are wallowing in debt that they need to pay $300 per month to own whole life insurance when they could have the same death benefit for $100 with a term policy is WRONG. That's $200 of debt repayment that can't happen each month. The number one reason for life insurance is so loved ones aren't left with debt if the main source of income passes away. Why not work to reduce debt now? Yes, it's responsible for you to have life insurance to remove debt from the picture if you pass away, but what's more responsible is working to eliminate the debt NOW.

I realize there are reasons to own life insurance other than eliminating debt. Life insurance can protect business owners from having to liquidate their business if one shareholder passes away. Life insurance can pay capital gains upon death of a farm/cottage owner so his/her children can keep the farm/cottage. Although most of this can be accomplished with "plain vanilla" term insurance, there are more complex estate planning issues for which permanent insurance could be the best option. I'm not saying people shouldn't have SOME permanent/whole life insurance, but the amount they "need" depends on both their ability to pay premiums now and their estate planning needs in the future.

If you need to keep your life insurance premiums low, keep in mind **most term insurance can be converted to permanent insurance later,** often easily and without proof of health. However, this ability to convert term to permanent life insurance usually expires around age 65 or 70. Before purchasing term life insurance, understand your conversion options.

Keep in mind the commissions on whole life and universal life policies are HUGE!!! Ask yourself *"Is this a mutually beneficial transaction or do I feel like this person needs to make this sale more than I need this policy?"*.

If what I just said is hitting home, and you suspect you may have the wrong type of insurance for your needs, consider reducing your whole life coverage and replacing the death benefit with term insurance. You'll still have the same death benefit without all the bells and whistles and you'll have more money to pay off debt and save for your future. Like I said, **I wouldn't look to a whole life or universal life cash account to save for** your future unless you've maxed out your TFSA and RRSP. If you're thinking right now about cancelling your permanent life insurance policy, I wouldn't do that if I were you. Especially if you bought the policy less than seven years ago. I'd look at reducing it is all.

Corporately owned life insurance

I won't get into this, but if you have a corporation, there are many amazing ways to utilize life insurance to reduce or eliminate estate tax bills and/or get money out of the corporation tax-free. If you're interested in learning more about this, I've provided a few links to articles describing scenarios at **barriefinancialconsulting.ca/resources** > **Corporately owned life insurance**.

Be confident you own the right type and amount of life insurance.

Key 38

Here's a great tool to help you accomplish this: **barriefinancialconsulting.ca/resources** > **What's your life insurance need?**

If you find you have too much insurance, consider donating your no-longer-needed life insurance to charity.

If you find yourself in a situation where you no longer need the amount of life insurance you own, have a conversation with a financial professional about donating what you don't need to charity before surrendering the policy. Why? Because you have no choice but to give. May as well choose

VOLUNTARY GIVING (charity) over INVOLUNTARY GIVING (tax). When you choose voluntary giving, you get to decide who the money goes to. Plus donating life insurance or any other financial asset to charity can mean a nice tax credit. Know your options.

Make sure to calculate your life insurance need annually or when your financial situation changes. If you always know you're adequately covered, those conversations/sales-pitches with life insurance sales persons in grocery stores (or at family reunions) can end quickly.

It's time to wrap it up!

It's not just life insurance sales persons who have a tendency to sway us to the "more is never enough" way of thinking. It's everywhere. It's the key reason why I chose to reduce my exposure to media. Less media exposure helps, but it's human nature to always want more.

How much is enough?

How much of what? What do you want? We've come full-circle to the question we began with. My hope for you is that you have a clearer idea of what you want and how to achieve it.

I know what I want. I want to have the ability and the freedom to make a positive difference. I know opportunities will come my way to make a difference which won't result in financial compensation. I don't want or need to make money from everything I do, but I still need to pay my bills. *That's why I* ***need*** *to be financially free.*

- I need many income streams from my core talent.
- I need to have control of my spending.
- I need to understand the risks in my **what ifs** and have protection against them.

I've learned that my answer the question *"How much is enough?"* is *"I don't know."* I don't think I'll ever get enough of this. By "this" I mean learning, sharing and giving to others. That's why I wrote this book: to encourage you to **strive every single day to use your thrill of the chase instinct for good**.

What do you want?

Do you want to achieve your goals? Do you want to have the financial flexibility to be able to switch gears when the perfect opportunity presents itself? Do you want to gain true fulfillment by changing lives for the better? I bet you don't want the "stuff" that everyone else wants. **You want something rare: true fulfillment**.

Be ready for the opportunities that will come your way. Whether this means investing in a new endeavour or creating a new product or service, you **want to be 100% ready for the next opportunity to experience true fulfillment.**

Be ready by being financially free!

Once you've achieved it, never stop using and sharing your financial freedom to create money and health for others. I promise you that nothing else will bring you more fulfillment, both from a soul perspective and an **income tax** perspective.

Yes, I'm going to end my book with "tax talk"!

You have no choice but to give.
Involuntary giving = tax.
Voluntary giving = charity.
Key 39

Choose voluntary giving!

I promise the next book in my "39 Forever Mom" series will help you with this, but you can start learning now at **barriefinancialconsulting.ca/resources** > **Choose voluntary giving.**

No matter the amount of money, how you earn it and what you do with it can make you happy or unhappy. The choice is yours.